STRIKE FORCE 10

STRIKE FORCE 10

Heinz G. Konsalik

translated from the German by

Anthea Bell

G. P. Putnam's Sons
New York

First American Edition 1981

© 1979 C. Bertelsmann Verlag GmbH, München/54321

First published 1979 by C. Bertelsmann Verlag GmbH
under the title *Sie waren Zehn*.

English translation © 1981 Macmillan London Ltd.

Library of Congress Catalog Card Number 81-1557
ISBN 0-399-12615-5

Printed in the United States of America

Main Characters

Peter Radek, aged 25   Lieutenant
(Pyotr Mironovich Sepkin)

Berno von Ranovski, aged 24   Lieutenant
(Ivan Petrovich Bunurian)

Elmar Solbreit, aged 22   Second Lieutenant
(Luka Ivanovich Petrovsky)

Baron Venno von Baldenov, aged 28   Captain
(Leonid Germanovich Duskov)

Johann Poltmann, aged 21   Second Lieutenant
(Fyodor Panteleyevich Ivanov)

Detlev Adler, aged 25   Lieutenant
(Alexander Nikolayevich Kraskin)

Asgard Kuehenberg, aged 28   Captain
(Kyrill Semyonovich Boranov)

Dietrich Semper, aged 22   Second Lieutenant
(Sergei Andreyevich Tarski)

Bodo von Labitz, aged 31   Major
(Pavel Fedorovich Sassonov)

Alexander Dallburg, aged 20   Officer Cadet
(Nikolai Antonovich Pleyin)

Larissa Alexandrovna Khrulankova, aged 22   Tractor driver

Lyra Pavlovna Sharenkova, aged 20   Tram driver

Anya Ivanovna Pleskina, aged 27   Doctor

Lyudmila Dragonovna Tcherskassya, aged 29   Police lieutenant

Wanda Semyonovna Haller, aged 23   Building forewoman

Yelena Lukanovna Pushkina, aged 19   Secretary in the Kremlin

Igor Vladimirovich Smolka, aged 40   Colonel, Soviet
Intelligence

Yefim Grigoryevich Radovsky, aged 52   General, Kremlin
staff officer

Vladimir Leontinovich Plesikovsky
Nikolai Ilyich Tabun
Anton Vassilyevich Nurashvili
and Stalin

One

SINCE no one was expecting them, no one came to meet them.

After crossing the border and passing the East German police checkpoints they stood at the windows of the last carriage in the interzonal train looking out at the fields, the neat villages with their well-kept streets, and the brightly coloured cars which drove for some of the way parallel with the train, as if racing it.

An elderly man came stumbling along the corridor. Suddenly he flung up his arms, then began opening compartment doors, shouting ecstatically, 'We've made it! We're in Germany!' He hugged the other passengers, kissing them on both cheeks. Then, exhausted, he leaned against one of the corridor windows, pressed his face to the smeared glass, and wept quietly.

They had left Moscow four days before, fearing endless formalities. They were at an assembly-centre, having come from all points of the compass with their wives and children, carrying suitcases, bags and cardboard cartons; half a lifetime — in some cases three-quarters — shrunk to the amount 'that one person can carry'. Now they were standing side by side outside the huts: twenty-seven men with their wives, fifty-three children, seven old men and nine old women, looking at the Comrade Commissar, listening to him in silence.

'Well, so you're the ones,' said the man who had introduced himself as Kyrill Abramovich Konopyov. He was fat and heavy, with cheek-pouches like a hamster's and small eyes almost buried in rolls of fat. He wore good, well-polished boots and a full, dark-blue linen jacket over brown trousers. His hair was short, grey and curly, and he scratched his head when he had something important to say. 'And just how many years has Russia fed you, eh? How long has Russia been your father and your mother? Haven't you had all you could wish for? Don't you have the most power-

7

ful nation in the world behind you? Isn't the Soviet Union the safest place on this planet to be? Oh, no, that's not good enough for you; you must be off to the capitalist West. Suddenly you remember you're Germans. Germans indeed!' He spat. He marched along the line of silent men, stopping briefly in front of each and looking at him with his small, piggy eyes. 'And just what do you expect of the West?' he asked. 'What's so great about it, eh? We Russians were the first in space; we lead the world in technology, medicine, cybernetics, mathematics, agrarian reform. Who has the best chess players in the world? The best gymnasts? Who has the most powerful army? But what's the use of talking to you, standing there with your bits and pieces, thinking: Never mind him, never mind Comrade Kyrill Abramovich; we're Germans, we are.' He kicked a suitcase and laughed rather breathlessly. 'Is *that* all you've kept of Russia? I call it a bloody shame.'

Nobody wavered. They filed through his office to pick up their papers: train tickets; the final rubber stamp on the permit for a person of German origin to emigrate; their signatures on a document in which they gave assurances that they no longer had any claims whatever on the Soviet Union; and, last of all, their passes for crossing the border and the export permits for their much-inspected luggage.

Not one of the emigrants was in a position to pay an air fare to Germany. Nor could they afford rail tickets for the international express trains. They were quite prepared to leave Russia together in a special carriage. They would have to change from the Soviet broad-gauge track to the standard European gauge in Poland, and they must then change again in East Germany, where they would be connected to the train travelling through Thuringia and over the border into the free West.

Free West?

Konopyov did not see it that way. He sat in his office, behind a mountain of documents, producing a personal file on each man who passed his desk.

'Ah, it's you, is it?' he said, as a grey-haired man of medium height came up to the desk and presented his passport. Konopyov looked up, and the two men's eyes met. Then Konopyov glanced at the woman standing beside the man, with a younger woman who, according to the records, must be the couple's daughter.

8

'Now, Kyrill Semyonovich Boranov, you're an intelligent man. You and I even share the same first name — that makes a link, doesn't it? Can you tell me why, after thirty-four years, you suddenly decided you're German?'

'I've always been German, Kyrill Abramovich.' The man tapped his passport. 'It says so here: my name is Asgard Kuehenberg. Birthplace, the estate of Thernauen in Livonia. I held the rank of captain in the German Army.'

'I know, I know.' Konopyov's face twisted. 'The whole thing came out at the time of that ridiculous application of yours. Very successful, wasn't it? Sentenced to ten years in Siberia! Pardoned after three years because of intervention by the West German Government. Still, you've lived here as a Russian citizen for thirty-four years. Lived pretty well, too — you were high up in the Moscow tramline service. So why, I wonder, did you get the crazy notion, after such a long time, of admitting you were a German, a spy and saboteur?'

'Homesickness, Comrade Konopyov.'

'Homesickness?'

'Surely a Russian can understand that.'

'Your wife Lyra Pavlovna is Russian.' Konopyov stared at the woman by the man's side. She wore a simple cotton dress and summer sandals, but no stockings. She looked younger than her fifty-four years: a slender woman with brown hair still unstreaked with grey. Her face was oval, with slightly raised cheek-bones. 'And your daughter Tamara Kyrillovna — she's Russian, too,' said Konopyov. He looked at the girl. She was taller than her parents, very slim and pretty. A waist a man could span with his hands; breasts like the first autumn apples; long, shapely legs. 'I call it disgraceful,' said Konopyov. 'And just how did the West German Government find out you were still alive?'

'It's a long story, comrade.'

'Oh, I can read it all in here.' Konopyov tapped the file. 'Kyrill Semyonovich Boranov, I am now asking you in my official capacity: will you give up this idea of emigrating?'

'No.'

'Very well, then; I'm asking these ladies, who are Russian: do you really want to leave your native country for good? All right,

9

it may sound old-fashioned, but don't you ever want to see Mother Russia again?'

He paused, scratching his grey curls. The women did not react with the emotion he had expected. Their faces were unmoved.

'He is my husband,' said Lyra Pavlovna at last, in a clear voice, 'and I go where he goes.'

'And he is my father,' said Tamara Kyrillovna, equally gravely. 'Anything he does is right.'

'Well, you've certainly trained your family well,' said Konopyov. He rummaged among the papers and produced those to be signed. 'What work will you do in Germany?'

'I don't know.'

'You think the German tramline services can't wait to get you?'

'No.'

'Or are you going to take up your army commission again?'

'I'm too old for that.'

'You certainly are — too old for any of it. Too old to go emigrating, I can tell you. Here, in the Soviet Union, you could have ended your days peacefully. In the West, you'll be an outsider. "What's he after here?" they'll say. "Why didn't he stay in Russia? He remembers he's German after thirty-four years, and now we have to support him out of our taxes." Kyrill Semyonovich, you're going back to a country you don't know any more. Everything's changed there. Those who are no use to the economy of the West go to the wall. Free West? It's the authorities who decide what freedom means there! Oh, yes, I can see in your eyes what you're thinking. "Same as here." Right?'

'Your words, Comrade Konopyov, not mine,' replied Kuehenberg cautiously.

'We're speaking in private. I ask you: what's so much better about the West? You think they'll pay you an officer's pension?'

'We shall see.'

'There's a good deal you'll see. Did you never feel at home here?'

Kuehenberg nodded. He put one arm round his wife and the other round his daughter, and drew them close. No doubt he had often stood like that in his little garden in one of Moscow's new housing estates, where they were bulldozing great areas of forest flat to build simple, neat little houses to be let to good officials, reliable comrades. He must have stood in the sun, looking at the garden with its cherry-trees and vegetables, and been happy.

'I love Russia,' said Kuehenberg. 'It hurts to leave.'

'But you're leaving all the same?' snorted Konopyov. 'You're sick, comrade. Mentally sick.'

'There comes a time in any man's life when he wants to be himself. His real self. It's just a dream to most people; they go on living the lives that fate has declared for them. But I have the chance to be a German again. Do you honestly think I could let it pass?'

'You're a fool, Boranov.' Konopyov slammed down a rubber stamp on a piece of paper which had already been stamped many times over and was thus obviously an important document. 'You know what that was?'

'A rubber stamp.'

'Your death as a Russian citizen. Now you're nothing – until the Germans acknowledge you. That action stamped you out. Kyrill Semyonovich Boranov no longer exists, and your new name of Asgard Kuehenberg is only conditionally recognized. It's the name you gave, but you can't prove it; your government will give you no more than vague assurances. From now on, you and your family are nothing.' Konopyov pushed the papers over the desk to Boranov. 'How do you feel now?'

'Not too good, I must admit.' Kuehenberg gathered up the papers and put them in his coat pocket. 'Are those all the formalities?'

'That's all.'

'When can we leave?'

'Tomorrow morning, from the Leningrad Station. Platform 3. The last carriage is reserved for those of you who've just discovered you're German.' Konopyov coughed and leaned back. 'And there's no way you can ever return.'

'I realize that.'

'Then get out,' snapped Konopyov. 'Kick Russia in the arse, that's right. I like to think they'll be doing the same to you in the West.'

That had been four days ago.

Now they were travelling through Germany, the land they had

11

longed to see, towards Bebra where their carriage would be coupled to a train bound for Göttingen. They would reach their journey's end in Friedland. The old man at the window, a farmer called Herbert Zimmerman who had battled with the authorities for his repatriation for seven years, was still weeping, unable to grasp the fact that he was finally back in the country the Zimmerman family had left scarcely a hundred years before to settle by the Volga. Kuehenberg himself, with his wife Lyra and his daughter Tamara, stood by the window of their compartment, watching the landscape flit past.

'Your country is very beautiful,' said Lyra Pavlovna; her husband's silence made her uneasy. She winked at Tamara. The girl nodded and pointed to a vehicle which drove along beside the train until the road went downhill and it disappeared.

'A yellow van. Do look — bright yellow!'

It was a postal van. Kuehenberg passed a hand over his eyes. 'Well, that's something that's changed. The postal vans used to be red.'

There were coaches waiting for them at Friedland railway station.

Two Red Cross nurses, an ambulance man, a policeman, and a civilian who introduced himself as representing the reception-centre organizers, took the little band to the coaches, with their bags and cases, and drove with them to the barrack-like centre. The coaches drew up in the forecourt of the administration building. The ambulance man, a cheerful young fellow who had been sitting with the Kuehenbergs, said, 'Well, here you are, then. Welcome to Germany.'

And then they were standing out in the sun, which was as hot as it had been in the suburbs of Moscow, although the air was not so fragrant with the scent of flowers and vegetables, fruit and herbs as in their own sunlit garden, where Kyrill Semyonovich used to go around with a hose, watering his plants.

'Barracks,' said Lyra Pavlovna. Now that they were in Germany she spoke German, with a harsh Russian accent. 'I thought this was freedom. Barracks, like the ones at Kolposheva.'

Kolposheva, on the River Ob, the Siberian penal labour-camp of the notorious Narym district, a town of the living dead. Those who ended up in Kolposheva were forgotten.

12

Kuehenberg took the luggage out of the coach: suitcases, three cartons, a jute bag. He piled it up in front of the women, and then took Lyra's face in his hands. 'It's just for a few days, Lyranya,' he said. Overcome by tenderness, he kissed her eyelids and caressed her cheeks. 'As Konopyov said, we have no identities here yet; they'll be giving us numbers! We know what the administrative process is like, don't we? This is only a transitional phase, Lyranya.'

A senior organizer of the reception-centre made them a short speech of welcome. They had come a long, hard way, he said, and a hard way still lay before them as, although they were Germans, they were in an unknown country now, very different from Russia. But they must not be discouraged; they would be given all the help they needed in settling in.

Then they were allotted their rooms. The Kuehenbergs had two rooms and a shower. The big centre, which had once been a reception-camp for returning prisoners of war, was almost empty, most of its buildings closed. Only a trickle of German immigrants was coming back now.

They fetched supper from the communal kitchen: goulash and noodles, then vanilla cream with raspberry sauce. Afterwards they strolled through the deserted barrack-town, saw the bell-tower with the famous Friedland Bell, sat in the evening light on a white-painted bench by flower-beds in the main square of the camp. When the sky became darker, and lights came on here and there in the buildings, they went back to their rooms and unpacked their cases. Tamara showered first, and put on her night-dress, then Kuehenberg got under the shower, soaped himself, and waited for Lyra to join him. She still has a beautiful body, he thought. Smooth, taut skin, firm breasts, not an ounce of superfluous fat anywhere. We've been married thirty-four years and I love her as much as on the day I met her. But has she always been happy with me? She's gone through so much with me: falling in love and getting married; then learning the truth, that I was a German; her difficult labour with Tamara, when she nearly bled to death; our years of contentment, but always with the fear of discovery; her struggle against my wish to go home to Germany; and then my application to emigrate—the interrogations, arrest, beatings, my conviction, our time in Siberia, my pardon, another

13

application, more threats, more interrogations, until at long last they allowed me to leave. Now we are in Friedland, to start a new life in a strange world. Lyranya, I have asked so much of you over the years!

He reached for her under the shower, pulled her towards him, her smooth, naked body wet against his; the water sprayed over them.

'Kyrillushka, what are you doing?' she cried, clinging to him as if she were afraid of falling. 'You're out of your mind. Suppose Tamara came in? Oh, you old bear! I tell you, don't. We'll get water all over the place and you'll have to pay for repairs. Kyrill, we aren't twenty any more.'

She was laughing, enjoying his lovemaking; she sighed like a girl when he stroked her breasts and gently took her erect nipples in his teeth, then clutched him as he pushed her against the wall of the shower, and put her legs firmly together. 'You're crazy,' she gasped. 'What are you doing? Lie down decently, can't you?' She pushed him away, laughing, a velvety undertone to her voice, covered his erection with a towel and ran to the door, dripping with water, to lock it. Only when she had rubbed herself dry did she lie down on the bed, looking expectantly at her husband.

'It's just as good as it was all those years ago,' she said softly, a catch in her voice as he bent over her.

'I love you, Lyrashka. I love you more and more every year. I....'

He buried his face in her throat and fell silent; the sensation of entering her was as intense as thirty-four years ago, when they had first made love behind a grassy mound in the Lenin Hills, on the outskirts of Moscow, the vast blue sky above seeming to sing as he felt her warm skin against his own.

I would have stayed in Russia if she had been set against leaving, he thought, feeling her lips on his own shoulder and neck. But she went along with everything I did; she never complained, never reproached me, never opposed me.

They showered again, unlocked the door, and went to bed. All was quiet around them. It was far quieter than their little house in Moscow, where there were always neighbours with something to celebrate. And far quieter, too, than Kolposheva labour-camp where you heard men weeping in the huts at night, and the sound

14

of stammered prayers, hoarse gasping, snoring, growled curses. This silence, such a vacuum of sound, oppressed them. They wanted to sleep, they were bone tired, but the silence prevented it.

'Our first night in Germany,' said Lyra Pavlovna. She was lying on her own — they were single beds. 'It's uncanny, Kyrill.'

'You'll find it's different once we're out of this centre. The world outside is noisy.'

'Noisier than in Russia?'

'Much noisier. Russia will seem quiet as an empty church by comparison.'

'How do you know?'

'I can tell, simply from the traffic in the streets.'

'Are we going to live in a big city, darling?'

'I don't know.'

'In your application forms, you said you were going to Cologne. Is Cologne a large place?'

'Very large.'

'Larger than Moscow?'

'No, much smaller.'

'Then how can you say it's large?'

'Well, Cologne is large by German standards.'

'Then everything is smaller in Germany than in Russia?'

Her logic was unassailable. He smiled in the dark. 'Yes,' he admitted. 'Many things are smaller here.'

'In that case, why should Germany be such a great place compared with Russia?'

'Who says so?'

'Oh, everyone here. They say America and Germany and France are all better than Russia.'

'It's not the actual size of the countries.' He stretched and yawned. 'Go to sleep now, Lyranya.'

'Good night, Kyrill.' Her voice sounded childishly thin. 'I hope I dream of your Germany.'

During the night the door opened softly, and Tamara tiptoed into the room. She slipped into Lyra's bed, just as she used to do when she was a child, and nestled close to her mother.

'I'm scared, Mamushka,' she whispered. 'I'm scared of these strange people and this strange country.'

'So am I, dochaska,' whispered Lyra Pavlovna back, 'but don't say so. Put a brave face on it. This is your father's native land, and we must respect it.'

The first day began with much official questioning, the filling in of long forms, the taking of photographs for identification papers, and preparations for transport on from the centre. Most of the immigrants were luckier than the Kuehenbergs in having relatives with whom they could stay, or they were being sent to jobs on the land where they could get acclimatized to their new life. The artisans were going to factories where they would learn to adapt their skills and be integrated into the work-force.

Asgard Kuehenberg received different treatment.

He was the last to be summoned to the administration building, and did not pass through the various individual departments. Instead, he was taken to a room where a man was waiting for him. This man, who wore a good, light-grey suit, was middle-aged, with keen eyes under a high forehead. His brown hair was rather long, in the modern fashion. He rose to his feet at once as Kuehenberg came in, and bowed slightly.

'I'm Heinz Wildeshagen,' he introduced himself, 'and I'm glad to meet you. Well, how are you feeling?'

'All right,' replied Kuehenberg cautiously. He took in the situation at a glance. They were alone in the room; there was a document on the table, and a black briefcase beside it. Despite the heat, the window was closed. The curtains were drawn, too, and the pleasantly dim light softened the bleakness of the furnishings. Heinz Wildeshagen indicated an upholstered chair in front of the desk.

'Shall we sit down?'

'If you like.'

Kuehenberg sat. As he did so, his glance fell on the cover of the document. He could read the words there quite clearly: *Wild Geese — 1944*. And a stripe right across the cover indicated that the document was top secret.

'Oh, God,' said Kuehenberg, 'must we go into that? Where did you get it?'

Heinz Wildeshagen put his hand over the document.

'Didn't you know that all Canaris's files survived the war? After the Admiral's execution the new Intelligence chiefs, Kaltenbrunner and Schellenberg, seized all written records. When the SS took over the whole of Military Intelligence, a new wind began to blow, but not a better one. Of course, you weren't around then.'

'We heard about it, though.' Kuehenberg leaned back. Wildeshagen offered him a cigarette, and he accepted it, inhaling several times as he tried to get used to its sweetish aroma, so different from the acrid fumes of Russian machorka cigarettes, or the long papyrossi. 'What's the idea of this? It was thirty-four years ago.'

'This file on Operation Wild Geese was found in the records that fell into American hands. When the Gehlen administration began getting to work in the Federal Republic, the files were returned to us—first photocopies, then the originals. Did you know General Gehlen?'

'Only very slightly. We had very little to do with the Foreign Armies East department. We were a special commando unit.'

'We know that. What we don't know is who planned it, or how. The Federal Information Service has been making inquiries for years without success. Apart from this thin file—it has only three pages in it—we haven't found any material.'

'There isn't any to be found.' Kuehenberg ground out his cigarette in a glass ashtray. 'Exactly what is in that file?'

'A list of ten names. Another list, of the names of Russian towns or country areas. And a memo from the Führer's Rastenburg headquarters, signed by Field-Marshal Keitel. That consists of just one sentence: "The Führer approves this operation." That's all.'

'Quite enough,' said Kuehenberg, satisfied. 'Well, what do you want now, after thirty-four years?'

'I hold the rank of captain—your own rank at the time, Herr Kuehenberg.' Wildeshagen pushed the file over to him, but Kuehenberg did not touch it. 'I'm with the Federal Information Service. The events of the Second World War and all the background material relating to it have been most thoroughly studied; we've used documentary matter, the evidence of eyewitnesses, historical research. There are hardly any mysteries or unanswered questions left. But there *is* this solitary and no doubt highly interesting shadowy area, waiting for you to illuminate it.'

'You put it very nicely, Herr Wildeshagen.' Kuehenberg smiled faintly. 'You're almost lyrical. Personally, I'm glad that no one knows about it. Let us leave the shadows alone, shall we?' He rose, but Wildeshagen remained seated, and drew the thin file back towards him.

'Captain Kuehenberg—'

'Please, I've been Kyrill Semyonovich Boranov for many years, I have only been answering to the name of Asgard Kuehenberg again these last five days, and it's still only conditionally mine. I have no German papers yet, no official recognition that I'm a German citizen.'

'Then you may consider me the bearer of the news that, in Germany's eyes, you have always been Captain Asgard Kuehenberg. Even when you were reported missing in action, you lived on in this file. You—and the other nine officers. You're the only person who knows their fate.'

'Yes, that's so.'

'Tell me about the Wild Geese.'

'Ah, well, geese, Latin zoological name *Anserinae*, are members of the anseriform order. Large aquatic birds, feeding on plants which they grub up with the ends of their bills, masticating them with the notches in the sides of their beaks. The sub-genus *Anser* includes the northern brown Bean Goose, the White-Fronted Goose, so called because of its white forehead, the Chinese Goose, and the Greylag or Wild Goose, native to the larger waters of Europe and northern Asia. The Wild Goose nests on the ground and emigrates to north Africa and India in winter.' Kuehenberg smiled reminiscently. 'Fancy remembering all that. Yes, they made good ornithologists of us. I know all there is to be known about geese.'

Wildeshagen smiled wryly. 'Well done,' he said. 'But we can hardly suppose that ten German officers were sent into Russia, with Hitler's approval, to give instruction in the breeding of geese.'

'Where do those documents say anything about German officers being sent into Russia?'

'Herr Kuehenberg, this file has been through the hands of our top experts. The list of Soviet place-names—that second sheet of paper—shows them encircling Moscow like a ring. It was perfectly clear, even with no other clues, that Operation Wild Geese was closely connected with Moscow. However, no Soviet military

18

historians of the war say a word about a German commando unit operating in the Moscow area. And even General Gehlen, a close friend of Canaris, knew nothing about it.'

'I'm delighted to hear it.' Kuehenberg looked down at Wildeshagen. 'Am I going to be denied repatriation in Germany now, and sent back to Russia? I came back because I was homesick, not to dig up a piece of folly again. Can I go now?'

'My dear Captain, of course, any time. You're a free agent here. You're not in Russia any more.'

'After this conversation, I begin to doubt whether that's such a good thing.'

Wildeshagen now rose himself and put the file away in his black briefcase, which had a combination lock. 'What are your plans, Herr Kuehenberg?'

'I have no plans yet.'

'You named Cologne as your destination.'

'I had to say I was going somewhere. I picked Cologne because I once had a good friend who came from that city. The only man in our year at military academy who couldn't say "general" the standard German way, with a hard *g*. He always pronounced it "yeneral".'

'Lieutenant Willy Hecht.'

'My turn to congratulate *you*. You're very well informed.' Kuehenberg went to the door. 'Yes, it was Willy Hecht. Do you happen to know if he survived the war?'

'Sorry, I can't help you.' Heinz Wildeshagen shrugged his shoulders. 'Where are you going to stay in Cologne?'

'I thought I was a free agent?'

'I meant well, Captain—'

'For God's sake, I'm plain Asgard Kuehenberg. Captain Kuehenberg was buried somewhere in Russia in 1944.'

'In Moscow.'

'You do stick to your guns, don't you, Herr Wildeshagen? But don't get too hopeful. You may not know it, but we Baltic Germans were always fervent patriots. Up there on our estates in the East, in the wide fields of Latvia, Livonia and Estonia, we never set eyes on the Rhine, but we worshipped it. Don't ask me why, because I don't know. Now that I'm back, I'd like to be left in peace. Can you understand that?'

19

'Listening to you, yes, I can.' Wildeshagen took an envelope out of his breast pocket and handed it to Kuehenberg, who hesitated before taking it. 'This is for you.'

'What is it?'

'A welcome home from the Retired Officers' Association.'

'H'm.'

'Four weeks' free accommodation for you and your family in the Blum Hotel in Cologne, and a cheque-book: you have a bank account to draw on, containing five thousand Deutschmarks, for a start.'

'For a start ...,' said Kuehenberg thoughtfully. 'You expect a lot of me, don't you?'

'Come, now — do you have any fluid assets?'

'Well, yes,' Kuehenberg grinned. 'A bottle of vodka.'

'Glad to see you haven't lost your sense of humour!'

'Why should I? The Russians are a happy people, naturally inclined to sing and dance and make merry.' Kuehenberg opened the door. 'Very well, then, I'll leave for Cologne tomorrow. Where is the Blum Hotel?'

'Right opposite the Cathedral.'

'Wonderful.' Kuehenberg laughed wholeheartedly. 'They'll certainly stare at us in those marble halls when we turn up with our shabby luggage.'

'You're expected.' Wildeshagen came round from behind the desk. 'Your return is being most discreetly handled.' He himself opened the door for Kuehenberg. 'I'd like to come with you, if you don't mind.'

'I don't mind.' Suddenly he looked at Wildeshagen with a plea in his eyes. 'In fact, you'd be a help. My wife and daughter — their first encounter with the West is bound to be a shock for them. A world of such plenty!'

'How about yourself?'

'It will be difficult for me, too.' Kuehenberg placed his hand on Wildeshagen's shoulder. 'So perhaps you'll teach us how to swim when we plunge into the warm waters of Germany tomorrow.'

Kyrill Semyonovich, or Asgard Kuehenberg as he now was, told his family, 'Well, my dears, we're being driven to Cologne.'

'By whom?' asked Lyra Pavlovna dubiously.

'An army officer, little pigeon.'

'So we're not to be left in peace?' Her dark eyes looked sad. 'What did they ask you?'

'They're interested in wild geese.'

'What did you tell them, Papushka?'

'I gave the officer a lecture on ornithology, with the result that we're to be put up at the best hotel in Cologne. We've been invited there by a Retired Officers' Association; we shall spend our first few weeks in Germany as guests of the State. They're trying to make out it's a kindness. In fact they want to know about Operation Wild Geese.'

'Are you going to tell them?'

'No.'

'They won't be pleased.'

'We shall see.'

'We can't go back to Russia now, Kyrill Semyonovich.'

'We'll find a place somewhere to live in peace.' He drew Lyra towards him and stroked her slightly wavy hair. 'Are you afraid?' he asked.

Lyra Pavlovna nodded. Officers again, she was thinking. Twenty-eight years of fear that Kyrill Semyonovich's real identity might be discovered, and then he told them of his own free will. That was when their troubles began. Interrogation, threats, questions, questions all the time: officers and yet more officers besieging the Boranov family. Once or twice a general came from the Kremlin, drove around with them in a Volga limousine, and asked Kyrill, 'Now, can you tell me how you organized it? All the details? All we want is a complete record, for the sake of history. It will remain under lock and key in the Kremlin archives. You have nothing to fear. It was wartime, and we all did our best for our countries.' But then they were sent to Siberia, after all. However, Kyrill Semyonovich's spirit was not broken.

'What can they do to you, Papushka?' asked Lyra. She was repacking the suitcase. Tamara had already taken out their other items of luggage, among them the jute bag, full of top-quality goose-down plucked from their own birds. They had kept geese in their little garden, too. Four birds, always four, for the last seventeen years. Could one keep geese in Germany?

'Nothing, Lyranya,' said Kuehenberg. He had just seen Captain

Wildeshagen arrive. 'We shall have a great many visitors, that's all — very polite people. They'll all have something to offer: a good job, money, the guarantee of a carefree old age. Then things will leak out. There'll be reporters, people from publishing firms, film, television and radio people, offering us even more money and pretending it's my moral duty to let the world know about Operation Wild Geese.'

'And will you tell them?'

'No.'

'Not for all that money?'

'Do you think I can be bought, Lyranya?'

'Were we ever as poor as we are now, Kyrill?'

'Believe me, we shall be all right.'

'Yes, darling.'

'You're a wife in a million.' He kissed her again. Tamara rushed into the room.

'There's a car here,' she cried. 'Oh, my goodness, what a car! Do look, Papushka!'

Kuehenberg went to the window. As he might have expected, it was a Mercedes. Its black bodywork gleamed in the sun. It had thick, dark-grey, ribbed fabric upholstery. There were neck-rests for both front and back seats, and a long aerial. Not just for a radio, thought Kuehenberg. No doubt there's a radio telephone or something of that nature, too. Wildeshagen himself was opening the boot and loading it up with the Kuehenbergs' luggage: vinyl suitcases, the two cardboard cartons, the jute bag. He closed the boot, mopped his sweating brow with the back of his hand, and slightly loosened his tie. It was early summer, and very warm. The vine growers of the Rhine and Mosel needed more rain; heat and humidity would produce a good vintage.

Kuehenberg stepped back from the window. Despite her twenty-eight years, Tamara's cheeks were glowing like those of an excited child.

'That's right, Tamarenka,' he said, putting his jacket on. 'We're going to Cologne. A few hours on the motorway.'

'To the little city of Cologne. . . .'

'Perhaps we could buy new dresses,' said Lyra Pavlovna.

He thought of the bank account. I'll pay it back, he resolved. I haven't come home to accept charity. I shall regard what I use as a loan. I'm a healthy man; I can still work. As soon as my papers come through, I shall look for a job. And Tamara is a trained hairdresser; it will be easy for her to find work, too.

Heinz Wildeshagen kissed the hands of Lyra Pavlovna and Tamara, to their secret amazement: they had never seen a man kiss a woman's hand except in films about the decadent times of the Tsars. They got into the Mercedes, hardly daring to sit on the beautiful upholstery. Kuehenberg sat in front, with Wildeshagen, and fastened his seat-belt. Almost soundlessly, the engine started.

'Good God,' said Kuehenberg, as Wildeshagen moved off. 'You mean we can leave just like that—no formalities?'

'They've all been dealt with, Herr Kuehenberg.'

'I'd have liked to say goodbye to the centre organizer.'

'No need. He's busy, and he doesn't know you personally; you were just passing through.'

'I see.' Kuehenberg leaned back and, following Wildeshagen's example, loosened his own tie. 'So now I can do as I like?'

'You could put it that way.'

'Then there's something I'll ask you to do: drive quite slowly along the motorway, and stop somewhere where there are plenty of people around.'

Puzzled, Wildeshagen looked at him, then nodded and drove on. After a few minutes, they joined the motorway to Kassel. As requested, Wildeshagen drove the big car slowly along the right-hand lane. Columns of other cars, tankers and trucks overtook it, and once or twice, when a small car purred past, its occupants looked back at them in surprise. A Mercedes 350 crawling along in the slow lane—what was wrong?

'Stop,' said Kuehenberg. In the distance, they saw a rectangular blue sign with a large white P. 'Can we get out there?'

'Yes, of course.'

Wildeshagen drove into the parking-place. It had a picnic-area surrounded by woods; birds were twittering, and there was a scent of newly mown grass. Several holidaymakers sat around the stone tables, eating their packed lunches: families with laughing children. A dog was barking. Nearer the exit, four long-distance trucks were parked, their drivers sitting on the footboards drinking coffee from Thermos flasks.

'Just the place,' said Kuehenberg, getting out. Baffled, Wildes-

23

hagen followed him. 'Plenty of people of all sorts.' He loosened
his tie yet further, and undid the two top buttons of his shirt.
'Now, I've read that the most popular politicians in the Federal
Republic are Schmidt, Kohl, Strauss and Scheel. And your Fin-
ance Minister is Apel, is that right?'

'He's Minister of Defence now.'

'Even better.'

He walked towards the tables, hands in his trouser pockets,
looking for all the world like a boy bent on mischief. The confused
Wildeshagen followed, wondering what on earth Kuehenberg was
about to do.

It was like nothing Wildeshagen could have expected.

Kuehenberg gave the picnicking drivers a friendly nod. 'Having
a good lunch?' he asked, loud enough to be heard all over the
parking-place.

The picnickers nodded, looking curiously at him. The old boy's
had one too many, they thought. Amiably, one of them raised a
plastic coffee-cup and toasted him.

Suddenly Kuehenberg said, very loud, 'Chancellor Schmidt is
a bastard!'

Silence. He waited, staring at the faces, which were all turned
to him now. Behind him, Wildeshagen plucked at his jacket, but
he wrenched himself free, and walked into the very middle of the
picnic-area. A couple of men smiled at him; the women began to
giggle. The children stared. What did the funny man want?

'And Kohl is solid bone between the ears,' said Kuehenberg,
even louder.

No reply. By now, the women were laughing out loud, and the
men grinning. He mopped his sweating face. 'And Strauss is just
a loudmouth,' he shouted at the smiling faces. 'And as for Apel
—he's been busy dipping into your pockets. The whole Government's a load of shit.'

A man right in front of him raised a cup, roaring with laughter.
'Cheers!' he said. 'Hey, there's a whole lot of names you forgot
to mention.'

The crowd laughed, heartily amused. Kuehenberg walked away
from Wildeshagen, who was trying to restrain him again, and
went over to the long-distance truck drivers.

'You heard me?' he shouted. 'Here you all sit, stuffing your

24

faces, while your government is tricking you, lying to you, making use of you. Criminals, all of them.'

One of the truck drivers reached inside the cab of his vehicle, produced a bottle of beer, opened it, and offered it to Kuehenberg.

'Here, have another on me, mate,' he said amiably. 'Don't get so worked up. Better cover your head; sun's a bit hot today.'

Kuehenberg did take the bottle. He put it to his mouth and drank half of it. Then he handed it back to the truck driver, saying, quite soberly, 'Thank you. The best drink I've had in thirty-four years.' Slowly he went back to the car. Wildeshagen was standing beside it, looking rather pale, and Lyra and Tamara stared at him as if he had just walked out of a lunatic asylum.

Kuehenberg straightened his tie again.

'That', he said, 'was something I had to do. Can you see why, Wildeshagen?'

'Frankly, no.'

'No, how could you? It wouldn't have been possible here in 1944: I'd have been put up against a wall and shot for treason. And it's not a thing I could have done in the Soviet Union. But you saw what happened just now. No one hit me. They just sat there laughing. No police car came to take me away. Even if it wasn't true – well, no one minded.' He leaned against the car. 'I really am in another world, a new world. I wanted to be sure of that, see it and feel it. Now do you understand, Wildeshagen? I felt the air of freedom blowing. *I am a free man.*'

He did not wait for Wildeshagen to reply, but got back into the car, fastened his seat-belt again and closed the door. 'You can drive faster now,' he said, as they rejoined the motorway. The people in the picnic-area waved cheerfully to him. Odd old bloke, they thought. Pissed as a newt! Really seemed to have it in for the Government. 'As fast as you like. I feel like a bird escaping from its cage.'

Wildeshagen put his foot down and the speedometer rose to 180 k.p.h.

He's still more of a Russian than a German, though, Wildeshagen was thinking. He was twenty-eight when he was reported missing. Now he is sixty-two. He's lived most of his life as a Russian, and it shows. He thinks, feels, sees and acts like a Russian. He will believe in nothing but what he can touch and hold.

25

They did not talk much on the way to Cologne, but watched the countryside, marvelling at the alarming amount of traffic on the roads, the streamlined cars, the amazing variety of sweets and souvenirs on offer at the filling stations and service-areas, and the menu of the motorway restaurant where they stopped for lunch.

'You mean we can have anything on this menu?' whispered Tamara, as if even asking were forbidden.

'Anything you like,' said Kuehenberg.

'Without queuing up for it?'

'They'll come and serve us.'

'As much meat as I want?'

'You can eat until you burst, my angel.'

'It's like Paradise, Papushka.'

'I don't know about that.' Kuehenberg turned to Wildeshagen. 'Would *you* say you were living in Paradise?'

'Definitely not.'

'No. A man can have so much that all he wants is spaciousness and silence.'

'Things you've left behind, Kuehenberg.'

'Ah, but in Russia I could never have got up in public and called Brezhnev a bastard and a criminal.'

'Well, if that's your idea of happiness—'

'Just at the moment it is.' Kuehenberg had a cold beer and a pork chop, with chips and cauliflower. Tamara tackled an enormous porterhouse steak, while Lyra Pavlovna happily applied herself to a large meat roll stuffed with bacon and gherkins. Like Christmas-time, she thought. Christmas the whole year round.

'But of course', said Kuehenberg, 'I may get acclimatized to this sort of life faster than any of us would like.'

It was all as Wildeshagen had said it would be.

They were welcomed to the Blum Hotel discreetly and with the greatest courtesy. No one laughed at their jute bag or vinyl cases, the women's cheap dresses or Kuehenberg's crumpled suit. One of the hotel managers took them up to the first floor himself and showed them their rooms. Lyra Pavlovna was reminded of a visit they had once paid to Tsarskoye Selo, the Tsar's summer palace in Leningrad. Moscow Tramways, First to Third Districts, had taken their staff on an outing to that city — a great occasion. There had been a chartered Aeroflot plane to Leningrad from Moscow, then special coaches to take them into the city and all around it, from the Fortress of Peter and Paul to the fabulous palace. They had seen everything there, all the pomp in which the Tsar lived, draining the lifeblood of his people while he himself slept under sable covers. There were silk wall-coverings, and thick carpets which muffled the sound of your footsteps. Huge cut-glass chandeliers hung from the gilded ceilings. It had been a memorable experience. To think that a man who squeezed the very last rouble out of his people had been able to live like that.

Lyra Pavlovna waited until they were alone in their rooms, and then, timidly, touched the wall. Kuehenberg looked at her in surprise.

'What is it, Lyranya?'

'This is like silk,' she said. 'Just the same as at Tsarskoye Selo. And look at those chandeliers, and the carved furniture. Did a Tsar live here, too?'

'I don't think so. It's an ordinary hotel.'

'Ordinary?'

'Yes.'

'And these are our rooms?'

'Yes, you can see they are.'

'Kyrill Semyonovich, they must have mixed us up with somebody else.'

It took some time to convince Lyra Pavlovna that there was no mistake. She bathed in the pink bathtub, put on her best dress, brushed and combed her hair, and looked into Tamara's room next door. Her daughter had been quicker to get her bearings. She was sitting by the window in one of the handsome chairs, also wearing her best dress, watching the door expectantly.

'He should be here soon,' she said.

'Who?' asked Lyra Pavlovna.

'The waiter. There's a telephone there. I picked the receiver up, and someone asked if I wanted anything, so I said yes, would they bring me a samovar? I can't wait to see if it really works, Mamushka!'

'Oh, you silly girl,' cried Lyra Pavlovna, 'asking for a samovar here in Cologne.'

There was a knock at the door. 'There – now they'll come and laugh at you,' whispered Lyra. But she called out, 'Come in.'

A waiter opened the door and pushed in a trolley. 'Your samovar, madam,' he said, stepping aside. Sure enough, the trolley did hold a samovar, a genuine samovar of brightly polished brass, the boiling water bubbling away over a little spirit flame.

'I took the liberty of bringing some biscuits, too, madam,' said the waiter politely.

Sitting stiffly in their chairs, Lyra and Tamara watched as he placed the samovar and teacups on the table, arranged the plate of biscuits beside them, and then laid a large bouquet of flowers on the table. There was a deckle-edged card: *With the Management's compliments. Wishing you a pleasant stay.*

Tamara did not move until the waiter had left the room.

'It's like being in a film,' she said. 'Some sort of fairy-tale film where a magician grants all your wishes.'

'I just don't understand.' Lyra Pavlovna rose and approached the samovar cautiously, as if it might explode any minute. 'Why all this? *We're* not Tsars!'

Next morning, Wildeshagen came to fetch Kuehenberg directly after breakfast. He brought his wife with him, to look after Lyra and Tamara. Their programme was to include a visit to Cologne Cathedral, a shopping expedition, a taxi ride around the Cologne ring road. 'They'll be dazed by the end of it,' Kuehenberg remarked. 'Well, what are you and I going to do?'

'Drive to Bonn.'

'Without the ladies? Why?'

'I'd like to show you the Hardthöhe.'

'What's so special about it?'

'The Ministry of Defence is housed there.'

'Ah. I see.' Kuehenberg looked past Wildeshagen and out at the square, where a multi-coloured flock of pigeons was pecking up the grain and breadcrumbs scattered by passers-by. 'And suppose I'd rather go shopping with my wife and daughter?'

'You're expected in Bonn, Herr Kuehenberg.'

'I'm a free agent. Don't forget that.'

'It was only a request; but a very earnest one.'

'From whom?'

'The operations staff of the Federal Armed Forces.'

Kuehenberg sighed. 'Well, this'll all pass over in time. One thing you do learn in Russia, Wildeshagen, is a certain fatalism. Master that and nothing can shake you any more.'

While Frau Wildeshagen was preparing Lyra Pavlovna and Tamara for what lay ahead, Wildeshagen and Kuehenberg got into the Mercedes again. They did not go into Bonn itself, but turned off the motorway from Cologne and drove up the Hardtberg to the Ministry of Defence buildings. Wildeshagen had a pass on his windscreen; they went through three checkpoints without being stopped, and finally drew up in a kind of inner courtyard. Kuehenberg looked around.

'Nice place you have here,' he said. 'Bright, airy, positively cheerful. The Bendlerstrasse in Berlin was a much gloomier spot; nobody who went in there thought there was much to laugh about.' He got out and stretched.

Wildeshagen looked at the time. 'We're ten minutes late.'

'Well, there's an attitude that hasn't changed,' Kuehenberg laughed with pleasure. 'My dear fellow, *I* have all the time in the world. No use anyone who wants to talk to me clock-watching. You know what the hunters of Siberia say? A bear can run for three days — you must be able to run for four.'

Some things were the same as ever: long corridors, room succeeding room, functionaries of various degrees of seniority hurrying about, secretaries carrying files, men smoking on the stairs, scraps of conversation. . . . Then a door with no name on it, only the words *Please Apply to Room 1012.*

Wildeshagen did not apply to room 1012. He knocked, opened the door, and nodded to Kuehenberg. 'You can go in.'

'What about you?'

'I'll stay out here.'

'Who's in there?'

'A lieutenant-general.'

'Suppose I don't go in?'

'No one can make you.' Wildeshagen's smile was rather strained. 'You *are* a free agent.'

'Then I will.'

Kuehenberg entered the room, flinching slightly as Wildeshagen closed the door after him. The room itself was large and sunny, with a photograph of President Scheel on one wall. Hanging opposite, very much to Kuehenberg's surprise, was a picture of Admiral Canaris: a yellowed picture in a frame which was obviously old. There were easy chairs around a circular table, which held coffee-cups, a coffee-pot keeping hot under a cosy, cigars and cigarettes, an enormous onyx ashtray, and a bottle of French cognac with two big balloon glasses.

A man in civilian clothes rose from a chair and came towards him, arms outstretched.

'Asgard, old fellow,' he said. 'So miracles do still happen. Imagine seeing you again. Good Lord, you've gone grey. Have you shrunk? I seem to remember you as taller.'

'No, it can't be.' Kuehenberg stayed by the doorway. 'Wait a minute – don't come any closer! My God, if it's really you, old chap, you've put on weight. You used to have a figure like a Greek god. Try saying "general"!'

'Yeneral.'

'Willy Hecht! Willy!'

They embraced, hugged each other, then went over to the group of chairs arm in arm.

'A brandy to celebrate,' said Willy Hecht. 'Yes, I'm a "yeneral" myself now, and I still can't pronounce it properly! Sit down, old fellow. My God, how long has it been?'

'Thirty-seven years, Willy.' Kuehenberg took the cognac-glass and sniffed the contents. 'The same brand you always used to drink?'

'In your honour, Asgard. Here's to you.' Willy Hecht drank, and dropped into his own chair. 'The old days – ah, what times those were! I wouldn't have missed them for anything.'

'*I* would. When I look back now. . . . God, we were blind, mindless idiots. We believed all we were told. We were prepared to die for a gigantic deception.'

'It's easy to philosophize about it half a lifetime later. But, when we were young officers, don't you remember how we loved the Army – even more than we loved the girls? These days' – Willy Hecht waved a hand – 'career soldiers, they're just career soldiers, ready to shove aside anyone who stands in their way. Well, I'm due for retirement myself next year. I shall be a good civilian, go for walks, grow roses, sunbathe in Tenerife. By the way, thanks.'

30

'What for?'

'Giving your destination as Cologne when you emigrated.'

'I *was* thinking of you. Just coincidence, Willy; all my other friends were from the Baltic, you see.'

'There were ten of you, weren't there?'

'Now, don't *you* start, Willy.'

'I know how you feel. I've had a report.'

'From Wildeshagen?'

'He's a good man. Coffee?'

'Please.'

'So you don't want to talk about it?'

'No.'

'You're the only man who can give us the answer to one of the very last riddles of the war. We've taken this thing over from the Federal Information Service. The Americans don't know about you and your return yet. If they find out, I doubt if they'll handle you with kid gloves. They suspect something of tremendous historical importance behind Operation Wild Geese.'

'Well, I suppose it might be of some historical importance.'

Kuehenberg drank his coffee and ate a piece of cake; it was the old-fashioned type of seed-cake, and it brought back memories of the Thernauen estate. The terrace looking out on the grounds, its roof supported by columns. The box hedge around the rose garden, clipped into large globes at the four corners. The gravel path leading to the stables and the paddock where the horses were broken in. And Fräulein Selma, in her lace-trimmed apron and starched cap, asking if the young master would like another piece of cake.

Livonia in 1938, a blessedly peaceful place.

'We know about Operations Eagle, Barbarossa, Siegfried — each had its name, they are all on record,' said Willy Hecht.

'And they cost thousands of lives. Some of them even millions.'

'Wild Geese was smaller, wasn't it?'

'There were the ten of us.'

'We know that. But just what did the ten of you do?' General Hecht reached under the table and produced the familiar thin folder from a shelf below it. He pushed his brandy-glass and coffee-cup aside and placed the file in front of Kuehenberg.

'All it contains is our ten names, Hitler's approval in writing, and a list of Russian place-names.'

'Ten places around Moscow. Which gives one something to think about.'

'Then think away, Willy.'

'Your own personal records have disappeared without trace — all ten of them.'

'I know.'

'We tried following up that lead. But your personal files had been withdrawn from your divisional headquarters, from all the record offices, and they ended up at Oberkommando der Wehrmacht. And Canaris, there at OKW, took them over. We think they must all have been burned after the attempt on Hitler's life. After 20 July there was nothing left but this thin file, which came into the hands of Kaltenbrunner at SS staff headquarters. From there it was sent on to Bavaria when the Russians were approaching Berlin, and the Americans got hold of it. They were practically out of their minds about it for years. Here was this Operation Wild Geese, and no one had the faintest idea what it was about. At the Nuremberg trials, the Americans tried discreetly pumping the Russians. Not a word out of them. Contact with Russia on the subject has been attempted again and again. No luck.'

'And now I come back.'

'Yes, the last of the ten.'

'No, you're wrong. There are still four of us.'

'Asgard!' Willy Hecht reached for his brandy-glass with a shaking hand. 'You sit there and say that as casually as if it were the score of some game. There are still *four* of you alive?'

'Yes.'

'In Russia?'

'Only three in Russia now. I'm the fourth.'

'Good God in heaven! Why didn't the others come back, too?'

'They're quite happy as Russian citizens.'

'Happy? German officers?'

'You forget Germany's traditional urge to go east — from the knights of the Middle Ages, through the Hanseatic League, the German scholars and officers who entered the service of the Tsars, the farmers who settled on the Volga and the Don at the time of Catherine the Great. In Kazakhstan there are districts bigger

32

than Bavaria whose people speak good German with a Swabian accent, as well as Russian. Leaving politics aside, Russia's a country where a man can still feel in touch with Nature.'

General Hecht opened the file. 'There are still four of you,' he repeated, breathing deeply. 'Who are the others?'

'Willy, the Wild Geese are tame, domestic geese now. Don't ask me any more questions — there's no point in it. Let's drink our coffee and our brandy, and you tell me how *you* are. Yeneral Hecht, by God!'

The General reached down to the shelf beneath the table again and placed another folder beside the coffee-cups. It had a white cover with a red cross on it. Lips compressed, Kuehenberg leaned back. His face did not move; the deep lines in it were like scars from old sword-cuts.

'Do you know what that is?' asked Hecht.

'I can guess.'

'It's compiled from the literature of the German Red Cross's Missing Persons Service. The first request for help in tracing a man dates from 1946. The applicant is still hoping, still searching, and has been for thirty-two years, Asgard. You know, there are still people — mothers and fathers, brothers and sisters, wives and children — telling themselves that "missing" does not necessarily mean "dead".' General Hecht opened the folder. Letters, forms, questionnaires, yet more letters. Old photographs, showing laughing young men with cheerful, boyish faces. Group pictures, pictures of individuals. A lock of curly fair hair in an envelope.

Kuehenberg looked away when Hecht took out the lock of hair and held it out to him.

'His mother wrote: "Perhaps this lock of hair may help. I cut it off when my son had to go to Russia again. He was twenty-one then. He had been a lieutenant for six months, and he was proud of his fair curls. He was such a cheerful lad. I feel sure his friends must remember his hair, and the way he laughed...."'

'Johann Poltmann,' said Kuehenberg dully. 'Or, rather, after 3 June 1944, Fyodor Panteleyevich Ivanov. Married to Wanda Semyonovna Haller. She was forewoman of a construction brigade.'

33

General Hecht dangled the lock of fair hair in front of Kuehenberg.

'Won't you talk, Asgard?' he asked quietly. 'His mother is seventy-nine now, living in an old people's home in Bremen. And hoping – hoping. Every year she applies to the Red Cross again. They all do. You are the only person who knows the real story. Asgard, you *must* talk – that is, if you have any heart left. Do you want to read the letters?'

'Yes.' Kuehenberg took the lock of hair between finger and thumb and put it back in the envelope. Johann Poltmann, with his fine head of curly hair. He almost wept when he was threatened with having it shorn for Operation Wild Geese. Here was his mother's last memento of her only son. . . .

'Is anyone looking for *me?*' asked Kuehenberg, closing the folder.

'No. You're the only one with no family left. You probably know that your family's estate at Thernauen was overrun when the Russian tanks suddenly broke through. The buildings were burned down; everyone was killed.'

'My poor father.' Kuehenberg looked up at the strip lighting on the white ceiling. 'He thought his Russian neighbours were good friends. Many Russians came to visit us, treated the place like home. He thought a white flag of truce would enable him to survive the war. A white flag, and a peace-offering of bread and salt for them. No one could persuade him otherwise. He had a missionary's faith in human nature.' Kuehenberg held out his brandy-glass. 'I'll have another, please, Willy. Will you give me time?'

'You'll tell us, then?'

'I'll try. Not for you or your military archives – for these mothers and brothers and sisters. Is Bodo von Labitz's wife still alive?'

'Yes. Living in Vienna.'

'Did she ever marry again?'

'No. She's still hoping.'

'He was celebrating the birth of his first child at the time.'

'A boy. William Heiko von Labitz. He's a lawyer in Vienna now; his mother lives with him.'

'I'll write it down,' said Kuehenberg, sipping his cognac. 'I'll let the Wild Geese fly once more. But after that, Willy, I never

34

want to hear about it again. I came back out of homesickness, for no other reason. Who's going to read my account?'

'Only a very few people, I promise you.'

'You must remember that three of us are still living in or near Moscow — good Russian citizens with wives and children.'

'No one will learn their names. I give you my word.'

'You'll be disappointed, you know. Wild Geese was the craziest, most hopeless operation of the entire war.'

Two

RADEK, Peter, aged twenty-five, Lieutenant
C Company had dug in north of Pleskau. It was a wretched
position: scattered foxholes linked by shallow communication-
trenches. There were only a hundred and nine men strung out
along a line which would normally require a whole battalion to
hold it. Weary, exhausted, dirty, hungry men, tired to the bone.
The deep penetration of the Soviet armies into the German
Army Group North sector, extending from Leningrad to Velikiye
Luki, might have come to a halt here on the eastern bank of Lake
Peipus and Lake Pleskau, but farther south, where the 16th Army
was facing General Popov's 2nd Baltic Front, the activity was like
a kettle boiling over.

Night and day the front was under fire from thousands of guns,
massed particularly densely in the Russian 22nd Army area. Spearheads of T34 tanks, those steel Soviet monsters against which the
Germans had no real defence, were churning up their scattered
positions, flattening foxholes or chasing the fleeing men who ran
for it. It was a cruel game: the Russians let them run, drove after
them, shooting to miss for a while, and then, when they could run
no longer and raised their arms in surrender, the heavy machine-
guns mounted on the tank-turrets were turned on them.

It was much the same in the north, where, in General Merets-
kov's Volkhov Front zone, the Russians suddenly stopped as if to
get their breath back after their uninterrupted and victorious progress from Leningrad to Lake Peipus. Illusory optimism spread
among the German troops, and was nourished by the articles
Goebbels wrote in *Das Reich,* and by the speeches of those Nazi
Party staff officers recently introduced into the Army.

The Soviet 'pinprick policy' was paying off. All along the front
dying had become an anonymous business.

Yes, a quiet front. Now and then the slow, heavily armoured Soviet reconnaissance-plane nicknamed 'the coffee-percolator' droned past above the German foxholes, not afraid to fly so low that you could see the pilot. The men had tried shooting at it, but it just droned along its observation-path like a giant insect, stubborn and invulnerable. You got used to it in time. You even missed its *tuck-tuck-tuck* when it stopped.

The foxholes of C Company were so far apart that Lieutenant Radek had said, 'If the Ivans attack with their T34s, they won't even notice we're here.' Radek was back in the company bunker after a tour of inspection. 'Bunker' was rather a grand name for this pit, roofed with planks and earth, rather larger than the men's foxholes, but crammed to bursting-point with a folding table, a field-telephone, three crates of hand grenades, two heavy machine-guns, and a folding stretcher with the Red Cross conspicuously painted on it.

Radek was tired. Early that morning he had run, ducking low, along the communication-trenches to his men, and had stayed out there with them until evening.

'We're in a hell of a spot here,' said Staff Sergeant Hagemüller. The days when a lieutenant commanded a platoon were long past. 'You watch this, sir.'

He put a steel helmet on the end of a stick and poked it above the edge of the foxhole. Less than a second later there was a whooshing sound, then a clear, metallic impact, and the helmet flew through the air as if propelled by a ghostly hand and struck the edge of the trench. 'Straight through the head, that would've been,' said Hagemüller. 'They've got plenty of ammo, and they're bloody obstinate. They shoot at anything that moves.'

Lieutenant Radek lay flat in the shallow pit in the ground. 'Surely we can find out just where the hell they are?' he said.

'Somewhere in that scrubby terrain over there.'

' "Somewhere" isn't good enough as a target-designation.' Radek pushed his gas-mask cover over the edge of the foxhole. Instantly, a shot tore it out of his hand. 'Christ!'

'I was thinking, sir,' said Hagemüller, 'that we might get a better idea if Sections 3 and 6, on the right and left, gave us cover with their machine-gun fire, and we had three men crawl up to

37

within throwing distance. Three or four package-charges, and we'd have 'em.'

Radek shook his head. The same old story: he had been hearing it for weeks.

'I know, sir, I know. Fifteen shots per man per day. Hand grenades for use only in emergency. Machine-guns for use only in defence. Hell, it's like expecting a toothless old lady to bite her way through iron bars.'

'Not my damn silly order, Hagemüller. They'll be shortening the front in two days' time. Our bridgehead's being withdrawn.'

'Two days is a hell of a long time, sir.'

Radek shrugged his shoulders. 'Sorry, we have to stick it out here. Then we get back to a nice consolidated rear position.'

Lieutenant Radek had spent the day crawling along the trenches, from foxhole to foxhole, visiting his company. The Russian troops facing them had just been relieved; now they had to deal with a crack regiment of Siberian sharpshooters. They even sang at night, their songs echoing through the moonlight to reach the German lines.

'And, damn their eyes, they're roasting meat,' said Corporal Emil Happes. 'Smell that? They've got a pig roasting on a spit, while we're licking out our canteens.'

Just before Radek crawled back to the company bunker and the men detailed to fetch rations from the field-kitchen came along, there was a clatter of tin cans tied together with string. It came from Section 1.

The alarm signal. Ivan was coming.

It was only an exploratory raid. They were shooting as they ran, throwing hand grenades, and yelling their unnerving Russian cry. Then, equally suddenly, they retired to their own position.

Nothing gained—but it was yet another of those pinpricks intended to let the Germans know: We can get you any time we want.

At last, Radek stumbled into the company bunker and flung his helmet against the mud wall. Sergeant Lehmann saluted as if he were on sentry duty outside a barracks.

'Nothing to report, sir,' he announced.

'Never mind the formalities, Lehmann,' said Radek, sitting down on his bed, which consisted of a pair of crossbars and two boards nailed together. 'Listen to what I'm going to tell them at Battalion HQ!'

He wound up the field-telephone, waited, and then said, 'Radek here. I want to speak to the commanding officer. . . . I'm to do what? Get back there to you – at once? Come off it – you must be crazy! *Who* said so? OKW – High Command themselves? Oh, I like that, I really do like that. You're dead drunk back there, and we can't even venture to get our heads up above the ground. . . . Oh, all right, I'm coming, I'm coming.'

Radek hung up, and fished his steel helmet off the ground with his foot.

'It seems the CO has a burning desire to see me, Lehmann. I'll be back at dawn. If anything special comes up, ring me at Battalion HQ.'

Again, he had to crawl along the trenches until he reached the company's supply-depot and field-kitchen; not until he was past the next chain of hills could he rise from the ground. The Company Sergeant-Major was waiting there for him. 'Jeep ready and all tanked up,' he reported. The German version of a jeep was a converted Volkswagen, a vehicle around which many legends were gathering.

'You know anything about this, Ratterfeld?' asked Radek, getting behind the wheel. 'I dare say you've had a word with your mate in the battalion orderly-room.'

'All I know is, something or other came from OKW, sir.'

'Something to do with me?'

'Looks like it, sir.'

'That's ridiculous. I ask you, why would OKW bother about me. Must be a mistake, if you ask me.'

It was no mistake.

Major Sauer was waiting for Radek at the battalion command-post. He looked him up and down, and shook his head. 'You'll have to get that uniform cleaned for Berlin.'

'Best-quality Russian mud and blood, sir.' Radek put his helmet down on a camp-stool. 'Look, surely this Berlin thing is some kind of joke?'

'That's what I thought' – Major Sauer picked up a piece of paper and put his glasses on – 'I got the phone call taken down in shorthand as it came through. It was Vangenheim himself, the

39

Divisional Commander, representative of God the Father Almighty, on the line. He said they'd just had a radio message from OKW sent on by Army High Command. Urgent. You are to be withdrawn from the front at once and go to Eberswalde. Division will see to the papers for the journey. Squadron 2 has a courier-plane ready to fly you in. Got an uncle in OKW, Radek?'

'No, sir.'

Major Sauer poured two glasses of cheap brandy. 'Eberswalde, too,' he said.

'What about Eberswalde?'

'The Brandenburg Officers' Riding School is in Eberswalde.'

'It's not the moment for practical jokes. Haven't they heard there's a war on?'

'Your birth-date is right; Vangenheim added that to your particulars, obviously to be on the safe side. You *were* born in Riga?'

'Yes.'

'Well, then, it's no joke.' Major Sauer raised his glass to Lieutenant Radek. 'Perhaps they're going to train you as a Cossack. Well, send me a postcard after your first riding lesson.'

Radek looked over the rim of his glass at his battalion commander. 'What about C Company?' he asked. 'Who'll take them over?'

'I'll send Second Lieutenant Heinze from D Company to replace you.'

'Heinze's only just out of military academy, sir.'

Sauer sighed. 'I know. I know,' he said impatiently.

Next morning, Lieutenant Peter Radek was reporting to Colonel Vangenheim, the Divisional Commander. A large and handsome car, a Horch, rushed him to Squadron 2's airfield.

At 1420 hours the courier-plane, a Fokker, rose into the sky, heading for Berlin. Only Radek and the pilot, a Luftwaffe acting pilot officer, were on board.

At 1437 hours, Staff Sergeant Hagemüller reported from the front line: 'Second Lieutenant Heinze just fallen. Shot through the head. Those bloody Siberian marksmen. . . .'

RANOVSKI, Berno von, aged twenty-four, Lieutenant
They were lying in woodland south of Orsha. Ahead of them, the railway tracks gleamed faintly in fitful moonlight. The single great

40

railway from Brest-Litovsk to Moscow, passing through Minsk, Borisov, Orsha and Smolensk, ran almost parallel to the Brest-to-Smolensk highway, the most important road in central Russia. Two lifelines along which German supplies were travelling. Provisions, ammunition, weapons, tanks, spare parts. And there were men going home on leave, men returning to their units from leave, raw young recruits, still little more than children, rapidly trained and now staring, wide-eyed, at the landscape rolling past them; the wide, beautiful, terrible country of Russia. They were to dig themselves into its soil and hold on, for the honour of the Fatherland, and by the Führer's orders.

Without the road and the railway, the German divisions in action here would soon have been paralysed. As long as blood was flowing through these two vital arteries, the thin lines of German soldiers would get transfusions of new strength. After the winter and spring Soviet offensives in the north, the Crimea and the Ukraine, they were expecting another major strike here in the central sector of the Eastern Front, an attempt by the Russians to make a massive breakthrough to the Polish border. But as long as the Germans had the road and the railway it would be difficult.

In the area around Orsha and Borisov, where German supplies were accumulating, and every village along the railway line had become a huge storehouse, General Shankovsky, with painstaking attention to detail, had built up an invisible troop of saboteurs. Officers who looked like weather-beaten peasants, or like village idiots unfit for active service, had infiltrated the area, parachuting in by night, made their headquarters in the Dobryn and Sobrino forests on either side of the Dnieper, and were gathering the people around them. Unobtrusively, in small groups, there were men and women being trained to use weapons, lay mines and make home-made time-bombs. They learned to creep up on an enemy in silence, camouflage themselves with grass and twigs, dig holes in the ground where they could suddenly vanish; they practised throwing knives, and strangling a man with thin steel wire, a silent method of killing. A special detachment of women and young girls was told that it was no disgrace to lie down to make love with a German in the bushes on the embankment.

'Keep thinking: I make this sacrifice for Mother Russia,' Shankovsky's officers told the silently listening women. 'You can wash it off afterwards, comrades, you can wash it all away. It does not touch your souls, only your skin. Your brothers are giving their lives — what's this sacrifice by comparison? Every German for whom you open your legs means a blow struck against the Nazis. At that moment, your brave menfolk can move in for decisive action.'

To the Germans, these Russian partisans were a silent, deadly threat. 'We've had 2359 acts of sabotage and attacks on the railway line over the last two months,' said Major von Habner. He was a grey-haired, genial man, who had been put in charge of supervising the Orsha-to-Borisov section of the railway line because he was unfit for service at the front. Now he would gladly have exchanged his position for one in the front line. His troops were pathetically inadequate. A battalion of Bulgarians, mostly stationed in bunkers along the railway to patrol the line, who somehow were never in the right spot when a bomb blew up part of the track. Three companies of Germans, 'convalescent units', as they were called: those who had been unlucky enough to get wounded, but not severely enough to be sent home. In addition, there were three hundred Russian volunteers, who would work for the Germans for bread and a bowl of soup. Uncomplainingly, they did the heavy work, repaired tracks, rebuilt portions of the embankment, dug new bunkers along the line, erected barbed-wire fences, laid mines on the embankments — and passed on sketches, showing just where those mines were, to the partisans in the woods and marshes.

'2359 acts of sabotage,' said Major von Habner, his pointer travelling over the big map of the area which hung on the classroom wall of Orsha Primary School, an old brick building with tall, narrow windows, dating from Tsarist times. The classroom forms were too narrow for grown men, so the officers and NCOs he was addressing perched on the desks. 'Partisan activity is increasing daily,' the Major went on, tapping the railway line on the map. 'It suggests that things will be pretty hot here, too, before long. The immediate execution of captured partisans does nothing to keep our volunteers friendly, and we need them to do the repair work. We must act; we must comb the whole area where the partisan command-posts are hidden and wipe them out. I plan to operate using three battalions. We shall encircle

42

areas and go over them metre by metre. Anyone carrying a weapon to be shot on sight. All suspect persons to be immediately sent to Goloshevka, where they'll be interrogated. Gentlemen,' said Major von Habner, putting down his pointer, 'I don't like killing civilians, but a Russian who's friendly by day may be a cold-blooded murderer by night.'

So now they were lying along the railway line, by night, motionless, camouflaged by bushes, observing the terrain. They were in small groups of four, with enough space between them to allow any partisans who turned up to slip unsuspectingly out of the woods. Once they were on the tracks, the Germans would open fire.

Lieutenant Berno von Ranovski was one of a group some way from the rest of the company. It was a warm night with a good deal of cloud; the moon floated in silvery cotton-wool. They had been searching for partisans for two days, unsuccessfully. All they found in the scattered peasant huts were terrified women and children, who cowered at the sight of German soldiers and were anxious to assure them that they had no chickens or pigs left, not so much as a bag of barley or rye.

'Where are your men?' Ranovski had asked.

'No men,' cried the women. 'Gone. Gone Orsha. Gone Germany. Not know. No men more. Alone here. Hungry. . . .'

There was no answer to this.

'There they are,' whispered Sergeant Meier suddenly into Ranovski's ear. 'To your right, sir. See those shadows? At the edge of the trees.'

Ranovski stared at the forest. At first, he saw nothing but darkness. Then he caught sight of slow, cautious movement in the shadows.

'Get the flares ready,' Ranovski whispered back.

'Ready now, sir.'

'Let them reach the tracks first.'

There was movement again at the edge of the wood. Figures slipped out and made for the tracks. Figures in long, full skirts, smaller shadows hopping along beside them like dwarves.

Lieutenant von Ranovski swallowed. 'Those are women and children!' he whispered hoarsely. 'No flares, Meier.'

'Partisans, sir.'

'Women, Meier. And small children. Are you going to shoot children?'

'This is a hell of a thing, sir. The women take the children along to protect them, see? They're counting on our tender hearts: we won't shoot kids. So the children form a circle while their mothers lay explosives on the tracks. You've only been here a month, sir, you don't know the place yet, but I've been dealing with these partisans for a year. We know their little tricks, and this is the nastiest of the lot—using kids as a shield.'

'I can't give the order to fire,' said Ranovski in hollow tones. 'No one can ask me to do that.'

'Then we'll take the women prisoner. Anyone found in possession of explosives goes to Goloshevka anyway, where the Special Unit men see to them.'

'And what happens to the children?'

'No idea, sir.'

'Really, Meier?'

'Word of honour, sir. I've heard rumours of transports of children being sent to Germany, mostly ten- to fourteen-year-olds who can work.'

'That's not true, Meier.'

'Only rumours, like I said, sir.' Sergeant Meier drew his right leg up, ready to move forward. 'Shall we get 'em?'

'No.' Ranovski looked at the group of women and children. They were crossing the rails now, making their escape through the camouflaged German company lying there in ambush. An NCO from the nearest group crawled up to Ranovski

'Lieutenant von Ranovski, sir,' he stammered, 'that—that's them. The partisans. Why don't we fire?'

'Assemble at the departure-point,' said Ranovski curtly. 'How would you like it if someone shot *your* mother, Sergeant?'

Half an hour later, the company was in its trucks on the way back to Orsha. Among the reports delivered to Major von Habner in the morning was one from Ranovski 'No incidents in control sector,' ran the brief report. 'Grid reference 7—9: 29 houses. No occupants but women and children. No weapons found. No evidence of partisan activity.'

'Odd,' said the Major at his midday conference. 'The tracks were loosened at four points along your sector of the line last night, Ranovski. An ammunition-train was derailed at 0325. Only damage to material, thank God.'

At 1400 hours, the Divisional Commander rang Lieutenant von Ranovski. 'Can you be ready to leave at once?' he asked.

'What?' Ranovski was thinking rapidly. They didn't transfer an officer for disciplinary reasons as casually as that – not without interrogating him first.

'You're flying to Berlin today,' said the Divisional Commander. 'Orders from OKW.'

'Berlin, sir? OKW? What on earth am I to do at High Command?'

'How should I know, Lieutenant? The telegraph message says: minimum baggage, report to the Officers' Riding School in Eberswalde.'

'But I *can* ride, sir. And I never put in for a cavalry course.'

'Better ask OKW.' The Divisional Commander seemed to be in a hurry. 'When can you report to Divisional HQ?'

'At once, sir.'

'Good. Your CO is being informed by us. Whatever they want you for in Berlin, it must be very urgent, so don't waste any time.'

Berlin, thought Ranovski, with sudden pleasure. I left Lilli in Berlin. Little green-eyed Lilli with her round breasts. She squealed like a piglet when you made love to her, and when you thought she'd had enough she'd bury her face in your stomach and threaten to bite her initials there. ...

He was to be disappointed. He never saw Berlin again.

SOLBREIT, Elmar, aged twenty-two, Second Lieutenant
He was covered with mud from the top of his head to the toes of his boots. Dried mud, bits of waterweed and green algae covered his uniform. His boots themselves were squelching with water, his face was a muddy grey spotted with green. Weary to the point of collapse, he crouched on the ground, tossed his sub-machine-gun aside and took off his helmet. His short fair hair was stuck together as if with glue.

The men who had come back with him looked the same. Figures out of some legendary world of fable: the Marsh King's sons.

'It's a real bastard,' said Second Lieutenant Solbreit. He took

45

off his wet boots and threw them after the gun. G Company was used to such apparitions in its camp; all patrols coming back from the Pripet marshes looked like that. Sergeant-Major Maritzka bellowed for the NCO on kitchen duty and demanded tea and vodka. Captain Voggenreiter emerged from his reed hut, which was additionally camouflaged with a net, and squatted down beside the young lieutenant. Two men brought a bucket of water and washed Solbreit's face. When they had finished, a thick liquid remained in the bucket. The other members of the patrol made their way to their own dugouts, took off their clothes and stood under the watering-cans tied to a string which formed improvised showers. A lance-corporal ran back and forth with buckets, replenishing the watering-cans. A delicious smell came wafting out of the cookhouse. Bean soup with bacon, specially ordered by Captain Voggenreiter. 'If the lads get back, we'll have a good meal to celebrate.' He laid emphasis on the word 'if'. *If* — everyone knew what that meant, and no one would have laughed at a man who went into the Pripet marshes to scout for Soviet positions, or capture a prisoner for questioning, if he had knelt down to pray, even after his return.

They knew almost nothing about the enemy around them, except that he was there — and popping up where least expected. At their backs, where the battalion staff should have been. Or to the west, where the 3rd Battalion had been building strong positions for months. Or straight out of the impassable swamps, where, by ordinary human standards, no one could live, because there was no firm ground underfoot, just the quaking mud, lakes full of rushes, marshes with a treacherous carpeting of flowers, reedy hollows where millions of birds nested: wild duck and divers, pheasants and cranes, partridges and grey-green mallards. The war did not disturb the birds; its noise was muted in the marshes, which swallowed up its sounds. Grenades sank in mud as soft as blancmange before exploding.

It was man-to-man fighting here, not tank against tank or gun against gun. The marshes covered an area as large as Prussia, and the Russians lay somewhere in this jungle of reeds and rushes, willows and poplars, furze and giant ferns, while the Germans lay somewhere else. The first tiger to leap was victorious.

Lieutenant Solbreit mopped his face with a large towel. In

spite of his face having been washed in a whole bucket of water, the towel still came away yellow with mud. He started to rise, but Captain Voggenreiter made him stay where he was.

'Sit down for a bit, Solbreit. No more information yet, then?'

'Combat patrol, Solbreit section, back from reconnaissance: no enemy movement, own losses none,' said Solbreit formally, reaching for the tin mug the NCO was holding out to him: tea laced with vodka. He drank greedily, and then belched. 'Sorry, sir.'

'A good healthy sound,' Voggenreiter laughed. 'B Company's patrol is back, too. I've spoken to Leifheim; they saw none of the enemy, either. We're attacking a vacuum. But there they suddenly *are*, materializing like marsh spirits. Damn it all, they must be somewhere. They can't turn into so many reeds.'

'They *use* reeds, though.' Solbreit lay down flat on his back. Christ, I'd like to sleep, he thought. Close my eyes, close my ears, close my mouth and sleep. 'We found a corpse.'

'An Ivan? My God, Solbreit, what unit did he belong to? That would at least give us a clue.'

'First Bare-Arsed Battalion, I guess. No, not quite right; he had swimming-trunks on, nothing else. He was decomposing. Could have been three weeks dead. An advanced post, I suppose. But at least he showed us how the Ivans do it.' Solbreit raised his head, drank the rest of the tea and let his head sink back again. The sergeant grinned at him, his round face like a moon in the pale-blue sky. 'Seppl, just how much vodka did you put in that tea?' asked Solbreit sleepily. 'God, I'm drunk.'

'Half and half, same as you usually have it, sir.'

'Too strong after a day like this, you fool.'

'Tell me about the reeds, Solbreit.'

'They — the Ivans, I mean — they plug their nostrils up with beeswax, put a hollow reed in their mouth, sometimes two reeds, and go right under the surface of the water or the swamp. They breathe through the reeds, which look just like millions of others. In theory, there could be hundreds of Russians lying underwater in the reeds around us ready to emerge when they want. Hence the sudden attacks out of nowhere. I mean, we can't grab hold of every reed we see and give it a tug to find out if there's a Russian head the other end.'

'Solbreit,' said Voggenreiter. 'You've made an invaluable tacti-

47

cal discovery. Pity you won't be around to see us use it to smoke the Ivans out of these marshes. Are you all right?'

'I'm worn out, sir, and I'm drunk.'

'Too bad. You have to be at Divisional HQ this evening.'

'Oh, no.' Solbreit closed his burning eyes. 'Tomorrow. . . .'

'It's a summons from OKW. The Division rang three hours back. You report as soon as possible to Eberswalde.'

'Eberswalde? Do you know the place?'

'No, but the Divisional Commander does. He asked, had Lieutenant Solbreit applied to join the cavalry?'

Solbreit sat up, sniffing the bean soup. 'Why? Is there a cavalry school in Eberswalde?'

'Yes.'

'Oh, marvellous! You can bet there'll be a pile of horseshit waiting for me.'

BALDENOV, Baron Venno von, aged twenty-eight, Captain
It was a wonderful summer in Estonia.

The grass grew thick and tall. The estate's accountant was already reckoning on a record year: plenty of hay, turnips, lucerne, clover. The oats, wheat and maize were filling out nicely in the ear, too. It all meant good sturdy cows, healthy horses, winter feed for the pigs, more chickens and eggs. And money in the coffers of Neu-Nomme estate, a thriving, self-contained little world: a cleverly contrived piece of Paradise. Two hundred years ago there had been nothing here but the weed-grown steppes with their tangled bushes, useless land, open to the winds blowing in off the sea. The first settlers who came to the River Brigitten, with permission from the Tsar of Russia, were farmers from Mecklenburg and Pomerania, among them the youngest scion of a family of country gentry, Baron von Baldenov.

His picture now hung in the big hall of the manor-house at Neu-Nomme; it showed a stern-faced man, with long mutton-chop whiskers and watchful blue eyes. And he still kept watch over his family. From whichever angle you looked at the picture, you always met his gaze.

These fine days had to be used to the full. All the able-bodied people on the estate were out in the hayfields mowing, loading the carts, erecting the tripods on which the hay was heaped up to

48

dry. Extra help had come in from neighbouring farms. Johannes von Baldenov had promised a festival with a whole roast ox at the end of the hay harvest. A whole ox roasted on the spit, in the sixth year of the war, the summer of 1944! And there would be music, and dancing, and home-made fruit wine; and the lusty maidservants of Neu-Nomme, who liked a bit of fun, would be wearing nothing under their full, brightly coloured long skirts.

Venno, the eldest son of the family, was home on leave at just the right time. He had three weeks' leave to mark his winning of the Iron Cross, 1st Class.

Decorations were taken for granted in the Baldenov family. Whichever son went into the Army was duty bound to his ancestors to win them.

Captain Venno von Baldenov, acting as officer commanding his battalion of the former 2nd Cavalry Regiment—the Ösel Hussars—had performed his act of heroism during a Soviet tank attack north of Kishinev in Moldavia, shooting down nine T34 tanks with the handful of seven men he had left and a light anti-aircraft gun. He'd done it in sheer desperation. Ahead of him were the Soviet armoured spearheads within range with heavy machine-gun fire, and behind him was the River Prut.

So it was not heroism, just the instinct for survival, when Venno von Baldenov, seeing the T34 tanks of the 4th Ukrainian Front under General Tolbukhin, told his seven weary men, 'If you ever want to eat your mothers' home-made brawn again stick it out now. Don't think of anything, just load and fire, load and fire. Either the Ivans will retreat or we'll be done for. There's nothing else to do.'

His men hammered away at the T34s under cover of a small hill into which the tanks' shells thudded, throwing up fountains of earth into the blue summer sky, forming crater after crater, until the hill resembled a huge Swiss cheese. Shell splinters whistled through the hot air, shearing pieces off bushes and trees. Baldenov had taken over the gunsight himself, and was crouched in the iron seat, adjusting its aim and shouting his orders.

At every hit they scored, the seven men and their captain uttered a shout of triumph.

As the sixth tank was hit, the Russians halted their advance, concentrating their fire on that death-dealing hill before them.

'They're stopping!' said Baldenov. 'Pick off the third from the right.'

After the ninth tank was disabled, the Russians lumbered away. The eight men looked incredulously at the retreating monsters.

One small gun and eight men had halted a Soviet tank advance.

Venno thoroughly enjoyed his home leave. The Baldenov family had never been saints, though they duly went to church on Neu-Nomme estate, sitting in the front pew on Sundays. The men were great womanizers; they made happy and stable marriages because their wives were wisely magnanimous in this respect, knowing that, in due course, the masters of Neu-Nomme would have spent their superfluous ammunition. During his first two weeks at home, Venno had given little Baroness von Ebenhausen, Baron von Riguldi's daughter, and the widowed Baroness von Soulepp cause to admire his remarkable virility, without ever arousing hopes of a more permanent relationship after the war. He visited the neighbouring estates, rode across country and through the woods with the ladies, found sunny, secluded spots, got his two dogs to patrol the place so that they would be sure of privacy, and then gave the enthusiastically co-operative young ladies a display of his prowess.

Today, Venno had gone out to the hayfields with the others. The young master stood on a mountain of hay in one cart, nimbly wielding his pitchfork, and waving to the girls down below, as if challenging them to tire him out.

He was a strong man; he stood there with his chest bare, wearing faded, close-fitting drill-trousers. His muscles rippled beneath the skin of his upper arms, back, stomach and thighs.

The girls who worked on the estate admired him from afar, eyes shining. As yet, the young master was out of their reach. During these three short weeks' leave, he spent his time going around with baronesses. But, once the war was won, Venno would have leisure to carry on the family tradition and go chasing skirts on his own estate.

The hay-cart was three-quarters full when Lance-Corporal Hans Briszliszky, his batman, came galloping over the field, waving a piece of paper.

'Telegram for you, sir!' shouted Briszliszky, reining in his sweating horse. 'Just this moment come. Urgent!'

Venno kneeled on the pile of hay. The girls with their pitch-forks clustered around the nervous, prancing horse.

'Official news of the Knight's Cross come through?' asked Baldenov.

'No, sir. First thing tomorrow you report to Eberswalde, sir.'

'To where?'

'Eberswalde, sir. The Riding School.'

'Are they out of their minds? I could ride while I was still in nappies.'

'It must mean a job on the General Staff, my boy, what else?' said Johannes von Baldenov proudly. 'If OKW themselves.... Well, my boy, your whole family will be proud of you.'

'The family would do better to put its mind to evacuating Neu-Nomme while you can still take everything with you,' said Venno, reading the telegram yet again. 'Listen, Father, you should set off after harvest. We expect a vast Russian offensive this summer. We're too enfeebled to hold out against it.'

'*You* held out against thirty T34s, on your own.'

'In peculiarly lucky circumstances. Listen to me. Get yourself safely into the Reich. There are nine Soviet armies facing us here in the north. And how many do we have? Two. The 20th and 16th Armies. And they're under strength.'

'Good God, boy, what a way to talk! The Führer knows what he's about. Our wall of iron—'

There was no way Venno could get through to the old man. He could only beg him to go.

Next morning, Venno von Baldenov flew to Berlin from Reval airfield. He never saw his father or Neu-Nomme on the River Brigitten again.

POLTMANN, Johann, aged twenty-one, Second Lieutenant
So far, Lieutenant Poltmann had been wounded three times, each time too slightly for the injury to justify his being sent home. The army doctors who treated him, at the field-hospital at Mogilev behind the lines, shook their heads in sympathy. 'Hard luck again, old fellow. Quarter of a pound of flesh off your backside, but otherwise you're fine. Five centimetres higher up, now, right through the buttock, and you'd have made it home this time. As it is, nothing doing.'

51

Second Lieutenant Poltmann enjoyed a kind of erotic notoriety in the field-hospitals of Mogilev. Not that he was endowed with particularly amazing potency. The secret of his mysterious success with women lay in his hair. Almost platinum blond, it curled so naturally and endearingly that women longed to plunge their hands into it. At the moment of climax, a girl would not cling to his shoulders or dig her fingers into his back, wind her legs around his hips, or her arms around his neck: she would thrust her fingers into those blond curls.

'All very well for Johann,' said his officer friends, raising a cheerful glass to him. 'He simply has to take his cap off.'

Mogilev's 2nd Field-Hospital, where Poltmann was now a patient, was generally known to be the hospital with the best-natured nurses. They came in two categories: the 'old hands', nurses who had worked for months in the big field-hospitals, and were beyond being surprised by any tricks the men thought up to get under their skirts; and the nursing ancillaries, young girls being trained and undergoing their first baptism of fire here near the front. Idealistic as these young girls might be, Lieutenant Poltmann's fair hair weakened their moral fibre. After five days lying on his stomach, he was allowed to move around normally, and went about the hospital to take his pick. There was a pretty little brunette, but she had an overpoweringly strong Saxon accent which put him off. His next favourite was called Elfriede, a very Germanic blonde, with lovely if rather sturdy legs, and breasts which strained so hard against her blouse that its buttons were always popping out of their buttonholes. She walked through the hospital like a Valkyrie. There was a large company of hunts-men after this sporting trophy, but none of them successful. Elfriede's feminine pride surrounded her like an aura of in-vulnerability—until Second Lieutenant Poltmann was admitted, with his ludicrous wound in the buttocks. When he happened to meet Elfriede outside the laundry-room where he had gone to hand in a shirt, she asked him, 'Is it real, Lieutenant?'

'What?' asked Poltmann, baffled.

'Your hair. The colour, I mean. Or do you bleach it?'

'At the front?'

'Oh dear, what a silly question.' Elfriede smiled, embarrassed;

52

the effect was to make her look less formidably Teutonic. 'May —may I ... ?'

'May you what?' asked Poltmann.

'Touch – touch you.'

'Where?'

'Your hair, of course,' said Elfriede. Her eyes tried to flash with indignation, but her full, beautifully curved lips were smiling.

'Yes, if you want to.' He bowed his head, and Elfriede stroked his silky, pale-gold curls with both hands. Her breath was coming faster, and her breasts rising and falling like pistons, as he could see very clearly with his bowed head so close to them. He could feel her hands trembling.

'Thank you,' she said, in a husky, much deeper voice. 'Well, now, let's have your dirty shirt, Lieutenant Poltmann.'

Poltmann left the laundry-room with strangely mixed feelings.

That evening he chose a particularly lovely poem from his volumes of Hölderlin, wrote it out in his best handwriting, folded up the sheet of paper, cut off a long lock of his curly hair, put it into an envelope with the poem, sealed the envelope, and that night slid it under the door of duty-room 6. He had made inquiries, and found out that Elfriede was on duty from four in the morning till twelve noon.

His missive had a remarkable effect.

The next day Elfriede was free, she and Poltmann met in a little hut by the Dnieper. They did not waste much time talking, but their lovemaking, on a straw mattress laid on an old wooden bedstead, was tempestuous.

'I'm wearing your hair on my breast, next to my skin,' she said, and so she was. She had tied the pale-gold curl together with cotton, hung it from a small silver chain like a pendant, and now it lay between her beautiful breasts. 'So I can feel you all the time,' she whispered. 'Every time I move you're there beside me, stroking my breasts.'

Their idyll lasted five days. Then the medical supervisor of the hospital, an army doctor with the rank of colonel, summoned Johann Poltmann to his office and looked him up and down. Colonel Beckmann had a reputation for being strait-laced.

'Well, Lieutenant, there's going to be no more rutting in my hospital for you.'

'Colonel Beckmann, sir, I—'

'No excuses, please, Lieutenant. I know the rules of the game, even if I don't take part. I gather you were the successful hunter, Lieutenant Goldilocks – did you know that's what they call you?'

'Er ... yes, but I can hardly help it, sir.'

Dr Beckmann picked up a small piece of paper and waved it in front of Poltmann.

'You're to take off directly, Lieutenant, with the minimum of baggage.' The doctor let the slip of paper flutter back to his desk. 'Orders from Berlin. A plane will take you from Mogilev to Minsk, and then you fly on to Eberswalde in a Fokker.'

'OKW? But that's impossible.' Poltmann stared at Dr Beckmann.

'Perhaps OKW wishes to put your curls to tactical use,' Dr Beckmann suggested.

Poltmann went round to the orderly-room. The chief orderly grinned. 'You'll need to take off in secret this evening, sir,' he said. 'Our little airstrip here won't be big enough to hold all the weeping females.'

ADLER, Detlev, aged twenty-five, Lieutenant

In the fjords of southern Norway the war had taken an extremely leisurely turn in 1944.

Now and then there were sounds of activity in the fjords, mainly evidence of the presence of the English flying their bombers over the mountainous terrain from Tromsö in the north to Stavanger in the south, dropping their deadly cargo. In Narvik, Namsos, Trondheim, Andalsnes and Bergen, the sirens sounded quite often, and there was work for anti-aircraft guns to do. But you could hardly call it war any more. As you lay there dozing in the sun by Sauda Fjord, casting your fishing-line into the water, you could thank your lucky stars you had not been posted to Russia or Italy or to face the Yugoslav partisans. France smelled of gunpowder, too, and something was brewing in England; there were rumours of a big Allied invasion.

None of this troubled Lieutenant Adler.

He and his men, forming a signals section, were billeted in the wooden houses of the small town of Sauda. He had his lines laid, and kept a constant check on them: even in Norway there were saboteurs. However, Sauda was too remote even for them; it was a very unimportant place. The Germans stationed there were so bored they even willingly did parade-ground drill. Apart from that, like their commanding officer Lieutenant Adler, they lay by the fjord fishing, or rowed an improvised pontoon along its narrow waters, singing German folk songs.

Detlev Adler was not a great fisherman or huntsman. He generally lay in a small mountain pasture in the sun listening to music broadcast by the German army transmitter in Oslo. When the political programmes and the war bulletins came on, he would switch off the radio and put on a gramophone record. Listening to *Swan Lake* or *Coppélia* or Beethoven's First Piano Concerto, he quite forgot he was here in a Norwegian meadow, and once again he was only the young man who wanted to study music but had to go into uniform instead. 'My dear boy,' a colonel at Military District Command had told him, 'there'll be plenty of time to scrape away at strings later. We have a war to win first.'

In fact, Detlev Adler became a good officer, and had soon won the Iron Cross, both 1st and 2nd Class. He was never wounded; he did not suffer so much as a scratch. On combat patrol in France, he had been the only man of his party left alive, and he still did not know how he had managed to crawl back to safety, alone and unharmed. It was not as if anyone could overlook him. He was a very tall, sturdy man, with angular features and high cheekbones. 'You look like an Ivan,' a friend had once told him. 'Put you in a Russian uniform and they could print your picture in the *Reich* as an example of Himmler's racial typing.'

'Well, I was born in Dursupe,' he replied. 'That's in Latvia. Do you know Latvia? Well, you've missed something. Lake Angern on the Bay of Riga, and the birch woods, the wide fields, the Baltic beaches—you can still find amber in the white sand there. I hope to God Latvia never falls into Russian hands.'

This morning Sergeant-Major Kreutzer, one of the radio operators, came running down the narrow path to the meadow where his commanding officer lay naked in the sun, listening to Puccini's *Madame Butterfly* with Maria Cetobari and Helge Roswaenge on his gramophone. Sergeant-Major Kreutzer clicked

55

his heels and announced punctiliously, 'Radio message from Bergen HQ. You're to report to Oslo, sir.'

'Good Lord, they must be drunk in Bergen,' said Adler. He stretched, put his hands under the nape of his neck, and blinked up at the sun. Sergeant-Major Kreutzer looked helplessly down at his naked superior officer.

'Sir, I did query it. Got bawled out for my pains. Nothing to joke about, they said. Order came through from the Commander-in-Chief in Oslo himself, they told me.'

'What does Oslo want, then?' said Adler.

'Wants you to report to them there, sir, and then you go on to Berlin, and then you go straight to the Officers' Riding School in Eberswalde.'

'They're off their heads!' Adler switched off his gramophone and got up. Still naked, he ran up and down the little meadow, went to the edge and looked down, over a drop of several hundred metres, at the fjord. The pontoon his men had filched was rocking on the sunlit water. The black dots which were men's heads bobbed round it: his men on morning swimming-instruction duty, though they could all swim like fish already.

'Damn it, I suppose I'll have to go to Oslo, if it's an order,' said Adler. 'But I'm not letting them put me on any bloody horse! I'll be back on Monday, Kreutzer.'

But Adler was not back on Monday. Officially, he was never seen again.

KUEHENBERG, Asgard, aged twenty-eight, Captain
Elmfried Kuehenberg had been happy for a whole day: his son Asgard, a captain serving on the Russian front, at Orgayev in the south Ukraine, had come home on leave. The occasion was the award to him of the German Cross of Gold, disrespectfully known by the privates as the 'Fried Egg', an order given only for personal courage of the highest degree, and valued by many officers more highly than the Knight's Cross, often awarded to them on behalf of their troops. General Schörner, commanding the South Ukraine Army Group, had personally pinned the Fried Egg to Asgard Kuehenberg's uniform, and given him three weeks' home leave.

'Where do you live?' he had asked Kuehenberg.

'Livonia, sir. North of Dünaburg.'

Schörner made no direct reply, merely pressed Kuehenberg's hand very firmly and said, 'Well, come back to your men again safe and sound, Captain.'

Kuehenberg thanked him, turned and left. He knew, from Schörner's second-in-command, what the General himself could not say: the position they were in was hopeless. The Russians might begin their major offensive at any moment. If Canaris was to be believed, they were bringing up massed troops, tanks and artillery which constituted the biggest military force ever brought together in a war. Only Hitler regarded the lull on the Eastern Front as a sign that the Russians were exhausted after the winter offensive. They had halted in April. How could they be capable of an even stronger offensive in June?

Asgard Kuehenberg went home to the small manor-house in Thernauen intending to make good use of his leave, not to spend it relaxing or telling family friends tales of the front, or even devoting much time to his fiancée, Luise von Serlock. In Livonian society it was taken for granted that Asgard and Luise would marry as soon as the war was over.

Asgard Kuehenberg did spend a day visiting neighbouring landowners, and receiving congratulations. He shook hands, let people take photographs of him, danced with various ladies, accepted the good wishes of the servants, including their seventy-four Russian farmworkers, who kissed his hand in the traditional way and wished the young master health and happiness. Then he said, 'That's enough, Father.' He took a bottle of red wine and two long-stemmed glasses of cut crystal out of a cupboard.

They sat facing each other by the empty hearth.

'I know what you're going to say,' Elmfried Kuehenberg began. 'Things look bad at the front.'

'Very bad, Father.'

'But the Führer will know what to do.'

'Father,' Asgard stared at the old man, 'you don't actually believe the stuff Goebbels writes in the *Reich* every week, do you? We've been in retreat ever since Stalingrad — in Italy, on all Russian fronts, in south-east Europe. We've lost more in one year than we won in six, and that's just the beginning. This summer of 1944 will see the end of Germany's Russian venture.'

'I don't believe it,' said old Kuehenberg stubbornly. 'And I certainly don't want to hear such talk from any German officer who wears the Cross of Gold, least of all my own son.'

'Father—'

'Prove your point.'

'Very well. I can. Schörner's second-in-command told me in confidence when he heard where I came from.'

'Schörner.' Elmfried Kuehenberg gestured contemptuously with his long-stemmed wine-glass. 'Scaremongering.' He waved the glass around him. 'Does this look like war? We have peace here. Are our Russian farmworkers discontented, rebellious? Do they scent their Soviet brothers coming? Nothing of the kind — they're working harder than ever. No insolence in their manner; these people know very well this is German land, and German it will stay. This is a good place to be, and they're well off here.' Elmfried Kuehenberg put his glass down. 'Well, what do you say to that?'

'I can only offer you facts and figures. From Narva to Vilna we have the Narva Group, at half strength only, the 18th Army in and around Pleskau, the 16th Army at Rossitten, the 3rd Panzer Army north of Vilna. They comprise the Army Group North, under General Friessner.'

Old Kuehenberg nodded his approval. 'Good.'

'But as for the Russians. . . .' Asgard leaned towards his father. 'At Narva, they have the Leningrad Front under General Govrov, with three armies. At Pleskau, the 3rd Baltic Front is ready with four armies, under General Mazlennikov. The 2nd Baltic Front, under General Yeremenko, is outside Idriza and Rossitten with three armies. South of Dünaburg is the 1st Baltic Front, with six armies, under General Bagramian. And then there's the 3rd Belorussian Front — Marshal Cherniakhovsky has three armies in readiness opposite Vilna. Father, that makes nineteen Soviet armies, fully equipped, against four exhausted German armies. They have over a million Red Army soldiers: well-rested troops, with plenty of ammunition and plenty of petrol. Our own tank divisions are squabbling over every petrol-can, and in the foxholes at the front we have to count out the ammunition and keep a record of every shot fired.' Asgard drew a deep breath and looked

58

at his father, who seemed a little disconcerted after all. 'Will those figures do for you, Father?'

'What about the Führer?' asked Elmfried quietly.

'He's given orders that we are not to retreat a step.'

'There! You see?'

'And suppose those nineteen armies start to move, all at once?'

'Ah, we're not important folk, my boy.' Old Kuehenberg re-filled their glasses. 'We can only see things from ground level — but the Führer has a view of the whole situation from above. So do Keitel and Jodl and Goering.'

Asgard rose to his feet. 'Father, your blind faith in the Führer will be your death sentence if you don't act now.'

'Act?' Old Kuehenberg looked at his son, perplexed. 'What do you mean?'

'I've come home to spend my leave helping you evacuate Thernauen.'

'Evacuate Thernauen?' repeated the old man incredulously.

'Yes, Father.'

'Run, you mean? Run away? Show the Russians our backs? Abandon everything we've built up here over two hundred and fifty years? The estate, the woods, the lake, the horses, the land. Just run away? And where do you suggest we go, my dear boy?'

'To your brother in Essen.'

'Oh, yes? He has a four-roomed apartment. Very glad he'll be to see me turn up with a hundred and seventy horses, a hundred and twenty head of cattle, four hundred and sixty-seven pigs, and a whole army of chickens, geese and ducks!'

'Father, you may think yourself lucky to be able to get away with a couple of suitcases. I beg you — once the Russians start to advance it will be only about a week before they're at our door. And our Russian farmworkers will set fire to Thernauen well before the first armoured spearhead arrives, to light the way for them.'

'They'd never do that. Never.'

'They'll *have* to, Father, or their comrades will liquidate them. They'll burn Thernauen to save their own skins — and, if you're to survive, you must get inside the Reich in good time.'

'You want me to leave your mother?' asked old Kuehenberg softly.

'Mother has been dead for seven years, Father.'

'But she's buried in the grounds, under the sycamore-tree. You want me to leave her to the Russians? How can you ask a thing like that, my boy?'

'Listen, Father,' said Asgard quietly. 'You could take Mother's bones with you, in a zinc coffin. But you must go—you must do it very soon. I know there's not much time left.'

'Once you're back at the front, I give you my word I'll go,' his father replied after a pause. 'But I want you to have these three last weeks here. Let's hope, Asgard. Miracles do happen in war.'

Two days later Elmfried Kuehenberg was holding the miracle in his hand. He showed it to his son, beaming with paternal pride.

'The Liezere postman brought this by bicycle an hour ago. A telegram!' Old Kuehenberg could not resist reading it aloud. '"Start immediately for Berlin. Report to the Riding School, Eberswalde. All available means of transport to be at your disposal. This telegram represents marching orders and all official passes. Signed: Kettner, Operations Staff, OKW."'

Asgard took the telegram from his father and read it through twice without a word. Then he handed it to Luise.

'Don't you have anything to say?' Old Kuehenberg's face was working. 'My boy, it's a miracle. You're being withdrawn from the front! Do you think they want you as a riding instructor in Eberswalde? Well, in any case, it means you'll survive the war—you'll *live*!'

'But this is ridiculous,' said Asgard. 'In 1944, with an invasion of France and a big Soviet offensive in the offing, they'll hardly be needing riding instructors.'

'When do you leave?' asked the old man. Saved, he was thinking. My only son, saved. And, even if the Russians do break through and we lose the Baltic, they'll never reach Eberswalde. They'll be crushed long before they reach the East Prussian border—no Red Army man will ever set foot on that ancestral German soil.

'It says "immediately".' Asgard folded the telegram and put it in the pocket of his hacking-jacket. 'I'll get myself taken to Riga in an hour's time, and then find a plane to fly me to Berlin. Now, Father, don't forget: leave the place this week. Start getting ready to evacuate it at once.'

'All right, my boy, I will.'

'I'll get in touch when I'm in Eberswalde.'

But Asgard Kuehenberg did not get in touch from Eberswalde. And Elmfried Kuehenberg did not leave Thernauen estate. On 29 July 1944 three Soviet soldiers clubbed him to death with the butts of their rifles, under the big sycamore-tree beside the grave of Asgard's mother. All around him the manor-house, the stables and farm buildings, the stud, the coach-houses were burning.

The Russian farmworkers of Thernauen had fired the place as soon as the Soviet armoured spearheads reached Gostini on the Düna.

SEMPER, Dietrich, aged twenty-two, Second Lieutenant

'Gawd, there's a pig in here!'

Corporal Sepp Hölzerlin crawled down into the hole and pulled out the pig by its hind legs. The Russian peasant whose remote house they had just searched was wailing and wringing his hands, calling upon the saints, tearing out his grey hair, gathering his wife, three daughters and two sons-in-law around him, and getting them all to weep in chorus, too.

'Germanski not kill,' cried the peasant. 'We die. Die of hunger.'

'Nice little sow, this, sir,' reported Corporal Hölzerlin. He had the pig clamped firmly between his legs, and he now saluted smartly. 'Lieutenant Semper, sir, this here pig resisted capture. That's enemy action, that is!'

The Kovel area, south of the Polesye moors, was a place already drained of its resources. Three and a half years of German occupation had done nothing to make good the damage done to the land when it was overrun. The criminal policies of the racialist Nazi functionaries, and the 'cleaning-up' operations of the SS in the occupied areas, had emptied the countryside.

Corporal Sepp Hölzerlin untied the string from the beast's snout. It began squealing and squeaking deafeningly, trying to free itself of the grip of Hölzerlin's legs, even attempting to bite him.

'That proves it, sir,' bellowed Hölzerlin, beaming. 'There'd be fresh bacon, with sauerkraut. And he would make blood puddings and liver sausage, too, to say nothing of roast pork.'

Lieutenant Semper nodded. Two men hauled the pig away.

Now there was no sound but the voice of the peasant, still praying to some saint or other, while the women continued their wailing.

'Look, I don't like doing this,' said Lieutenant Semper, in fluent Russian without a trace of German accent. The peasant stopped praying at once, and the women cut their wailing short. They stared at the German officer in amazement.

'Comrade Lieutenant ...,' stammered the old man. 'You—you speak Russian?'

Dietrich Semper merely nodded, not wishing to enter into a discussion on the subject. A man born east of Dorpat and within sight of Lake Peipus, growing up with the children of Russian labourers, was bound to speak Russian like a native. 'I only want to explain that we're fully within our rights in seizing your pig; you know it's illegal to keep one. So stop that row, and be glad you're still alive and won't be punished.'

'But what shall we live on now, Comrade Lieutenant?' faltered the old man.

'On whatever else you've hidden around the place here.' Lieutenant Semper shook his head, smiling slightly. 'I should know your tricks by now. The pig was an error of judgement; you shouldn't have tried hiding anything so valuable as that so near the house!'

Semper turned away, and strode after his scout patrol. One pig would not really go very far between forty-three men; still, this was a day to celebrate, and the field-kitchen could produce a banquet.

It was decided to divide the pig into three, one-third going to the field-kitchen (those parts suitable for soup and sauerkraut dishes), one-third going to the Company Sergeant-Major in the form of joints to be roasted on iron bars, while Hölzerlin set to work on the remaining third to make his brawn and sausages. But before Semper himself had a chance to pronounce judgement and distribute suitable praise in all three pork-butchering departments, the radio operator started frantically waving both hands at him.

'Here, it's for you, sir. The battalion. They're crazy. They want you to leave us.'

Dietrich Semper went over to the radio transmitter and put the earphones on.

The commanding officer of the battalion, Captain Hatterscheidt, answered at the other end of the line. 'Here, what's your radio operator's name, Dietrich?' he asked as Semper came through. 'I may say I heard that lot. I am not crazy. Kindly bring a report on that radio operator with you. What were you up to just now?'

'Well, sir, I was about to give my expert opinion on boiled belly of pork, roast pork loin, and a nice bit of brawn.'

'Do you mind my asking if by any chance you're drunk, Dietrich?'

'We just picked up a partisan, sir. Pig weighing a couple of hundredweight. Like a good joint of pork sent over, sir?'

'You can bring it yourself, Second Lieutenant Semper. Divisional HQ has passed on orders, from OKW. You're to go to Berlin at once. Top priority. No, I'm not crazy – but OKW may be. D'you know Eberswalde?'

'No.'

'Nor do I. Officers' Riding School, it says here.'

'You're right, OKW certainly must be crazy.'

'Well, nothing we can do about that, Dietrich. You come over here to the battalion, and then you can have my jeep to get you to Regimental HQ. I suppose there'll be some explanation. Perhaps they mean someone else called Semper. And Dietrich – don't forget my joint of pork.'

But Second Lieutenant Dietrich Semper ceased to exist once he left the battalion command-post in Captain Hatterscheidt's jeep.

LABITZ, Bodo von, aged thirty-one, Major
The aim of National Socialist population policy had always been to produce many healthy Nordic children, the future world leaders.

South of Tiraspol in the south Ukraine, a bare seventy metres from the advanced Soviet foxholes, the commissariat officer of the 6th Army had finally been persuaded to provide the ingredients for a celebratory party. Along with its usual supplies, the battalion had received ten cans of meat, twenty bottles of brandy, and two cakes from the divisional bakery. The baker had piped on the cakes, in sugar icing: *Happy Birthday to Our CO 30 Years On.*

63

Major von Labitz was deeply touched. It was a surprise party as far as he was concerned; his fellow-officers had kept it secret till the last minute, opening the door of the room where it was to be held only when everything was ready. The room was no more than a barn, cleared out for the purpose, but now it held tables with white cloths, chairs, cut crystal glasses, china, knives and forks. Orderlies in starched white jackets served the meal: oxtail soup, goulash and dumplings, blancmange flavoured with woodruff and vanilla sauce. A princely meal for a great occasion: Major Bodo von Labitz had become a father.

His first child—a son! William Heiko von Labitz. The baby's mother, Enrica von Labitz, *née* Baroness von Saalsfels, had managed to get a telegram sent to Army Group A under Field-Marshal von Kleist, and despite the overloading of the telegraph lines it actually arrived. 'Healthy son born. Weight 3856 grammes. Mother and child both well. Long live Germany!'

Perhaps it was the last sentence which induced army personnel to pass on news of no military or tactical importance, though it filled Major von Labitz with delight. A sturdy boy! He was born rather late in his parents' marriage—at least, his father was thirty-one and his mother twenty-eight—but Labitz had been expending most of his energies on furthering his army career, carrying on the traditions of the Labitz family.

And now came the birth of a son to crown his career so far. William Heiko was, one might say, the fruits of his last home-leave. Not really intended, because Labitz still had that career-ladder to climb, but Enrica had been so avid for love during that last leave, had shown such passion, that Bodo's caution was flung to the wind during their fervent embraces and the *coitus interruptus* he planned never happened. When she wrote later to tell him she was pregnant, he indulged in much philosophical reflection and a letter which began: 'My darling—you're always in my heart. So we are to have a child. A true child of love. May God protect our child and grant that it lives in happier times than these. Once we have won this war, there will never be war again. We shall rule the world, bringing peace, happiness and prosperity to all nations! Pray God that our first child may be a boy. Germany needs strong sons....'

And so he went on, for three pages.

If the drunkenness of the guests were taken as any criterion, the party in the barn was a huge success. All the officers of the regiment's four battalions were invited. As a special surprise, the Divisional Commander arrived in his Horch car, bringing six bottles of champagne. The other officers were not particularly pleased to see General Labbroth. It meant they must drink more moderately, could not bawl rounds at the tops of their voices, and could not, unfortunately, slip a few women in through the back doors. Tiraspol was a small town, but the women here near the Romanian border, not far from the Black Sea, were classic beauties, dark-haired, bright-eyed, slender and supple, with pointed breasts—and like cats on heat once darkness had fallen.

As for the war itself—well, the front had been quiet since April. Small skirmishes, a few men lost every day, but that was all. Ivan had had a bellyful. Everyone said so, including the Russian deserters and prisoners.

So life was good in Tiraspol. Odessa cognac was famous. The country was normally a huge and fertile orchard, but the war had carved lines through it and ploughed up the fields. The vineyards were overgrown with weeds. There were no men left now; anyone not serving in the Red Army had been taken off to Germany in goods-trucks, to make German shells instead of wine, or hew German coal out of the seams of German mines. The Ukraine could have fed all Germany and the German armies; the policy of treating Russians as subhuman was rebounding on Germany herself like a deadly boomerang.

To the officers at Labitz's party, however, all seemed well.

It was almost midnight when General Labbroth, an avuncular arm round Major von Labitz's shoulders, drew the proud father aside. 'Cigar?' he asked.

'Thank you, sir.'

'Well, it's midnight, Labitz. Another day ahead. Yesterday was for you—and your lovely wife, and your son. I've acted against orders, I'm afraid, but I felt a few hours couldn't matter. I have something for you.'

'Yet another present, sir? I'm quite overwhelmed.'

'I wouldn't know whether it's much of a present.' He put his hand in his pocket and produced a piece of paper. 'An urgent telegram from OKW. They want you in Berlin.'

'For another general staff training course, sir?'

'Shouldn't think so. You're to go to the Eberswalde Riding School.'

'It must be some sort of joke, sir.'

'Never noticed the OKW were a particularly humorous lot myself. And the wording's clear enough. You're to go to Eberswalde at once; you'll be flown from Kishinev at seven tomorrow. Well, Labitz, old fellow, let's have another glass of champagne to drink your son's health – and then off you go to Kishinev and Berlin!'

Bodo von Labitz was not to drink much more champagne, and he never set eyes on his son.

DALLBURG, Alexander, aged twenty, Officer Cadet

Officer Cadet Alexander Dallburg was having the time of his life in France. Fresh from military academy, he had been posted to the 914th Regiment of the 352nd Infantry Division, guarding the Western Front, and happened to arrive in Normandy at a time when the most serious injury likely to befall you was a dose of the clap.

Dallburg, aged twenty, had a boyish face with large, innocent blue eyes. He moved into a small requisitioned apartment in Grandchamps-les-Bains, an idyllic little seaside town with a beach, a small bay and a harbour, a café on the promenade, and a bar called the Bistro St-Jacques.

The duties themselves were boring. Drill, weapon cleaning, training marches, the building of bunkers along the coast, the mining of certain sectors, the erection of tank barriers.

'Though they'll never come across,' said the officer commanding the company, Lieutenant Lippe. 'They'd be crazy to try it. This coast can't be taken. We'd be shooting our Allied friends down while they were still bobbing about out at sea. And we have Rommel, too. No, you'll have to find other ways of passing the time while you're guarding this front, Dallburg.'

Lieutenant Lippe himself practised what he preached with enthusiasm: he was living with a bosomy young French widow in a pleasant house on the promenade. Thanks to plenty of wine and good food he was putting on weight, despite his energetic exercise in bed. He went around in civilian clothes much of the time, wearing a beret, an open-necked shirt and worn plimsolls, a cigarette hanging from the corner of his mouth, as if he had grown up in the fresh sea-breezes of Normandy. He knew nothing about his generals' worries; he did not know that an American army under General Bradley and a British army under General Dempsey had assembled in England, across the Channel. He had no idea that Montgomery, Rommel's old adversary in north Africa, had taken over command of the invasion forces, and that the American General Eisenhower was Supreme Commander of the operation known as Overlord. The Allies were only waiting for good weather. There were a hundred and seventy-six thousand men stationed along the south coast of England, looking up at the sky, and they had vast amounts of equipment.

But there was no one to explain that to young Officer Cadet Dallburg. The entire company was busy making sure that life in the healthy climate of Normandy was not *too* bracing and Sergeant-Major Felix Bülles, feeling responsible for the well-being of little Dallburg, said, after he had been there four days, 'Got to do something about this, mates. The lad seems scared of girls — could be he's never had one yet. Real little innocent, he is. Tell you what: we'll send him round to Gabrielle. She'll make a man of him.'

Gabrielle was the star attraction of the Bistro St-Jacques. Small, delicate and fragile in appearance, with bright, shining eyes, slender legs and a provocative wiggle. There was something touchingly childlike about her, an impression of saintly innocence, which was the cleverest of her accomplishments, for anyone who went up to Gabrielle's little attic bedroom came out so exhausted he had to report sick next day, while Gabrielle herself, chirpy as ever, was bustling around the Bistro St-Jacques.

Alexander Dallburg was carried off to the bistro by the Sergeant-Major. He looked dreamily at Gabrielle. Gabrielle's eyes, an equally dreamy expression in them, met his.

'Bonjour, mademoiselle,' said Dallburg. His French was excellent; up in the Baltic, the better-educated families automatically mastered two foreign languages — Russian and French. 'How beautiful you are.'

To which Gabrielle replied, 'Merci, monsieur. How kind *you* are. Not a bit like the others. They all want it after just five minutes. . . .'

And, from then on, Gabrielle would have nothing more to do with the rest of the company. Dallburg came in for respectful admiration, and Sergeant-Major Bülles for a great deal of abuse.

Three days later, Gabrielle moved into Dallburg's little apartment. She was genuinely in love with him; it was like nothing she had ever known before. Her past might have been wiped out. 'Amazing,' said Sergeant-Major Bülles. 'Mind you, I saw something like it once before. In Cologne. When a tart really falls in love. . . .'

In fact, you might have mistaken Grandchamps-les-Bains for Paradise. But even Paradise has gates, through which people may come in — and go out.

Lieutenant Lippe, who visited his orderly-room once a day, looked at the NCO on duty in alarm when the man held out a note.

'Telephone message, sir. I took it down. It's from the division.'

'From where?'

'Our Divisional HQ, sir. The 352nd.'

'Neumann, I can smell the Calvados seeping out of every pore of your skin.' Lippe took the note from him. 'I'd been counting on the division forgetting we even existed. . . . Hullo, what's this? Dallburg? Good Lord.' He glanced through the telegram, and then stared blankly at the NCO. 'Have you read this, Neumann?'

Lance-Corporal Neumann stood to attention. 'Took it down, like I told you, sir.'

'There must be a mix-up. Dallburg going to Berlin? I'll call them.'

The 352nd Infantry Division, its staff quartered in a beautiful little château, had more to worry about than Officer Cadet Dallburg or the doubts of Lieutenant Lippe. The latest reports indicated that an Allied invasion was very close indeed. They shouted impatiently down the line at Lieutenant Lippe. Yes, of course the order came from OKW. Why on earth should he doubt it? It was highly urgent business, and Officer Cadet Dallburg ought to have been well on his way by now.

Lippe hung up. Sergeant-Major Bülles, who was with him, scratched his nose. 'Where *is* Dallburg?' Lippe asked.

'In bed with Gabrielle, sir. Stands to reason,' said Bülles. 'I'll fetch him.'

'No. I'll go.' Lieutenant Lippe got into his jeep and drove down to the beach. Dallburg's apartment was not locked. Gabrielle was pottering around in a silk dressing-gown, her dark hair loose, whistling like a little bird, a picture of happiness. There was a smell of strong coffee and fresh croissants. Dallburg was standing in the bathroom naked to the waist, shaving. Brush in hand, chin covered with lather, he stood to attention at once when he saw Lippe. Gabrielle's eyes flickered nervously all of a sudden. Her feminine instincts were alerted.

'Dallburg,' said Lippe in kindly tones, 'look, I'm sorry to tear you away from your idyll, I really am, but there's a war on, you know. You've got your marching orders.'

'Russia?' asked little Dallburg quietly.

'No.' Lippe shook his head. 'Back to Berlin. Eberswalde. The OKW wants you.'

'High Command? What on earth for?'

'Better ask Keitel that! Come on, finish shaving, fuck Gabrielle again, because it'll be the last time, and then we're off to Divisional HQ. If they had their way, they'd shoot you off to Eberswalde by rocket.'

Most of them arrived at Eberswalde in single-engined courier-planes such as Fokkers, which could land on the improvised airstrip, a field rolled flat. Dallburg was the last to come in – not because it was any farther from the Normandy coast than from Russia, but because General Dollman's 7th Army, to which Dallburg's division had sent him on, kept the insignificant young officer cadet waiting. A courier-plane to Berlin for a single man – for God's sake, they'd just got the new air-photographs in from the reconnaissance-planes, showing the south coast of England to be one huge army camp. If there were only a few bomber squadrons available, with fighters to escort them, every bomb would have found a target. But the air belonged to the Allies; Germany had lost the battle for air space long ago. The moment of invasion seemed to be coming very close. But neither Field-Marshal von Rundstedt, Commander-in-Chief of the West, nor Rommel and Blaskowitz, commanding Army Groups B and C, were getting anywhere with their warnings to Hitler. The last reserves of men had already been scraped up. You might rely on the old saying that one German soldier was worth ten of the enemy, but that did not take the enemy's enormous superiority in munitions and supplies into account. And they were supposed to take time off to worry about an officer cadet. OKW could bloody well send a plane themselves if they wanted him that badly.

The ten men were housed in the living-quarters of the Officers' Riding School, isolated in one wing as if they were suffering from some highly infectious disease. As they arrived, they were all greeted by an officer who introduced himself as Lieutenant-Colonel Hansekamm and behaved as if they were old friends. He shook hands with them, asked if they had had a good journey, made a few jokes to lighten the atmosphere, which still remained tense. But when each man asked the obvious question — 'What's this about? What are we supposed to be doing at a riding school?' — Lieutenant-Colonel Hansekamm said evasively, 'I'm afraid I have no authority to tell you that. Colonel von Renneberg will talk to you about it as soon as he's back from the Führer's head-quarters.'

The Führer's headquarters? Something to do with them?

They soon got to know each other. Second Lieutenant Semper, who had brought two bottles of vodka from Kovel with him, as a consolation prize for missing the roast pork, produced one of them as soon as Labitz mentioned the birth of his son. They had gathered in Asgard Kuehenberg's room, which was the largest, with a fine view out over the paddocks into the countryside of the Brandenburg Mark.

Dallburg turned up in the middle of this improvised party, fresh from meeting Hansekamm and going through the hand-shaking, joke-cracking routine. The others welcomed him as if he had been especially sent as a mascot, and he resigned himself to the familiar rôle. 'Lieutenant-Colonel Hansekamm tells me I'm the last to arrive,' he remarked.

Baron von Baldenov looked round. 'So there are ten of us,' he said thoughtfully.

'With the Führer's bright, beady eye on us,' said Solbreit, cheer-fully disrespectful as ever, even here in Eberswalde. 'I ask you, what have we done to deserve it?'

70

No one laughed; no one could even summon up a faint smile. Asgard Kuehenberg leaned forward, poured himself another vodka, and gazed into the clear liquid. 'There's one thing that does strike me, you know. We're all from the Baltic.'

'You're right; that can hardly be coincidence,' said the fair-haired Poltmann, quite excited.

'Perhaps they want us to form a Baltic Male Voice Choir,' suggested the irrepressible Solbreit. He had drunk rather more vodka than the others, and now jumped up on his chair, put his hands on his hips, and let fly, in a not unmusical voice, with an extremely bawdy song. The others applauded.

'Not bad at all,' said Berno von Ranovski. 'We ought to try that one on the Führer.'

Solbreit climbed down from his chair. They all knew he was as worried as they were. They all sensed that Lieutenant-Colonel Hansekamm's geniality masked something very serious indeed. OKW ... the Führer's headquarters ... ten officers, all from the Baltic ...?

'I know,' said Detlev Adler suddenly. 'We're being told off to boost morale in the Russian units of our own forces. The Vlasov Army, or Pannwitz's Cossack regiment. Making good German soldiers out of freedom-loving Russians. Oh, shit!'

'How about another song?' said Solbreit in hollow tones.

'In Samoa the girls go down
Without skirts or blouses to dance in town.
They don't wear knickers, they don't wear bras,
Just a fig-leaf — with a hole in it — to cover the arse.'

'That'll do,' said Labitz harshly, pulling rank on the others for the first time. Solbreit shut up. 'Tomorrow I'll tackle Hansekamm and try to get something out of him. Now, let's go to bed.'

'I've got a better idea than bed. Let's open my other bottle of vodka,' said Semper. 'After all, once we've drunk it no one can take it away, and for all we know OKW is going to insist we drink nothing stronger than the milk of human kindness from tomorrow.'

The motion was carried, and they set to work on the second bottle of vodka. It was passed around Kuehenberg's room, while the moon shone brightly down over the Mark outside. Horses whinnied wearily in the stables, shuffling their hoofs and snorting. The solitary figure of a sentry, rifle slung round him, marched up and down among the buildings. Far away, there was a dull thudding. Flak. An air raid.

At about three in the morning, Solbreit gave the company another song, and then they went to their own rooms and fell into bed, dazed with the vodka.

Only Kuehenberg still sat at his window, looking out over the paddocks, pale in the moonlight. If they get out of Thernauen in good time, he was thinking, they could take the stud stallions and a few good brood mares with them. Don't leave it too long, Father.

Next morning they appeared at breakfast with puffy eyes and furred tongues. Two attentive orderlies served them in silence. A dining-room had been set aside especially for them, on the same isolated corridor as their own rooms. Breakfast was a rather silent meal; they peered at each other with their red-rimmed eyes, and Peter Radek said, 'Semper, old chap, that vodka of yours must have been distilled in Hell. Were you and your men drinking the stuff the whole time out at Kovel?'

'That's right.'

'And you could still actually see the Russians?'

'Sure. In fact we saw them double. Made us practically bullet-proof. We scared Ivan silly.'

A few of them grinned wearily, thinking of life with their men. They had been in the thick of it only the day before yesterday, and now they were sitting at a table with a white cloth, breakfasting off china plates, their eggs served up with the elegance of a five-star hotel.

Hansekamm joined them when they had almost finished drinking their coffee and the orderlies were offering cigarettes. Flat little Oriental cigarettes, with a straw-like flavour. Solbreit, Ranovski and Semper, who still had Russian cigarettes with them, declined the Oriental variety and smoked Russian papyrossi. They were used to the acrid tobacco and the almost sulphurous yellow of its smoke. 'We never had any trouble with midges in the Pripet marshes if we all smoked these,' said Solbreit.

72

Hansekamm wished them good morning, indicating with a wave of the hand that they were to remain seated. He sat down beside Solbreit, rather to the alarm of the others, who had quickly become used to his outspokenness.

'You won't be using cutlery like this much more,' he said. 'At lunch, we shall provide you with a spoon – if necessary, a knife, too – but you'll have to get used to eating sausage with your fingers and licking them clean afterwards; not too bad at all, I assure you.'

They stared at him blankly, and Labitz shot Solbreit a warning glance.

'Oh, so I was right,' said Detlev Adler. Hansekamm raised his eyebrows. 'Training Pannwitz's Cossacks – though I don't see why they're making such a big secret of it. That's nothing new.'

'I'm afraid you've jumped to conclusions,' Hansekamm laughed genially. He was a tall, thickset man; you could tell merely by looking at him that he enjoyed the pleasures of good food, a decent claret, and the embraces of his wife, who was billeted with him in a three-roomed apartment in a farmhouse near the Riding School. 'Whatever you may have been thinking, gentlemen, it's wrong.' Hansekamm took one of the Oriental cigarettes, and Solbreit gave him a light. 'I can't tell you anything yet. We must wait until Colonel von Renneberg comes back from the Führer's headquarters. But please consider yourselves honoured guests of OKW until we have the Führer's blessing.'

'And when we do have it, then what?' Solbreit speaking.

'We get down to work.'

Kuehenberg said, 'I didn't imagine we've been withdrawn from the fronts simply to adapt our table manners in the way you've just indicated, sir.'

Hansekamm waved the implied query away, and smoked his cigarette, lost in thought. 'Renneberg should have been back long ago. Looks as if things aren't going so smoothly as we'd hoped.'

'Must be a very delicate mission, breaking it to the Führer that his officers have to eat sausage with their fingers.'

Solbreit, of course. Labitz glared sternly at him, and Solbreit shrugged his shoulders apologetically. But Hansekamm had no intention of letting himself be provoked into indiscretion. He merely laughed heartily again, and then looked at his watch. 'May I ask you gentlemen to join me in the instruction-room?'

The instruction-room was not unlike a small school classroom. Ten chairs were set out in two rows, there was a huge map on the wall, and a desk and another chair in front of it. Hansekamm stepped out in front of them and leaned against the narrow desk.

'Yes, gentlemen, a map of Moscow and the area surrounding it. Please sit down. You will not take any notes on anything you hear in this room. We are relying on your intelligence, which we know to be above average.'

'Glad to hear it.' Solbreit again. 'My maths master at school used to reckon I was as stupid as they come.'

Hansekamm smiled in his avuncular manner. 'A man's intelligence is developed by life, not by his school achievement. Many men of genius were dunces at school.'

'You mean we're to become men of genius, by order of the Führer?' inquired Kuehenberg.

'Metaphorically speaking, yes.' Hansekamm looked at them in silence, and then turned back to the huge map of Moscow and the area round it. 'I'm sorry to have to ask for your forbearance,' he said, 'but until Colonel von Renneberg returns I can't tell you any more. Perhaps the whole idea will fall through, and then you can return to your units. All I *can* tell you is that you have been picked for the greatest, most dangerous operation of the war. An operation which, by ordinary human standards, is impossible to carry out. Your isolation here is because the slightest indication of the nature of your mission might set everything at risk, and with it the final victory. When Colonel von Renneberg comes back from the Führer's headquarters, and you have been told everything, you will realize that you are of more value to Germany than any army group.'

They said nothing, but sat looking at the map of Moscow. It had been drawn up on the basis of greatly enlarged air-photographs, and the position of every house was indicated, every barn, the course of every stream, every little bridge, forest path, woodland clearing and pond.

'That's the general view of the area, gentlemen,' Hansekamm went on. 'You'll see some photographs later showing even more detail. There's one real beauty, with a couple making love in a

74

cornfield—you can see them quite clearly. Our reconnaissance-planes ventured as low as that, merely to provide you with this material.'

They warmed towards Hansekamm. Let's hope this Colonel von Renneberg has a sense of humour, too.

Hansekamm took out his cigarette-case. 'Any suggestions as to how we should occupy our time now, gentlemen?'

'We could go to the cinema in Eberswalde,' suggested Radek.

'Out of the question. No one is to see you.'

'In civilian clothes, I mean.'

'You would still be noticed in Eberswalde.' Hansekamm chewed at his cigarette. 'We don't want to be neurotic about this, but I'm afraid you must resign yourselves to ceasing to exist, gentlemen.'

'You mean we can't write letters home?' asked little Dallburg.

'Good Lord, no. Certainly not.'

'My wife had a son three days ago,' said Labitz quietly.

'We're aware of that. Colonel von Renneberg will be having a word with you.'

'But a phone call to my wife can hardly endanger security.'

'I'm sorry.' Obviously Hansekamm could be firm when he wanted.

Kuehenberg rose, went slowly over to the huge map of Moscow and stood in front of it. 'I hardly like to say what I'm thinking,' he commented.

Hansekamm nodded. 'Then don't, Captain Kuehenberg. You're sure to be on the wrong track.'

'I was in Moscow eight years ago myself.'

'We know that. Just before the Berlin Olympics here.' Hansekamm was jovial and avuncular again. 'We know everything about every one of you, gentlemen, from the day you were born.'

'And who thought up—whatever it is we're to do?' asked Berno von Ranovski.

'I *am* allowed to tell you that. Operations Command at OKW, working in close collaboration with the Intelligence Bureau.'

'Canaris!' said Kuehenberg.

'Yes.'

'Jesus Christ!' Solbreit exclaimed. 'We really *are* in the shit.'

75

Three

IN NORMAL CIRCUMSTANCES, Colonel von Renneberg would not have thought it worth mentioning the fact that he had now been kicking his heels at the Wolf's Lair, Hitler's Rastenburg headquarters, for two days, waiting for a chance to present his case.

Escorted there by Keitel himself, Colonel von Renneberg resigned himself to an even longer wait when he saw the Commander-in-Chief of the West, Field-Marshal von Rundstedt, turn up on 5 June 1944. Rundstedt was admitted to the Führer's bunker at once, and the doors remained closed for hours. General Schmundt, Hitler's army adjutant, seemed to be the only person who had not forgotten Renneberg. He came into the barrack-hut acting as a waiting-room and sat down beside the Colonel.

'This is like a newsreel,' said Renneberg sarcastically. 'One doesn't often see so many prominent people all at once. Still no appointment for me, I suppose?'

'Rundstedt has arrived.'

'Yes, so I saw.'

'Do you know why?'

'I can't say I actually *know*. I can guess. The situation in the west—'

'Is critical. Canaris sent reports in yesterday. The Führer flew into a rage. What's your notion of things, there in Berlin? You obviously differ from the Führer in your view of the situation as a whole.'

'Maybe because we're not "the greatest military commander of all time".'

'Careful!' said Schmundt, a note of warning in his voice. 'I'll forget that remark.'

'Well, Rundstedt is in there telling the Führer the kind of

76

trouble we're in, and Busch, Model and Schörner will all back him up — and here I sit, with a plan in my briefcase which, in the right circumstances, could put an end to all our worries. Keitel's in the know, and so is Jodl, and of course Canaris. No one else.'

'Except you.'

'Correct.' Renneberg nodded his head. 'Let's just say only a very small circle indeed knows what we propose, and I need half an hour to put it to the Führer, that's all.'

'Half an hour?' Schmundt smiled pityingly. 'Do you know who gets to speak to the Führer for as long as half an hour? Goering, maybe, or Himmler. What on earth are you thinking of, Renneberg? If you do get shown in — and I think Keitel will get you that far — what you do is bow, bark out your business in telegraphic style, and then the Führer will do the talking.' Schmundt looked out of the window. Himmler, accompanied by three SS Obergruppenführers, was walking through the tall pines. 'Trouble brewing today. There goes Himmler, looking as if he knew all the answers. Can't stand the man....'

Schmundt stepped back from the window, with every appearance of disgust. Renneberg was surprised. Have I misjudged the man? he thought. 'Forget I said that, will you?' added Schmundt quietly.

In his mind, Renneberg rapidly went over the facts that few people knew: 11 February 1944, the plan to blow up both Hitler and Himmler, which could not be carried out, because Himmler did not turn up for the envisaged conference; 9 March 1944, a plan to shoot Hitler during a discussion of the present situation at his big map-table, but the officer whose mission it was to do the shooting had not been allowed into the room, and this plot, too, failed; 15 May 1944, a secret meeting between Field-Marshal Rommel and General von Stülpnagel, commanding Paris, to discuss the possibility of a commando unit seizing Hitler, to be tried later by a German court of law, after the elimination of the SS. General Schmundt would have been present if any of these plots against Hitler had been carried out, either at the Wolf's Lair or during one of the Führer's brief visits to Berlin. And now Colonel von Stauffenberg was planning to assassinate Hitler at the next favourable opportunity. Which meant that, if it were a bomb attack, Schmundt might be killed, too. He stood near the

Führer at most conferences. Was he against Himmler? Bormann might have the ear of Hitler, but Himmler, with his army of SS men, had power affecting all Germany. What exactly will happen if Hitler is removed? Renneberg wondered. The one thing we can depend upon is the armed forces. Field-Marshals Rommel and Busch, Generals Hoeppner, Stülpnagel, Field-Marshal von Witzleben and his circle of officers. . . .

Still, that's not my business now, he thought. Mine is a plan of almost unheard-of daring. A plan which, if it's successful, will be doubly effective, bringing about the end of the war and, close upon the heels of that, the end of the madness of National Socialism.

At last, on the afternoon of 5 June, as Colonel von Renneberg was drinking a cup of lemon tea in the officers' mess of the Wolf's Lair, a major came up to him. 'The Führer wants to see you,' he said.

Renneberg's head shot up. 'When?'

'Now.'

Renneberg leaped to his feet, tightened the buckle of his belt, put on his cap, and attached his black briefcase to his wrist with a steel chain — a security precaution he automatically took, even in the Führer's headquarters.

It was the first time Colonel von Renneberg had been inside the bunker, which was really a barrack-like hut in the middle of the inner security circle, surrounded by tall pines and birches, with camouflage-nets hanging in the tree-tops. From the air, the Wolf's Lair was practically invisible.

Keitel himself met Renneberg at the door. 'You have a whole fifteen minutes,' he said.

In officer circles, opinions about Keitel differed. He was a Nazi and a careerist, no doubt about that, devoted to Hitler, ready to act as audience for the Führer's outbursts of rage. Most army officers considered Keitel as Hitler's creature. On the other hand, he was sufficiently receptive to new ideas to approve plans such as the one Renneberg had in his briefcase. Not just because it came from OKW and he himself was Chief of High Command, but also because he saw the desperate nature of the present situation, and knew any chance must be seized.

'What's the atmosphere like in there?' asked Renneberg, in a tone of rather surprising familiarity, from a colonel to a field-marshal — but, when Keitel himself was a colonel, Renneberg had joined his staff as a raw young lieutenant, and over the years Keitel had developed a paternal liking for the younger man.

'Not very pleasant, Renneberg. The Führer is rather tired, after listening to what Rundstedt had to say.'

'Have you told the Führer the details of the plan?'

'No, that's your job, if he wants to know them. I've only prepared the ground.'

'What were his first reactions like?'

'He thinks it sounds crazy.' Keitel nodded briefly. 'A word in your ear, Renneberg. If the Führer starts to speak, don't interrupt.'

'Of course not.' Momentarily, Renneberg closed his eyes; he knew by repute about Hitler's dreaded monologues.

Keitel preceded him. It was all just as Renneberg had imagined it from the photographs he had seen: a long table covered with maps in the middle of the room, white-washed walls, a few chairs. A spartan place.

Hitler sat at the table, looking smaller than Renneberg had expected. Indeed, he was surprised to see Hitler seated at all. The Führer had a cup of herb tea beside him, and wore glasses — another surprise for Renneberg — though he took them off as soon as the Colonel clicked his heels and announced, 'Colonel von Renneberg, Operations Staff, OKW, reporting, mein Führer.'

Jodl was leaning against the table with the telephone. Keitel stood beside Renneberg. There was an orderly hovering in the background. No Himmler present, no Bormann. For a long moment, Hitler and Renneberg looked at each other. Hitler had aged badly; his face was wrinkled, and his nose looked broader than in his photographs. He must be very tired.

'Field-Marshal Keitel here' — Hitler glanced at Keitel standing beside Renneberg — 'has told me what you've brought. Go on.'

That voice: it sounds deeper over the radio, thought Renneberg. He undid the briefcase from its chain, and placed it on the table in front of Hitler. Why, he thought suddenly, it could be as simple as this. If I had a bomb here now instead of a folder, the world would be changed. But all I have is this thin file. . . . Well, let's hope Stauffenberg has the same incredible luck, and gets the chance to place his own briefcase on Hitler's table.

79

Hitler rose, and at a glance from Keitel the orderly left the room. Now there was no one there but Hitler, Jodl, Keitel and Renneberg.

Hitler waited for Renneberg to take out the file, and then picked it up. It contained only two sheets of paper: a list of names and a list of places. He looked at them in surprise, and then at Renneberg, his tired eyes suddenly flaring. 'Are you mad?' he asked abruptly. 'Is this all?'

'Mein Führer' — Renneberg did not know whether he should still be standing to attention, and decided to stand at ease — 'Field-Marshal Keitel has explained the basic plan to you. For the sake of the strict security measures required, no written plans for Operation Wild Geese exist.'

'Wild Geese — I like the name,' interrupted Hitler. 'Why Wild Geese?'

'Many wild geese fly north, mein Führer, but they do not all return.'

'H'm.'

Renneberg took a deep breath. Keep going, he told himself. Hitler's glance is enough to unnerve anyone.

'Go on.'

'If I may elucidate, mein Führer — in view of the present situation, Operation Wild Geese aims to change not just the situation at the fronts, but also the whole aspect of world affairs at a single blow. The shock arising from the success of this mission will lead to the paralysis of Russia, and symptoms of disintegration will follow rapidly. With the collapse of the Eastern Front, the Allies will have no chance either in the south-east or in any invasion plans they may have. Our gain in morale itself will demoralize the enemy. Mein Führer, our plans are already so far advanced that the ten officers whose names you have there are ready to be dispatched on Operation Wild Geese within a very short time. The other list, mein Führer, is that of the areas in which they would infiltrate the country.'

Hitler put the folder down on the table, and Keitel placed a map of the Moscow area in front of him. Hitler leaned over it. He swept his right hand across the map. 'Your suggestion is madness, Colonel,' he growled.

'Yes, mein Führer. But it's feasible.'

'It will never succeed.'

'We can but try.'

'If it *does* succeed. . . .'

'We'll have won the war,' said Renneberg.

'And if it doesn't?'

'No commander goes into a battle envisaging defeat.'

Jodl glanced at Keitel. Oh Lord, said that look, now for another tirade. When Rundstedt had left Hitler had raved on and on, and did not calm down until he drank his tea. Surprisingly, however, Hitler said nothing, but scrutinized Renneberg keenly.

'Who's behind this?' he asked suddenly. 'Canaris, no doubt?'

'The plan was made by a number of experts, working in collaboration, mein Führer. With your permission, the Wild Geese are ready to take off.'

'It's nonsense,' said Hitler harshly. He swept the map of Moscow aside. Then he sat up straight, put a hand in his pocket, and the monologue began. Keitel, Jodl and Renneberg listened without a word. At the end of the speech, however, and much to the surprise of them all, Hitler said, 'Very well, you have my approval. But Operation Wild Geese is to have top secret status. Whether it succeeds or fails, none of us here knows anything about it. Colonel, can you guarantee that there will be no written records of it whatever?'

'Absolutely none, mein Führer. The personal files on the ten picked officers are at OKW, and will be destroyed the day the operation begins. These ten men will cease to exist. If they fail, we report them missing in action.'

'And if they succeed?'

Greatly daring, Colonel von Renneberg said, 'I shall leave the manner of their reward to you, mein Führer. *If* these ten officers should change the course of world history. . . .'

'Mad!' Hitler made a dismissive gesture. 'Completely mad! However, your people can have what facilities they need, Colonel. *If* it succeeds. . . .' Hitler looked at Renneberg, head on one side. That searching glance seemed to rest on him for an eternity. '*If*—well, even then, those ten men must remain anonymous, but they may be sure of the gratitude of the Fatherland and of the world.' It was the voice of the Hitler whose propaganda speeches so hypnotized his hearers.

Renneberg breathed a sigh of relief. 'Then may we consider ourselves free to act, mein Führer?'

'Yes.'

'Thank you, mein Führer.'

Heels together, a salute, one last glance into those slightly narrowed eyes. Hitler nodded. Jodl showed no reaction at all. Keitel was already going to the door. Renneberg turned and went out of the bunker. He heard a chair being pushed back.

Hitler sat fiddling with his glasses. When the door had closed, he raised his head. 'What do you think of all that, Jodl?'

'I think we should forget about it, mein Führer, and let it come as a surprise.'

'An excellent notion, Jodl.' Hitler put his glasses on. 'Damn Rundstedt! As if any enemy forces could ever take my Atlantic Wall!'

'You could have put it more forcefully, Renneberg,' said Keitel outside the Führer's headquarters, under the tall pines. 'You could have aroused more enthusiasm for Wild Geese in him.'

'I have permission, sir; that's all I wanted.' Renneberg saluted punctiliously. 'And I'd like to thank you very much.'

'Yes, all right, all right.' Keitel dismissed the subject. 'Now what?'

'Now the Führer's given permission for us to go ahead, we can do as we think fit. We shall act as soon as possible.' Renneberg glanced at his watch. 'When can I have the Führer's approval in writing, sir?'

'Fetch it from me in an hour's time.'

That evening, Colonel von Renneberg flew back to Berlin in a courier-plane with the memo giving Hitler's written approval in his briefcase, which was still chained to his wrist. On landing, he got into a waiting car and was driven to Eberswalde. He was passing through a landscape lit by bright moonlight. The peace of the countryside, the scent of new-mown hay, harvested early after a rainy spring, the smell of the first roses rising from front gardens, the apparent security of this pleasant part of the world aroused long-forgotten romantic sensations in him. He got the car to stop and, much to the surprise of its NCO driver, walked off the road and a little way into the fields, drawing in deep breaths of the fragrant night air.

How lovely Germany is, he thought bitterly. And, assuming the reports from the west which Hitler refuses to take seriously are true, what will all this look like in a few months' time?

Quarter of an hour later, the Officers' Riding School at Eberswalde came into view. Its buildings lay quiet in the moonlight. Renneberg had telephoned from Berlin to tell Lieutenant-Colonel Hansekamm his news, and the ten officers, roused from their beds, were waiting in the instruction-room. Down in the hall, Hansekamm met Renneberg.

'So it's all clear?' he asked briefly.

Renneberg nodded. 'All clear.' He pointed upward. 'Do they know anything?'

'No, but of course they're speculating.'

'Do they come anywhere near the truth?'

'No, none of them. Who could think of something like *this*?'

'Well, at least we can put them out of their misery now.' Renneberg went upstairs and walked briskly into the instruction-room. Lord, he's pretty bright and chirpy for three o'clock in the morning, thought Ranovski.

'I'm Renneberg,' the Colonel introduced himself. He had taken up his position behind the desk. In the light of the powerful bulb hanging from the ceiling, something strange happened: Renneberg and the map of Moscow and its surroundings behind him merged together, and he looked as if he had just stepped out of the map. 'Gentlemen, I'm very pleased to meet you, and glad to see you looking so well. I should like to put an end to your speculations, and tell you, very briefly, why you've been asked to come here.'

Asked is good, thought Labitz. They practically conveyed us to Eberswalde by rocket.

'I have just seen the Führer,' said Renneberg gravely, but in matter-of-fact tones. There was no drama in his brisk voice. 'I have with me his permission for our operation to go ahead. In the near future, gentlemen, you are to assassinate Stalin.'

On 6 June 1944, at 0200 hours, thousands of parachutes dropped from the sky between Montebourg and Caretan, Caen and

Cabourg, landing behind the supposedly invulnerable Atlantic Wall. The night was full of the drone of bombers and Spitfires, heavy transport-planes and fast escort-aircraft. Hundreds of gliders circled soundlessly above Normandy and came down in the fields west of the River Vire and east of the Orne, bringing equipment, light artillery, mortars, ammunition, provisions, medical supplies, tents and spare parts.

The 82nd and 101st US and the 6th British airborne divisions had jumped in, along with the 3rd and 4th parachute brigades. The German troops, taken by surprise, and some of their units, such as those at Ranville and in the marshy area of Chef-du-Pont, only at half strength, could do nothing but try to shoot down a few of the massed parachutes floating to the ground. Once landed, the Allied forces immediately established firm positions, set up bases, dug themselves in or went directly into action, attacking the Germans in the rear.

And everywhere the French population came to their aid. They brought wine for the soldiers, took American or English paratroopers injured in the drop to their farmhouses to be tended, told the invaders where the German positions were and showed them how to approach the enemy bunkers unobserved.

At 0314 the next wave of invaders came in. Over two thousand bombers, commanded by Air Marshal Leigh-Mallory, rained bombs down on the bunkers of the Atlantic Wall, on the beaches, on the hinterland just behind the German positions.

Soon afterwards, at 0550, six hundred warships of all sizes, from battleships to destroyers, appeared in the morning mists, raking the coast between Quinneville and Nerville with their powerful guns.

At 0630, the sea itself came to life as if a huge shoal of grey, steely monster fish were coming in to land. The first of the Allies' landing-forces: the first specially built landing-craft coming to shore and disgorging American, British and Canadian troops, with mortars, flame-throwers and light artillery. And still the bomber squadrons droned over the countryside, attacking German supply-lines, the gliders hovered down, the airborne divisions jumped. Amphibian tanks climbing up out of the sea like great prehistoric monsters landed to join the attack on the Atlantic Wall.

Telephones were ringing frantically at the headquarters of

Field-Marshal von Rundstedt, Commander-in-Chief in the West. Field-Marshal Rommel got straight into his jeep and raced north to the front. At 0520, as the six hundred warships were taking up their firing positions, Hitler was woken in the Wolf's Lair and told of the landings of Allied airmen in Normandy and the heavy bombardment in progress.

'It's a diversion,' shouted Hitler. 'Kill them. Kill them all. I want no enemy paratrooper left alive. Those are my orders.'

At 0630 the first wave of landing-forces had stormed the coasts. There was appalling bloodshed, for after the first shock the Germans fought back, often without orders from their divisional commanders. By now, Rundstedt and his staff, as well as the staff at the Führer's headquarters, knew that D-Day had begun with a vengeance.

At 0630, too, General Eisenhower, Supreme Commander of the invading forces, issued his order of the day, informing his men that the eyes of the world were on them and that, with their brave allies on all the fronts, they would succeed in crushing the German forces and the tyranny of National Socialism. Eisenhower wished them all good luck, and prayed for God's blessing on their great and noble enterprise.

When Eisenhower's order of the day was read to Hitler by the unfortunate adjutant picked to do the job, he was momentarily turned to stone. Then he bawled out orders to annihilate the invaders. The maps of Russia on his big table had been exchanged for maps of Normandy. 'Tell Rommel I expect total victory over the invading troops,' he shouted.

Colonel von Renneberg appeared at breakfast on that morning of 6 June as if the world had not changed at all, took a seat at the head of the long table, and watched the orderly pour his coffee. It was real coffee, and there was cream from the nearby farm to go with it, and crisp, fresh rolls, good butter, and golden honey from the Mark, as well as sliced salami and real Hungarian ham flavoured with the smoke of juniper wood.

Colonel von Renneberg spread a roll with butter, placed a slice of smoked ham on it, and then looked up and round the table.

'I can see, gentlemen,' he said calmly, 'that you've already heard this morning's news.' He smiled ironically. 'Evidently I'm not the only one who regularly listens to the BBC. Please don't let this spoil your breakfast. The invasion is no surprise to us. We've known for weeks what troops were being mustered in England and where the landing would be. However, our reports to the Führer's headquarters were dismissed as fanciful. Well, there's no point in crying over spilt milk, gentlemen, but D-Day is certainly of great importance to us. If you look at the actual situation — not the situation as described for public consumption in OKW's daily bulletins — you will see how essential your task is.'

'I did rather want a word about that, Colonel,' interrupted Baron von Baldenov. 'You come back from the Wolf's Lair, introduce yourself to us in the middle of the night, point to a map of Moscow and tell us baldly that we're to kill Stalin.'

'Later, my dear fellow; we'll come to that later,' said the Colonel. 'Do go on with your breakfast, gentlemen.' He looked at the text of Eisenhower's order of the day, which he had with him. 'General Eisenhower tells his men that their enemies are well trained. Wrong. The 7th Army, under General Dollman, with eleven infantry divisions, is all we have in the invasion-area. Other divisions are probably on their way by now, but unfortunately our men in France have little fighting potential: they are either too old or very young. Eisenhower also says we're "well equipped". Wrong again. The SS divisions are fully equipped, and they are all farther south, in Paris or in central France. By the time they reach Normandy, the invading troops will have a firm footing there. As for the Luftwaffe — a disaster, gentlemen!' Renneberg looked at another note in front of him. 'We have just ninety bombers and seventy fighters capable of going into action. According to the intelligence we receive from England, the enemy has three thousand one hundred bombers and five thousand and forty-nine fighters. In addition, there are some five thousand transport-planes....'

'My God,' said Kuehenberg, 'does the Führer know all this?'

'He's been told. He says it's lies.' Renneberg looked briefly into his companions' dismayed faces. 'And then there's the Navy. Stationed along the coast of France and ready for battle, we have the following. Battleships: none. Cruisers: none. Destroyers: three. Torpedo-boats: thirty-six. U-boats: thirty-four. Now for the invading forces. Battleships: seven. Cruisers: twenty-seven. Destroyers: a hundred and sixty-four. Landing-craft of all kinds, many of them armed vessels: roughly over six thousand.'

'God help us,' said Labitz, in hollow tones.

'Even that isn't likely.' Renneberg tapped the text of Eisenhower's order of the day. 'God's been dragged into it already — Eisenhower's applied for His blessing. As for fighting men, the first wave of landing forces this morning comprised forty Allied divisions and, according to our information, there are eight hundred thousand men ready in England; at this moment, more soldiers and equipment will be crossing the Channel, and there is almost nothing we can do to stop them. Well, that's been the situation in the west since early this morning.' Renneberg drank his coffee with every appearance of enjoyment, and then rose.

'I rather think I've lost my appetite,' said Semper.

'I lost mine in the small hours.' Detlev Adler rose, too. 'You mean the invasion was already in progress when you got us out of bed to tell us we were to kill Stalin, Colonel?'

'Yes, although I didn't know it. I had a phone call from Berlin at four, and I've been sitting by the telephone ever since.' He walked past the eleven officers to the door. 'May I ask you to join me in the instruction-room? Hansekamm will explain the eastern situation to you, though some of you may already have a fair notion of how things stand there.'

A few moments later all ten of them were facing the huge map of Moscow again. Lieutenant-Colonel Hansekamm was at the small desk, while Renneberg perched on a stool on one side. Somewhere a rooster was crowing, and the neighing of horses came in through the open window. A lovely, sunny morning, with the tree-tops swaying in a light breeze, and clouds like tufts of cotton-wool sailing across the blue sky.

I just hope to God that Father realizes what is going on, thought Kuehenberg. At least the invasion ought to alert him to get out of Thernauen.

Hansekamm said, 'We consider it certain that the current invasion of France marks the beginning of a new offensive on the Eastern Front, especially in its central sector. Probably in the second half of June; that would be good tactics from the Allied point of view. By the end of June, the invading troops will have spread all through Normandy, Army Command will be paying increasing attention to the Western Front, and the Eastern Front, comparatively quiet, will seem to be of secondary importance. Then the Red storm will break over us. We have some figures from the Foreign Armies East department of the Intelligence Bureau; they're unconfirmed, but they could well be right. According to those figures, the Russians have mustered in the central sector a hundred and twenty-six infantry divisions, six cavalry divisions, sixteen motorized brigades, forty-five tank brigades. The number of planes is estimated to be four thousand; we think it is more. The estimated number of tanks may be too low as well.'

Hansekamm continued after a pause, 'Facing the Russians, we have forty divisions, and no reserves at all; eight hundred and twenty-nine aircraft, not all of them fit for combat; and one tank division.'

Labitz rose, his face working. 'But this is appalling,' he cried. 'If those figures are correct, how can anyone continue to believe in our Final Victory?'

Renneberg smiled grimly. 'We're in private here, Labitz. We can say what we like to each other; not a word will get outside. It's more than likely that the figures are correct. In other words, 1944 looks like being Germany's year of reckoning, the year we face collapse on all sides. This morning's invasion signalled the start of the final battle for the Reich. I impress this upon you so urgently, gentlemen, to illustrate the importance of your mission.'

'But why us?' Peter Radek was staring at the map of Moscow. 'What makes us potential murderers, out of so many thousands of officers and millions of men?'

'That's not the way to look at it, gentlemen. This is not murder; it's a commando operation. The fact that we are striking at a single man does not turn an act of war into the crime of murder.' He took Hansekamm's place at the desk.

'But the thing can't be done,' said the fair-haired Poltmann. 'It's as impossible as it would be to kill the Führer.'

Hansekamm went to the window and looked out. 'No, it's not,' said Renneberg calmly. 'I saw a remarkable number of vulnerable spots at the Führer's headquarters. There are as many chinks in

Stalin's own armour. It should be possible for you to carry out your mission successfully.'

'Subsequent Ascension into Heaven all inclusive.' Solbreit's ever-ready tongue slightly relaxed the tension.

'That's right.' Colonel von Renneberg looked at each man in turn before he went on. 'The operation is code-named Wild Geese. Many wild geese fly north, but some of them never return.'

Baron von Baldenov rose, went over to the big map of Moscow, and then to the window where Hansekamm was still standing. 'Who picked us?' he asked frostily.

'A small team of experts. The final decision was mine, as initiator of Operation Wild Geese.'

'Oh.' Kuehenberg, too, rose to his feet. 'So *you* thought this up, Colonel, did you? Send a few officers off to Moscow – bang, bang, Stalin's dead – the Soviet front collapses, the shock paralyses the Americans and British, the entire world is scared shitless – and Germany's saved. As easy as that.'

Renneberg smiled patiently. 'You're right, Kuehenberg. Basically, it *is* very simple. Not so much the assassination itself as your previous infiltration into Moscow. We have that all worked out in detail. You were chosen, from a great many other officers, because you all have the necessary qualifications. You all speak Russian as fluently as you speak German; some of you even speak with a Russian regional dialect. You know the Russian mentality, you have always had personal contact with Russians, six of you have Russian mothers. It will be easy for you to turn yourselves into genuine Russians at the drop of a hat. Once inside the country, you can merge with Russian society at once.' Renneberg looked at them all. 'Does anyone disagree with that?'

'No,' said Labitz, speaking for all of them.

'Incidentally, Major, you had been picked as leader of this commando unit, but the birth of your son does alter things. I can't ask you to take the job on now. We had carefully excluded fathers of families from the operation. You can withdraw if you choose; the decision is yours alone.'

'There's no need even to ask me, Colonel,' said Labitz stiffly.

'Well, give it till tomorrow, Labitz; sleep on it.' Renneberg prepared to deliver his second blow. 'A decision to go ahead would place you in the same position as all the others: you would cease to exist.'

'What exactly do you mean?' inquired Kuehenberg.

'From now on, your identities are wiped out. Lieutenant-Colonel Hansekamm indicated as much to you yesterday in general terms; today I can speak more plainly. If you agree to take part in Operation Wild Geese, you will have gone missing so far as your families are concerned. Your personal files will be destroyed at OKW headquarters on the day your mission begins. There will be no written records of Operation Wild Geese. You will no longer exist. Please think that over, Labitz. Your wife would be getting news this very month that you were reported missing in action.'

'That could have happened to me any time on the front, at Tiraspol,' said Labitz, his voice rather rougher than usual.

'In the normal course of military action. This time, you will be volunteering. Your consent means obliterating your own identity.'

'Well, is anyone else backing out?' Labitz looked round, and the others looked awkwardly back at him. 'Dallburg, you're the youngest — why are *you* throwing your young life away? Solbreit, don't you ever want to see that girlfriend of yours again? Kuehenberg, who's going to see to the stud and the horses?'

'Stop it, please, Major,' said Detlev Adler firmly.

Labitz turned back to Renneberg. 'Well, I don't know why anyone should bother to ask any more questions.' He sat down again and crossed his legs. 'So now, obviously, we learn Moscow off by heart. Streets, squares, buildings, hideouts, contacts—'

'All but the last. You'll have no contact with anyone outside. Each of you will be on his own until he reaches Moscow; only once he is well established there will he make radio contact with the others — assuming they, too, have reached the city. But those are details. First for the basics,' said Colonel von Renneberg. 'You're about to undergo a series of tests, gentlemen; we want to keep the risks you run down to a minimum. We'll take a break now until after lunch. Then we'll meet again here, and we'll be wanting you to try on some Soviet uniforms.'

Renneberg and Hansekamm left the instruction-room. The ten men stayed there. Young Dallburg tore open his collar as if he felt it were choking him. Poltmann ran his fingers through his fair curls. Ranovski searched his pockets for a packet of papyrossi.

And Semper said wistfully, 'That brawn will be just about ready to eat by now.'

The men's measurements, taken from their personal files, had been so exact that all their Soviet uniforms fitted.

'Instant transformation,' said Hansekamm, walking round them. 'You look Russian right the way through. Except for you, Poltmann; it's that curly head of yours.'

'There are plenty of fair-haired Russians.' Poltmann's voice held a note of something like panic. I'm damn well not shaving my head for this job, he thought.

'We'll have to cut it shorter, Poltmann — just a little shorter,' said Hansekamm kindly, in the tones of one soothing a child. 'It'll grow again, but you can't go parachuting into Russia with curls that length. Later, you can grow them for the benefit of your girlfriends again.'

Later, Hansekamm was thinking. Would there be any 'later'? He avoided looking directly at the men. He thought: I could ask each of them separately: 'Why are you doing this without a word of complaint?' And in each case the answer would be: 'I could die anywhere, at the front or in a Moscow street — this is war.'

Colonel von Renneberg strode briskly into the instruction-room and flung a thin looseleaf folder down on the desk.

'The latest news from Normandy: the invading troops have a firm hold on five of the beaches now. The airborne divisions are operating in our rear, and supplies are being dropped to them by plane and parachute. Three SS Panzer divisions are coming up to relieve our men — but, by the time they get there, there should be about a hundred and seventy thousand of the Allies along the coast.'

Renneberg looked at the ten men. 'Tomorrow we're going on a little expedition to Frankfurt an der Oder, where there's a prison-camp for Russian officers. You'll be used to your Russian uniforms by then. You'll be taken there as new arrivals, and stay there for three days. That will show whether there are any tiny errors in your use of the language which could prove fatal in an emergency.' He opened the folder and leafed through the papers inside it. 'Now I'm going to give each of you his new curriculum vitae. Names, dates of birth, job or profession, parents, grandparents, home towns, childhood memories, love-affairs, Soviet army units, names of your commanding officers and your friends, when and where you started your military service. And then, for your arrival in Moscow, when and where you were discharged from the Red Army, reasons for discharge; there'll be papers showing professional qualifications, identity cards, certificates of discharge, application papers for new labour deployment.' Renneberg picked up a sheet of paper and held it at eye level. 'Major von Labitz!'

'Yes, sir.' Labitz stepped forward. Renneberg looked hard at him.

'Your name is now Pavel Fedorovich Sassonov. Please learn this curriculum vitae off by heart, by noon tomorrow, when I shall hear you say your piece and then burn the paper. The same applies to all of you.' He handed Labitz the closely written sheet of paper.

Labitz took the sheet of paper, turned away, walked slowly to the open window and read it. The sun stood high above Eberswalde; it was a warm, windless day, and the bitter-sweet scent of mown hay rose from the meadows and wafted into the room. Renneberg picked up the next sheet of paper.

'Lieutenant Radek, your new name is Pyotr Mironovich Sepkin.'

'Very good, sir,' said Radek quietly, taking his new life away into a corner.

'Lieutenant von Ranovski. You are Ivan Petrovich Bunurian.'

'Georgian name, sir?'

'That's right. You have a slightly Georgian look about you.' Renneberg picked up the next sheet. 'Second Lieutenant Solbreit. Luka Ivanovich Petrovsky. That suit you?'

'Certainly, sir. I can just imagine a woman whispering it. . . . Lukushka!'

'Thought so myself.' Renneberg smiled briefly. 'Captain von Baldenov. You are Leonid Germanovich Duskov.'

'Why Germanovich?' asked Baldenov.

'Your grandfather admired the Germans and called his son after them. His bad luck, and yours. Second Lieutenant Poltmann. Fyodor Panteleyevich Ivanov. I dare say the girls will call you Fedya.'

'Do I *have* to cut my hair, sir?' asked the still crestfallen Poltmann.

'I'm sure you'll have enough left to attract the girls. Lieutenant Adler. Alexander Nikolayevich Kraskin.'

'Harsh-sounding sort of name, sir.'

'Not if you get called Sasha for short. Captain Kuehenberg. Kyrill Semyonovich Boranov.'

'Thank you, sir,' said Kuehenberg.

'Second Lieutenant Semper. Sergei Andreyevich Tarski.'

'Not a bad name, sir.'

'Officer Cadet Dallburg.'

'Yes, sir.' Little Dallburg was the only one to make the mistake of instinctively clicking his heels, despite the Russian uniform he wore 'Sorry, sir,' he apologized, going red.

'Your name is Nikolai Antonovich Pleyin.' Renneberg gave him his sheet of paper. 'Yours is a particularly attractive curriculum vitae, Nikolai Antonovich. We knew you have a good singing voice – a light lyric tenor, isn't it? So you are a music student who was called up for the front. As you have never actually been wounded, the reason for your discharge from the Red Army is a mysterious disorder of the eyesight: none of the doctors at the front could explain it, but it made you unfit for combat. Well, read it for yourself.' Renneberg attempted a joke. 'Perhaps we shall be hearing of you some day: Nikolai A. Pleyin, rising young star of the Bolshoi, singing Rudolf in *La Bohème*!'

'I'll do my best, sir,' said little Dallburg, trying to reply in kind. 'Perhaps Stalin will be in a box in the audience, and I can reach round behind Mimi's back and shoot him from the stage in the middle of the big love duet.'

'I'm afraid we don't have that amount of time in hand, gentlemen. The faster events take place at the front, the less time you have yourselves. There'll be no point in killing Stalin if the Russians are already lighting their camp-fires at the Brandenburg Gate. You are to be parachuted into Russia this month. Then you must get well established in Moscow before you attempt to strike – but remember, it's a race between you and the Soviet offensive.' Renneberg closed the now empty folder. 'From now on I must ask you to speak only Russian and address one another by your Russian names.' And, to the surprise of all except Hansekamm,

93

he broke into excellent Russian himself. 'Kindly learn the contents of those papers off by heart before we start for Frankfurt an der Oder, comrades; after that we shall burn them.'

'Not mine,' said Solbreit, ready with a reply even in Russian. 'It's a lovely piece of paper, this. What on earth are you thinking of, comrade? I could roll at least twenty papyrossi out of this. Though newsprint is better—I guess *Pravda* tastes best.'

'Very good,' Renneberg congratulated him, laughing.

Solbreit stared at the Colonel, frowning. 'Just what I said, comrade, didn't I? Tastes very good. What's so funny about that?'

Before lunch next day, Colonel von Renneberg questioned each man. They had thoroughly absorbed their fictional lives. To men from the Baltic, familiar with Russians from early childhood, shedding their German skins presented hardly any problem at all. As for the political ramifications of the projected deaths of Stalin and Hitler, they did not, and most of them never would, know anything about them.

A closed truck was waiting outside the door of the isolated wing of the Riding School. Two corporals were sitting in the cab. They had orders not to get out. The tailgate of the truck was down, and there were steps leading up to it. Inside the truck were two long benches. Once the tailgate was up there were no windows or ventilation, only the small barred slit through to the driver's cab.

'Tight security, eh?' said the driver's mate to his companion. 'You think it's for prisoners, or what?'

'In the Officers' Riding School, idiot?' The driver, a corporal who had been wounded nine times and seconded to home duties, tapped his forehead.

'There's a maximum-security jail in Frankfurt—for deserters and so on. Could be someone's going there.'

'Here they come.'

Both men peered out of the cab. Hansekamm came out of the door first, followed by ten Soviet officers, with Colonel von Renneberg bringing up the rear. They all climbed the steps into the truck, the tailgate was drawn up, and Colonel von Renneberg knocked on the barred window with his fist. It was the signal to start.

94

The driver stared at his mate. 'See that?'

'Not blind, am I? Officers. Ivans. Said so, didn't I?'

'On their way to be shot or hanged, that's what.' The corporal started up. 'We're to stop just before we get to Frankfurt.'

'Don't look too good for 'em.'

'That's what I said.'

The truck drove out of the forecourt of the Riding School, and lumbered along the drive until it reached the road from Eberswalde to Frankfurt an der Oder, passing through Freienwalde, Wriezen, Marxwalde, Seelow and Leubs. Right through the Brandenburg Mark. Beautiful countryside: hills, lakes, pools, moorland, sand, pinewoods, birch groves, gentle undulations, all shining in the bright summer sun. The twelve men in the dark truck saw none of it. They were talking quietly to each other in Russian, and Colonel von Renneberg was reminding them yet again of what they might expect to encounter in the Russian officers' camp.

As planned, they spent three days in the camp.

No one knew or guessed the secret of the ten men, from the camp authorities to the teams of guards, the interpreters, or the senior Soviet officers in the place. To their German guards they were just ten new arrivals sent on by OKW, apparently after thorough questioning. Colonel von Renneberg had half an hour's private conversation with the camp commandant, a major.

'Here are the papers,' he said, taking several files out of his briefcase. 'We've interrogated all the prisoners; Army Group Centre sent them on to us in Berlin, suspecting that several of them might be carrying misleading papers and weren't in fact men with the ranks and duties of ordinary army officers.'

'Ah, political instructors, eh?' said the Major.

'So we suspected. However, the interrogations produced no results. They stuck to their stories, and so we decided to put them in here. If they *are* political commissars, they'll try to make trouble in the camp — form secret groups, give illegal periods of instruction. These are tough, fanatical men.'

Renneberg was purposely presenting his men in a bad light; the more closely they are watched, he thought, the more thoroughly

Russian they must be, and the sooner they will win the confidence of the Soviet inmates.

The ten were soon accepted by the Soviet prisoners; not surprisingly, it was the ready tongue of Luka Ivanovich Petrovsky, otherwise Solbreit, that broke through the Russian officers' initial reserve. Newcomers, especially small batches of newcomers like this one, were always suspect at first. After captured Russian officers had seen good friends of theirs go over to the Vlasov Army, they all feared treachery in the prison-camps.

Lieutenant-Colonel Konstantin Dmitrinovich Sakmatov, the secret political officer in the camp, shook hands with the new arrivals and got a brief account of their stories. 'Hopeless lot, the Germans,' said Luka Ivanovich, spitting. 'You can't even roll papyrossi with the paper they provide. Haven't got a decent cigarette, have you, Konstantin Dmitrinovich?'

'Sorry, Luka Ivanovich; only German ones.'

'They still make me throw up.'

A simple but effective bit of dialogue. To be on the safe side, however, the Russians separated them, and they were given beds in different huts. The huts were of a fair size, each containing up to ten officers. Little Dallburg, now Nikolai Antonovich Pleyin, found it easiest to make new friends. Once they found out that he was a good singer, his companions instantly begged him to perform for them. Nikolai Antonovich did not object. What Russian with a good voice would hesitate to sing a few songs about his native land in captivity?

His clear voice attracted officers from the other huts, and soon they were all listening intently, doors and windows opened wide to the sound, as Nikolai Antonovich sang the song of the Siberian horsemen, the song of the cornflower, the ballad of the maiden who threw maize up to the sky where it turned to stars. When he had finished his recital, no one applauded; they walked quietly away to their huts, heads bent, and many of them had tears running down their cheeks.

That evening, Pleyin got three times his ration to eat; everyone contributed. 'Eat up, comrade,' the men urged him. 'It's good for the voice. Eat up, little brother. Have some more bread and margarine. Have some sugar in your tea—it's not real tea, some sort of dried German leaves, but put plenty of sugar in and it's drinkable. Don't be shy. We like you to have it; we want you to enjoy it.' Pleyin ate his fill, and then lay on his wooden bunk with its hard seagrass mattress, folded his arms behind his head, and thought.

Only five days ago he had been with Gabrielle — Gabrielle and her soft, tender, supple and passionate body, her shining eyes, pointed breasts and little mouth which could utter such wild cries, her whispered words of love, her sunny laughter. And there had been the sound of the sea, the wind driving pale-yellow sand over the dunes, and Gabrielle's lips were salty when he kissed them.

Five days ago — and now he was a Russian. Nikolai Antonovich Pleyin. Alexander Dallburg would never exist again. Never. He would never see Gabrielle again, or hear her voice sigh, 'Chérie. . . .'

A man can lie in his own coffin and never know it.

'What are you thinking of, Nikoshka?' asked the man beside him.

'My mother, comrade. She'll be heartbroken. She must think I'm dead.'

'It's the same for us all. They'll be all the happier when we come home.'

'You think you'll see Russia again?'

'I live for nothing else, Nikolai Antonovich.'

Pleyin, who had once been Alexander Dallburg, turned his face to the wall.

Maybe he will see Russia again, he thought, but I shall never come back to Germany.

After three days the men were moved from the camp again. The senior Russian officers had been informed four hours before the truck drew up near the camp once more. They had been told the ten new arrivals were being transferred to a detention-camp and regarded as political prisoners.

'That's ridiculous,' protested Lieutenant-Colonel Sakmatov, and even General Iswarin, the senior Russian army officer in the camp, intervened, asked to speak to the German commandant, and assured him that their ten comrades were perfectly legitimate army officers, not political commissars. The camp inmates formed groups around their new friends, wondering whether there was

97

any point in staging a protest and trying to argue with the German officers.

'No, I know what they're like, comrades,' said Pavel Fedorovich Sassonov, who had once been Bodo von Labitz. 'There'd be no point in it. We have no rights at all now. Don't put yourselves in danger on our account. You're good comrades, real friends, but don't make trouble. I dare say this will all turn out to be a mistake.'

They said good-bye as if they had all been friends for years. A platoon of German soldiers with machine-pistols at the ready was waiting by the camp exit. Everyone could feel that the atmosphere in the camp was explosive; one small spark might set off a catastrophe.

Colonel von Renneberg was waiting beside the truck, its tailgate let down again. Hansekamm remained inside. The ten men turned once more to wave, the Soviet officers waved back — one even made the sign of the cross — and then they clambered into the truck and sat down on the benches. The tailgate was put up, Renneberg shot the bolt on the inside, and the truck clattered away. The last they heard was a rhythmic cry uttered by many throats.

'*Rossiya! Rossiya!* Russia! Russia.'

'Highly successful,' said Renneberg in the darkness of the truck. 'Congratulations. You've exceeded all our expectations.' He was speaking in Russian.

Everything was the same back at Eberswalde.

The Allies now had a million men landed in France. Colonel von Renneberg gave them only a brief résumé of the situation in the west. Their concern was Moscow now. The huge map of the city and its surroundings hung there on the wall. It showed the smallest alleyway, the tiniest footpath.

'Comrade Hansekamm, I can't wait for that photograph of the couple in the cornfield you promised us,' said Luka Ivanovich Petrovsky.

'I have something rather better in store for you.' Renneberg nodded to Hansekamm, in the manner of a theatrical producer signalling to his stage manager. 'Just one thing: please remember the ten of you are comrades, all in this together, and we don't want any trouble between you.'

'Why on earth should there be?' asked Kyrill Semyonovich Boranov, once called Kuehenberg.

Hansekamm opened the door of the instruction-room. They heard the click of heels in the long corridor outside, and then their hearts seemed to leap into their throats.

A woman came in. She had short black hair, she wore a simple blue linen skirt, a yellow blouse, and sandals with medium-height heels. And from her dark head to the soles of her feet she radiated such physical perfection, such a bitter-sweet kind of sensuality, such sparkling animal vitality, that Fyodor Panteleyevich Ivanov put both hands to his fair head and said out loud, 'Good Lord above!'

Petrovsky turned to Renneberg and said reproachfully, 'Comrade, we're ready to do what you like, but there's really no need to add the tortures of Tantalus, too.'

The young woman smiled, and looked at the ten men without embarrassment. Her eyes were slightly slanted, with an Asiatic effect. She put her hands behind her back. Her blouse was stretched over her full, round breasts; two nipples the size of hazelnuts strained against it. Her waist was slim, her hips well rounded, her long, firmly muscled, tanned legs showed that she was fit and athletic.

The ten men, standing in a semi-circle, responded to the woman's glance each according to his temperament. Sergei Andreyevich Tarski, formerly Second Lieutenant Semper, said in matter-of-fact tones, 'Well, at least one of us is out of the running — he's just become a father.'

'You're all out of the running,' said Renneberg, obviously pleased by the success of his surprise. 'May I introduce Milda Ivanovna Kabakova?'

'What a beautiful name,' said Leonid Germanovich Duskov.

'As you know, we had not intended to provide you with any contacts in Moscow,' said Colonel von Renneberg. 'Each man was to run his own risks. But, after much thought, we changed our minds, and decided that you should have just one contact in the city after all. Milda Ivanovna has an apartment at number 19, Lesnaya Street. The street runs from the square in front of the

Belorussian Station—you'll see the Gorky Monument in the middle of the square—to Novoslobodskaya Street.' As Renneberg spoke, Hansekamm pointed out the places named on the map of Moscow, but none of the men was watching his pointer; they were all staring at Milda Ivanovna. 'This is where number 19 stands.'

'When do we get to Moscow?' asked Ivan Petrovich Bunurian, formerly Lieutenant von Ranovski.

'Comrade Milda will be parachuted in in a couple of days' time. The rest of you must learn how to make a parachute-drop first. Have you memorized the address?'

'I certainly have,' Petrovsky gave Milda Ivanovna Kabakova a cheerful nod. She looked back at him, brows raised, both chilly and challenging, very much keeping her distance. 'Comrade, nothing on earth will keep me from number 19 Lesnaya Street.'

'Comrade Kabakova will be your mutual contact; you will report to her, and get in touch with each other through her. You will be approaching Moscow from ten different directions, and after establishing yourselves in the city—we are reckoning on a period of four weeks for this—you will all meet at Milda Ivanovna's. If you are lucky.'

'There'll be no holding me,' promised Alexander Nikolayevich Kraskin, formerly Detlev Adler.

'And now,' Renneberg continued brusquely, 'let's put our minds to Moscow. Comrade Kabakova will tell you all there is to know about the city and its surroundings.'

They enjoyed their lesson. Milda's voice was low, melodious and vibrant, and it was a pleasure to listen to her. As for her appearance—there was a magic around her that took the men's breath away. She talked for two hours, sometimes leaning on the long pointer, which reached her chin and nestled between her breasts when she rested one end of it on the floor. She did not react at all when Alexander Nikolayevich Kraskin, called upon to repeat various place-names, took the pointer from her and caressed it tenderly before going up to the big map. The others grinned. Lieutenant-Colonel Hansekamm shook his head in silence. Renneberg sat at the desk, making notes.

'Thank you, Milda Ivanovna,' said the Colonel, at last, looking at his watch. 'The same time tomorrow, please.'

She nodded, put down the pointer, smiled shyly at the men and left the instruction-room, her hips swaying slightly as she walked.

Renneberg looked round at his protégés. 'Now, then,' he said gravely, and in German for once, 'I know you're all young men, and I can make allowances; but you are officers, and you should surely understand the serious nature of our task. Forgive my saying so, but some of you were behaving like adolescent schoolboys. As far as you are concerned, Milda Ivanovna is sexless.'

'Really, sir, we'd have to be less than human to accept that,' protested Luka Ivanovich.

Renneberg rose. 'By the way, to save you fruitless nocturnal prowling, Milda Ivanovna is *not* staying in the Riding School.'

'Comrade Renneberg.' Alexander Nikolayevich Kraskin rose from his own chair. 'Did you say Milda Ivanovna was parachuting into Russia in a couple of days' time?'

'Yes. We are short of time. The Americans and English are making a lot of headway in France, while there is this suspicious lull on the Eastern Front. Now, if Stalin can be assassinated while the Allies are intoxicated by the imminent certainty of victory, the shock will be all the greater.' Renneberg went to the window. They could hear a car starting outside; Milda Ivanovna being driven to her quarters. 'Comrade Kabakova is a native of Moscow. There's no need for you to know how we came to be in touch with her, or how she got here, but she cannot go back the same way; it would take too long. That's why we're dropping her in by parachute.'

'Why is she doing it?' asked Kyrill Semyonovich Boranov.

'Her grandfather, a White Russian officer, was executed by firing squad after the Revolution. Her father, a naval captain, was shot during Stalin's purge of the armed forces, when Marshal Tukhachevsky was executed. Her mother went mad; she is still alive, in a Moscow mental hospital. I think that's enough to explain why Milda Ivanovna does not love the present régime.' The Colonel cleared his throat. 'Incidentally, she doesn't much love the Germans, either. Her involvement with us is of a purely private nature. She is obsessed by a desire to be revenged on Stalin; the political aspects of our operation, as such, don't interest her at all. When you have killed Stalin, Milda will thank you — and then spit in your faces.'

'Sir, that sounds like a dangerously weak link in the chain to me,' said Pavel Fedorovich Sassonov thoughtfully. 'Privately motivated fanatics always constitute a risk.'

'We all know that.' Renneberg searched his pockets for cigarettes and a lighter. 'But one can't visit Hell without consorting with the Devil.'

'When are we likely to drop into Russia ourselves?' asked Duskov.

'As soon as you have had parachute training. There's a good deal for you to learn by then, and you must learn it very fast.'

Milda Ivanovna came to continue instructing them next day, this time wearing a yellow skirt and a red blouse, its top three buttons undone because of the heat, so that her smooth, tanned skin was visible, as well as the edge of a white bra, and the upper part of her rounded breasts. The swell of them beneath her blouse gave the imagination plenty of scope. She wore some make-up, and had tied a flower-embroidered ribbon round her glossy black hair. It was absurd to try to think of her as sexless. It will pass over, thought Renneberg; they may not have much longer to live, so one might as well allow them this small erotic pleasure.

They were now studying the area around Moscow, into which they would be jumping. Milda and Hansekamm took turns to describe the various districts. Detailed photographs were projected on a screen — including that long-awaited air-photograph of the couple making love in the cornfield.

'Hullo, what's that?' inquired Petrovsky. 'Milda Ivanovna, can you explain that one, my little Moscow pigeon?'

'This cornfield is near Stupino,' said Milda soberly. 'It lies south of Moscow, on the road to Tula in the west and Ryasan in the east. It belongs to the collective farm known as "The Honour of Lenin Farm".' She tapped Petrovsky's chest with her pointer. 'The feature which interests you so much, Comrade Luka Ivanovich, shows two people engaged in conceiving a new Russian citizen, so that Russia may live for ever.'

'Ah. I like the sound of that,' said Petrovsky. 'A usual part of the programme on collectives, is it, comrade? And how high is productivity? Do tell us more.'

'Comrades,' said Hansekamm rather feebly, 'this is not a cabaret

102

show. Your job is to learn certain facts. Remember, one slip could be fatal. This picture was taken last year. The identical field is growing a grain crop again this year, and it could turn out to be a hiding-place for one of you. Kindly take all this more seriously, comrades.'

Finally, the picture of the cornfield slipped off the screen, giving way to a photograph of a woodland area, with a road visible at the bottom of the picture. 'The Latashino district.' Milda pointed with her stick. 'To the south of this wood you can see the Rzhev-to-Moscow road, which joins the famous Smolensk-to-Moscow highway at Golitzyno. There is a deserted hamlet in the wood; it is better avoided, since it is often used by—'

'By comrades engaged in conceiving sons for the Russian people,' interrupted Ivan Petrovich Bunurian, 'and none too keen on having a few onlookers dropping in by parachute.'

Milda Ivanovna put her pointer aside, and leaned against the whitewashed wall.

'Now you've insulted her,' said Petrovsky. 'You shouldn't have done that, comrade.'

'I shall expect you to make contact with me in due course at 19 Lesnaya Street,' Milda Ivanovna went on. 'No doubt your friends will explain how that is to be done.'

She walked proudly past the ten men and out of the room, leaving a faint trace of perfume behind.

'Oh Lord!' Sergei Andreyevich Tarski exclaimed. 'And I thought she was to be our little Russian mother.'

Colonel von Renneberg left the window, his face like a thunder-cloud. 'If time were not so pressing,' he said in Russian, 'I should interrupt your training, turn you back into German officers and see you suitably disciplined.'

'Sir, we apologize. Please try to understand.' Major von Labitz, alias Sassonov, rose. 'It's only natural to—'

'Can't you get it into your fat heads that what you learn here will increase your chances of survival?' shouted Renneberg. For once, his reserve and patience deserted him. 'I should be able to expect a certain maturity from *you*, of all people.'

'Just a moment, comrade,' Duskov suddenly interrupted. 'As you know, I come from a poor background in Kazan. My father works on the roads; my mother makes shirts in a collective combine factory; my sister's already widowed, with one child – her husband died of liver disease, poor fellow. I was trained as a cobbler myself, but I'm off to a job as a railway shunter now I've been discharged from the Red Army on account of that bullet I got in my hip, making me unfit for active service as a driver at the front. Now, comrade, I ask you – show me a woman like Milda Ivanovna, and how do you expect me, as an ex-Army shunter, to react? Or take Comrade Petrovsky here, who used to work in a warehouse. What does he know of the finer things of life? A glass of kvass, his newspaper, the crates and cartons he stacks at work, his girlfriend in the evenings – that's what fills his life. Or do you think he's used to spending his time philosophizing about long-range agricultural policy in Kazakhstan? Who's talking about the behaviour of German officers? We're Russians – small fry, all of us. So we behave like the men we are. If we didn't, would we be the genuine article?'

Colonel von Renneberg had listened, his face flushed but unmoving. 'Have you finished?' he asked at last, nervously clicking his cigarette-case open and shut.

'Yes,' said Duskov.

'You're right.' Renneberg put his cigarette-case away again. 'I should thank you for pointing it out. I was thinking along the wrong lines. No doubt because I don't have to turn into a Russian myself.'

That evening's meal became a party. Not so much because of the food, or the Crimean wine, or the candles on the table, but because Milda Ivanovna came to join them.

She was looking beautiful. 'I shall hope to see you all again in Moscow,' she said. Her face constantly changed as she spoke; it was full of vitality. Now and then she ran a hand through her dark hair; when she laughed she pressed her hands to her breasts, as if to hold their beautiful curves in place.

'Moscow,' said Kraskin suddenly, at one point, looking at Milda Ivanovna with concern for her in his eyes. He was remembering what had been said before. 'When *are* you being parachuted in?'

'Tomorrow night.'

'My God!'

'I'm not afraid.'

'At what time?' asked Duskov.

'Why do you want to know, Leonid Germanovich?'

'So that we can all be thinking of you, Milda Ivanovna. Some of us might like to pray, too.'

'Do you believe there's a God?'

'Don't you?'

'No.' Her face, with its Asiatic cheek-bones, became harder, darker, more angular. 'I think God was never in Russia. Only the Bolshevists.'

'Sometimes out at the front, when you're in the middle of the firing-line, it's possible to feel the kind of belief in God a small child has.'

'Then you're lucky, Leonid Germanovich.' Milda stared at the flickering candle in front of her. 'In such a situation, I should curse a God who calls us his children, but lets us slaughter each other. What sort of father is that?'

'Yes.' Kyrill Semyonovich Boranov put down his wine-glass. 'We all have fathers. Did they fight tooth and nail to stop us going to the war? Far from it: they were proud. My boy in his uniform. My son the lieutenant. My lad with his Iron Cross 1st Class, his Cross of God, his Knight's Cross, or whatever it was!' He looked around, rather confused. 'Sorry, comrades. I was momentarily in the wrong country. I suppose I was talking about Captain Asgard Kuehenberg, who knew so many people full of patriotic pride. But is it any different in Russia? Fathers are a species apart as soon as their sons put on uniform, Milda Ivanovna, so why should God be any different?' He cleared his throat, and poured himself more wine. 'What time will you be jumping?'

'Between two and three in the morning, if all goes well.'

'We'll think of you,' said Kraskin. 'We'll be standing at our windows, looking out at the night — though whether that will be any help, comrade. . . .'

'It will be a great help.' She attempted a smile. 'I shan't feel so alone.'

'And how will you know when *we* have been dropped in?' asked Bunurian.

'She won't,' Renneberg answered for Milda. 'She won't know whether the Wild Geese have reached their journey's end until it's time for you to make contact with her.'

105

'And suppose no one at all makes contact?' The question came from little Pleyin.

'Impossible.' Renneberg was smoking a cigar, watching the round smoke-rings he blew. 'By all the laws of probability, at least two out of ten men *must* come through.'

'A soothing thought,' said Boranov, his voice husky. 'We only need time to get used to knowing we're pawns in a game of chance. . . .'

That night, they all went to the door and said good-bye to Milda Ivanovna in the Russian manner, kissing her on both cheeks. A large car was waiting in the drive. The driver and his mate were baffled.

'Hey, Gustav, this is your big moment,' said the driver. 'Our passenger's a tart — Russian top brass, for the use of.'

'One between ten? Bit stingy, isn't it?' The lance-corporal stared at Milda, who was walking towards the car and turning back now and then to wave.

'Shut your mouth!' hissed the driver as Hansekamm came round to the other side of the car and opened the door. And then, out loud: 'Corporal Hämmerle on duty, sir!'

'To Berlin,' said Hansekamm. He helped Milda into the car, closed the door, got in the other side and sat beside her. They moved off down the road. A clear June night, with moonlight over the hills and pinewoods of the Mark. Hansekamm wound down his window and breathed in deeply. There was a scent of resin and fresh grass in the air.

'You're very quiet, Milda,' he said.

'I'm tired,' she said. She had leaned back, partly covering her face with her silk scarf.

'Try to get some sleep,' said Hansekamm.

Milda Ivanovna nodded, and put the scarf right over her face like a curtain, leaning back against the upholstery.

She was crying, very quietly.

The men began their parachute training next day, jumping first from a tower, with a safety rope, then from an aircraft, linked to an experienced paratrooper who would know what to do if anyone forgot to pull his rip-cord. They wore German uniforms, without any indication of rank, and were taken to the air-base in a truck.

106

At the end of that first day, when they were back at the Riding School, they sat at supper as if they had been stunned, listlessly pushing the food around their plates. Little Pleyin had been so frightened when he first jumped from the tower that he had thrown up; he was ashamed, but no one thought any the worse of him for it.

'Only a question of getting used to it,' said a paratroop lieutenant in charge of their training, cheerfully. 'You'll soon love it. Hovering in between heaven and earth — it's like an orgasm.'

'Christ, the man's a pervert!' groaned Ivanov. But after a while, when he found himself floating through the air as if gravity did not exist, he was surprised to discover that he did feel a curious pleasure in it, though despite their practice in rolling over and over he had not expected such a hard impact on landing.

As usual after the evening meal, they spent an hour or so sitting companionably together with Colonel von Renneberg, drinking wine or brandy, smoking, and listening to the latest radio news. OKW's bulletins were not at all like Renneberg's own accounts of the situation.

'Well, I'm pleased with your progress, gentlemen,' said Renneberg that night, raising a glass of Russian cognac to them. 'If all goes according to plan, we should be able to drop you into Russia between the eighteenth and the twenty-fifth of June.'

There was silence for a while, until Sergei Andreyevich Tarski suddenly said, 'Two o'clock.'

'Two o'clock?' Renneberg put his glass down on the table.

'That's when she's jumping.'

'Please don't worry. Milda Ivanovna runs less risk than any of you. No one is likely to stop a woman farmworker and check up on her. You're a different matter; people will naturally wonder why you're not in the Army.' He switched over to the BBC; cheerful dance music emerged from the radio set. He turned down the volume slightly, and crossed his legs. 'However, we do have a certain amount of trouble,' he said casually.

'With whom?' asked Boranov.

'With the Führer's headquarters. Himmler and Kaltenbrunner, who are not among the few who know about Wild Geese, have got wind of something, and are sniffing around like hounds on a scent. For reasons I won't go into, gentlemen, it is best they should *not* know. Keitel and Jodl won't say anything, and the Führer himself has probably forgotten all about us; he thought the enterprise an idiotic one. Still, the SS has sent OKW an official query. OKW is not saying anything—but I do ask myself, where's the weak spot? How did any rumours leak out? I'm telling you this so that you will realize that the slightest attempt by any of you to smuggle out a message—a letter to your families, say—could be fatal to yourselves.' Renneberg folded his hands on his crossed knees. 'I should also tell you that letters to your relatives, reporting you missing and expressing great regret and sympathy, are ready to be mailed. They'll be sent off the day after tomorrow.'

'The day after tomorrow,' said little Pleyin quietly.

'So then we shall be dead,' said Duskov, raising his glass.

Sassonov held his own wine-glass in both hands, and looked at Colonel von Renneberg. 'Speaking as a dead man, there's one thing I'd like to know,' he said.

'What is it?' asked Renneberg.

'I have a young wife. My first child was born only a few days ago. My first child, and obviously my last. How—how will they be cared for?'

'Your widow will receive a pension. Your son's education and training are guaranteed, whatever career he wishes to pursue.'

'And suppose we lose the war?' It was the first time any of the company had said it out loud.

'There will always *be* a Germany,' he said, 'and, whatever kind of country it may be, Germany will keep its promises.'

'A Communist Germany?'

'That's an impossibility.'

'How do you know?'

'Moscow will never gain a foothold on the Rhine. It is too near to Paris and London.' Renneberg swirled the cognac in his balloon glass. 'But global politics are not our concern now, gentlemen.'

'No,' said Sassonov quietly. 'I'm only interested in my wife and child. Our estate is in Latvia, and if we lose the war they'll be as poor as church mice.'

'As I told you at the start: fantastic as it may sound, you could be the men who change the course of world history. The name of the figurehead of a new age today is not Adolf Hitler but Joseph

Stalin. The Western Allies do not know just what they are bringing into their own houses along with their Soviet friends, though they will find out in time. However, the apparently inexorable progress of Stalinism could be halted by a single shot, a single hand grenade.'

'In which case,' said Boranov, 'the name of the figurehead *would* be Adolf Hitler.'

Renneberg looked gravely at him. 'No. Since you are officially dead men, you may as well know this much: Adolf Hitler will not determine the way world history turns, either. Once you have killed Stalin, much else will change in Germany, too.'

At two in the morning, the ten men were standing at the windows of their rooms, looking out into the night.

'Good luck, Milda,' said Ivanov softly.

'Shall we ever see her again?' wondered little Pleyin. 'Do you think we'll get through?'

Colonel von Renneberg stood at a window beside Boranov. He, too, was looking eastward, at the moonlit night sky, and he was talking quietly, but not about Milda Ivanovna.

'I could still get you out of this, Captain Kuehenberg,' he said in German.

'I don't understand, comrade,' replied Boranov in Russian.

'Never mind all that for a moment, Kuehenberg.' Renneberg drew closer to him. 'I've seen your personal file, your family history, everything, and now I have come to know you. You are an intelligent man, and you love your country.'

'Who doesn't, comrade?' Boranov was still speaking Russian, and Renneberg did not persist in using German.

'Even now, I could keep you here. Get you on General Oster's staff.'

'And what would I be doing there?'

'Well—you'd get to know Witzleben, Stauffenberg, Goerdeler, Hoeppner, the Kreisau Circle. . . .'

'Who are they?'

'That would all be explained to you—at all events, you'd get to know the people who believe that Germany can still survive. After Hitler. Canaris is one of them. And Stülpnagel, and Rommel—'

'Rommel, too?' Boranov turned away from the window. Twelve

minutes past two. Milda could have landed by now. 'Why do you put this to me?'

'Because we need men like you, Kuehenberg. Strong men, with wide-ranging minds and innate political intelligence, along with the courage to take risks. You are still young. Only twenty-eight. You are the future, Kuehenberg. Over the last few days I have asked myself again and again: can we afford to lose this man in Moscow? Because, even if you survive Operation Wild Geese, your life will be virtually over—you're quite clear about that?'

'There are ten of us, Comrade Colonel,' said Boranov firmly, 'and ten we will remain. We will kill Stalin—you deal with Hitler—and perhaps we shall meet again some day, and wonder whether it was all worth while.'

'Only a passing thought. Well, it was interesting talking to you, Kyrill Semyonovich.' Renneberg went to the door.

'Thank you, Comrade Colonel.'

Boranov turned and looked out of the window again. The door closed, behind his back. He was still not quite able to grasp what he had heard: Witzleben, Canaris, Rommel, all against Hitler? Stalin's death to usher in world-wide changes? He shrugged his shoulders, leaning his hands on the window-sill, chilled by the nature of the task ahead.

The little night-flying reconnaissance-plane hummed at a fair height above the Minsk area, making for Smolensk and Moscow. German searchlight batteries probed the sky, but up here it was cloudy; the fingers of light became entangled in cloud as if absorbed by cotton-wool, and gave only a dim, milky glow. The gunners waited ready by their anti-aircraft guns, but no orders came to fire: the aircraft was flying too high, and was on its own, too.

It passed the German lines, and was soon flying over Smolensk. The Soviet air force didn't react to the distant hum. It could hardly be German. What would a solitary German plane be doing in their air space?

It went on its way towards Moscow. It had no number, identifying mark, or sign of its nationality. It was painted grey-green and hardly showed up at all against the sky. Once past Vyasma it lost height, climbing down through the cloud cover, and took

110

its bearings from the broad ribbon of the highway, along which convoys of trucks and artillery were moving westward.

'We're going to approach Moscow from Kaluga,' said the Luftwaffe sergeant piloting the plane. 'I'll drop you over the Lopassyna river valley. Ready to jump?'

'Yes.'

Milda Ivanovna checked her equipment once again. The harness fitted well. Wearing a leather cap, and a tracksuit over her peasant clothes, she was still miserably cold at this height, and kept beating her hands together to keep them warm. An old scarf knotted to form a bag hung round her neck. Later, she would carry it in her hand, as Russian peasant women did when they had something to transport. The one big risk was that some policeman might stop her and ask to see what was inside. He would be very much surprised. Instead of a few black-market eggs, he would find a small but powerful short-wave radio transmitter, two keys, one for the door of an apartment building and one for an apartment inside it, a novel by Tolstoy with certain groups of letters on certain pages acting as the key to a code, and a packet of five thousand roubles in notes of small denominations. But perhaps the most important piece of Milda's equipment hung in a gold locket between her firm, beautiful breasts: a gelatine capsule filled with potassium cyanide.

The sergeant pointed down. 'The River Oka.'

'I can see it.'

'Another ten minutes. I'm coming down to jumping height for you.'

'Right.'

Milda Ivanovna looked down. The aircraft was gliding soundlessly, the ground coming closer: her country, Russia, the land that had asked so much blood of her family and which, none the less, she loved with all her being. The woods of Michnyevo. A ribbon wound through the dense green trees, faintly shining: the little River Lopassnya.

'Ready now?' asked the pilot.

Milda checked all the straps of her harness yet again. The pack on her back felt like a lump of ice. She had folded the silk parachute herself. It had struck her, at the time, as a ceremonial which meant the entry to life or death. A few tangled lines of rigging,

111

the failure of the rip-cord to perform, and the pack would not burst open with the loud crack familiar to all paratroopers. For a second you would feel like a bird, actually sailing through the air with arms and legs outstretched, until the air itself became hard as a board, beating at your head like a hammer, and the monstrous, rushing darkness opened up before you.

Milda Ivanovna remembered what the young paratroop company commander had told her; it was a comfort. 'Most people whose parachutes fail to open when they fall from such heights are already unconscious before they reach the ground; they don't feel anything.'

'Here goes,' said the sergeant. The plane described a wide arc over the little River Lopassnya and came back, gliding silently. 'Now!'

'Now. Thanks.'

'I'll pray for you,' said the young pilot unemotionally.

Milda Ivanovna pushed off. She tumbled head first into the night sky. For a split second she really did feel as if she were hovering weightlessly. The weird illusion of floating freely in the sky filled her with a sense of potentially deadly euphoria. Then she knew she was falling; she spread out her arms and legs in the correct position, counted – twenty-one, twenty-two, twenty-three, twenty-four – and pulled the rip-cord.

With a sound like an explosion, the pack on her back broke open and the parachute hissed out and unfolded, expanding to a vast dome against the night sky, turning Milda round and round in the air. She hung helpless in her harness for a moment or so, and then got herself into the vertical position, taking hold of the strap around her, kicking her legs, and looking down. The woods and the river were slowly coming towards her.

The reconnaissance-plane, still gliding, circled lower. Eyes and lips narrowed, the pilot stared at the falling parachute: the most beautiful woman he had ever seen in his life, dropping to an unknown fate.

'Damn this bloody war,' said the young sergeant. He described another arc, turned away, and then switched the engine on again, climbed steeply, and turned towards Kaluga.

On 18 June 1944, the ten men sat in the instruction-room again, looking at the now familiar map of Moscow and its surroundings; the area it showed extended for a hundred kilometres around the city.

Hansekamm, holding the pointer, was waiting for Colonel von Renneberg. There was something in the air; they could all feel it. The moment's coming, thought Boranov. The Wild Geese will be set loose to go on their suicidal flight east. My God, every day this mission seems more obviously crazy.

Renneberg came in at last, a blue briefcase under his arm, went to the desk and opened the case. Hansekamm approached the map with his pointer.

'Gentlemen,' said Renneberg in German, 'I have here the final plans of your mission.'

Petrovsky instantly put up his hand. 'Not understand,' he said in Russian-accented broken German. 'Not speak Germanski.'

'Damn you, I forgot. Sorry.' Renneberg smiled ironically, and continued in Russian. 'As I call out your names, please come up and indicate the place I have mentioned on the map. It shouldn't take long; the map must be imprinted on your brains by now.' He took a sheet of paper out of the briefcase and held it up. 'Pyotr Mironovich Sepkin.'

'Yes.' Lieutenant Radek rose.

'You will be dropped in at Moshaisk, in the Uvarovka district. Please show us where that is on the map.'

Sepkin took the pointer from Hansekamm, went up to the map and indicated the spot without the least hesitation.

'Good. Ivan Petrovich Bunurian.'

'Yes.' Lieutenant von Ranovski got to his feet.

'You'll jump in near Maximovo.'

A few steps up to the map, and the pointer went straight to the place named.

'Good.'

The process was repeated eight more times. It was like working a slot machine: Renneberg fed in a place-name like a coin, and a robot went up to the map of Moscow and indicated it with automatic precision.

Renneberg put the sheet of paper back in the blue case while Pleyin was still standing by the map of Moscow, pointer in hand.

'You know what those areas look like, from the air-photographs.

Moscow can easily be reached from any of them, either by road or by rail. Just to encourage you – and I can tell from the look in your eyes you'd like to know – Milda Ivanovna has reached Moscow.'

'Thank God!' cried Petrovsky.

'But the aircraft from which she jumped is reported missing.'

'Genuinely missing – or only for the record?' asked Boranov hoarsely.

'Genuinely missing. We imagine it was shot down by Soviet fighters.'

'The first casualty of Operation Wild Geese.' Kraskin lit a cigarette, inhaling the smoke as if to soothe his nerves.

Renneberg closed his briefcase. 'You will soon be getting Russian civilian clothing, papers, a few roubles, and the sort of everyday objects anyone might carry around. Anything else you'd like to ask?'

'No,' said Sassonov.

'We shall drive out to the airfields tomorrow.'

'Then this is our last evening together?'

'Yes.'

'We'll make it a good Russian farewell party, comrades,' said Bunurian, his voice low. 'Who knows if we'll ever see each other again?'

Renneberg said, 'I've had Crimean champagne put on ice for you – a souvenir of the days when we had the Crimea in our hands. But it must be bed for you at eleven, gentlemen. I think' – his face softened – 'each of you will want a few quiet hours to himself.'

Later, Renneberg and Hansekamm themselves handed out the civilian clothes: trousers and jackets made of harsh fabrics, clumsy shoes, hand-knitted socks, checked or striped shirts, all well worn and correspondingly shabby – clothes for labourers, peasants, lower-grade clerks. That evening, they drank their Crimean champagne, Pleyin sang folk songs, Tarski and Sepkin linked arms to dance a *krakoviak*. Kraskin had even got hold of a balalaika; he held it between his knees, and played the instrument as if he had been doing so all his life. Petrovsky was in good form, with an inexhaustible repertoire of dirty jokes; despite the noise, Bunurian and Sassonov played a game of chess which ended in a draw; Ivanov turned out to be something of an acrobat, and performed an act good enough for a circus; Duskov did a hilarious mime of a rider with his horse falling under him.

But, at the appointed time, Renneberg looked ostentatiously at his watch. The party was over.

'We shall be leaving in five groups, setting out at six in the morning,' he said. 'Sleep as well as you can.'

They nodded, and left the room in silence. Renneberg locked the door after the last man and put the key in his pocket. It was all over.

It was a cool morning, with a good many clouds in the pale-blue sky driving westwards, lit up by the milky radiance of the sun, which had just risen. The weather was colder than it had been for the last few days, and the air moister. There was dew on the grass. Larks rose from the fields, and a group of bustards, wings flapping, circled a small, reed-grown pond.

Just before six o'clock, ten civilians in shabby clothes and dirty shoes were gathered in the hall of the isolated wing of the Officers' Riding School at Eberswalde, smoking acrid cigarettes made of machorka tobacco wrapped in newsprint. They could have been miles away as they leaned against the walls in silence. They had handed in the last proofs of their old identities a quarter of an hour ago: their watches and underclothes, a cigarette-holder, a seal ring, wallets with photographs of their parents, brothers, sisters and girlfriends, their purses, identity cards, a few handkerchiefs, matchboxes and lighters. These things were all collected in bags and taken away.

Pavel Fedorovich Sassonov had hesitated for a moment before taking off his wedding ring. It was more than the mere act of handing it over: it was the last step in the complete obliteration of his identity. Hansekamm waited patiently with the bag until Sassonov finally took the ring off and dropped it in to join the other things.

'What will happen to those things?' asked Sassonov, getting the question out with difficulty. 'You're not going to keep them, are you?'

'If you really want to know, we shall either bury them or hand them over to the Berlin refuse disposal service.'

Then Hansekamm gave them Russian matchboxes, Russian penknives, even Russian keys. Nikolai Antonovich Pleyin, who was supposed to have worked as an army electrician after being called up from music college, even got a complete electrician's toolkit. He opened it, looked at the tools, and closed it again. 'Let's hope this works out,' he said.

'We know you're good with your hands. Your mother said you were quite a child when you built a radio set out of old parts, and it worked.'

'So I did.' Pleyin suddenly swallowed. 'You mean you talked to my mother?'

'Our files on each of you were complete.' No one else asked for any details. And now they were standing in the hall smoking, waiting to leave. Renneberg had not appeared yet. It was just before six. They heard cars drawing up in the forecourt outside.

'Hell, we're not dead yet, comrades,' said Petrovsky suddenly. 'Why are we standing around looking so glum? Let's look on the bright side. In a few hours' time, as far as we're concerned, the war will be over. We take a nice little walk to Moscow; we have our certificates of discharge from the Red Army and, whatever happens in Europe, it's none of our business now. We're hardworking, peaceful citizens, and those of us who reach Moscow may well survive.'

'And Stalin will obligingly walk up to us and invite us to put a bullet through his head, will he?' Boranov ground out his halfsmoked cigarette on the tiled floor. 'One of us at least must get really close to him; the thing can hardly be done from a distance.'

'How can we be sure in advance?' Sassonov was pacing calmly up and down. 'We shouldn't be thinking so far ahead. First we have to drop safely into the country. Then we'll see how things work out.'

At three minutes to six, Renneberg came downstairs from the first floor, a leather coat round his shoulders; he, too, was expecting rain. 'The cars are waiting,' he said. He put down his briefcase, and produced a small chrome box from the left-hand pocket of his uniform. It was a little like a cigarette-case, but thicker.

'I don't want to make much in the way of a speech just now. We've learned to know each other well enough to dispense with that kind of thing. But there's one certainty: we shall not meet

116

again. I wish you the very best of luck. And another thing, gentlemen — I've been putting it off until now. If you are in trouble, real trouble, and you're sure there is no way out, there is a rapid solution to all your problems, one which I know you'd all prefer to dishonourable surrender.' He opened the chrome box, and went up to Sassonov first. 'Please keep it in a place where you can always lay hands on it, although I hope none of you will have to use it.'

'At last,' said Boranov frostily. 'I was wondering when we were coming to that.'

'Potassium cyanide,' said Renneberg calmly. 'It takes effect at once. It has a strong taste of bitter almonds, but that is the last thing of which you will ever be aware. You will feel no pain.'

He gave a capsule to each of the men, then he picked up his briefcase. It was five past six. 'Ready to go?'

The men looked at each other, and then they all came together and embraced each other, Russian fashion, kissing on both cheeks. It was a silent and moving farewell. Even Petrovsky held his tongue for once. Ivanov was the only man to say anything; simply 'See you in Moscow, then.'

Sassonov, who was in command of the group from now on, waited until they had all finished saying good-bye. Then he said firmly, 'All ready.'

Renneberg opened the door, and morning sunlight flooded the hall. The air, heavy with dew, smelled of fresh grass and earth. Five closed cars stood on the forecourt, very correctly drawn up side by side. They were painted grey-green. Two Adlers, two DKWs, a large Horch. The drivers, standing beside them, stood to attention when they saw Colonel von Renneberg. They also looked surprised. Two officers and ten civilians — but very curious civilians, in very shabby clothes. They thought of their instructions to drive the men to various airfields. What could civilians like these have to do with the Luftwaffe? Could they be bomb experts, working on some new weapon? Goebbels had been talking about a miracle weapon for months.

Five minutes later, they started.

Car 1 took Sepkin and Kraskin to Fürstenfelde airfield.

Car 2 took Boranov and Petrovsky to Frankfurt an der Oder airfield.

Car 3 took Renneberg, Bunurian and Pleyin to Stettin airfield.
Car 4 took Hansekamm, Tarski and Ivanov to Küstrin airfield.
Car 5 took Duskov and Sassonov to Muskau Heath airfield.

Inside one of the Adlers, Petrovsky stretched on the cracked upholstery and tapped the driver's shoulder. The corporal jumped. 'What is it?' he asked.

'What sort of news have you been hearing?'

The driver stared at the road ahead. Careful, now, he thought. 'What d'you expect me to hear?' he asked. 'The Final Victory is near.'

'Hell, why don't we get him to stop and we'll go on foot?' said Petrovsky to Boranov. 'I'm not keen on having a bloody fool for a chauffeur.'

The corporal hunched his shoulders. Better keep my mouth shut, he thought. Too clever by half, this bloke; the sort to provoke you into saying things. He turned the car into the Fürstenfelde road and put his foot down.

Clouds were banking up in the sky like huge white mountain ranges, illuminated by the summer sun.

'Do you think there'll be rain?' Boranov asked the driver.

'Not likely.'

'Why not?'

'Too much wind.'

'You understand the weather?'

'I'm a farmer from these parts. Could be we'll have a summer storm — not a lot of rain, though.'

'Do you have any children?'

'Four. And, if you're all that interested, I'm not at the front on account of getting a shot in the lungs. Still in there, that bullet is. Seems like they can't get it out. Let it wander, they say. Ever heard of bullets wandering round a person's body?'

'Yes. But they can be there for years and do no harm.' Boranov put his hand in his jacket pocket and brought out a handful of banknotes. He tossed them over the back of the front passenger-seat.

'What's that?' asked the corporal in some alarm.

'About two thousand marks. For you.'

'Me? Why me?'

'Well, for your four kids.'

'But I can't – I mean, two thousand marks, just like that.'

'I shan't be needing them.'

The corporal said nothing. Something very odd here, he thought. Some kind of a trap, is it?

Petrovsky leaned toward Boranov. 'I thought you'd handed everything in?' he whispered.

'Not the cash. I mean, it seemed a shame to let the refuse disposal machines mince it up. I thought I'd give it to someone who needed it.'

They had a shorter way to go than any of the other cars, and so theirs was the first of the five to reach its destination: the military airfield of Frankfurt an der Oder. The corporal waited until the two civilians had got out and been met by the commanding officer of the air-base. Then he got behind the steering-wheel and drove at full speed back to the highway.

I can send Erna a postal order for two thousand marks tomorrow, he thought. She won't believe her eyes.

'You'll be setting out so as to arrive over the target-area about two in the morning,' the commanding officer of the reconnaissance squadron stationed at Frankfurt an der Oder told Boranov and Petrovsky. 'Now, would you come into the folding-room? You'll want to fold your own parachutes. They're parachutes captured from the Russians.'

Four

PARACHUTE on his back, Ivan Petrovich Bunurian crouched by
the exit-hatch under the transparent roofing of the gun-turret. He
was in a Dornier bomber converted for use as a long-distance
reconnaissance-plane. With a crew of only two, and no heavy
bombs to carry, the aircraft could fly fast and climb higher.
Bunurian had taken up his position here in the turret to try to
get a glimpse of the countryside over which they were flying.
However, he could see nothing. They were up above cloud, which
did thin now and then, but never gave much of a view of the
ground below. In fact the cloud was useful, since it rendered the
Soviet anti-aircraft defence powerless. Now and then, and especially when they were crossing the front line, searchlights groped
into the sky, but they could not penetrate that thick white wall.
Once past the front, no one took any notice of a solitary plane.
Had there been any central organization co-ordinating anti-aircraft precautions, it might have been noticed that ten unidentified
aircraft were approaching Moscow from ten different directions,
in a pattern radiating towards the heart of the Soviet Union, and
that could hardly be a coincidence. As it was, the single planes
went their way unmolested, approaching their target-areas at
about two in the morning.

The aircraft carrying Bunurian tilted sideways, flew in an arc,
and lost height. It was coming down through the cloud, but still
he could not make anything out yet. The country below was
black, a bottomless abyss. If he had to jump now he would be
casting himself into boundless space, without any sense of direction. A hell of a thing, not being able to see where you're going
as you float through the air, he thought.

The co-pilot, a Luftwaffe sergeant, made his way along to the
gun-turret. Bunurian was standing by the hatch, his Russian cap

well down over his forehead, clutching the handle beside the exit. The engines were throttled down, and the circling plane was losing height all the time.

'We're there,' said the sergeant. 'That's the Maximovo forest down below. The town of Turginovo's north of it; you want to skirt around that, so don't go due north. We'll drop you near the road to Volokolamsk. You can get to the railway line to Moscow there.'

'Don't worry, I know the place a lot better than you do,' said Bunurian, quite cheerfully, feeling the tension of these last few moments easing. He was surprised to find that he did not feel the slightest fear, only a burning desire to get that hatch open at long last and tumble out.

'Well, best of luck, mate.' The sergeant patted Bunurian's shoulder. 'What's your name, by the way?'

'Ivan Petrovich—'

'Oh, come off it! Want me to give anyone a message?'

'Who?'

'Well—your parents, wife, a girlfriend. How should I know? You must have someone back at home.'

'No. I'm not leaving anyone.' Bunurian opened the small hatch. The slipstream almost tore him out of the plane. He clutched the handle and braced his feet against the metal floor. 'Now?' he shouted.

'In a minute.' The converted bomber tilted slightly sideways and flew in another circle. A whistling signal sounded from the cockpit. 'Now!'

The sergeant slapped Bunurian on the back. Ivan Petrovich ducked, let go of the handle, and pushed himself off. Head over heels, he fell into empty black space, spreading out his arms as if he could fly unaided, like a bird. Then he pulled the rip-cord, involuntarily holding his breath. Would the parachute unfold?

There was a clear, hissing sound above him. The white silk shot out of its pack, billowing and expanding to form a huge dome. Then he felt the jerk as his harness pulled up his body and then left it dangling limply underneath the parachute lines.

Bunurian let out a deep breath. Done it! Now for a few moments of weightlessness, the delightful sensation of floating.

Overhead, very faintly, he heard the sound of the aircraft's engines. It was climbing steeply up through the cloud cover again, going back westwards.

The pilot, a second lieutenant, had a logbook on his knees. He entered: '0205 hours. Mission accomplished. Parachute-jump successful. On our way back to Polozk air-base.'

He closed the book and tossed it into a corner of the cockpit. The co-pilot climbed into his own seat and strapped himself in again. 'Called himself Ivan Petrovich. Wouldn't give any other name. You think he was really Russian?'

'Not likely, speaking perfect German like that.'

'Intelligence uses some pretty weird characters these days.'

'Yes, there's something funny about this one,' agreed the pilot, making the plane climb steeply. 'Daftest mission we ever flew on, if you ask me. And all that secrecy lark, too. Talk about making mountains out of molehills. . . .'

After a few seconds, when his eyes had become used to the darkness, Bunurian realized that he was approaching a densely wooded area. Shapes stood out: tree-tops, clearings, an almost circular little lake, glades, paths, one of them leading to an area where trees were being felled. Tall stacks of trunks stood there, stripped of their bark. He saw tractors, and three log-cabins.

Hell's bells, thought Bunurian, I'm coming right down into a woodcutters' camp. Just the thing I needed! Hullo, there, brothers, thought I'd drop in for a bite to eat. The name's Ivan Petrovich, baker by trade, just discharged from the Army, sent along to bake you some of my nice crusty bread. . . .

Bunurian kicked out, tugging at the lines. He knew it was possible to influence the drift of the parachute slightly like that — not much, but even drifting a little way from the woodcutters' camp could save his life. Gritting his teeth, he stared down. He felt as though he were falling faster now. But he did drift away over the huts, towards the forest, over the path leading to the clearing, and into an area where the trees stood close, their tops like a green, multi-crested sea.

Well, they had been trained in landing in forested areas. He drew up his legs and hoped the branches would cushion his impact. He felt the first of them brush his feet. Now, he thought, if I can get hold of a stout branch and cling to it. . . .

The initial impact with the tree-tops was gentle enough. He flung out his arms, clutched at a thick branch, got his legs around it, and then felt the billowing parachute on his back tugging at him, forcing him on, almost crushing his ribcage. He pressed his face into the leaves, groaning slightly — the straps around his chest and thighs seemed to be trying to tear him apart — as the tremendous force of the parachute tried to drag him away from the tree. At last, the silken mushroom collapsed, spread itself picturesquely over a tree-top as if covering it with a white tablecloth, and left Bunurian free to climb down.

He got out of his harness, still clinging to the top of the tree like a monkey. Then he heard a crack. He was horrified to see the branch giving way under his weight. He fell backwards into the depths below, brushing past other branches. He flung out his hands and grasped one. It broke his fall, but could not stop it.

His whole body seemed to be burning as if he were being flayed alive. He fell on and on, struck another thick branch, and abandoned himself to the pain. My back, he thought, my back — it must be broken!

Another branch caught him, tossed him back, flung him to the ground.

Bunurian's left foot twisted under him. He fell full length on his face, buried his fingers in the soft earth and clung to it as if the ground itself might give way beneath him. He lay there perfectly still for a while, racked with pain.

But I'm alive, he thought. Cautiously, he tried turning over and, much to his surprise, he managed it. He lay there on his back, trembling. Can't have broken my spine after all, he thought. But my ankle's broken all right. He waited, without moving, to see what his body would do next. The throbbing pain was concentrating on his left foot now, ebbing away from the other parts of his body.

The sky seemed lighter. Not that it was near dawn yet, but his eyes had adjusted to what little visibility there was. He saw that he had fallen into virgin forest, and was lying on ground soft with the leaf mould of many years. He could not see his parachute, but it was certainly still somewhere up there in the branches. Very carefully, Bunurian sat up. His clothes were badly torn. That meant he must find other clothes, fast.

Left leg outstretched, he pulled up his right leg and tried to stand up, leaning all his weight on it. A savage stab of pain from his left ankle pierced through him. Sighing heavily, he fell back again, and sat there on the soft ground.

I must make myself a splint, he thought. Tie up that broken ankle, support it with bits of wood, get two stout branches under my arms for crutches and move forward on one leg. It should be possible. If I can just get moving, then I can wait for my ankle to mend.

But that could take weeks. Long before then, the others would have met in Moscow.

He lay down on his back again. The pain, no longer localized in his left foot, was spreading right through his body again. He looked round for a piece of wood. He found one and put it between his teeth. Then he turned on his right side and began inching his way forward.

The pain was appalling. Despite the wood between his teeth, he groaned out loud. Sweat broke from every pore of his skin, ran over his face and into his eyes. After a metre or so he lay still again, face pressed to the ground, chewing on the wood like a starving dog with a bone.

It's no good, he thought. I'll never get anywhere like this. Another few metres and I shan't be able to stop myself screaming. I must lie quite still, somewhere in the shelter of the bushes. Lie still and wait for the pain in my ankle to lessen. Two or three days should do it. I must be patient—patience is a very Russian virtue.

Bunurian managed to drag himself the necessary metre or so farther on to a group of bushes, where he collapsed. He was weeping with pain, unable to keep the tears back any longer.

Leonid Germanovich Duskov made a perfect jump, landing in a gentle dip in meadowland, among a chain of hills. He rolled over, just as they had been taught, got underneath the parachute, gathered it together, and then lay there beside it in the long grass for a few minutes, getting his bearings.

Colonel von Renneberg would have applauded. Duskov had

come down right on target, in between the towns of Kolchugino and Alexandrov. To the north-west, about ten versts away, the Yaroslavl-to-Moscow highway ran through the forests and the marshes around the River Nyerl. Once he reached that road, he was as good as in Moscow already. He could either hitch a lift or catch a train from Alexandrov.

Dragging the parachute behind him, Duskov stuffed it under some stones beside a stream, and then covered it with enough earth to hide it. The night sky was clear now, a vault of twinkling stars. He sat by the stream, washed his hands and face, and experienced a sensation of great relief. He had solid ground underfoot again. He was a Russian now, a Russian discharged from the Red Army, and anxious to get to Moscow and start his new job as soon as possible.

Right, here goes, he thought. This stream will be the Pyeshka. Farther downstream there's a brickworks, and beyond that it's all forest until just before you get to Kolchugino. Milda Ivanovna's intensive training sessions with that map were paying off. He must go north towards Alexandrov, wait outside the town until day-light, then walk boldly through the streets, stopping for a chat here and there, perhaps trying to cadge a lift on a creaking wooden cart going to the city.

He checked once more to make sure that his parachute was well hidden, and then walked along a small path beside the stream until he came to a wood. He decided to go through it. He was going north-west: the right direction.

After an hour he stopped to rest, sat down under a tree and rehearsed what he was going to say when he met his first Russian. Streaks of light formed on the horizon, and then the sky turned pale blue shot through with yellow. The dawn of a lovely sum-mer's day. Duskov nibbled the end of a twig. You don't get breath-taking great skies like this anywhere but Russia, he thought. Difficult to say what makes the Russian sky so unique; it's a thing you simply feel, with your whole soul.

When the sun was up, a golden disc in the blue sky, and bitter-sweet scents were beginning to rise from the ground, Duskov went on in the direction of Alexandrov. He reached a lane, rutted with cartwheel tracks. He stopped to examine his clothes and make sure they showed no traces of his landing, brushed off a little dirt, and went on along this lane.

He saw the first houses of a little village appear in a slight valley ahead of him: thatched cottages surrounded by small gardens with wooden fences. He heard dogs barking and hens clucking. A beautiful little horse was galloping up and down a paddock far too small for it, pushing its head and chest against the palings and neighing now and then: a clear, challenging sound. The painted shutters over the windows were still closed, and dew sparkled on the rough carving of the gables.

Yes, it's still very early, thought Duskov. Travellers are not out and about at this time. It could look suspicious to turn up now. He sat down on a fallen tree by the side of the road, wiped his shoes on the damp grass, and deliberately rolled himself a papyrossa from coarse tobacco and a scrap of newspaper.

He found that the cigarette almost turned his stomach. I'm hungry, he thought. That's what it is. When did I last eat? Fourteen hours ago. In the plane, he had refused the chocolate the young second lieutenant piloting it had offered him. Be meticulous about details, Renneberg had told them again and again. Even the smell of your breath could give you away. You can't smell of vodka in a place where there's no vodka to be had. Similarly, there is no chocolate to be had in Russia.

He ran both hands through the dewy grass and licked the moisture off them. Then he washed his face and neck in the dew. It was wonderfully refreshing and, despite his pangs of hunger, he felt strong and cheerful.

The shutters at one of the cottage windows were thrown open, and a head appeared, its hair tousled. Its owner coughed, stretched, and scratched his chest under the grey shirt he was wearing. Then he shouted something to a barking dog. He was an old man. He leaned out of the window and spat vigorously. This seemed to make him feel better. He yawned again, and went back into the room.

Duskov rose to his feet. The old boy's sure to have a crust of bread and a bowl of milk, he thought, and I'll persuade him to find me an egg. With a nice fresh egg inside me, the world would look a very pleasant place. Perhaps I can wangle a bit of bacon, too. . . .

He made a detour, so as to approach the little village by way of the road. A chorus of barking dogs greeted his arrival. He reached the first cottage in the place, where an old woman with a scarf round her iron-grey hair, wearing clumping wooden-soled shoes and a long, patched skirt, was just hobbling over to a little shed, carrying a bowl of corn mush. She had not noticed the stranger approach, so she uttered a quavering scream when Duskov remarked, in a friendly tone, 'Nice morning, little mother. Lovely air you have here!'

She dropped the bowl, and corn mush splattered everywhere. Eyes wide with alarm, she stared at Duskov. Her gap-toothed mouth fell open, and she crossed her hands over her pendulous breasts. Then she leaned against a decrepit handcart.

'I was going to throw it away, and that's the truth, comrade,' stammered the old lady. 'It had gone bad, you see, and it stinks.'

'Waste of good corn mush,' said Duskov. The old woman rolled her eyes in terror. 'Even if it has fermented a bit, corn mush like that can be good food these days. . . .'

'Ah, but mine's an old stomach, comrade, a very old stomach,' wailed the old woman. 'I must be about eighty or so, I'm not too sure, but when the last Tsar was shot — Tsar Nicholas, you know — well, I was already a grandmother then, and at my age, comrade, I can't digest stuff that's gone off. That's the truth, comrade, I swear it is. Come inside, comrade, look anywhere you like. Oh, Blessed Virgin Mary, I've always been an honest soul, I never had trouble with the authorities in all my born days. . . .'

Duskov leaned against the birchwood fence, smiling amiably. He realized that she took him for some kind of official who had arrived to check up on something or other.

'Got any milk, little mother?' he asked.

'Oh, only a drop or so, that's all the old goat will give now.'

'And an egg?'

'An egg! Dear me, an egg. Just look at those fowls, comrade. If I wasn't sorry for the poor things, I'd wring their necks, so I would — scratching around, eating good grain, but will they lay eggs? Not them.'

'Well, I'm hungry,' said Duskov, without more ado.

'Hungry?'

'And thirsty. Not surprising, surely, little mother? Everyone has to eat and drink every day. What do *you* live on?'

'Oh dear, an old woman like me doesn't need much.'

'Nor do I. So let's go shares.'

Duskov moved away from the fence, went to the cottage door, and waited for the old woman to unbolt it. He entered a large room with a huge stove, a bench, a long table and two stools. Duskov sat down at the bench by the table, legs spread wide, and looked around him. The old woman's clothes hung from nails on the walls, there was a bed made of wooden planks in a warm corner behind the stove, and a kettle was singing on the stove's iron hotplate. Duskov raised his head and sniffed: there was a smell of perfectly good corn mush in the room.

'Oh!' cried the old lady suddenly. 'Just fancy, comrade, I've found an egg after all.' She was in transports of delight. 'Hiding there right behind the stove. You can have it, Comrade Inspector.'

'With a nice rasher of fried bacon, little mother?'

'Bacon? Where would I get bacon?' The old woman folded her hands, gazing artlessly at her uninvited guest.

'Shall I show you? Bacon still alive and kicking! Let's go out to your shed, little mother. Don't you keep a pig hidden away there, so no one will hear it squeal or grunt? A nice little pig who gets fed on good corn mush?'

The old woman looked terrified again; she collapsed against the stove.

Duskov waited for her to recover. 'Now, little mother,' he said, 'isn't it possible you might find a little bit of bacon hiding somewhere, just like that egg?'

The old woman became appreciably calmer. She sat there hunched on the bench, calculating the risks of adding a rasher of bacon to the egg she had 'found'. The Inspector would do one of two things. Either he would bellow, 'Aha, so you *do* keep a pig here – an illicit pig around the place, in this year of 1944!' or he would say, 'That was a good plateful of egg and bacon, little mother. You have a kind heart, so I'll turn a blind eye for once.'

'I can always look,' she said, her reedy voice ingratiating.

'That's a good idea, little mother. Have a good look, and do hurry up – I'm ravenous. You never know, if you look really hard you might find a bit of bread and some butter, too, and a pot of last year's raspberry jam. Those are very fine raspberry canes out by the fence, little mother.'

The old woman, sighing deeply, got up from the bench with remarkable agility for someone of her age, and went out.

Duskov leaned comfortably back and looked out of the window. The countryside gleamed in the morning sunlight. A good breakfast, he thought, and then we'll see what develops. So long as I'm an inspector sent to see whether the peasants are keeping their pigs for themselves, no one will ask questions. They'll be only too glad to help me go on elsewhere. That's one way of getting to Alexandrov.

Stupino, on the River Oka, constitutes a major traffic junction to the south of Moscow. A main railway line passes through the town: the railroad running from Moscow through Tula, Kursk, Kharkov and Stalinov to Rostov on the Don, linking Moscow to the Sea of Azov and the whole fertile southern country between the Crimea and the basin of the Don. There is also a good highway from Kashira on the Oka, which runs through Stupino and on into the very heart of Russia.

Alexander Nikolayevich Kraskin had dropped safely into wooded countryside at five past two in the morning, between Stupino and Syerpukhov, landing in the shallow bed of the little River Lopanassya. Its sluggish current bore up the parachute; he waded to the bank and pulled it in, hastily folded it, and hid it under some of the loose stones washed away by the river from its banks over many thousands of years. Then he undressed, hung his clothes on a tree to dry, and waited for morning. It was a warm night, and he ran up and down to keep his circulation going.

When the sun rose he dressed again. His clothes were still clammy with moisture, but they would dry on him in the course of the next few hours. The trouble was that the fabric of his jacket and trousers stank of goat once it was wet. Kraskin wondered how he could venture to mix with other people if he was smelling like this. Explain that everything was fine in the Red Army until you got demobbed, on account of an honourable wound, and were then issued with civilian clothes which stank to high heaven when exposed to a drop of rain? Possible, but Kraskin decided to avoid such discussions.

He walked through the Stupino forest all morning, beside the babbling Lopanassya river, and then turned east, taking minor roads, and reached the little town of Stupino at three in the afternoon. It was a rather bleak place. It boasted a small park, with Siberian elms and plane-trees, a few benches, and a painted plaster monument to Stalin. It also had a hospital, a Party Palace complete with pillared façade, and a small hotel whose rooms were almost always empty. Emil Benyaminovich Privalzev's one profitable sideline was the illicit still in his back cellar. He was delighted when a guest walked into the hotel asking for a room. Had peace suddenly broken out, or what?

Unfortunately his guest stank like a herd of goats, but he'd have to put up with that. He opened a large register and made great play of leafing through it as though searching for a vacant room. Then he beamed at his guest.

'Room 4,' said Emil Benyaminovich expansively. 'Lovely room. Nice view of the station. Only come vacant just this moment. What with all the comings and goings here, comrade, I can tell you, I could do with fifty rooms, but how many d'you suppose I have? Nine — just nine. Sometimes I get people queuing all the way to the station for the privilege of sleeping in one of my beds for the night. You're in luck, though, comrade, you really are in luck. That'll be four roubles.'

'Two,' said Kraskin amiably. 'Do I look like a general?'

'But it's room 4.'

'Then how about room 9, comrade?'

'Three roubles, then, seeing as it just happens to be free,' said Privalzev, wrinkling up his nose. At three roubles or less, he could permit himself to notice the smell. Observing this, Kraskin stretched, thus intensifying the aroma given off by his damp clothing.

'Two roubles! I'm only passing through. I'm a mechanic by trade — been working in a sugar-beet processing plant.'

'Ah, so *that's* it.' Privalzev retreated to the wall behind his reception desk. 'Sugar-beet — rotting sugar-beet. Gets right into the pores of your skin, eh? How do you cope with the smell?'

'Oh, you get used to it.' Kraskin laid his hand on the desk, palm upwards. 'Two roubles for you, little brother, and the key for me. How about a meal?'

'Got your ration card on you?' Privalzev pushed the register over. 'Here, write your name down – and mind you do it properly; they come to check up.'

This was a valuable piece of information. Kraskin entered his name, licking the point of the pencil once or twice as though to write better with it. Privalzev read the entry and nodded, satisfied.

'How many coupons do you have, Alexander Nikolayevich?'

'I'm all right for coupons, but I'd like to save them. Food's short in Moscow, and that's where I have to go. Transferred to a factory making armour plating for tanks. That's promotion if you like – tanks instead of sugar-beet! I'm proud of that, comrade, I can tell you. What do *you* think?'

'I think they'll have to decontaminate you first.' Privalzev handed Kraskin the key of room 4. 'What d'you expect in the way of a meal without any coupons?' he asked.

'I could manage another two roubles if you can find something, comrade – what's your name, by the way?'

'Emil Benyaminovich Privalzev.'

'OK, Emil Benyaminovich – well, I like you, see? The moment I came in and I saw you standing there, I thought: That's the kind of man I like! He's bound to be able to find a decent meal for a couple of roubles. . . .'

It had been a good idea to stop at Privalzev's hotel, although it had taken some courage to enter his name in a register checked by the police. Privalzev did indeed manage to produce an excellent meal. There was a chicken thigh with beetroot, followed by a pudding made of curdled milk and dried fruit, and since Kraskin belched in such a gratifying way, and seemed a good fellow (apart from the smell), Emil Benyaminovich warmed to him enough to offer him a couple of glasses of his home-distilled liquor. Kraskin coughed and then rolled his eyes to heaven. 'That's really something,' he said. 'Who distilled it, Emil Benyaminovich? Whoever it was, he certainly knows his job. How about another, little brother?'

They drank until evening, embraced, kissed, and had sworn eternal friendship by the time the sun set. They sang song after

131

song. To his surprise, Privalzev found that one could indeed get used to the smell of his guest's clothes.

Late at night Kraskin, by now lachrymose, allowed Privalzev to support him on his way to room 4, where he collapsed on his bed, still lamenting his bad luck, and then fell into a sleep broken by sobs. Privalzev covered him up and quietly left the room.

Kraskin waited until Emil Benyaminovich was downstairs again, then got up, bolted the door and sat by the window.

It was an excellent observation-post. The railway station was directly opposite. He could watch the trains arriving and departing, and had a clear view over to the goods-station. Kraskin intended to get to Moscow by rail, and thought the least conspicuous way would be to steal a ride in a goods-truck. He felt sure he would be the first to reach Moscow, and in the course of time, once settled in, he meant to be the first at number 19 Lesnaya Street.

Towards morning, a goods-train bringing cattle up from the south arrived at Stupino goods-station. It was shunted off to a siding, and Kraskin saw it as soon as he got up and went to his window at daybreak.

A train carrying cattle, he thought. What could be safer? They don't check up on cattle-trucks. Beef for the people of Moscow will get through all right.

He put his clothes on — they did not stink any more — and went downstairs to wish Privalzev good morning.

It's no use merely hoping for luck, thought Kyrill Semyonovich Boranov; you must take what comes and try to turn it to your own use. That, at least, was how he felt as he stood ready to jump at the hatch of the long-distance reconnaissance-plane, hanging on to the iron bar above the exit, and waiting for the go-ahead. 'Ready? Now!'

But no word came from the cockpit. Instead, the co-pilot, a sergeant-major, came crawling along the low fuselage of the plane and got to his feet beside Boranov. 'We're in the shit,' he said.

'Hell.' Boranov could tell from the sound of the engine that

132

they were gathering speed again, and the plane was climbing. 'Overshot the mark?'

'No, your target-area's right down there. Vieryevo. But if you jump now you're going to land on top of a huge Soviet convoy. Truck after truck, all going along the Volshenki-to-Borovsk road. We can't see just what's in the woods round about, but there seem to be several fires, looking a hell of a lot too like army camp-fires for comfort. Better avoid the place.'

Boranov nodded. Milda's thorough training was already paying off for him, too. He had the map inside his head, and could see the picture of the landscape as if it were projected on the big screen: forested areas with roads running through them. The River Nara, crossed by the road from Roslavl to Moscow. Scattered farms. The big Simbukhov collective. The Nazaryevo sawmills. But there was another place suitable for a parachute-jump, and closer to Moscow: the turnip-fields of Plesenskoye.

'Make for Naro-Fominsk,' said Boranov.

'That's crazy. There's a major road there, and the railway from Kaluga to Moscow.'

'And a huge turnip-field at Plesenskoye. I'll jump in there.'

'Let's hope there isn't another convoy sitting in your field making turnip soup.'

'There'll be ways to avoid them.' Boranov clung to the bar over the exit-hatch again as the plane turned sharply left and tilted over. 'If all else fails, just drop me out where you don't see anything much around the place. But I do have to get out of this old crate of yours – that's the main thing.'

The sergeant-major raised two fingers. 'OK. Let's look for these turnips of yours, then – though I call it risky, myself.'

Boranov did not reply. Risky, he was thinking. Laddie, if you knew what our mission really was. . . .

The co-pilot crawled back the way he had come. The plane swerved again, climbed, and hummed away through the night sky towards Moscow. Kyrill Semyonovich listened to the sound of the engine. It reminded him of the clear humming of the wind-driven pump at Thernauen. He had grown up with that sound; as a boy, he used to lie in the grass under the towering iron skeleton of the pump, watching the wind whirl the shining, silvery wings around until they were only a humming silver blur.

He started when the co-pilot tapped him on the shoulder. 'We're over Plesenskoye,' said the sergeant-major.

'Any military convoys down there?'

'No. No lights.'

'Can you make out that turnip field?'

'Sure.' The sergeant-major grinned. 'Four hundred and thirty-two plants to a row, if I counted right.'

'Very funny.' Boranov checked the position of his parachute harness for the last time

'Coming down to correct height,' said the sergeant-major. 'When we see your turnip field, we'll rock the wings for a moment, and then out you go.' He put a hand on Boranov's shoulder. 'Good luck. You'll be OK. See you some time, maybe.'

'No. No, you won't.'

The co-pilot nervously fingered his leather jacket. 'You mean you know you won't be coming back?' he asked quietly. 'No chance at all?'

'Hardly any.' Boranov clung on. The plane was diving steeply now. He smiled slightly. 'Have a good flight home. And listen — try to survive. It won't be long now.'

'That's just what I say. Once we start using our new miracle weapons—'

'Good Lord' — Boranov hunched his shoulders — 'how can you be such a fool? I suppose you believe that stuff Goebbels puts out?'

'I know we're in a hole at the moment, but the Führer knows what he's doing,' the man replied obstinately. 'Reducing the front, massing more troops in a smaller area — it's a brand-new tactical notion. The Ivans' strength will just bleed away.'

'Well, you'd better keep trying to believe that,' said Boranov, 'even when you're lying under your birchwood cross. Is your mother still alive?'

'Yes. In Wuppertal.'

'Then write to her when you get back to your base. Tell her: "Up in the air, less than fifty kilometres from Moscow, I met a man who said that every day the war goes on is another crime against humanity. He was really out to demoralize the forces, Mother, and — would you believe it? — he was an officer. Thank God, we chucked him out over Russia, and *he* won't be back." '

The plane began to rock. The young sergeant-major swallowed. 'Sir, it's time. You — you must jump now.'

Boranov pushed open the narrow hatch. The wind almost tore him out of the plane. There was a hollow roaring sound all round him. 'Good luck,' he shouted.

'Good-bye,' said the sergeant-major. He clung to the iron bar with his left hand, and saluted smartly with his right.

Kyrill Semyonovich Boranov pushed off into the darkness, spread his arms and legs, and fell into the abyss. He felt a jolt bring him swinging round in the air as the parachute unfolded, billowing out overhead.

Looking down, he could make out the plain south of Plesenskoye, now that his eyes were getting used to the darkness. There was no need to try changing direction. The turnip fields were coming closer down below. The nearest houses were about two versts away, a small group belonging to a collective farm. There was a wood in between him and the houses; he would not be seen. The silence was total. When he did land, the ground was soft with the green foliage of the turnip leaves. His parachute dragged him a little farther on. He was caught in its harness, unable to roll over as he had been taught when a gentle wind puffed out the silk, pulling him over the field. Then he dug his hands into the ground, clutching at the thick stems, got hold of a large turnip protruding above the ground, and clung on to it to brake himself. The parachute sank to the ground and collapsed.

Boranov stayed there for a moment, recovering from the impact. Then he rose, gathered up the parachute and dragged the crumpled bundle away from the middle of the field to the narrow stream on its western boundary.

Boranov strode along a path used by tractors and trailers, and saw the first roofs of the collective ahead in the darkness. He listened. There was nothing moving. He approached the outhouses, and found a shed whose door stood open, swinging in the gentle breeze. Its rusty hinges creaked, drowning out the sound of his footsteps on the rough paving of the farmyard. He saw that the shed was stacked full of old crates. Putting the parachute down by the door, he burrowed himself a way through the crates to the back wall, then returned for the parachute, stuffed it into a large crate at the very back, put a lid on the

135

crate, and blocked access to it as he made his way out again.

He hurried away through the darkness. Not until he had gone several hundred metres, and was out of sight of the collective, did he stop near a wood to rest for a moment or so, leaning against a birch-tree and breathing heavily. Done it, he thought. There's a train from Naro-Fominsk to Moscow, but the police do check up on trains, and they're likely to ask a healthy young man why he isn't in uniform. And, even though my papers are all right, I might as well avoid any arguments.

The tram would be a good way to get into Moscow. Trams go right out to the suburbs, they're crowded, and no one checks up on them. Boranov decided to risk a brief train ride to the tram terminus.

He walked on, and reached the unmetalled road to Plesenskoye. After going about four versts, he saw the first houses in the village. And outside the second house he spotted a bicycle. Casually, Boranov walked into the front garden of the house, which was surrounded by a fence, waited in case a dog began to bark, and mentally composed a polite greeting for anyone who opened the door and came out threatening him with an axe. But all was well. Boranov took the bicycle, pushed it out of the front garden, and mounted its dilapidated saddle. A couple of powerful kicks, and he was off and away, the chain squealing so loud that he caught his breath in alarm. But nothing happened.

Boranov cycled fast at first, but when he reached the wide road leading to Naro-Fominsk he slowed down, pushed his cap back on his head, and found he was feeling positively cheerful. Almost imperceptibly, the sky began to turn pink. Dawn was coming. It was daylight by the time he was cycling through the streets of Naro-Fominsk towards the station.

It was a pretty little station; it even had a clock which told him the time was ten to five. Some peasants were assembling, with hampers full of chickens and ducks, which they were obviously taking to Moscow.

Boranov sat down on a bench with a group of factory workers going to work at Rassudovo. He took a large onion out of his pocket (no one could tell that the onion had been grown in Mecklenberg), and began to peel and eat it. A policeman appeared on the platform three times before the Moscow train came in at nearly eight o'clock, glanced at the waiting passengers, exchanged words with a few acquaintances, and left again.

At eight-thirty, the train finally started off. Boranov got a seat in a compartment containing six peasants, fifty-three chickens, a small, thin, but vociferous piglet, and a fat woman smelling of stable manure who told him she had been widowed for three years.

Boranov expressed his sympathy, leaned back and closed his eyes. About seventy kilometres to Moscow, he thought. If an inspector comes along, it'll all depend on how convincingly I can talk.

More people got into the already crowded train at Peredelkino. There was some squabbling, a police officer had nine peasants thrown out of one compartment so as to occupy it himself. Boranov made himself popular by announcing that he was getting out at Okhakovo, so his seat would be free then.

'Okhakovo — that's not far,' two men told Boranov, patting him on the shoulder. 'Let us have your seat now, little brother, and travel outside — it's a warm day, you won't mind. Fresh air's good for the lungs.'

So Boranov rode the last part of the way on the footboard outside the door, clinging to the window-frame, and safe from the eyes of any inspector. He jumped down on the tracks as soon as the train stopped at Okhakovo and passed the policeman standing by the station gateway with a cheery, 'Fine day, comrade!'

The terminus of the suburban tramline into Moscow was right outside the railway station. A big old tram was standing there, covered with such pithy slogans as 'Stalin Means Victory' and 'Your Courage Makes Russia Immortal'. A crowd of passengers waited to be let on. At the only open door of the vehicle, like an archangel at the gates of Paradise, stood the tram driver herself. The rush for a seat could not begin until she gave the word. Since only two-thirds of the passengers would get a seat there would be a chaotic scramble.

Boranov looked at the crowd of people, put his hands in his pockets, and strolled towards the tram. He stopped to read the words, 'Your Courage Makes Russia Immortal', nodded approvingly, and went right up to the door. The people behind him seemed to be holding their breath. The tram driver stared at him incredulously. She was a pretty girl, with mid-brown, shoulder-length hair held back over her ears by two slides; she also had a nicely curved figure, so far as Boranov could tell from the baggy blouse, unflatteringly cut skirt and heavy shoes she wore. And there was no hiding her long, slim legs.

'Are you blind?' she inquired. She had a pleasant voice, though her manner was not friendly.

'Far from it. I was just taking to heart those beautiful words you drive around with you, little sister. "Your Courage Makes Russia Immortal." '

Boranov put one foot on the running-board. The tram driver hesitated, then raised her own foot and trod, hard, on Boranov's. The crowd watched in quiet suspense. This encounter between the tram driver and a stranger was as good as a play.

Boranov withdrew his foot. 'You've got a kick like a kangaroo,' he observed. He peered hopefully into the tram. 'When can one get in?'

'When I say so.'

'And when will you say so?'

'When I think it's time.'

'And when will *that* be?' Boranov smiled at her. 'Do you need a calendar, or what?'

'Idiot!' said the tram driver. She stepped back, took refuge herself behind a metal barrier, and raised her hand. 'Right—now!'

Boranov took a running jump into the tram, and wedged himself into a seat by the window. No sooner was he sitting down than the crowd of waiting passengers rushed in after him. The driver got into her place and stepped on the bell. All of a sudden the tram was off, leaving behind a few passengers who had been unable to get in, while some of those clinging precariously on outside had to jump off again.

Sitting by the partition between the driver's cab and the rest of the tram, Boranov watched the tram driver's profile. He wondered how old she was; in her mid-twenties perhaps, probably younger. There are red lights in that brown hair when the sun falls on it. Lovely slim neck, with downy hair at the nape of it. Damn it all, she really *is* pretty.

138

That was how Boranov met Lyra Pavlovna Sharenkova, the Moscow tram driver.

The pain had won.

When he was able to think clearly again, Bunurian did not know whether he had actually fainted, or whether his brain had simply blotted everything out, numbing his nerve ends. But he was thinking clearly now. Less than five hundred metres to his right stood those three log-cabins, surrounded by stacks of newly cut wood, and there was the broad path along which the woodcutters went to their work in the clearings. He could hardly hope to fool them into believing he had sustained so complicated a fracture of the ankle simply by stumbling over a tree root. Even if they believed that, he would still have to explain away the state of his torn clothes and badly grazed skin.

Bunurian raised his head, with difficulty. The bushes where he had taken refuge were thick, but close to the path along which the woodcutters would bring their logs. He was out of sight, however, and so long as they did not have a dog to get wind of him he should be safe enough here. He could stick it out for a day or so. The pain would keep his hunger at bay, and he could quench his thirst by licking dew from the leaves.

His ankle was badly swollen. Teeth chattering, Bunurian tried to get the torn sock off it. It felt like skinning himself: a burning pain shot through his whole body, and he had to bite on a piece of wood again as he freed his ankle from the sock. Then he lay back once more, tears in his eyes, waiting for the worst of the pain to disperse all over his body, as before, leaving him merely with the sensation of lying permanently on a bed of nails.

It will stop some time, he told himself. It will get better when the swelling goes down.

He tore strips off his shirt, moistened them by dabbling them in the dewy grass, and wrapped them round his misshapen foot. The cool sensation was delicious, the pain ebbed, and he felt almost happy to realize he could open his mouth again without that chattering of the teeth. He saw the day dawn: a pale-yellow sun rose and immediately flooded the countryside with warmth. Hundreds of living creatures woke in the woods: there were birds twittering overhead, and little animals scurrying through the dry branches. He heard the sound of voices from the log-cabins, and then a clattering noise, like an old tractor engine protesting at being put to work.

Bunurian listened intently. He heard laughter from the wood-cutters' huts. The tractor engine was turning over smoothly now; work was beginning. He remembered his parachute, stranded somewhere high up in the branches. If the wind rose, it would billow out like a white banner, visible for miles around.

He realized that he was in a virtually hopeless situation. If he were not found today, he would be tomorrow or the day after. It was crazy even to think of hopping through Russia on one leg. But give me a day or so more, he thought, and things will look different. A day or so more, and I'll be a new man.

He lay down on his back again, resting his broken ankle on a thick, springy branch, analysing every sound he heard. The screech of the saws, some way off; the creak of breaking wood as a tree tilted, swayed, and then fell to the ground with a majestic crash; the stuttering of the tractor engine; men's voices—and then Bunurian felt the hair rise at the nape of his neck as he heard dogs barking. It was the first time he had heard that sound.

He groped for the poison capsule, which he had hung round his neck in a little leather bag—and found nothing. The cord must have broken as he fell from branch to branch of the tall tree. Icy horror overwhelmed him, making it difficult for him to breathe. His escape route into painless oblivion was gone. If he were found, he would have to suffer the torments of any defence-less animal.

Bunurian closed his eyes, fighting down his choking terror. They'll batter me to death like a rabid fox, he thought. Dear God in heaven, I didn't want to die like that.

He wondered whether to try crawling farther on during the night, supposing they did not find him today. Even a few hundred metres would increase the distance between himself and the wood-cutters, and every metre gave him a little more chance to escape discovery.

They came towards evening.

Bunurian had slept for a while, although he tried to force himself to remain alert, but his tortured nerves had relaxed slightly under the soothing influence of the cold compresses and, with that small degree of respite from pain, weariness overcame him. He woke in alarm to find himself looking into a red-gold sunset sky. A great cloud, tattered at the edges and looking like smoked yellow glass, stood almost motionless above the forest. There was hardly a breath of wind, and it was very warm. The ground gave off a bitter-sweet fragrance, as if it had been baked dry in the course of the day.

There were confused voices, gradually coming closer. Twigs cracked. The woodcutters were striking the trees with cudgels as they walked along, as if to flush out game lurking among them. They were calling to each other.

So they're coming, thought Bunurian, lying quite still. Combing the place for me, like beaters covering the ground metre by metre, strung out in a chain. They're bound to find me. He felt quite calm. Any notion of escape was pointless.

However, his heart did contract when he heard a voice, quite close. 'Hey, comrades! There's a shoe here — just the one. He lost a shoe.'

Bunurian nodded, resigned. Oddly enough, the utter hopelessness of his situation made him a cool observer; he found himself following with intense interest the efforts of his persecutors to find their victim. So they had found a shoe now. They must have been alerted by the sight of the parachute, and then started searching. He heard more men coming up, talking to each other. Then one of them, a man with a deep voice, called out, 'Look at that — there's blood on this shoe. He's injured. We should be able to find him.'

'That's a Russian shoe, though,' said someone.

'But not an army shoe. A civilian's shoe.' The deep voice rose above the rest. 'One thing's for sure, comrades: if that was an emergency parachute-jump, he should've been wearing army boots. Civilians don't drop by parachute, do they?'

'Comrades from the Party, maybe. . . .'

'What, jumping in here? Just because the countryside's so pretty? Use what brains you've got, Oleg Viktorovich!' The man with the deep voice laughed. 'Heard an explosion, did you? Heard a plane crashing? No, whoever came down here wanted to keep it quiet — so form that chain again and keep on looking.'

Bunurian sat up in the thick bushes, cautiously placing his

injured foot on the soft ground. Suddenly, he saw the woodcutters. They were coming towards him, a line of them, carrying stout cudgels and long-handled axes. One of them had a pistol and was holding it out in front of him, finger on the trigger. And then, at last, they were face to face with him. The man who first saw him let out a yell, and pointed his cudgel at the bushes.

'There!' he shouted. 'There he is. He crawled in there.'

The man with the pistol—he was the owner of the deep voice —fired into the bushes, but well wide of Bunurian.

'Right, that was just a warning,' shouted the man. 'You're surrounded, so hands up, and out you come.'

'I can't,' Bunurian called back.

His reply seemed to have them baffled. 'He *is* from the Party after all,' whispered the man called Oleg Viktorovich. 'And you shot at him, Pal Tikhonovich, you did. Here, we're going to be in trouble. I mean, why shouldn't a civilian drop in by parachute these days? Perhaps that's the way they send inspectors in now. Different methods in wartime. . . .'

Pal Tikhonovich, whose fine singing voice made him much in demand at parties, cautiously raised his head. 'Are you armed, comrade?' he asked, rather foolishly.

'No,' said Bunurian, summoning up a faint smile. 'Why should I be?'

'Where d'you come from, then?'

'The front. I was at Smolensk.'

'And you just dropped out of the sky? Right here?'

'By accident.'

'H'm. You mean you got the wrong door in the plane? Wanted to take a pee and suddenly found yourself flying through the air, and it just so happened you had a parachute on your back? Oh, come off it, comrade. You think we were born yesterday?'

'I can explain,' said Bunurian, without much hope. 'I'm hurt. My ankle's broken. When you're not used to dropping by para-chute. . . .'

Pal Tikhonovich approached the bushes. Bunurian parted the twigs, and they stared at each other. The rest of the woodcutters surrounded the spot. Oleg Viktorovich, a sturdy, hunchbacked little man, snorted and wagged his head. This stranger was no inspector; he'd have said so if he were. An inspector would have bawled them out right away. Oleg Viktorovich raised his cudgel and shoved it into Bunurian's ribs. Bunurian gritted his teeth.

'Stand up,' snapped Oleg.

'I can't, I tell you.'

'Who are you?' asked Pal Tikhonovich.

'My name's Ivan Petrovich Bunurian.'

'Armenian,' said Oleg contemptuously.

'No, I'm Georgian, comrade.'

'What's the difference?'

'Generalissimo Stalin comes from Georgia, too. . . .'

'Some of you hold him tight.' Pal Tikhonovich waited until three men forced Bunurian down on his back. They began to strip him, pulling his trousers down over his broken ankle so roughly that Bunurian had to clench his teeth again. They ripped off his underclothes and searched his jacket, putting everything they found in a pile. Pal investigated it, nodding several times. 'Papers seem all right,' he said. 'Discharge from the Red Army, and so on. But what's this?'

He picked up a tin and held it in front of Bunurian's eyes.

'A tobacco-tin, of course,' said Bunurian. 'There's still some tobacco in it. Help yourselves, comrades. Good army tobacco.'

Pal Tikhonovich weighed up the tobacco-tin in his hand. Bunurian watched uneasily. That tin had a false bottom, with a miniaturized radio transmitter underneath it: not a Russian transmitter, but the latest and most sophisticated of American electronic equipment. If Pal Tikhonovich pressed the hinge of the lid, the false bottom would spring out – and there would be no explaining that away.

'Give it here,' said Oleg, the hunchback. 'Maybe he's Georgian, but his tobacco could be all right.' He snatched the tin from Pal Tikhonovich and tapped it hard. 'And then you can tell us how come you fell out of the sky, mate.'

The tin did not stand up to that hard tap. There was a soft click, and the false bottom flew up. Alarmed, Oleg stared at the transmitter under it, without understanding what he saw. Bunurian sighed. He felt frozen inside. Pal Tikhonovich, obviously the most intelligent of the men, pushed Oleg aside, grabbed the tin back, and looked at it more closely.

'I can explain about that,' said Bunurian through gritted teeth.

'It's a long story, comrades. It began in Leningrad. I was one of the defenders of the city, and the—'

Pal Tikhonovich pressed a tiny button, and the tobacco-tin began to hum, very quietly. He held it to his ear. All the other woodcutters were gaping at him. Then he clenched his fist on the little transmitter.

'Bastard,' he said tonelessly. 'Stand up, you rat.'

Pal Tikhonovich took hold of Bunurian — he was a strong man — and hauled him to his feet. Appalling pain shot through Bunurian again. His broken ankle gave way when he was forced to put some of his weight on it. It was more than the bravest of men could stand. Bunurian screamed, his red-rimmed eyes bulging from their sockets, the spittle running from his open mouth. He clung to a branch, lifting his injured foot from the ground, the tears still running down his twitching cheeks.

'Please ... please ...,' he stammered. 'Listen to me, please. ...'

It was Pal Tikhonovich who struck the first blow, with his stout cudgel. Oleg Viktorovich instantly followed his example, striking Bunurian's injured leg, which Bunurian was holding in the air above the ground.

Bunurian screamed again, in torment, and would have fallen, but three of the woodcutters caught him and held him upright to take their blows — on his head, on his neck, his forehead, his shoulders, his face. Blood spurted from his nose and mouth, his scalp was split open, a torrent of blood flooded his head and ran down to his body. Silently, grimly, as if felling a particularly stubborn tree, the men battered away at him. When the three who were holding him finally let go, he collapsed to the ground, curled up like a worm, a shapeless and bloody heap. 'Smash his guts out,' growled Oleg Viktorovich. 'He's a spy, that's what — a filthy spy.'

There are limits to human endurance, and Bunurian was past feeling pain now, but he could still think. Mother, he thought. I'm dying, Mother. Thank God you'll never know how I died. You'll think of me as reported missing, and as long as you live you'll be hoping for me to come back. It's a cruel word, 'missing'. Those who love us will never give up hoping for a miracle. Oh, Mother, Mother. ...

At last a heavy blow crushed his skull in. The woodcutters did

144

not realize at once that he was dead, and went on battering his body until Oleg, the hunchback, swung up his axe and split the already shapeless head with a single blow.

'That did for him,' screamed the little man. His eyes were gleaming feverishly. 'Can't do no more spying now. Can't send no more radio signals now.'

'Where *is* that thing?' bellowed Pal Tikhonovich.

Absorbed in their murderous work, they had forgotten the tobacco-tin. Now they searched for it, and found it lying in the grass beside the corpse. It had shared its owner's fate; it lay in a pool of blood, shattered by blows, as if it had been a living thing itself.

Oleg picked it up and handed it to Pal Tikhonovich.

'You damn fool,' said the big man, wiping his hands on his trousers. There was blood everywhere. 'Throw it away. No, better bury it. You know what we've done? We've gone and destroyed important evidence. That means trouble. They'll want to question us. They won't like it if we say that radio thing got smashed, so not a word about that, little brothers, OK?'

'Not a word about *any* of it?' suggested Oleg, rather subdued. 'I mean, nothing much happened, right? Nothing important.'

'No, we have to report it, don't we? That parachute, a stranger —how do we know what's behind it all? But don't mention that radio. Get it?'

Eyes narrowed, he looked at the dead man, then turned away and went back to the log-cabins. The others followed their leader in silence.

Oleg buried the tobacco-tin with the smashed transmitter after removing the tobacco inside and wrapping it in a handkerchief. There was a bit of blood in it, but he supposed that wouldn't make much difference to the taste.

About noon next day, three brown cars arrived at the wood-cutters' settlement north of Maximovo. The political commissars' office in Kalinin had been alerted by the brief report, which ran simply, 'We found a parachute and then we picked up this suspicious civilian, so we did him in.'

'You did *what?*' the commissar in Kalinin had shouted, when Pal Tikhonovich phoned him with this story from the little Maximovo post office.

145

'Only doing our duty,' said Pal, feeling rather uneasy.
'Is the man dead?'
'You could put it that way, Comrade Commissar.'
'Did he say anything first?'
'Wanted to tell us some story about Leningrad, but I could tell straight away that was just to put us off the track, so like good Soviet citizens we—'
'We shall be coming over,' shouted the commissar in Kalinin, obviously very nervous, 'and just don't touch a thing till we get there. Acting like a bunch of bloody woodcutters.'
'We *are* woodcutters,' said Pal Tikhonovich, distinctly subdued, and hung up. The postmaster, a wrinkled man with a sallow face, stared at the giant with the beautiful deep voice, unable to grasp what was going on.
'What happened?' he asked, when Pal Tikhonovich leaned against the counter, as if for support.
'How many dead in the war so far?' asked Pal.
'How would I know? Shouldn't think anyone could count 'em. Hundreds of thousands, anyway. Maybe millions—better not to talk about it.'
'So just one more can't make much difference, right?'
'Don't suppose so.'
'Well, they're carrying on in Kalinin as if we'd gone and pinched Lenin right out of his glass coffin. I tell you what, comrade, whatever you do, you can't be right. It's one hell of a life, little brother.' Against all the rules, Pal Tikhonovich spat on the post office floor.
The postmaster, about to protest, looked into Pal's eyes and thought better of it.
The giant searched his pockets. 'How many kopeks for the phone call?'
'It's free, comrade—official business. Are the commissars coming?'
'You bet they are.'
And a kind of silent alarm-bell went off in Maximovo. Commissars from Kalinin—everyone knew that commissars never confined themselves to what they were supposed to be investigating. The local Maximovo district Soviet, in particular, took every opportunity to put its house in order.

As yet, no one in Moscow knew about the incident. It had occurred in the Kalinin district, and the local office of the NKVD, the People's Commissariat of the Interior, was hanging on to it. If there *should* be anything behind this story of a spy, they wanted the honour and glory for themselves. Their Moscow comrades got quite enough decorations as it was.

Those men who knew Milda Ivanovna Kabakova — and she had a wide circle of acquaintances — clicked their tongues appreciatively when they met her. Women were polite to her, while secretly bursting with envy. Every Saturday evening, a group which consisted mainly of artists and writers met at her little apartment in number 19, Lesnaya Street, near the bus-stop and the numbers 5 and 25 tram-stops, to talk, listen to the radio, read or discuss their own works. There were not many of them now — most were at the front themselves, but wrote letters, which were read aloud at these gatherings and often enclosed poems or stories.

Milda was pleasant to everyone. She moved like a gazelle on her long, slender legs; she arranged her skirts so that they showed just a little of her thighs under the light fabric as she swung provocatively around. But no one ever got any farther with her. Ask around: you wouldn't find a single man who could boast of sharing Milda's bed.

And so her acquaintances were all the more surprised to see a man venture to take her arm and go walking with her in Gorky Park. The man — who on earth could he be? — was actually seen kissing her, in broad daylight, behind a high evergreen hedge. Then, one Monday morning, a major in full uniform was seen coming out of number 19 and going towards the Metro station, walking briskly, though he looked as if he had not had much sleep. And the windows of Milda's apartment on the second floor were opened, to air the place after a Sunday of sultry passion.

It was all only too clear. 'An army officer, of course,' said Matvey Petrovich Ptcholkin, a poet whose tuberculosis kept him out of the Army himself. 'Imagine Milda Ivanovna falling at last. Well, there's no accounting for women. That major — how old would he be? About forty, I'd say, and she's only twenty-four!'

What no one knew was that this major belonged to a small

group of hand-picked officers on duty in the Kremlin who saw Stalin every day. They were always around him, like a kind of military court, under the command of General Yefim Grigory-evich Radovsky. Radovsky was a man who set much store by his appearance and his smart clothes, and Major Yanis Mikhailovich Volonov, though inclined to think about his own appearance a good deal, was careful not to compete too hard with his superior officer in this respect. As it happened, he could have wished he looked more elegant when he first met Milda Ivanovna. She was feeding the pigeons in the huge forecourt of Moscow University, crouching down and enticing the birds with a velvety coo of her own. When a little gust of wind came along, he glimpsed her thighs and, for a split second, a pair of pale-blue knickers, before her full skirt fell back into place. But before Major Volonov could approach the beautiful girl, a pale youth — Matvey Petrovich, the poet — came up and said something to her, and they laughed and walked away together. A lovely girl, and a young man in a crumpled suit which was much too big for him; Volonov disliked him on sight.

For three days, he went about dreaming of the girl he had seen: those thighs, those pale-blue knickers, her lovely bosom, her full, red lips. When he was not on duty, he hung around the University forecourt, but she did not come back.

On the fourth day, Volonov decided to drown his sorrows in music. He went to see a Tchaikovsky ballet at the Bolshoi — and there he saw the girl again. She was there in the foyer, wearing a long, clinging pink dress, modestly high-necked, with embroidery, in the Uzbekhistan style. But the modesty of the dress in no way hid her alluring figure. Volonov was bewitched. He was glad to see that the pale youth in his appalling suit was not with her. Indeed, she seemed to be there on her own, leafing through a programme printed on greyish wartime paper, waiting for the bell to ring for the first Act.

Major Volonov went up to her and said, 'Don't you have a grain to spare for me, too?' Then he blushed scarlet. His beautiful, sublime, enchanting girl raised her head, looked straight at him, closed her programme, and said, 'I don't think I quite understand you, Comrade Major.'

148

'I saw you feeding the pigeons outside the University. I couldn't help wishing I was a pigeon myself.'

'What a sad thing to wish for.' She was smiling. 'Don't you know they want to reduce the number of pigeons in the city? Half of them are to be put down.'

'But you still go to feed them? I love creatures, too. Believe it or not, I used to talk to my own fleas at the front!'

Now she was laughing, and to Volonov the sound was like a joyous peal of bells.

'My name's Yanis Mikhailovich Volonov,' he said. 'I went back to the University three days running, hoping for a miracle — hoping to see you again. And now here you are.'

'I'm Milda Ivanovna Kabakova.' She looked past him, idly playing with her programme.

'That day I saw you — you went off with a young man.'

'Oh, yes. Matvey Petrovich. He's a poet. He has tuberculosis, poor lad; he won't live much longer, and he knows it.'

Volonov caught himself thinking nastily: That's good. 'And you look after him, do you, Milda Ivanovna?'

'No, he's just one of a group of friends who meet at my place. We feel the war has brutalized our people; we hope to see a poetic renaissance in Russia once it's all over. Our country has so many sensitive spirits. . . .'

Volonov was feeling ill at ease. He was not on very familiar terms with poetry, and did not think he could hold his own on the subject. She asked, 'Where are you sitting, Yanis Mikhailovich?'

Volonov was in transports of delight. 'In the stalls. In row 17.'

'I'm in row 24.'

'I'll wait for you out here in the interval, Milda Ivanovna. And after the performance . . .?'

'Oh, I don't think. . . .'

'Is that poet fellow meeting you?' Volonov's throat was dry with jealousy.

'No.' She smiled radiantly at him, a golden spark seeming to leap in her dark eyes, though it was really only the reflection of the lights in the foyer. But Volonov felt as if a small personal sun had beamed down on him. 'Well, let's see. After all, Yanis Mikhailovich, the performance does last three hours.'

Volonov endured heroically. In the interval, he raced to the foyer, bought the only drink on sale — a glass of sticky pinkish lemonade — and waited for Milda Ivanovna. She came in, graceful as an angel, accepted the glass from him, sipped· the sickly lemonade, and then took his arm.

Yanis Mikhailovich spent the entire interval promenading around the Bolshoi Theatre, arm in arm with the most beautiful woman in Moscow. Once back in his seat, Volonov could not remember just what he had been talking to her about, but he was unable to take in much more of the performance. He closed his eyes from time to time and thought of her.

After the performance he saw her home, and made a date to go walking with her in Gorky Park.

And then, on the Sunday, he spent the night with her. Neither of them had put anything into words, but it seemed perfectly natural. He caressed her warm, naked body and covered it with kisses from head to toe before he lost all that remained of his reason, clasped in her arms, her legs wound round him.

Their passionate lovemaking lasted almost all night long, until the sky began to grow pale in the east. Then Volonov and Milda mopped each other's sweating body dry, smoked sweetly perfumed Azerbaijan cigarettes from the Kremlin supplies, and drank a glass of golden Georgian cognac from the bottle which Volonov had brought with him.

'I hardly feel like an ordinary human being any more,' he said, blissful and exhausted. 'Don't you think we should feel afraid?'

'Afraid? Why, Yatya?' She stroked his chest, winding her fingers into its hairs.

'There are thousands dying this morning, Mildushka, and here we lie, feeling so happy. . . .'

'But *you* won't have to go to the front again, will you?'

'I don't know.'

'I thought you said you had a good safe posting in the Kremlin? Isn't General Radovsky a friend of yours?'

'Yes — yes, we get on all right.'

'Then, so far as you're concerned, my darling, the war's as good as over,' she said. 'Soon the Red Army will be in Berlin, and the Germans will be whining for mercy. I mean, the big offensive's coming soon, isn't it, Yatya?'

'Yes. It starts on 20 June.'

'As soon as that?' She looked alarmed.

He nodded, stubbing out his cigarette. 'Yes, we're certainly going to crush the Germans. We're ten times stronger, and that's not counting the reserves coming up from Siberia.' He crushed her naked body to his, burying his face in her fragrant hair. 'You're right, my love, you're right,' he said. 'We've won the war already. The world will be amazed to find how powerful Russia is. Moscow is the centre of the world. World politics can no longer be conducted without us. Other nations will have to get used to that idea or perish.'

Milda Ivanovna said nothing, but caressed him, thinking of the ten German officers who must have parachuted into Russia by now, and should be on their way to the city, in a last desperate attempt to save the world from Bolshevism.

But would Stalin's death really usher in a new era?

Suddenly, she doubted it. Lying there in Volonov's arms, she shuddered at the realization that they were all suffering under an illusion. Russia did not just mean Stalin. It meant people like Volonov, all those thousands of Volonovs who believed that the world would belong to Russia. Surely they would carry on the work after Stalin.

'I love you, Yatya,' she said huskily. 'I love you so much, I could kill you with pleasure. . . .'

And she meant it. But Yanis Mikhailovich thrilled once again to her passionate lovemaking, and thought himself the luckiest man alive.

On Monday morning, not long after Major Volonov had been seen leaving Milda Ivanovna's apartment, she made radio contact with another agent. Her message was passed on from one short-wave transmitter to another, until the last link in the chain relayed it over the front line to the staff HQ of the Second German Army. The high-ranking officer who received it read the message thoughtfully. It was news to him that the big Soviet offensive was to start as early as 20 June. Other sources had given the date as the twenty-second. But, whether it came sooner or later, their present situation was pretty well hopeless.

'Date can't be right,' said the General, 'but what the hell does it matter? As for the political views reported — well, that's something for the next generation to deal with. Just file that message. Our anonymous informant may be right, and Russia intends to dominate world politics, but who's interested in that at the moment?'

In Moscow, Milda Ivanovna went shopping. She stood in line outside a baker's with a great many other women, waiting for her ration. The smell of freshly baked bread wafted out of the shop and over the road. It was hot and sultry in Moscow, but the sky shone like pale-blue silk.

That same day, Major Volonov was present at one of Stalin's discussions of the military situation. He heard the Russian plans for the next four weeks, and the aims the offensive had set itself. They intended to reach the Bug, the Narev and the Weichsel, take East Prussia in a pincer movement, march on to Poland, free the Ukraine, and sweep through the Baltic provinces in the north. They had been on the move in the south ever since the December of 1943, and Stalin planned to attack here in force: Romania and Hungary would be overrun, the partisans of Yugoslavia would be liberated. All along the front, from the Baltic to the Black Sea, the Red Army was to drive the Germans back.

Major Volonov absorbed all he learned like a sponge. That's something which will interest Milda, he thought, still intoxicated with happiness. She's such a patriotic girl. She has such a loyal Russian heart. She'll be delighted to hear about this. When we Russians carry the German flags through the streets of Moscow as victors, we'll get married, Mildushka. It will be a triumphal procession such as Russia has never seen before. Milda, I love you!

Ivanov, Sepkin and Petrovsky, otherwise Poltmann, Radek and Solbreit, reached Moscow from three different directions on the same day as they had parachuted into Russia.

The three men had landed close to railway lines running into Moscow. After hiding their parachutes, they waited until morning, and then set off, looking like agricultural labourers, for the nearby stations. Sepkin was even lucky enough to hitch a lift from a farmer in a cart, a friendly and talkative old man who did not stop to wonder where the stranger had come from. 'Off to fetch a piglet from my brother's,' said the old man cheerily. 'Not really supposed to keep a pig, of course, but who's to know? And suppose I meet any comrades from the Party — that piglet won't squeal, not it. If I pour enough vodka down it before I start for home, it'll be dead to the world.'

Ivanov was sitting by the roadside, his golden hair flapping in the breeze, when a cyclist stopped beside him. He was eating an onion, remembering the trouble they had had in Eberswalde, learning how to peel, slice and eat raw onions without the tears coming to their eyes. 'A Russian does not weep when he eats onions,' Milda Ivanovna had said, 'so you must practise, comrades.' Ivanov had never quite got the knack of it, and he kept his face averted from the onion as he ate it, drinking cold tea from a Soviet army canteen to wash it down.

The rider of the bicycle was a young girl. Her faded headscarf was fluttering in the morning breeze and her long skirt billowed out. She had sturdy legs, a soft body, and two dimples in her cheeks. When she leaned towards Ivanov, her breasts rested on the handlebars.

'Don't know you, do I?' she asked. 'Who are you?'

'My name's Fyodor Panteleyevich and, yes, you do know me.'

'I don't, though.'

'Sure you do. You've known me for one whole minute.' He laughed, and so did she. She was no beauty, but her skin seemed to glow when she laughed.

'Hey, where did you spring from?' she asked.

'I'm back from the war. Look at that.' Ivanov raised his shirt to display a scar left by a shell splinter he had picked up by chance a year ago, while sitting outside his bunker waiting to be shaved. It was not a bad injury, and had healed over quite quickly. What had really annoyed him was the fact that it turned out to be from a German shell which had fallen short.

The girl on the bicycle admired his scar, giggling coyly at the sight of Ivanov's navel. Fyodor Panteleyevich tucked his shirt back in his trousers and rose to his feet. He decided it was a good thing he had finally defied Colonel von Renneberg and refused to have his hair cut really short.

'I'm on my way to the station,' he said. 'I was looking for an uncle of mine, but I didn't find him. No one hereabouts seems to know him. My mother's eldest brother: Vitaly Platonovich Pupy-khev, that's his name. Should be about sixty.'

'Never heard of him,' said the girl. 'There's no one called Pupykhev lives here.'

'No, so I discovered. Well, now I have to get back to Moscow, report to the Medical Committee again, and they decide if I can rejoin my mates. I'm keen to get to Berlin with them, I can tell you.'

'It's another nine versts to the station.' The girl giggled, for no real reason. 'Why don't you climb up behind? On the bike, I mean.'

Ivanov put his half-eaten onion in his pocket, screwed up the canteen, and sat behind the girl on a wooden carrier. He had to put both hands round her to hold on, and in doing so he squeezed her breasts. The girl twitched, and her body went rigid, but then she began pedalling along, riding slowly down the bumpy road. She breathed heavily as Ivanov's fingers began to caress her, and rode in a wavy line, squealing now and then, 'No, don't, Fedya! I'll fall off! Don't do that, Fedya, we'll miss your train! Fedya, you're crazy!'

Ivanov and the plump girl — her name was Pelageya — reached Dubna station an hour before the train came in, which meant there was plenty of time to repay Pelageya for her kindness in an old storage shed, lying on a dirty blanket. As the train moved off, he waved to her, a happy smile on her broad face, and he blew her kisses. Then he sat down and looked round. The compartment was full. It stank of sweat, old clothes and warm urine. A woman occupying a corner seat, squeezed in next to the massive body of an old peasant who whistled through his nose as he breathed, was looking at Ivanov with a smile in her eyes. Oh, no, not again, thought Fyodor Panteleyevich, smiling back, but with some reserve. Pelageya had been hot for it — understandable, with all the young men away at the front. And here was another one. Moscow may be tough going, he thought, and not just on account of Stalin.

Ivanov leaned back and crossed his legs. The girl's eyes sparkled at him again, and she pushed back her red-brown hair from her forehead and fidgeted with her blouse, as if she needed more air.

'I'm Wanda Semyonovna,' she said.

'My name is Fyodor Panteleyevich.'

Wanda was certainly pretty. Even sitting down, she knew how to show off her slender figure to good effect. Unlike Pelageya, who was a buxom earth-mother type, she had pretty, youthful breasts under that blouse. Like firm little apples, thought Ivanov. Pelageya's had been more like melons.

'I'm forewoman in a construction brigade,' said Wanda Semyonovna proudly – and, indeed, she had done very well for a girl of twenty-three. In the old days, hardly any girls did such hard manual labour, but since the Revolution an increasing number of women had been making their contribution to Soviet society as workers. Wanda Semyonovna could climb scaffolding, lay bricks, mix concrete or plaster walls with the best, and had even become a forewoman because she was a good hard worker, with a talent for leadership. Also, though one did not mention this, she had twice gone away with the Comrade Section Supervisor – until his wife gave him a black eye, which cleared his brain wonderfully. Wanda Semyonovna was transferred to another section of the brigade, but she was still a forewoman.

Ivanov nodded. 'I don't have a job at the moment,' he explained, speaking loud enough to be heard by everyone in the compartment; that should forestall further questioning. 'The doctors can't seem to make their minds up.' He raised his shirt again, and showed off his impressive scar.

'A war hero,' breathed Wanda shyly. 'Comrades, we have a war hero travelling with us.'

'Oh, come on, don't exaggerate,' said Ivanov modestly, tucking his shirt back in. 'Just doing my bit.' His blue eyes rested limpidly on Wanda. 'I'm still on soldier's pay at the moment, but I'm not sure what next.'

'Do you want a job, then, Fedya?' asked Wanda Semyonovna. She's already calling me Fedya, too, thought Ivanov. The women are certainly fast workers here.

'Work never hurt anyone – if it's not too much for my wound.'

He found that a peasant was offering him a piece of sausage, in an access of patriotic fervour, and clapped the man on the shoulder gratefully. It was a well-seasoned and undoubtedly home-made sausage, the end product of one of those illicit pigs.

'I could do with a scaffolder in my own gang,' said Wanda

Semyonovna. 'It isn't heavy work, comrade. Just nailing planks together.'

'On a building site?' Ivanov looked thoughtfully at Wanda.

'You don't get vertigo, do you? That wouldn't be any good; we're working high up on one wall of the Kremlin just now.'

Ivanov munched his sausage.

'I have a very good head for heights,' he replied, keeping the excitement out of his voice. 'I could walk a tightrope if you slung it between the Kremlin towers. I'm pretty good with a hammer, too. In fact, Wanda Semyonovna, you'd be surprised to find how good I am with my tools.'

The girl blushed a pretty pink, and Ivanov grinned cheerfully back at her. He had a vision of chucking a hand grenade at Stalin from the scaffolding.

Wanda Semyonovna's mouth twitched at the corners, and her firm little breasts were rising and falling faster.

'Why don't we discuss it?' she said, her voice rather husky. 'I'm sure the Brigade Supervisor will sign you on if you show him your scar, Fedya. Here at home, we'd do anything for our heroes from the front.'

Kosterovo was a request-stop for the train from Gorky to Moscow. The stationmaster halted it by hoisting a yellow flag. This morning, Luka Ivanovich Petrovsky was one of four passengers waiting for the train. He had walked across country in the night without meeting anyone. He bathed in the River Kyasma, and felt refreshed and ravenously hungry. Just outside Kosterovo, he bartered a little tobacco for two cucumbers, and ate them greedily.

He introduced himself politely to the other waiting passengers, offered one of his cigarettes to the rather morose stationmaster, and found, to his alarm, that a great many Red Army officers travelled on this line. There was an officers' training school for special units in Gorky, where they also ran courses for general staff officers. A slight error on Milda Ivanovna's part, thought Petrovsky. She never mentioned that.

He told an interested audience on the platform about the stomach ulcer which supposedly made him unfit for further military service. 'It's a hell of a thing, comrades,' he said mournfully. 'Belching all the time. Not nice, is it?' And he did belch, without any difficulty, since he had just eaten two raw cucumbers. His fellow-passengers were suitably sympathetic.

'Why don't they operate, Luka Ivanovich?' asked the station-master. 'Dirty great ulcer like that, you'd think they'd operate.'

'Tell that to the doctors,' said Petrovsky bitterly. 'They X-ray me, they pump out my stomach, and then all they do is give me pills and tell me to drink plenty of milk. I ask you, where am I supposed to get plenty of milk in wartime?'

At this point the train came in and stopped for the yellow flag. Petrovsky actually found himself in a compartment where four officers were sitting playing chess. They merely nodded when he said a polite good morning and squeezed himself into a corner. I'm in luck, he thought. Men with their minds on a game of chess don't talk. He glanced at the two chessboards, and saw that the games in progress were likely to last a long time. The four officers were lost in thought. Petrovsky suppressed an impulse to tell one of them that if he moved his knight the way was open for him to take his opponent's castle. When they stopped at the next station, Noginsk, and he saw two police patrols waiting there, he felt a moment's uneasiness, but they were not there to check up on the train; they were passengers themselves.

Beyond Noginsk, in Kukhino, they were obviously approaching the city. Houses came right up to the railway line. Moscow was coming closer. Petrovsky rose and went out into the corridor, feeling almost unnerved by the way the whole thing had gone so amazingly smoothly. He rolled a cigarette and smoked it. They passed through a large shunting-yard, the carriages rattling over countless points.

He went forward to the door, and mingled with the officers waiting there to get out.

By the time his train came into the Belorussian Station, Pyotr Mironovich Sepkin had made several firm friends. The company had been a cheerful one. An elderly passenger had played the harmonica, while the others sang and beat time with their boots.

The train stopped in the huge station building with a squeal of brakes. Like all the stations of Moscow, it was more like a palace than a railway terminus, decked out with almost regal splendour. Sepkin said good-bye to his fellow-passengers, with much hugging

157

and kissing, and then he was out on the platform, his heart suddenly thudding, his eyes watchful.

Moscow. The end of the line.

He looked round for police, then strolled to the exit, bought himself a copy of *Pravda*, and read the reports from the front with interest. Not a word yet about the coming offensive.

Only a little later, Luka Ivanovich Petrovsky's train came into Kazan Station. He got out, inconspicuous among the officers, left the station as fast as he could, went straight to Lermontov Square and sat down on a bench in the sun. He was sharing the place with a few old men out enjoying the summer warmth, chewing sunflower seeds and spitting out the husks. One of them had a rough-haired dog which, surprisingly enough, had not ended up in a saucepan during these years of food shortages.

Petrovsky took several deep breaths, to calm his racing pulse. He remembered something Colonel von Renneberg had said. 'Once you reach Moscow, gentlemen, don't let euphoria make you careless. Settle into the city as inconspicuously as you can. Remember, you have a hard job to do.'

Petrovsky stretched his legs, looked round Lermontov Square, and sat back at his ease. No need to be in a hurry on one's first morning in Moscow.

An hour later, Fyodor Panteleyevich came into Yaroslavl Station. Out on the platform, he took Wanda Semyonovna's arm as if they were lovers of long standing. They shook hands with their travelling companions, and the old peasant gave Ivanov the rest of his sausage. Ivanov bought Wanda a mineral water at a stall selling drinks.

'Why don't you come home and meet my parents, Fedya?' she said. 'They'd love to meet a war hero. Or do you have to go and see the doctors right away? This is my day off. I can speak to the supervisor tomorrow. Wouldn't it be wonderful to work in the same gang? You on the scaffolding, me plastering walls.'

'And in the Kremlin, too.' Ivanov pushed his fair curls out of his eyes; there was a warm breeze blowing in the square. 'But surely they wouldn't take just anyone on, for a job like that?'

'I can recommend you. After all, I'm a forewoman.'

He nodded, and on impulse, there in the middle of the square, he kissed her. She stood still for a moment, and then rose on tiptoe and buried her fingers in his fair hair.

'Oh, I must be crazy,' she said breathlessly, when he finally let her go. 'Fedya, we hardly know each other, but I feel as if I don't ever want to let you go.'

'Don't worry, Wandushka,' he said tenderly, putting his arm round her slim waist, 'the doctors may well agree that I never have to leave Moscow.'

How true, he thought bitterly. I shall never leave Moscow again. Second Lieutenant Johann Poltmann has been dead these last two days.

They walked on, and turned into Lermontov Square. By an odd twist of fate, Petrovsky had risen from his bench there exactly seven minutes earlier, crossed the square and turned into Kirov Street, which led directly to the Kremlin. Going down Kirov Street, you passed the Post Office, Novaya Square and Marx Prospect, with the famous Metropole Hotel, built by British architects at the turn of the century. Then there was the vast complex of the GUM department store on your left; and then, if you were a good Russian, your heart beat faster because ahead of you lay Red Square and the Kremlin itself, with the red star on top of the Spassky Tower, the dark mass of the Lenin Mausoleum and, like a fairy-tale turned to stone, the great, brightly coloured onion domes of St Basil's Cathedral, built by Ivan the Terrible in thanksgiving for his victory over the Tartars.

Petrovsky was walking down Kirov Street quite slowly, and Ivanov could probably still have seen his back, but walking with a girl like Wanda Semyonovna he was not likely to be taking much notice of other people.

There was thick semolina soup for breakfast, with more water than milk in it, but, still, it tasted sweet, filled the belly, and brought back memories of better days, when you could have sliced fruit into it, or added thickened fruit juice or even crystallized berries. Privalzev, the hotel manager, had even made some tea when Kraskin came down.

'Well, and how did you sleep in our very best bed, Alexander Nikolayevich?' he asked cheerfully.

'Not too well,' said Kraskin, scratching his head. 'If I were to stay here any longer, Emil Benyaminovich, which unfortunately I can't, I'd have to ask for another room. Say, number 9.'

'A general slept in that bed of yours!' protested Privalzev.

'Pissed in it, more like. It smells of old goat.'

'That was your own damp clothes, comrade.'

Kraskin laughed. He held the sleeve of his jacket under Privalzev's nose. 'No smell now, is there?'

He thought of the cattle-trucks out there in Stupino goods-station. He had to decide whether to go on a passenger-train, running the risk of encountering a police patrol, or with the cows.

'If you have a bread coupon, I can give you a second helping,' said Privalzev, who liked a bit of bread with his soup. 'I'm doing it because I like you, Alexander Nikolayevich.'

'You old rascal!' Kraskin took a ration card from his pocket, tore off a bread coupon, and pushed it across the table. Privalzev went off, came back with a basket of bread, and crumbled a slice of bread into the soup. Kraskin looked round.

'No one else having breakfast?' he asked.

'No,' admitted Privalzev gloomily.

'I thought this hotel was fully booked!'

'Ah, well, that's the kind of thing one has to say, comrade. It's a good thing the place belongs to the State — as it is, I have to live on what's left after I pay the rent, and that's not much these days.'

A kindly soul, Privalzev gave his guest a little basket of things to eat when they said good-bye a couple of hours later. They parted like brothers, waving to each other until Kraskin entered the station. He prowled around it for a while, taking a long, hard look at the long goods-train carrying the cattle. He noticed, with satisfaction, that no one was bothering about it much. Now and then a fat railwaywoman stumbled over the tracks to couple or uncouple some of the trucks, but that was all.

A passenger-train to Moscow came in about noon, and now Kraskin had to make his decision. Seeing that one carriage was full of soldiers, and bore a slogan — 'The Fourth Voronezh Rifles Bound for Berlin' — he decided to stay with the cows.

He waited until the fat railwaywoman had disappeared, then clambered over the buffer of one of the trucks, hauled himself up over the side, and dropped in among the cattle.

160

The animals gazed at him, mooing in hollow tones, and nuzzled him with their soft mouths. Kraskin laughed, patted the heads around him, and then pushed them away. These were short-horned, heavy cattle with pale coats, from the south. They had been on the move for three days, and they were uneasy, although Kraskin did not sense that. As a townsman, he thought of cows only as the providers of milk, beef and leather.

He looked for the best place to spend the journey, and decided to perch on a narrow crossbar which someone had nailed inside one end of the truck — just why he had no idea, but it would support his buttocks. His perch was not particularly comfortable, but it helped to take the weight off his feet to some extent.

He propped himself there, and looked at the cows, who were still staring at him. Outside, he heard buffers collide, and the sound of iron on iron, then of steel cables being hooked on and air-brakes snapping into position. The fat railwaywoman was at work again. When she passed Kraskin's cattle-truck, he heard her singing. It was hard work for a woman, but evidently she enjoyed it. Kraskin pushed away the heads of the cattle again, and wished he dared to roll a cigarette.

He stared at the sky, growing red now as evening approached, and went over his favourite compositions in his mind. The Grail music from *Parsifal*; the *Meistersinger* overture; Beethoven's First Piano Concerto with Edwin Fischer, Bruno Walter conducting; Elly Ney playing Beethoven sonatas; Gieseking playing Chopin nocturnes; Bruckner's mighty Ninth Symphony conducted by Clemens Krauss. . . . Heaven surely consists of music; music is immortal, he thought.

Night fell over Stupino, soft and warm. The goods-train jerked as a locomotive was coupled to it. Kraskin heard a whistle blow, answered by another whistle, and then the trucks moved forward and back slightly. More jerking vibrated through the train as other trucks were attached, and suddenly they began to move, the wheels rattling over the rails. Off to Moscow at last.

The cows stood close together in the truck, as if supporting one another. The acrid smell of their urine and dung grew stronger. It suddenly occurred to Kraskin that, all things considered, the truck had been remarkably clean when he chose it as his hiding-place. It must have been hosed down at some point

161

on its way from the south to Moscow. Well, he did not imagine the train would be stopping again before Moscow. At its journey's end, railway workers might come along again with hoses to get the animals reasonably clean before they were trotted off to the slaughterhouse, but not before that.

He closed his eyes, and fell asleep with tunes from *La Bohème* going through his mind.

He woke to feel a searing pain in his foot, which shot right through his body. The train was clattering through the night, as fast as if it were fleeing from some disaster. The cows were restless, crowding together, shoving one another. Their heads were raised, and their big eyes seemed twice as large as before. Kraskin groaned: the beast in front of him had kicked his shin. Her large head was thrown back, and she was lowing frantically, spittle running from her mouth.

Kraskin was too close to the side of the truck to be able to move at all. The bodies of the animals, a restless but compact mass, would not give way, even when he struck out hard with both fists. Despite the loud rattling of the wheels, he could tell what was making them so uneasy. Soviet bomber squadrons were flying low above the countryside through the night. The mooing of the cows drowned out much of the sound of their engines. To the animals, those strange sounds in the sky meant danger.

The bomber squadrons went on thundering overhead, and the cows began to panic, trampling the floor, thrusting with their heads, flinging their massive bodies against the sides of the truck, an avalanche of bone and flesh trying to break its way out.

'Get back!' shouted Kraskin, kicking and hitting. He struck horns and noses, foreheads and eyes; he kicked soft bodies and hard bones. He shielded his face with his elbows as the cows butted him, ramming his knee into their flanks and udders.

'Get back!' he shouted again. 'They're only aircraft, you stupid creatures. It isn't even a thunderstorm. Get back!'

The bodies of the cattle were crushing him against the side of the truck. He could hardly breathe. He would have to get up on the wall of the truck and down again on the other side. I could ride on the buffers, he thought. Something warm ran down his body, like water from a tap.

162

Blood, he thought. Christ, I'm bleeding. They gored my shoulder. I must get out of here or I'll be trampled to death. . . .

He tried to leap up and grab the top of the truck-side, but the cows would not leave him enough room for a jump. Kraskin began to scream. His left arm started to quiver; the shoulder itself was numb, but he could not move it, and the blood was still running from the wound. He had been gored from behind, just below the nape of his neck.

Once again, Kraskin tried to reach the top of the truck-side, this time levering himself up against the beast standing in front of him. He braced his legs against the animal's body, and with his back to the side of the truck started working his way slowly upwards, like a rock climber tackling a chimney. He was halfway up when there was a crash in the sky overhead. One of the bombers must have a faulty engine; it was backfiring now and then with a sound like gunfire. At that, the cows became utterly frantic. They reared up, clambering over one another in the confined space, butting and trampling everything in their way in their panic.

Kraskin fell back into the truck, slipped on the floor, which was covered with urine and dung, fell to his knees, and was immediately kicked by one of the animals. Half unconscious, he tried to get up again, but then there were bodies all round him and above him, a mass of flesh forcing him down. He lashed out again, and the cloven hoofs trampled him and trod him into the dung. He kicked, clutched a fat udder and dragged himself just off the floor, hanging there between the cow's legs like a Cossack under his galloping horse.

It was only a momentary respite. He was flung to the floor again, and a hoof stamped on his right hand. He could hear the crunch of breaking bones. He bit his left forearm, and began to weep with hopelessness and mortal fear. A sob shook his body as the hoofs came thudding down on it, and then he was only an unconscious lump of flesh being crushed out of recognition by the frantic cows.

About five in the morning, the cattle-train came into the goods-yard in Moscow. The animals had calmed down by now, and were standing in the trucks, swaying slightly, allowing themselves to be hosed down. Three gangs of railway workers, mostly women wearing high gumboots, pushed the gates aside to hose the muck out of the cattle-trucks with powerful jets of water.

In due course they came to truck 27, pushed back the bolts and opened it. A stream of water spurted out of a hose, and gradually the sloppy muck flowed over the side of the truck and spilled out. But there was still a lump of something left in one corner. Antonia Nikolayevna, the woman wielding the hose, directed the jet of water full on the obstinate heap of muck. It still did not move.

Cursing as fluently as any working man, Antonia Nikolayevna wedged the hose into the doorway, letting its jet play over the cows, and leaned into the truck. Then she uttered a piercing scream, flung her hands up into the air, and ran away, gasping for breath. Two trucks farther on, she vomited, and then sat down on the tracks as if stunned.

Sergei Andreyevich Tarski had always been a cheerful character, and whenever he had succeeded in something which threatened to be difficult he was happy as a lark. He was delighted with his easy landing, in a meadow surrounded by woods near Latashino.

There was a minor road from Latashino to the main road running south-east from Rzhev, meeting the famous Minsk-to-Moscow highway at Vnukovo. Going that way meant a circuitous and possibly risky journey. Tarski decided it would be easier to walk to Volokolamsk and catch a train to Moscow there. It was not a main line but, as Milda Ivanovna had explained, it was used a great deal by goods-trains coming from the north-west and, in particular, it was currently used to transport supplies for the coming Soviet offensive. Day and night, ammunition-trains and trains carrying troops went westward this way. According to Milda, hospital-trains also used the line, and some of these had ordinary passenger-coaches for the walking wounded. He would be in good company with these men, happy to be on their way home with only a minor wound, not too dangerous, but bad enough to keep them from the front. They wouldn't be in a mood for asking questions, thought Tarski. Tarski's own cover-story was malaria, contracted in the Pripet marshes, dormant at the moment, but liable to strike again at any time.

In the red-gold of the sunrise, Tarski set off for Volokolamsk.

After walking across country for four hours, meeting nothing but six carts driven by women—he gave them a friendly wave—he reached the banks of the little River Lama. He stopped here to rest, took his clothes off, swam in the water, which was still cold, let the morning sun dry him, and planned the rest of his journey.

Again, he had a choice: he could go over the river and on across country, making a detour south to reach Volokolamsk, or he could carry on along the road from Rzhev. The latter was the more direct but the more dangerous way.

Looking up at the sun, again Tarski decided he had been amazingly lucky. Back at Eberswalde, listening to Renneberg's lectures, with Milda drilling them in memorizing facts, it had seemed complicated. But here he was, lying beside a murmuring little river, basking in the sun, the fear he had felt as he floated down by parachute forgotten.

Tarski allowed himself a brief hour of this peace. He had time on his side at this point; he thought safety more important than speed in reaching Moscow. Then, without getting dressed, he walked along the bank looking for a place where the current was not too strong.

He soon found a suitable-looking spot: there was a small sandbank in the middle of the river, which he estimated to be barely a hundred and fifty metres wide at this point; not very wide as Russian rivers go. He made his clothes into a bundle, tied it to his head with his belt, and waded into the water. As he had already noticed while bathing, the current was stronger by the banks than in the centre. Tarski drifted a little way, then swam to the sandbank and paused there. On the other side of the sandbank, a vicious little undercurrent seized hold of him and took him farther downstream than he liked. He fought it, kicking hard and making for the bank. Spluttering, and cursing the deceptively peaceful appearance of the river which had given him such trouble—and he was a good swimmer—he landed on the other side, where the water had carved a small bay out of its bank, with a steep little slope above it. He undid his bundle of clothes, shook out his trouser-legs, and was about to put his shirt on when he heard something cracking overhead. Then a voice called harshly, '*Stoy!*'

Tarski stopped exactly as he was, arms raised, shirt half over his head. *Stoy*. Tarski had shouted it often enough himself, when he was combing through the thickets of reeds in the Pripet marshes for camouflaged Soviet machine-guns with his scout patrols. If they stumbled upon a Soviet position and called '*Stoy!*' the Russians came out, hands up in surrender, grey-green with the mud of the marshes, their eyes pleading for their lives.

Tarski's heart beat as regularly as before, but he was thinking at lightning speed, wondering just who was up there in the bushes. Was it a civilian—a peasant? If so, he could explain, apologize if it was forbidden to bathe in the river, assure the man he hadn't meant to scare away the fish. . . .

Tarski put his shirt on, very slowly, not sure how the man up there would react. When he bent to pick up his trousers, the harsh voice above him said, 'Don't move. Now, come up here.'

'Without my trousers on, comrade?'

Tarski turned. Two policemen stood on top of the bank, armed with submachine-guns. The round mouths of the barrels were a menacing sight.

Police, thought Tarski. That's different. Where the hell did they spring from, spoiling a fine, sunny day like this? It's not so easy trying to talk your way out of trouble with the police.

Putting his trousers under his arm, he clambered up the sandy slope. One of the policemen even helped him up the last part of the bank. Tarski saw a jeep standing on a rough road beyond the slope. A third policeman sat behind the wheel, grinning. Yes, he supposed he must look comic without his trousers.

He held the trousers in front of his genitals, and looked appealingly at the men. 'Look, can't I put these on?' he asked. 'It'd be easier to talk to you then.'

'Where d'you come from?' asked the officer who had called '*Stoy!*' He pushed the barrel of his gun into Tarski's side.

'Kiev,' said Tarski promptly. 'I was in the 23rd Rifles till I got malaria. Did you ever have malaria, comrades? It's no fun, I can tell you. I—'

'Papers!' interrupted the hostile police officer, holding out his hand.

'Here you are.'

Tarski got his papers out of his jacket pocket. They were

impressive. His certificate of discharge bore many rubber stamps and signatures.

The policeman read the papers very thoroughly, holding them up to the light, though everyone knew that cheap wartime paper bore no watermarks, looked at Tarski, frowning, and put the papers in his own pocket.

'Where are you going?'

'To Volokolamsk, comrade.' Tarski began to sense that this was not about to turn out well. 'My papers are all in order, comrade, aren't they? Certificate of discharge stamped at the 1st Belorussian Front. Could be Marshal Rokossovsky himself who signed it—you can't make the signature out. I was discharged because of my malaria. They can't cure it. Read the medical report, comrade.'

'Why were you swimming in the river?' The police officer pointed his gun at the trousers. Tarski decided to take this as an order to put them on, and no one stopped him.

'I just felt like it,' he said, doing up his flies. 'A nice hot day like this. . . .'

'Why are you going to Volokolamsk?'

'Got an uncle living there. Dementi Russlanovich Kozeboshkin. He hates his surname, poor man. How would you like to be saddled with a mouthful like "Kozeboshkin"? Still, can't choose your father, can you? I was only going to visit my uncle, comrades.'

'You came all the way from Kiev on foot?' asked the unpleasant character with the submachine-gun.

Tarski shook his head 'No, part of the way by train, mostly by road—hitched a lot of lifts on army trucks. You want all the details? Most people were very friendly when they heard about my malaria.'

'We're friendly, too,' said the second policeman, with a broad grin, speaking for the first time. 'We wouldn't want you to get footsore, comrade. We'll take you on to your uncle in Volokolamsk. Less than an hour by jeep. Can't do less for a comrade invalided out of the Army so young, can we? So let's pay a call on your uncle.'

Tarski nodded, suddenly chilled to the marrow. He walked steadily to the jeep, greeted the driver, and climbed into the back seat. The unpleasant character who had been asking all the questions sat beside him and barked out a command to start. Their journey offered no opportunities for conversation; it was hard enough to stay in the jeep at all as it bounced and jolted over potholes in the road. The driver did not slow down until they were approaching Volokolamsk. Then he stopped as they reached the first houses.

'Right, where does your uncle live?' asked the policeman beside Tarski, his voice syrupy now. 'How pleased he'll be to see you!'

'How should I know?' Tarski kept quite calm. 'It's the first time I ever visited him. He did once come to see us in Kiev. Fat little man with a round head—nearly bald. He was dealing in decorating materials at the time, but he could have changed his job.'

'Not his name, though?'

'I shouldn't think so.'

The police patrol drove into the little place, and stopped outside a house which bore a notice proclaiming it to be the post office. Of course, thought Tarski. The obvious thing to do. My comrades here are no fools. The postmaster will know everyone in the place, everyone who ever gets a letter. Even if a letter were addressed to a dog, he'd know whose dog it is.

Tarski and the three men climbed out and went into the post office. A grey-faced woman with many wrinkles round her mouth was sitting behind the counter eating a large cold potato boiled in its skin.

'Yes?' she said, stuffing a piece of potato into her wrinkled mouth. 'What is it?'

'It's about one Dementi Russlanovich Kozeboshkin,' said the spokesman of the patrol. 'Where does he live?'

'Who?' The old woman chewed away, darting her head forward like a bird.

'Kozeboshkin.'

'Not here.'

'What do you mean?'

'There's no one called Kozeboshkin lives in Volokolamsk.'

'Sure?'

' 'Course I'm sure,' said the old woman crossly. 'No Kozeboshkins here.'

168

The police officers stared at Tarski, the look in their eyes boding no good.

Tarski displayed no agitation. He remained quite casual as he undid the top button of his shirt and opened the little bag he wore round his neck. 'I just remembered — there's another paper,' he said as he did so. 'Malaria makes you forget things. This should clear it up, and then we can all go home.'

Putting his thumb and forefinger into the bag, he grasped the little gelatine capsule between them. Second Lieutenant Dietrich Semper reporting off duty, Colonel von Renneberg, sir, thought Tarski with a kind of irony. Better strike my name off the list. Mother, Father . . . thanks for all you did for me. . . .

His hand, with the capsule in it, darted to his mouth. As he bit the capsule, he tasted bitter almonds. Potassium cyanide. Death within a second. My God, how long a second can be. . . .

The policemen seized Tarski, flinging him to the ground. 'His mouth!' one of them yelled. 'Get his mouth open!'

They tried, but Tarski's jaw muscles were tensed rigid, and his teeth clamped together as if they had never formed two separate rows. The men smashed their fists into Tarski's chin, until one of them had the bright idea of using his knife to prise the clenched teeth open. The sound of Tarski's jawbone cracking was clearly audible. His mouth finally dropped open, and the scent of bitter almonds wafted out. Tarski's body was still twitching and his nerves jerking, but he was dead by the time they forced his jaws apart.

The old woman crouched behind her counter, the remains of her potato crushed under her thumb. 'What's going on?' she faltered helplessly. 'Comrades, what's it all about? Just because no one called Kozeboshkin lives here?'

Then she saw Tarski's broken jaw, his wide, staring eyes, his distorted body. She put her thumb in her mouth and fell down in a faint.

When an inspector visits a village, word mysteriously gets around, God only knows how. Duskov had not seen the old woman raise the alarm, but somehow or other, while she was searching for eggs, she must have signalled by waving out of a window. From then on there was great activity in the village, as the peasants hurried to hide anything that might look at all illegal. A delegation consisting of two old men plodded off, with many misgivings, to the old lady's cottage, where the Inspector was, at that moment, mopping up the very last of the egg yolk from his plate with a piece of bread.

The delegation stopped outside the door, straightened its threadbare clothes yet again, and then knocked. Duskov lowered his head slightly, staring at the doorway. The old woman folded her hands and praised God for His goodness. Reinforcements! She would not be alone with the Inspector any more.

'Who's there?' grunted Duskov.

'A visitor, to be sure!'

'Then send him away.'

'Oh dear, what am I to say?' The old woman hobbled to the door. 'Perhaps they've come to help you. . . .'

'No one knows I'm here.' Duskov rose, went to the window, and saw the two old men outside, nervously stroking their moustaches and whispering together. They were unarmed, and did not look as if they had come to ask awkward questions.

'Dear me, no, of course not, as God's my witness.' The old woman wrung her hands.

'Well, let them in,' said Duskov.

He sat down again and stretched his legs out to show he was at his ease. He scowled. The old woman opened the door, crying shrilly, 'Oh, come in, it's so good to see you.'

The two old men came in and bowed respectfully at the powerful Comrade Inspector. There he sat, frowning. He must be from Moscow, or at least from Zagorsk, they thought. You could see he was a city dweller straight away, just from the way he sat there, and from his clothes. Look at his shoes — and he wore socks, too, and there wasn't a spot on that shirt. Stood to reason a comrade like that would have a very important job.

The two old men stood to attention and raised their fists in a silent greeting.

'Well?' asked Duskov.

'We must all make sacrifices for our country,' said the old man on the left. That sounded good.

The old man on the right added, in a high, quavery voice, 'Victory will be ours.'

Duskov nodded slightly. 'So I should hope,' he said sternly. 'But what exactly do you have to offer at the moment?'

The two peasants glanced at each other in silent agreement: this Inspector was a decent sort, open to reason. Must be quite a tough job even being an inspector these days, making sure all was as it should be in these difficult times. 'Anything we can do to help ...,' said the old man on the left, scratching his nose. That sounded vague enough.

Getting the hang of the situation, Duskov inwardly breathed a sigh of relief. 'Help? How?' he snapped. 'Any suggestions, comrades?'

That was a nasty one, because if they offered too little the Comrade Inspector would feel insulted and check up very thoroughly, and if they offered too much they might make the same unfortunate impression.

'*You* say, comrade,' said the man on the right. 'And anything we can do—'

'I need some means of transport,' said Duskov, frowning. The peasants looked utterly dismayed, and the old woman shook her head and sat down. Transport? Heavens above, what did he expect? A tractor? He must know that it's the collective that allocates tractors and all the other agricultural machinery to us. It's all centralized now.

The old man on the left nodded gloomily. 'What for?'

'What *for*? Do I ask you what invisible pigs in pits underground are *for*? Do I ask you what all the chickens you have here are *for*, when you know there's a precise breeding quota? What *for*?' Duskov thumped the table.

He knows everything, thought the old woman, much upset. How can we hope to deceive him? Oh, little brothers, do find him transport.

'All we have is a turnip-cart — a sort of trailer.' The peasant on the right looked pleadingly at Duskov. 'But we could harness a cow to it. We could tie her to the cart with ropes. Our last horse was taken six weeks ago, comrade, but if a cow would do. ...'

'The fact is,' said Duskov, less sternly, 'the car that brought me here had to go straight back to Kolshugino, because another inspector had to go on to Yuryev-Polsski, where the people had slaughtered three bullocks without declaring them.' The peasants

171

nodded sympathetically. Our poor comrades at Yuryev-Polsski!
'And now I have to get back to Moscow.'

The peasants nodded silently.

'I want you to get me to Alexandrov railway station,' said
Duskov.

'When did you want to go, comrade?'

'At once.'

This remark galvanized the delegation. A miracle had occurred;
the village would be spared! 'We'll fix it!' cried the two old men
in chorus, hurrying out, and the old woman surreptitiously crossed
herself.

Four hours later, Duskov reached Alexandrov station in a
turnip-cart drawn by a very ill-humoured cow, and driven by
Kuzma Mrykhin, head of the village Soviet, himself. Mrykhin,
who had failed to make much headway in his attempts at conversation with the taciturn Inspector, was dismayed as they
approached the station. It looked deserted. There was not a soul
in sight, let alone a train. An ancient and bedraggled duck came
waddling down the tracks. Mrykhin stopped the cow and sighed.

'What's up?' asked Duskov. 'Have they got the plague here,
or what?'

Just my luck, thought Mrykhin bitterly. The two men walked
to the station.

There was one man on the station platform, with three crates.
He greeted Mrykhin and Duskov with a gloomy nod, and pointed
to the closed booking-office. A notice hung there, bearing the
pencilled words: *Repairs to Line. No Trains Today. Departures
from Zagorsk or Kolchugino Only.*

'We weren't to know, were we, comrade?' said Mrykhin.
' 'Course, it takes time, all the reconstruction work after the
German planes bombed us.' He read the notice again, and shrug-
ged his shoulders. 'Well, can't be helped. Do you want to go to
Zagorsk, comrade? We'll never make it with the old cow here.
Look at the way her tongue's hanging out. Could be she has
heart trouble.'

Refraining from veterinary discussion, Duskov went over to the
solitary man with the crates. The man grinned foolishly and
shrugged his shoulders.

'How long have you been waiting?' Duskov asked.

'Three days.'

'Where's the stationmaster?'

'Don't know. He comes along now and then, uses the phone, tells me they've found they're still seventy metres of track short, and goes off again.'

'All right,' Duskov told Mrykhin. 'I'll find some other method of transport here in Alexandrov. Thanks, comrade. You and your cow did wonders. I won't forget.'

Mrykhin fairly hiccuped with joy, shook Duskov's hands warmly, wished him good luck, and started back homeward in his turnip-cart. A good morning's work, he thought. We shan't be seeing another inspector here for quite a time.

Duskov waited until cow and cart had disappeared round the corner, and then looked around the little station. In the fenced garden of what was obviously the stationmaster's house beside it, he saw a morose man watering some rather miserable tomato-plants. The man wore only trousers and a singlet, and his beard was several days old. He replied to Duskov's greeting with a grunt, and turned his jet of water on an apple-tree.

'If you're growing sunflower seeds between the tracks, you should get a good harvest,' observed Duskov. The morose man looked at him, pressing his thumbs over the end of the hose, so that the water sprayed out in a broad fan, displaying a spectrum of colours in the sunlight.

'Better ring Central Rail Administration in Moscow,' he grunted. 'Everyone bloody going on at *me*. Can't help it, can I? I'm doing my job here all right, but if no trains come in I can't have any to go out. That's logical, right?'

'Very logical. Well, I have to get to Moscow.'

'So do plenty of people. You leave from Zagorsk.'

'And how do I get to Zagorsk?'

'I know a very good way. You put your right foot forward. Then you put your left foot forward. Carry on like that for several hours, and you'll be in Zagorsk. Easy.'

'Remarkably easy. I just can't tell you how grateful I am.' Duskov turned away.

'Idiot!' commented the philosophical stationmaster, and turned his hose on a compost-heap where he had sown some marrows.

Alexandrov turned out to be a neat, clean little town. Duskov walked through it, making for the village of Strunino, where there was a big brickworks. He saw the tall chimney of the kiln rising into the blue summer sky in the distance. Well done, Milda Ivanovna, he thought. Another two hundred metres, and the road should fork.

Sure enough, it did. Duskov sat down on a boundary stone, wiped the sweat from his face, and looked at a farmhouse surrounded by a fence. Cherry-trees grew in the garden, the vegetable plot was well tended. But there was something that interested Duskov even more standing outside the garden gate.

A car. An old one, it was true, but since the wheels bore traces of recent dust it seemed to be in working order. Also it bore a Moscow number-plate. The headlights on the wings were covered in black waxcloth with small slits in it: blackout precautions. But only some very important personage would get a permit to drive a car by night. An official, or someone useful to the war effort, might get one, too. Who was important to the war effort here in Alexandrov? Maybe the manager of the brickworks?

Duskov thought it over, and then, discarding the advice of Colonel von Renneberg, who had told them to avoid any kind of risk until they were safe in Moscow, decided to try his luck.

He strolled over to the pretty farmhouse, examined the carved wooden gables, then wandered along by the fence and stopped beside the car. To his amazement, the ignition key was actually in it. The car was ready to start. What extraordinary luck, he thought; though he would have been even luckier if he had found it at night. Of course, he could jump in, start the engine and race off, but how far would he get? The alarm would be raised at once.

He opened the car door, got behind the wheel, and looked at the key. In the dark, I could have pushed it quietly down the road before starting the engine, he thought. But heaven knows what sort of noise this old banger will make. . . .

The door of the farmhouse opened. Duskov froze behind the steering-wheel. But it was not some official grown fat on his special privileged rations who came out into the front garden, but a creature the sight of whom held Duskov spellbound.

She was quite tall for a woman, with long, slender legs. Despite the stout shoes she wore, Duskov could admire the shape of those lovely legs pressing against the thin fabric of her bright-red cotton dress, which had a bell-shaped skirt. His gaze rested on every part of her: her full breasts, her shoulders, her swaying hips, which led on to the gentle but seductive curve of her buttocks, her bare arms, swinging gently as she walked. And her face! She had high cheek-bones and dark, slightly slanting eyes, a full-lipped mouth and a small, straight nose. Her long, black hair was tied back with a red scarf at the nape of her neck, and the ends of the scarf floated over her shoulders as she walked.

Sighing deeply, Duskov got out of the car. The woman stopped by the garden gate. The breeze blew her skirt against her legs, and Duskov had to force himself not to look directly at the top of her thighs.

'Were you thinking of stealing my car, comrade?' she inquired.

She had a low voice, and it was not shrill with accusation. Duskov stood there, perfectly motionless.

'Well, it was like this, comrade. You see, I drove cars in the Army for six years, comrade. I love them. Not just cars, any kind of motor vehicle there is. I've driven them all. I ended up chauffeuring a general; that was a lovely job. And then I got a bullet in my hip, and that was it. "Leonid Germanovich Duskov," they told me, "you may be a good driver, but we can't use you any more." They said that to *me* — when I know my way round the insides of a car better than any doctor knows the human body. So you see, after a few weeks without a car I feel deprived. I get this funny feeling whenever I see one. An irresistible impulse to get behind a steering-wheel, hear the sound of the engine. Why do you suppose Tchaikovsky never wrote a symphony for the internal combustion engine, comrade?'

'Because there weren't any in his day,' said the soft, cello-like voice.

'Well, to think what Tchaikovsky missed,' Duskov persisted. Keep talking, he thought; sheer impudence may get you out of this. 'Do you think I'm ill, comrade?'

'Quite possibly.' The beautiful creature laughed. She came closer, and tapped Duskov's forehead. He felt the tap of her forefinger as a tiny touch of fire. 'Anyway, we can soon find out,' she added. 'You're in luck, comrade. I happen to be a doctor.'

Duskov smiled broadly. Marvellous, he thought; she's a doctor. Hence the special permit for a car. A car with a Moscow number, too. Wonder what she's doing in Alexandrov? He wondered if he could persuade her to give him a lift.

'Do I get undressed?' he inquired hopefully. Her eyes were so big and black that for a moment he wondered, fancifully, if she polished them up every morning.

'I don't practise medicine in the road.' The low voice brought Duskov down to earth.

'In the car, then?' suggested Duskov, smiling faintly. 'Or in your consulting-rooms in there?' He pointed to the neat farm-house, but there was no doctor's plate. She must have been visiting a patient. 'A serious case, is it?'

'Yours? I should hardly think so. Anyway, that's not where I live.'

'That's what I meant. Do you have a serious case in there?'

'No.' She looked at him again, speculatively. 'It's my parents' house.'

'How about taking me back to your own consulting-rooms, then?' said Duskov boldly.

'I work at the Botkin Hospital in Moscow. I'm a surgeon.'

'Oh, no!' Duskov put out both hands as if to ward her off. 'One hole in my hip is quite enough. No more surgical knives for me, thank you.'

The Botkin Hospital, he was thinking. Not far from the centre of Moscow near the big Dynamos stadium. The Leningradskoye Chaussée runs through the whole area. The hospital complex is one of the biggest in the world. It's about fifteen minutes' walk from there to the Belorussian Station, and then not much farther to Lesnaya Street.

'Good,' said Duskov out loud. The doctor looked at him in surprise.

'What do you mean, "good"?'

'You work in a hospital—a whole collective of doctors. One has to go through any number of hoops to get into the Botkin Hospital as a patient. Which means you can't carve me up so easily. I assure you, that really sets my mind at rest, since I'm going to Moscow myself.'

The doctor did not deign to reply. She walked round Duskov, opened the door of the car, and then, looking back at him over

176

her shoulder, asked, 'Your name's Duskov? Where do you come from? No one of that name lives here.'

Duskov, who had been waiting for that question, had his answer ready. He went to hold the car door open for her, like a chauffeur attending on his employer. 'I'm from Kazan.'

'You're a long way from home, then.' She got behind the wheel and took it in both hands. She had long, slim fingers as well as long, slim legs. Everything about her is perfect, thought the enchanted Duskov. She should be a pianist, with hands like that.

'Do you play the piano?' he asked suddenly.

'Yes.' She looked at him in surprise, warmth in her black eyes for the first time. 'But how did you know?'

'Your hands. You could easily stretch three octaves with them.'

'How would you know? You're not going to tell me you play, too?'

'Well, I've had an eventful history, comrade. My father's a glass blower in Kazan, but I was the only son, brighter than most of the family, so I was supposed to be going to study, and I learned to play the piano from the local undertaker in Novo Rabinssk — that's where we live, near Kazan. Believe it or not, by the time I was twelve, I was playing the piano in the funeral parlour when they wanted a really solemn ceremony. Mind you, the corpses couldn't do much to protect themselves, and the undertaker thought it was beautiful.'

'Oh, for goodness' sake,' said the doctor. 'You talk far too much, and it's all nonsense.'

'No, really, every word's the truth, comrade. I was very gifted. However, as things turned out I never became a pianist, and I never studied, either. I trained as a cobbler instead. That's life for you. My uncle died, you see, and left us his cobbler's shop, and there was no one but me to take it on. Still, I did become a drummer in the town band, too.'

'Oh, get in,' said the doctor. 'Come on, don't gape at me like that. I have to go back to Moscow, so you can have a lift if you want. And you can tell me the rest of your life-story on the way — that is, if the journey to Moscow is long enough.'

Duskov went round to the other side of the car and got in. He had done it. The way to Moscow lay open. In Russia, a ready tongue would get you almost anywhere.

The doctor started up. The engine roared, the car leaped forward with a jolt, and then lurched off down the road. Duskov clung to the dashboard.

'Too much gas,' he yelled. 'And those gears send her shooting off like a catapult. And the steering needs adjusting, and the suspension. . . .'

'The car goes, though,' she said, her voice raised for once. 'If you want something more luxurious, you'd better go to America. This is Russia, after nearly four years of war.' She stopped the car. 'Can *you* do any better?'

'Will you let me?'

They changed places. Duskov took hold of the steering-wheel, engaged gear smoothly, and started off without the slightest jolt.

The doctor glanced at him. 'Well, so what are you going to do in Moscow?'

Duskov told her. His was a good, credible story. The old car, however, was getting harder to handle as they went along. It began to judder. Duskov tapped the steering-wheel and looked thoughtful. 'She's missing out on one cylinder — maybe two.'

Near the village of Kraznozavodsk the engine gave a low, almost human screech, and then fell silent. Duskov instantly turned off the ignition. 'H'm. Now what?' he wondered out loud.

The doctor sat there beside him, tall, slim and beautiful, staring at the hot, sunlit road ahead. 'What happened?' she asked.

'The engine died on us, comrade. I can sing you a funeral dirge if you like. No problem at all.'

'Idiot!' she said, opening the door. She got out and raised the bonnet. The acrid smell of hot metal rose to her nostrils, and she stepped back in alarm, wiping her hands on her lovely thighs. Duskov got out, too, and closed the bonnet again.

'Doesn't look too good,' he said.

'I have a special priority licence. I can get another engine.'

'What, here?' Duskov gestured at their surroundings. 'They do say God loves the Russians, but whether he'll send car engines like manna from heaven, I'm not so sure.'

'I wish you'd shut up.' Her warm voice had a metallic edge to it. Good, she's human after all, thought Duskov. 'We'll go into the village,' she decided.

'Kraznozavodsk?'

'Yes.' She looked at him, surprised. 'How did you know?'

A mistake, thought Duskov. The sort of mistake that should not occur. You were quite right, Colonel; one must think of such details the whole time.

'There was a signpost back there, comrade,' he said, 'and I have a good memory for names.'

This appeared to satisfy her. She hit the bonnet angrily, as if to punish the engine, and then walked down the road. Duskov watched her for a moment. Her hips swayed with every step she took, her long black hair floated back over her shoulders, her bell-shaped skirt blew out around her long legs. Good heavens, what a woman! Then he strode after her and caught up with her. 'Do you think it's wise to leave all your luggage in the car like that?'

'No one here would steal it. We don't all have the habits of people who come from Kazan.'

'Thank you. You misunderstand me, comrade; I wasn't going to steal your car, I was only allowing myself a little erotic satisfaction, because once I see a car—'

She stopped dead, her eyes blazing. 'Will you kindly stop talking like that, Leonid Germanovich? What makes you think your foolishness is going to impress me?'

'I could walk on my hands if you'd rather,' said Duskov, penitent. 'I was the best gymnast in my class at school. Just say what you'd like, comrade. I'd be happy to do anything to please you.'

'Then keep your mouth shut.'

It took almost half an hour for the smith and wheelwright of Kraznozavodsk to agree as to which of them should repair the car, and they eventually compromised, deciding to share the job. They towed the car to the village behind two cows. The smith assured the doctor and her companion that he would be honoured to give them shelter for the night, showed them into a room with a huge bed, and left them alone. The doctor sat down on the edge of the bed and tied her red scarf more firmly at the nape of her neck.

'Well, why are you hanging around?' she asked Duskov.

'Sorry — what would you like me to do?'

'You'd better go and find somewhere *you* can stay the night.'

'Right.'

Duskov left the room, walked around the smith's house three times, and then came back. By now, the smith had brought in a bucket of water, and the doctor was washing her hands. Duskov stood by the window, looking gloomy. 'I'll sleep beside the anvil,' he announced.

'What?' She looked up, drying her hands on a clean towel.

'They're a timid lot here in Kraznozavodsk. None of them wanted to offer a strange man a bed. Well, you can see their point. Most of the women are on their own, their men at the front, the old folk are no protection, and along comes a handsome young man like me, asking for a bed — I mean, what would *you* say?'

'We shall get this whole thing cleared up by tonight!' The doctor tossed the towel aside and went into the big living-room of the smithy. Lipa, the smith's wife, was standing at the hearth making shchi, a thick, fermented cabbage soup.

When Duskov, the smith and the wheelwright got the car engine stripped down, it turned out to be a write-off. The smith, who also acted as the village vet, had used the pulley he employed for getting sick horses and cows on their legs to lift the engine out of the car, and they placed it on a trestle, where it now stood, black, oily and hostile. The villagers clustered around it, gaping as if it were some extraordinary monster. Duskov had unscrewed the block and got at the pistons; two of the piston rings were worn right down to mere oily fringes. Meanwhile, the doctor was using the only telephone in the place to get through to Moscow.

'They can't send a new engine for a week, at the earliest,' she reported furiously. She looked with distaste at the oily engine. Covered with oil, his chest bared, his hands black, Duskov was sitting by the engine block smoking a cigarette the smith had given him. 'And I can't get hold of another car, either! We'll have to go to Zagorsk and catch the train to Moscow. There are only two ways of getting to Zagorsk, tractor or bicycle, and there's only one bicycle available, which means you'd have to ride it, with me on the back, and that's out of the question, so it only leaves the tractor. Good heavens, look at you! Will you ever be clean again?'

It was, indeed, a problem. Duskov sat in a wooden tub of hot, soapy water, scrubbed himself with a hard brush until his skin was reddened, then wrapped himself in an old but fortunately clean horse-blanket, and lay down on the vast wooden bed. When the doctor came into the room, he blinked wearily and yawned.

'Clean as a newly bathed baby,' he said cheerfully. 'Want to see, comrade?'

'Get out of my bed!' Her voice was dangerously low again.

'I think I have a temperature. Influenza epidemica, maybe.'

'*What?*' She leaned forward.

'Or it could be hypomnesis.'

She stared at him, speechless, then sat down on the bed beside him and placed her beautiful hands in her lap. Duskov, envying those hands, closed his eyes.

'Who *are* you?' she asked quietly. 'And please don't give me any more of your ridiculous tales about being a cobbler from Kazan.'

'Why should I lie to you? My papers are in my jacket pocket.'

'What would a cobbler know about hypomnesis?'

'Ah, well, I trained as an ambulance man, too, comrade.' Duskov opened his eyes again, directing an innocent gaze at the beautiful face over his. 'The undertaker insisted. I expect you know how many good people die sitting in their chairs. Well, their families seldom think to lay them out flat. So we had to do it, after they'd stiffened up. Can't take them to the grave in a sitting position, you know; you have to break the knee-joints. But our undertaker didn't say knee-joint — *articulatio genus*, he always called it. I bought myself a medical dictionary; rather enjoyed it. I learned quite a few medical expressions. There's spermatorrhea, for instance—'

'You,' she said, standing up, 'are a pig! Get out of my bed!'

She turned to look out of the window, and waited until Duskov was up from the bed and sitting in a chair, wrapped in the blanket. He was pleased to find that the three terms he had spent studying medicine at Griefswald University had not been entirely wasted.

'Right,' he said. 'The smith did say he'd put some straw down by the anvil for me.'

She nodded, looked at him, and then went over to him and placed the palm of her hand on his forehead. 'You have no temperature at all,' she said.

'Well, now I do. It came on just this minute.'

181

She hesitated momentarily, her hand still on his forehead, then rapidly withdrew it and gave him a sound slap on the cheek. Without a word, she left the room. Duskov was pleased. He had pierced that invisible armour of hers.

After supper — pirozhki stuffed with cabbage, and home-brewed kvass — they were back in their room, and stood there in silence, carefully avoiding looking at the bed. The smith had given them three candles. The doctor had seen no signs of any straw beside the anvil.

'Well, it's wartime,' she said at last.

'Yes,' agreed Duskov cautiously.

'We can't choose to do just as we'd like. We have to make allowances. Oh, all right, we'll share the bed. It's big enough. I shall put that chair in between us, and I warn you: if you push it away or try crawling round it, I have a sharp knife and I'll use it.'

'You're perfectly safe. I'm asleep on my feet,' Duskov lied, sitting down on his side of the bed. He looked hungrily at the doctor as she picked up the chair and placed it on the bed between them, right in the middle. 'I shall start snoring the moment I lie down.'

'Snoring?'

'Can't help it. It's hereditary. One of my ancestors must have slept with a sawmill.'

'Oh, for heaven's sake. Well, it's just for one night.' She, too, lay down, fully dressed, and blew out the candle beside her. It was warm in the room, although the window was open.

'You're not snoring at all,' she said suddenly.

'Perhaps it's the hypomnesis? I don't actually remember why I felt so sleepy now. Comrade . . . ?'

'My name is Anya Ivanovna Pleskina.'

Duskov took a deep breath. 'You're married?'

'My husband was killed in 1941, when the Germans attacked the Polish border.'

'I'm sorry.'

'Thank you,' she said briefly.

'It's a very hot night, Anya Ivanovna. Your dress must be sticking to you. Why don't you take it off? It's dark, and I'll turn over and go to sleep on my other side.'

'It's quite a thin dress.' But she did get up, and he heard the rustle of the fabric as she took it off and then came back to bed. He imagined what her body must be like: surely perfectly proportioned, with smooth, slightly tanned skin.

'Are you really interested in medicine?' she asked suddenly.

'I'm interested in everything. I'm a frustrated intellectual.'

'I mean, do you have to go and work on the railways?'

'They've transferred me there. It's for the war effort.'

'Hospitals are important to the war effort, too.'

'Yes. Yes, I should think they are.'

'I could apply to have you employed at the Botkin Hospital instead, as a nursing auxiliary. Would you like that? There are all sorts of ways you could be useful in a big hospital.'

Duskov's heart began to thud. 'An idiot like me, Anya Ivanovna?' he asked. He pressed his face close to the chair. He could see her own lovely face on the other side. Only the width of the chair seat separated them; its spiky legs hardly seemed much of a barrier any more.

'How old are you?' she asked.

'Twenty-eight, Anya Ivanovna.'

'Mm. I'm twenty-seven. Sleep well, Leonid Germanovich — and do cut out that stuff about hypomnesis.'

'By all means.' Duskov reached out a hand through the chair legs. She raised her arm and slapped his fingers away.

'No, this is the frontier. Behave yourself, will you?'

Early next morning, they were on their way to Zagorsk, rattling along on a tractor, to catch the first train to Moscow.

Pavel Fedorovich Sassonov had reached the highway from Ryasan to Moscow. A busy road, with convoys of trucks and military supplies passing along it to the capital day and night. One would not be conspicuous here, standing alone by the roadside trying to hitch a lift.

Sassonov's parachute-jump in at Yegoryevsk had gone so smoothly that he was still wondering why German Intelligence did not land more agents behind the lines. A specialist unit of saboteurs, properly disposed and operating as individuals, so as to be as inconspicuous as possible, could immobilize whole sections of the supply lines. Sassonov was busy with such ideas as he buried his parachute by the banks of a stream, washed in the gently flowing water, and checked everything once again to make sure he had left no traces behind.

After allowing himself a few moments of relaxation to smoke a cigarette, he set off, making for the highway. He had a clear picture of the area in his head, from Milda Ivanovna's description. The town of Yegoryevsk lay to his left, the village of Yiyinski Pogost to his right. He would have to go through a wood between them, and cross the Ryasan-to-Moscow railway line, so as to reach the Moskva river south of Vindgradovo. Then he must go on through another wood and across several fields, until he reached the main road at the tiny village of Starnikovo, which consisted of only nine houses.

Sassonov made good progress. He met no one on his way.

Now he was standing by the highway at Starnikovo, watching the trucks go by, counting those carrying munitions, and working out that, within the last twenty minutes, two batteries of heavy artillery and a whole battalion of men from the Asian provinces of Russia had passed by. My God, and we still hope to win this war, thought Sassonov. Well, perhaps only one desperate action such as the assassination of Stalin could do it.

He waited until some civilian trucks came along, and then started waving. One driver leaned out of his cab window. 'Can't stop, comrade,' he shouted, 'but I'll slow down, and you jump up behind.' Sassonov found himself in a truck full of clanking zinc buckets. He wedged himself in among them, and reached the Moscow suburb of Perovo safely, after an uncomfortable ride. He got out when the brakes of the truck squealed, and went round to meet the two drivers — an old man and a rather masculine woman with a harsh, angular face and short hair, wearing a blue boiler-suit.

'Thanks for the lift, comrades,' Sassonov said. 'This is Perovo, right? That's just where I wanted to go. Anyone know where the Maxim Gorky Steelworks is?'

'You'll find it all right,' said the woman in a harsh voice. 'Can't hide a steelworks that easily. Well, this is where we unload.'

Sassonov said good-bye, and walked into the city at a leisurely pace.

A great deal of reconstruction was in progress here. He saw

scaffolding and half-completed buildings everywhere. As he had been told, it was not difficult to find the steelworks. Sassonov inspected the administration building from a safe distance, and prepared to take the decisive step. It was four o'clock in the afternoon. His legs were tired, all his muscles ached from that long walk through the woods and marshes, and he longed to lie down somewhere and rest.

He thought: Do I have to get it all done today? Might it not be better to look for a bed where I can get a good night's rest? Still, the Colonel had emphasized the need for swift and decisive action. Sassonov made up his mind and crossed the street to the Maxim Gorky Steelworks. The transfer document in his pocket authorized Pavel Fedorovich Sassonov, mechanical engineer, to report to this steelworks following his discharge from the Red Army. The other members of the Wild Geese unit had a certain amount of latitude in their choice of work, but Colonel von Renneberg had wanted to know precisely where their leader would be.

Sassonov entered the administration building, gave his name and business to the man at the door, and was sent up to room 339 on the third floor. This was the personnel manager's office. Even in a Soviet steelworks, it turned out that the way to the boss lies past the secretary's office, and the personnel manager had a decidedly pretty secretary. Sassonov gave her a charming smile and introduced himself.

'I'm Lisanka Nikolayevna,' she replied.

Sassonov smiled at her again. 'I'm sure the Comrade Personnel Manager is very busy, but any chance of seeing him, Lisanka? I'm the new engineer. Just transferred from the 1st Belorussian Front.'

Lisanka Nikolayevna beamed at him, her red lips pouting prettily, rose and went into the next room, her hips swaying. After a brief conversation with her boss, Lisanka came back into her office, leaving the communicating door open. 'Please go in, Pavel Fedorovich.'

Sassonov strode briskly into the personnel manager's office. But the personnel manager was not alone. There was another man there, too, standing by the window, staring at the new arrival. Sassonov froze for a moment. Then he took his papers resolutely out of his jacket pocket.

He'd recognized the man standing by the window. He was Makar Prokofych Kutuzov.

The two men's eyes met for a moment. Then Sassonov handed his papers to the personnel manager behind the desk. The man looked through them briefly; obviously he was duly impressed by the rubber stamps.

'Glad to have you with us, Pavel Fedorovich,' he said, indicating a chair. 'I'm Oleg Abramovich Omelkov, and let me introduce Technical Director Makar Prokofych Kutuzov. You'll probably be meeting him again in the course of your work here.'

'No,' said Kutuzov harshly. He walked forward from the window and stared hard at Sassonov, frowning. Yes, it's the same man sure enough, thought Sassonov, feeling himself turn cold as ice.

Oh, my God, he thought, if only I'd obeyed my instinct. Found a bed for the night, not been in such a hurry to do it all today. Tomorrow morning, Kutuzov wouldn't have been standing here in this room. German efficiency is not always best. I should have been more of a Russian today; I should have known how to bide my time.

He remained standing by the chair he had been offered, and Omelkov stared at Kutuzov in surprise, shaking his head. Well, he'll soon be enlightened, thought Sassonov. Sorry, friends, I'm reporting off duty. Captain von Baldenov — I beg your pardon, Leonid Germanovich Duskov — you'll have to take over command of the operation. And good luck, all of you. If my son ever wonders about his father, I hope he may at least guess I died in action, and action of a unique kind in this unique war.

'And where did *you* come from, Herr von Labitz?' asked Kutuzov, speaking German with a harsh Russian accent but perfect grammatical fluency. Omelkov stared blankly at the pair of them, and sat down heavily in the wooden armchair behind his desk.

'What — what's going on?' he faltered.

Sassonov did not reply. He knew the time had come. Moving swiftly, he took the poison capsule from his pocket. But Kutuzov was too fast for him. He struck Sassonov's arm aside, grasping it tightly and wrenching it brutally backwards. The veins swelled at Sassonov's temples, but he did not utter a sound, nor did he let go of the capsule, and he clenched his fist over it when

Kutuzov, determined to make him open his hand, bent down and bit the flesh.

'What on earth are you doing?' cried the horrified Omelkov. 'Makar Prokofych, have you gone mad?'

The capsule squashed inside Sassonov's fist. Suddenly, a sharp smell of bitter almonds filled the air. Kutuzov stopped biting the hand, wrenched at Sassonov's arm again, dislocating the shoulder, and brought the point of his chin hard against Sassonov's skull. Only then did the clenched fist open. A couple of drops of liquid fell to the floor, and the scent of almonds intensified. Kutuzov ran to the window, opened it, and stared at Sassonov, who had collapsed helplessly in his chair.

'Ring the NKVD, Oleg Abramovich!' shouted Kutuzov, seizing Sassonov as he tried to get up. 'This man is a German officer. I know him very well. His name is Bodo von Labitz, and his family owned a factory in Riga where I worked as a technical draughts-man till they threw me out. I'd been distributing Communist leaflets. They wanted to haul me off to a concentration-camp, but I managed to get away. Well, that's him. A German officer.'

'German.... An officer....' Omelkov sighed, swallowed, and looked at Sassonov with incredulous amazement. Gradually, he took in that this appalling thing had actually happened in his own steelworks. The NKVD would turn the whole works upside down to find more spies, and then what else might not come to light? It didn't bear thinking of. Most people had something on their conscience, and the higher up they were the worse it was.

'The bloody bastard,' said Omelkov with feeling. He got up, came round the desk, and punched Sassonov three times on the nose, splitting the skin. The bone of Sassonov's nose broke with an audible crack, and blood poured down over his mouth and chin, staining his shirt.

'Get hold of the NKVD,' cried Kutuzov, quite beside himself. 'Don't you kill him, Oleg Abramovich. We'll need him alive. I've a feeling there's a lot more to be got out of him.'

They decided not to raise the alarm in the works. They made Sassonov sit down, his face still bleeding badly, and while Omel-kov rang the NKVD offices in central Moscow, anxious to estab-lish his reputation in high places as a good citizen, Kutuzov guarded Sassonov.

Sassonov sat quite still. After the first shooting pain, his dislocated arm had gone numb. His nose was swollen, and he had to breathe through his mouth, wiping the blood away with his left hand. The NKVD. Well, he knew what lay ahead, and he also knew he must escape interrogation at all costs. The NKVD's methods were notorious, and no one could endure them in silence. Somehow, somewhere, on the way in to Moscow, or in his NKVD cell, there must be some way to make up for the opportunity he had lost with the potassium cyanide capsule. There is always a way, if you are quite determined to kill yourself.

So I shall get to Moscow after all, he thought with bitter irony, while the red-faced Omelkov bellowed at him and Kutuzov kept him in the chair, both hands pressing down on his shoulders. How have the other nine got on? he wondered. It's like the nursery rhyme: now they were nine. Or was it less?

Omelkov paced angrily around his office, terrified in case the NKVD found out about the bartering circle, with several tons of steel secretly exchanged for foodstuffs. Out in the secretary's office, Lisanka Nikolayevna huddled behind her typewriter, wide-eyed, unable to make head or tail of it. That nice-looking man Pavel Fedorovich a German spy? A Nazi officer? What next?

In the NKVD offices, they had received the news from Perovo with what Omelkov thought extraordinary calm. An almost bored voice told him, 'Right, we'll send a car over. What's the German doing now? Sitting there bleeding? Good. Can you lock him up? What was that — you're keeping him there in your office? Yes, yes, that's all right. Just don't let news of the incident get out.'

In fact it was three hours before two cars containing NKVD officials arrived. Three long hours, during which Omelkov bawled intermittently at Sassonov, making dire threats or, when he was unable to restrain himself, kicking his prisoner's shins. Sassonov said nothing. His dislocated arm had gone numb; most of the time he just sat there with his eyes closed. When he opened them, he saw Kutuzov's face, the man's cold eyes watching every movement he made.

He was almost relieved when the men from Moscow came into the room. A man who introduced himself as a major leaned against the desk and looked through Sassonov's impeccable papers. Then he examined the remains of the potassium cyanide capsule, which Kutuzov had placed on a sheet of paper, sniffed it cautiously and pushed it aside.

'You are an officer?' he asked in Russian.

Sassonov looked at him, his eyes dull. 'Yes.'

'Name?'

There was no point in giving a false one now. 'Bodo von Labitz,' he said.

'Rank?'

'Major.'

'Serving with what unit?'

Sassonov was silent. The NKVD major waited, then shrugged his shoulders. To Omelkov's surprise, his tone was still courteous. 'Why did you come to Perovo?' he went on. 'What is your mission? Why were you to work in this steelworks? Are you in German Intelligence? Did Admiral Canaris send you on this mission?'

Sassonov still remained silent. He leaned his head back and stared at the ceiling. A good moment to cut his throat, thought Omelkov furiously.

But the NKVD man did not seem to expect answers to his questions. He gave Sassonov an almost friendly nod, as if he would have been disappointed to get anything out of him at this stage.

'Right, now you're coming with me,' he told Sassonov politely. 'And don't try to get away. It wouldn't guarantee you a quick death; we'd only shoot you in the legs. You see, we do understand our enemies' mentality. Can you walk?'

'Yes.' Sassonov rose from the chair, and when he staggered an NKVD man supported him. The dislocated arm was not quite numb after all; searing pain shot through his shoulder. 'My arm,' he said, as if apologizing.

'A doctor will see to that, but not till we get to Moscow.'

'Oh, I can stand it,' said Sassonov. He made his way to the door, leaning on the NKVD man, and turned to look at Kutuzov. 'My bad luck, wasn't it, Makar Prokofych?'

'I did my duty to my country.'

'Of course.'

In the NKVD offices in Moscow, a gloomy building with a neo-classical façade, Sassonov was taken straight to a kind of sick-bay. There was only one man on duty there. He looked at Sassonov's arm, did not say a word, but grinned, and jerked the shoulder round. Sassonov gritted his teeth. The pain seemed to be bursting his skull apart, and he felt very faint, but then he realized that he had the use of his arm back. He clutched it with his left hand, holding it close to his body. The Major, standing behind him, said politely, 'Yevsei here is an expert in such matters. He was a sports masseur before the war. Just a moment's pain, but then you find everything's in place again. Can you walk all right now?'

'Yes.' Sassonov turned. No good trying here, he thought; too many people around me.

They went up to the fourth floor in a lift, then walked down a long, whitewashed corridor, and into a room which was luxuriously furnished by Russian standards. A round table stood in one corner, with four chairs upholstered in imitation leather. There was a desk, and a picture of Stalin, beaming benevolently, hanging on the wall behind it.

Sassonov cast the picture a quick glance. Well, you're safe from *me* now, he thought, but there are nine others after you. That is, if they're still alive.

The door closed. The Major had entered the room with Sassonov, and he now stood to attention and saluted smartly.

A figure rose from one of the armchairs in the corner, grinding out a cigarette in a glass ashtray. He was a sturdy man of medium height, straight-shouldered, with stubbly, greying hair. He wore an olive-green uniform with large epaulettes and a double row of decorations.

He scrutinized the man in the bloodstained shirt for a few seconds in silence, then straightened his uniform jacket and introduced himself.

'I am Colonel Igor Vladimirovich Smolka,' he said. He had a pleasantly deep voice, without any note of threat in it.

'Pavel Fedorovich Sassonov, Colonel.'

So that's who he is, thought Sassonov. He remembered something Milda Ivanovna had said about the structure of the NKVD and Soviet Intelligence, the Russian counterpart of Admiral Canaris's German Abwehr. 'Though you don't need to remember that,' Milda had said. 'You won't be in contact with anyone of that rank; if you do encounter the NKVD, you immediately employ Method 2.'

Method 2 was the potassium cyanide capsule. It was enough to make a cat laugh.

Sassonov looked intently at Colonel Smolka, whose friendly manner did not deceive him. His next few hours or days would be a session spent in Hell.

'Sassonov — or wouldn't you rather be Labitz?' asked Smolka. He pointed to an armchair. The Major remained standing by the door, while Smolka and Sassonov sat down facing each other. Politely, the Colonel offered a packet of papyrossi, and Sassonov took one, leaning forward to the match that Smolka struck for him.

'Yes, well, you've made your mind up not to talk,' said Smolka, blowing out the flame. 'So we won't discuss that. I should be silent myself in your place.' He leaned comfortably back, crossing his legs, like a man sitting in a pavement café to watch the passers-by. 'But suppose we could come to an agreement? Tell me, where does your allegiance lie? With Adolf Hitler? Surely that would be ridiculous. A German officer taking a madman seriously?'

'I swore an oath to defend my native land.'

'And is that what you're doing? Germany attacked Russia, you know, not the other way round. You didn't swear to be a conqueror. Of course, now that Russia is winning, you *have* to defend your country. But all you are doing is shoring up a criminal régime. How do you reconcile that with your honour as a German officer? You've become the henchman of a criminal ready to plunge the whole world into disaster — and please don't talk to me about doing your duty. By means which we shall certainly discover, you came to Perovo disguised as a Russian, with papers in perfect order, presumably to carry out a special mission. I know you're not going to tell us about it, you don't intend to name names, or tell us who's behind it, or what contacts you have. But please don't think we are stupid enough to believe you were here in Russia entirely on your own.' Colonel Smolka knocked the ash off the tip of his cigarette. 'Am I right about that? I think I am.'

'No comment,' said Sassonov calmly.

'You know, I am constantly amazed by the German mentality.' Smolka crossed his legs the other way. 'Well, Major von Labitz,

I don't know why, but I like you. Please don't force me to have you taken down to the third floor of the cellars.'

Sassonov shrugged his shoulders.

'I wish you'd cut this short, Colonel,' said Sassonov, closing his eyes again. 'I've had — well, a tiring day.'

'How long have you been in Russia?'

'I've lost all sense of time and place.'

'When did you arrive at Perovo?'

'No idea. Around the time of Catherine the Great, possibly.'

Colonel Smolka leaned forward, smiling wryly. He shot questions at Sassonov as he sat there swaying in his chair, eyes closed.

'Were you planning to sabotage the Maxim Gorky Steelworks? Did you know we are producing armour plating for tanks there? Was it your job to sabotage the machinery? Or were you more interested in the new steel alloy being used for our T32 tanks? Do you have engineering qualifications in civil life? You're not working on your own, are you? No, that's impossible. How big is your unit?'

Sassonov wearily shook his head. 'Oh, why don't you go and ask the nearest pumpkin? It could give you more information than I can. I think I'll have a nap.'

'Well, we'll find out more tomorrow.' Colonel Smolka nodded briefly to the Major still standing silently by the door. Two NKVD soldiers came into the room and took Sassonov away.

The Major looked inquiringly at the Colonel, who was playing with a packet of cigarettes. 'We'll let him have his sleep out,' Smolka said at last. 'Anything we did to him now would seem like a blessed release, and we don't want that.'

Sassonov was taken to a small, windowless cell on the second floor of the cellars. He lay down on the wooden bed feeling a sensation of positive pleasure, and pulled the thin grey blanket over his feet. There was a hollow thudding in his head. Before he lost consciousness he thought: Good, they've knocked my skull in. It didn't hurt. Thanks, comrades, that spares me a lot of trouble. . . .

He woke wondering why, since he was dead, he could still feel pain in his right shoulder and his nose, and could hear distant sounds. It was a few seconds before he accustomed himself to the fact that he was still alive after all, lying on a bed in a dark cell of the NKVD building in Moscow. He was naked under the blanket; he had been stripped while he slept, and his clothes had been taken away. There was nothing in the cell he could wear apart from the blanket. He got his legs off the bed, wrapped the blanket round himself, and yet again bent his mind to the one voluntary action left to him: how can I kill myself?

Somewhere or other, a smoothly functioning alarm system must be observing his cell, because in a moment the door opened, and light fell into the dark room and on to Sassonov's huddled form. He blinked at the brightness, made out three uniformed figures, and stood up.

'Come with us,' said a harsh voice.

'Like this?'

'Yes.'

Sassonov picked up the blanket, clutching it around him, and went out into the corridor barefoot. A young lieutenant nodded gravely to him, and two soldiers fell into step one on either side of him. They led him six doors farther on. There, in a bleak room with walls painted green, sat Colonel Smolka, behind a plain wooden table. There was a chair in front of the table, placed so that it stood between two batteries of floodlights, four on either side. Politely, as if inviting him to a tea party, Colonel Smolka pointed to the chair.

Sassonov remained standing behind it. The floodlights were not switched on yet, but their presence told him what he might expect.

'No, thank you, Colonel,' said Sassonov calmly. 'What's the point of it? You won't get me to do anything but sweat under those lights, and what good would that do you?'

'We know rather more about you now, Major von Labitz,' said Smolka, leaning back, a rather morose expression on his normally avuncular face. '*You* may call it heroism to let yourself be destroyed here; *I* call it madness. In a few days' time there will be no German front in Russia any more. The Germans will be in retreat. We are about to launch a great offensive from the Baltic to the Black Sea. Our superiority of strength is crushing. No one can hold us back now.'

'I'm sure you're right,' said Sassonov, sitting down. 'Though I don't know why you bother to tell a naked man.'

'So you want to die for a lost cause?'

'No. You're not looking at it the right way, Colonel. I can't blame you; you don't understand the situation. I'm a dead man already, so you're asking for information from someone who doesn't exist.'

Smolka placed his fingertips together and laid his chin on them. 'We know you are a German officer. We have found that one of your shoes has a heel which will unscrew, and contains parts which can be assembled to make a small short-wave transmitter of American manufacture. I'll admit we hadn't come across one of those before. We tried it out, but we don't know either the correct frequency or your code. However, that transmitter proves you're not acting on your own in Russia. You are in touch with other spies or saboteurs. Also you were equipped with a potassium cyanide capsule — so yours is a very important mission, requiring absolute secrecy. And we also know that all your clothes and other items on you, right down to your pocket comb, were of Russian origin. There's nothing the matter with your papers, either. So whoever sent you on this mission made a complete Russian out of you. That means you are not involved in a military action of limited extent; your mission is something far more important.' Colonel Smolka smiled faintly. 'Our own methods with *our* top agents are not dissimilar. For God's sake, why don't you talk? Think how close the end of the war is.'

'The war's over already, as far as I'm concerned.'

'You're right there. Do you have any family?'

'Yes, a wife and child. A son. Only a baby.' He knew just what Colonel Smolka was about to say.

Sure enough, he said it. 'I can guarantee that you will see your wife and child again after the war. You will be perfectly safe. You'll be taken to an officers' prison-camp in Moscow, where you will meet men of the "Free Germany" movement — General von Seydlitz, to name only one. Officers with a real sense of honour, who realized, back at Stalingrad, that your Führer is a criminal madman.'

'Colonel, you might well doubt my own sense of honour if I were to betray others.'

'Aha. So there *are* others. You see, you play into our hands, Major von Labitz.' Smolka nodded, pleased.

194

Sassonov did not reply. He bit his lip. A mistake.

'Do what you like to me,' said Sassonov harshly, looking Smolka straight in the face. 'And those are the last words you will hear me say.'

The torture went on for nine hours, in a soundproofed underground room. Blows rained down on Sassonov's naked body, they put him on steel plates with electric currents running through them, they revived him with cold water when he fainted, they turned the floodlights on him, half-frying him, they hung him up by the arms, they twisted elastic bands which contracted when wet, inflicting unendurable pain, round his genitals — but Sassonov did not speak another word. He certainly screamed; his howls of pain re-echoed from the grey concrete walls, he uttered inarticulate sounds, shrill cries of torment, but when, in the intervals of respite, they questioned him again, he did not reply.

At last, after nine hours, he died. An electric current proved too strong for his tormented body to withstand. Sassonov's heart failed, releasing him.

Colonel Smolka declined to see the corpse again. Two hours later, an inconspicuous closed van drove it to the crematorium. An attendant scattered his ashes over a flower-bed, which bloomed behind the boiler-house with amazing luxuriance.

Semyon Tikhinovich Haller, a brawny man, was just washing himself from the tap in the corridor of the communal apartment which the Hallers shared with four other families. Each family had two rooms and a kitchen, and there was an extra washbasin out in the hall for communal use. No one could have expected Semyon Tikhinovich to come home from work clean: he spent his days standing by the gigantic steel saw in a rolling mill, and came back covered with metal filings. The worst of it was washed off at work, but he never felt really clean until he had been sitting in a wooden tub scrubbing himself well with a hard brush.

He was still up to his neck in this tub when his daughter Wanda Semyonovna opened the front door, pushed in a stranger, and said cheerfully, 'Hullo, there's Father, just come off shift.' She waved to the naked man and steered Ivanov closer to the tub. She was radiant. 'Father, this is Fyodor Panteleyevich.'

Semyon Tikhinovich grunted something indistinct, put the

brush down on the side of the tub and stared at Ivanov. He had greying hair, a broad face, and skin dried out by the constant heat of the rolling mill. 'How d'you do, Fyodor Panteleyevich?' he said in a deep voice. Then he had a fit of coughing. 'Bloody iron filings – getting everywhere,' he said, recovering. 'Up my nose, in my throat, into my lungs. You can even hear 'em when I pee.'

Wanda blushed and, unaccountably, whistled. Semyon Tikhinovich grinned. 'That's because I'm too vulgar, see, Fyodor Panteleyevich? If she thinks I'm being vulgar, she whistles. Offside! Just like a football referee. Take no notice of it. So where did you meet our Wandushka?'

'On the train,' said Ivanov, who had immediately taken to the muscular man in the wooden tub. 'I got in at Dubna, and we were in the same compartment. We – well, we started talking, and Wanda Semyonovna kindly asked me here.'

'He's a war hero,' Wanda cried, before her father could say anything. 'He's been fighting the Germans, ever so bravely. You show Father, Fedya.'

Ivanov, who was getting used to the exhibition by now, raised his shirt to show his scar. Semyon regarded it with obvious respect.

'I've been discharged from the Army,' Ivanov explained, 'and Wanda thought she might be able to get me a job with her construction brigade. . . .'

'Well, when Wanda says she'll do something, she usually does it.' Semyon gestured with a brush. 'You two go on in. I'll be with you in a minute.'

Wanda took Ivanov's arm and guided him down the long corridor. She opened a door with flaking green paint, and then they were in a room of medium size, with two windows. It was kitchen as well as living-room, and most of the Haller family's clothes hung from hooks and nails, but one wall was left clear for a picture of Lenin and a colour print of an icon showing a smiling, kindly Virgin. A woman, still quite youthful in appearance, stood at a coal-burning stove. She wore a blue skirt, a faded blouse over her ample bosom, and had her brown hair up in a bun.

'And here's my mother, Antonia Nikitayevna,' said Wanda. She ran to hug her.

'I – er – I wasn't really going to come,' Ivanov began, seeing

196

Antonia's critical gaze directed on him. But his sunny smile and fair hair soon made her friendlier. A practical woman, she asked, 'Did Wanda invite you to supper?'

'We — we didn't discuss it.'

'There's potato-and-onion soup.'

'Sounds like luxury, Antonia Nikitayevna.' Ivanov smiled apologetically.

Antonia stirred the soup, which certainly smelled good. Ivanov sat down, wondering how the problem of beds would be solved if he did stay the night. Semyon came in, clad only in a pair of trousers, a towel round his neck.

'Ah, there you are, Fyodor Panteleyevich,' he said. 'Make yourself at home. Would you like a game of chess?'

'There's nothing I like better,' Ivanov assured him.

Semyon Tikhinovich seemed pleased. 'Tell you something,' he offered. 'I'm used to our Wanda bringing home stray animals, but you're a new departure. Never knew our Wanda bring a man home before.'

'Don't worry,' said Ivanov amiably. 'I'll be off again directly.'

'No, you won't,' cried Wanda. She was laying the table with flowered china, and suddenly the whole room looked brighter.

'Hear that?' Semyon Tikhinovich tossed the towel down on a window-sill, beside a pot of geraniums. 'Like I was saying, our Wandushka usually gets her way.' He went into the next room to find himself a shirt.

The soup was good, if rather thin. Wanda beamed at Ivanov throughout the meal. When they had finished, she cleared the dishes away and ran water into the enamel sink beside the stove.

'Chess?' asked Semyon, and Ivanov nodded.

They sat up till quite late, playing three games. Semyon won them all, which left him in high good-humour. There were no difficulties about the sleeping arrangements; Semyon went to borrow a mattress from the neighbours and laid it on the kitchen floor. Ivanov lay awake on it for some time. The door to the main bedroom, where the Haller family slept, was not quite closed. He heard them whispering together. Suddenly Semyon's voice boomed out. 'Well, *is* he staying here?'

'Yes, Father,' said Wanda.

'You mean you expect us to get used to him?'

'That's right. I love him.'

'What the hell do you mean, you love him?'

'Ssh!' whispered Antonia Nikitayevna. 'He might hear you.'

'I love him the way you love Mamma,' Wanda whispered to her father.

'That's different.'

'Why?'

'Oh, for goodness' sake.... I'll tell you tomorrow,' said Semyon.

Ivanov stared up at the stained plaster of the kitchen ceiling. He was well pleased with his day's work.

The Comrade Supervisor of Reconstruction Collective Number 3 was a small, peaky man. His name was Viktor Leontinovich Skameykin. He had an office at one end of the long hut which housed the administration quarters, and he was forever hopefully pursuing the women of his brigade. Now and then, in return for lighter work, one of them would let him persuade her to sit on his knee and allow him to finger her above and below.

Skameykin looked at Ivanov without very much goodwill. He gave his certificate of discharge from the Red Army a thorough examination, viewed the scar (at Wanda's insistence) and then scratched his thin nose.

'It's difficult,' he said weightily. 'In fact, next to impossible. You'd have to get the Labour Office to send you here — otherwise you don't get your ration card. They need to file you away in their central card index before you have a right to eat. Anyway, we don't need anyone else here.'

'Yes, we do. We need scaffolders,' said Wanda firmly. 'Oh, go on, Vitya. You only have to scribble something on those papers. Please, Vitya.'

Skameykin sighed. When a girl called him Vitya so tenderly, his defences went down. He bent over Ivanov's papers again, hardly venturing to add anything of his own to those imposing documents. Finally he wrote, in the margin of the relevant paper, 'Requisitioned for work on erection of scaffolding by construction brigade of Reconstruction Collective 3, Central Moscow.' Then he pushed the papers back to Ivanov. 'You'll still have to go to the Labour Office for your ration cards,' he said. 'All right, off you go.'

Wanda put her arm through Ivanov's as they walked away. She was in her working-clothes: blue trousers splashed with mortar, heavy shoes, a pullover, and a scarf around her neck. Her hair was tucked under another scarf. 'Come on, Fedya,' she said. 'I'll show you the site.'

'In the Kremlin?' Ivanov breathed.

'We go in on a truck of builders' materials. The guards all know us; they'll let the truck straight through.'

'You mean it's as simple as that?'

'Why—did you think people couldn't get into the Kremlin without stripping naked first?' She laughed, and kissed his cheek.

'Something of that kind.'

'Why? Because of Stalin? Stalin isn't afraid of anything.' She looked at him, her eyes shining. 'Nothing can hurt Stalin. And his comrades in the construction brigade are his most faithful friends.'

'So we are,' said Ivanov, putting his arm round Wanda's hips. 'Have you ever actually seen him?'

'Oh, often. Once he even called up to me, when I was on the scaffolding. "Don't you get dizzy up there?" he asked. So I shouted back, "Yes, Comrade Generalissimo, but only now I've seen you."'

Ivanov was silent, feeling a strange chill pass through him as he thought that he might be the one near enough to Stalin to carry out the mission. Perhaps he would get, and should seize, the chance to do it before they were all to meet again as planned. Stalin could be dead well before then. And he would be dead, too.

'What are you thinking of?' asked Wanda. Ivanov smiled and kissed her.

'I want you,' he said softly. 'That's what I was thinking.'

'Later, Fedya.' She leaned her head on his shoulder, sighing. 'When we stop at midday. No one would see us over in the depot, behind the sacks of lime.'

The best place to hide is in a crowd, and Pyotr Mironovich Sepkin felt safest among all the people around the Belorussian Station and in the big square outside it. He walked around the

199

square, glancing down Lesnaya Street, but he did not venture near Milda's apartment. He spent the day strolling around Moscow and riding on the Metro, five kopecks bought him a ticket to travel underground, from station to marble-halled station, for four hours. Eventually, he surfaced again at the Belorussian Station. It was evening now, and Moscow lay in darkness under a warm sky.

Sepkin went down Gorky Street, crossed Sverdlov Square, and looked over at the Kremlin. Then he walked around the Bolshoi Theatre, and returned to Gorky Street to look for a place to buy a meal. He stopped outside the National Hotel, looking at its big, curtained windows. After a moment's hesitation, he entered the foyer of the restaurant, made his way past a heavy, dark-red curtain, and found himself in the dining-room. All the tables appeared to be occupied, but that would never deter a Russian, who hates to sit alone at a table anyway. Sepkin found an empty chair at table 23 and sat down.

'Warm evening,' he remarked to his table companions. They nodded by way of greeting. They were strangers here, members of a Party delegation from Bukhara, who had come equipped with special coupons and were all agog to see what they would get to eat.

The surly waitress serving table 23 glowered at Sepkin, pocketed her customers' coupons, and informed them that today's menu consisted of rybnaya solyanka.

At its best, this dish is a deliciously piquant fish soup, containing cucumber, capers, tomatoes, onion rings, lemons, olives and parsley, all simmered in fish stock with nicely seasoned chunks of fish, and eaten with little pasties made of puff pastry filled with curds, as well as black bread, mustard and salt. However, this was 1944, so when it arrived the soup was mostly water, with a few bits and pieces floating in it which smelled of fish but tasted like rubber. The soup, to the kitchen's credit, was certainly hot, and there was a thin slice of black bread to go with it, though the bread was rather underdone, but no mustard. The disappointed delegation from Bukhara looked at the soup, obviously thinking that, even nowadays, they could eat better than this back home in the Uzbek Soviet Socialist Republic, where you could get mutton off the

200

ration, and where the fish caught in the small streams might not be very big but still tasted of fish and were wonderfully fresh.

As Sepkin filled his stomach with the hot liquid, he was wondering where to spend his first night in Moscow. It was quite warm enough for him to sleep rough outside somewhere. He decided to look around. He paid for his meal, wished the Bukhara delegation a pleasant stay in Moscow (they looked at him rather askance at this), and went out into Gorky Street again. I could sleep on a building site, he thought. That's an idea. One good thing about an uncompleted building is that no one would be likely to take an interest in it. Tomorrow he would go to the Central Labour Office.

He turned off Gorky Street, walked down several other streets, and at last, on the corner of Kacalova Street, found the sort of thing he was looking for: a tall office block, still surrounded by scaffolding, builders' huts, piles of bricks, heaps of sand, and concrete-mixers. Sepkin clambered over the builders' materials, groped his way into the dark building, and found a wide concrete stairway leading down to the basement. He decided to sleep there. He would be able to get away quickly at dawn, before the construction gangs came back to go on with the work. There was no nightwatchman around, though with so much valuable material in the place there really should have been. Evidently the people of Moscow are honest, thought Sepkin, settling down on the concrete floor, leaning back against the wall and closing his eyes wearily. Well, now for some sleep; tomorrow will probably be a strenuous day.

He was just nodding off when he heard clattering and the sound of raised voices overhead. Startled, he sat up, jumped to his feet, and with a few long strides reached the shelter of the space under the stairs, splashing through some puddles and stepping on a plank which flew up and hit his leg.

Above him, in the big room at the top of the stairs, someone was screaming. A woman. Roars of laughter were the only response from whoever else was there—but the woman's scream was a piercing one, uttered in mortal terror. She was calling for help.

Don't ever get involved, Colonel von Renneberg had told them. Avert your eyes from anything that is none of your business. Think of your mission, and don't draw attention to yourselves.

Quietly, Sepkin went up the stairs. Am I really supposed to cower in a corner and listen to that? As he mounted the last few steps, he saw that only his own intervention could save the situation. Two drunken Red Army soldiers had dragged a girl into the building and were tearing her clothes off. One of them held her from behind; the other in front of her already had his trousers down and was brandishing his erect penis. He had just torn the front of her dress open.

'Carrying on like that,' said his mate. 'Hey, you should just feel her arse — it's quite something.' He roared with laughter again, clasping her round the waist. 'You get hold of her hair, Ignaz, and pull her over forward so I can get it in. Damn you, stand still, you little whore. Right little bitch, she is. Should be glad to get so much meat these days. Go on, Ignaz, pull her over towards you — keep still, will you, you bitch? You expect us to believe you never did it before?'

At this moment, Sepkin attacked. It was a clear June night, and now that his eyes were used to the dark he could see every detail. He descended on the two Red Army men like a huge bird of prey, his fist cracking down on their skulls while he brought his right knee up into Ignaz's genitals, with all his strength behind it. Stunned by the blows to his head, the man did not even feel the pain as he collapsed to the concrete floor.

The other soldier, standing behind the girl, had also been hit on the head, but he was not out of action yet. He pushed her aside and ducked, but Sepkin moved faster than he did. He brought the side of his hand down on the drunken man's temples in a karate chop. Silently, the soldier fell to the floor; there was a crack and a thud as he landed.

The girl had retreated to the wall. She was standing close to it, staring at Sepkin, wide-eyed. Her delicate, almost childlike face was quivering.

'It's all right; don't scream,' said Sepkin, standing perfectly still and speaking in the soothing tones of someone approaching a scared wild animal. 'It's over. Everything's all right.'

'Where — where did you come from all of a sudden?' Her voice was trembling. She began to cry, putting her head in her hands and turning to the wall.

202

'I was just passing, and I heard you scream. Now, listen, what can I do to help you?'

'I — oh, I want to get away from here — at once. . . .' She turned to face him, clutching her torn dress over her breasts, but not daring to step over the two soldiers lying on the floor. 'Suppose — suppose they wake up?'

'I've made sure they won't.'

'Have you killed them?' whispered the girl.

'I don't think so.'

'But suppose you have?'

'Let's not bother about hypothetical questions.' Sepkin held out his hand. 'Come on, you can trust me, comrade. I'll see you home.'

She nodded, and stepped over the two unconscious men without touching his hand, though the sight of it seemed to give her the strength she needed.

'You saved my life,' she said, her voice steadier now.

'I don't think that's what they were after.'

'They'd have had to kill me before they got it.'

'Is it worth that much to you?' He found a packet of cigarettes and offered it to the girl, who shook her head, looking back fearfully at the building. 'You only get one life, comrade,' he said.

'We'd better hurry up and leave before they wake up. Unless they *are* dead.'

'One can't tell for certain.'

'You hit them so hard.'

'There's a trick in it; it's a Far Eastern method of unarmed combat.'

'Have you been to the East?'

'Oh, the war takes you all over the place,' he replied vaguely. He came closer to her, and she did not flinch from him. She was holding her torn dress together with one hand while she smoothed down her thick, dark-blonde hair with the other. 'Where can I take you, comrade?'

'My name's Yelena Lukanovna Pushkina,' she said.

'And mine's Pyotr Mironovich Sepkin.'

'You were very brave, Pyotr Mironovich.'

'You shouted pretty loud yourself, Yelena Lukanovna. What else could a man do?'

Suddenly they were both laughing, quietly, in thankfulness and relief. They steered a way through the piles of bricks into Alexander Tolstoy Street. Looking down at herself, Yelena withdrew modestly into a doorway, where she tried to straighten her dress, but it was so badly torn over her breasts that pulling it together was no good. It was also torn behind.

'I have to take the Metro home,' she said. 'How can I, Pyotr Mironovich, looking like this?'

'There are two things we could do,' Sepkin replied. 'We can call the police and get them to take you home. That'll mean a great many inquiries, and they'll arrest the soldiers.'

'And you, too, Pyotr Mironovich, because you hit them.'

'Me, too, I suppose. . . .'

'I wouldn't like that.'

'Then I suggest you put my jacket on, and let me see you home on the Metro.'

'I just feel so ashamed,' she repeated.

'There's no need.' Sepkin took off his old jacket and helped her into it. She buttoned it up; it made her look like a sad circus clown. Sepkin said, 'Don't worry, Yelena, if anyone laughs at you, I'll shut him up.'

'You seem to like fighting people, Pyotr Mironovich!'

'Any time – for you.'

'However am I going to explain this at home?'

'Do you live with your parents?'

'There's only Father now. Mother died a year ago.' She glanced past Sepkin, and then stepped out of the dark doorway. He followed, putting an arm round her shoulders, and she did not object, though he realized that she was still very tense. 'Mother never got over Yuri's death,' she went on quietly. 'My brother. He was so good-looking – tall and fair and strong, and always cheerful, with such an infectious laugh. The Germans shot him in the big tank-battle at Gomel. A friend of his who got away told us about it. Yuri had already surrendered; he was standing on the tank with his hands up, but they still shot him, all the same. As if it was target practice for them.'

Sepkin stared at the road, feeling miserable. 'War's a cruel business, Yelena Lukanovna,' he said unhappily.

'It was the death of my mother. She just faded away. And one morning she simply stayed in bed and looked at us – her eyes were wide open, shining so brightly — and she said, quite clearly, "Look, there's Yuri holding out both hands to me. Always such a good son!' And she sighed and smiled, and she just wasn't there any more.'

'So now you hate the Germans?'

'Don't *you*, Pyotr Mironovich?' She stopped and looked at him, as if wondering for the first time just what sort of man he was. He's nice-looking, she thought, even if he could do with a shave — but how shabby his clothes are. A strange man, suddenly appearing out of nowhere and knocking down those two soldiers. 'Don't *you* hate the Germans?' she repeated. 'You must know what they're like?'

'Yes, I do. I'm just back from the front. Something to do with my lungs; the army doctor said I was unfit for active combat. Me. I was light-heavyweight champion of our division. I was unbeatable.'

'I'm sure you were, Pyotr Mironovich,' said Yelena Lukanovna, smiling and obviously mollified. 'It's a shame. What will you do now?'

'No idea.' Sepkin managed to look so downcast that Yelena gave way to a maternal impulse to stroke his forehead. He took her hand and held it tight. 'Well, I suppose I have to go off to the Central Labour Office and see what kind of job they can find me.'

By now they were walking down the Tverskoye Boulevard. They went down into the Metro at Mayakovskaya Station. At this time of night it was almost empty, and those few people around took hardly any notice of Sepkin and Yelena. They sat in a corner of a carriage by themselves. As they rattled along eastwards, he wondered if he had really killed the soldiers. If so, there would be a tremendous fuss when the builders found them next morning. But he had left no tracks, except perhaps for a few blurred footprints in the builders' sand.

'Where were you going to sleep tonight?' Yelena asked suddenly.

'I was just looking for somewhere when I heard you scream. I thought I'd try a hostel for soldiers on leave.'

'I know what. You can stay with us.'

'Won't your father mind?'

'Papushka's not rich, but we do all right. He has a good job.

205

He's a male nurse at the Sklifossovsky Accident Hospital. He knows a lot of influential people. I work, too,' she added. 'I'm a secretary in the Kremlin.'

Sepkin started. 'The Kremlin? Really?' he said, looking out of the window.

'In the Export Trade Secretariat. I'm in the Northern Europe Department.'

'Do you ever get to see Stalin?' asked Sepkin casually.

'I never have yet.' Yelena shook her head. 'He wouldn't be visiting our department. He has so many other problems.'

She actually works in the Kremlin, thought Sepkin, making an effort to keep his breathing regular. She could be my way into the place. He leaned back and looked at her. 'What would you do if you suddenly met Stalin in the Kremlin gardens, Yelena?'

'What would I do? I don't know.' She was thoughtful, like a schoolgirl trying to answer a question in a test. 'I might fall on my knees in front of him. He's our little father—where would we be without him? What would *you* do, Pyotr Mironovich?'

What I should do would only take seconds, he thought, and it would blow the pair of us sky-high. 'Stand to attention,' he said. 'After all, I'm a soldier.'

Luka Antipovich Pushkin was sitting in an old armchair, asleep over his copy of *Pravda*, when Yelena opened the apartment door. A table-lamp with a dim bulb was on, and there was a smell of tea and burned pirozhki. As the door closed, Yelena's father woke with a start, put down his newspaper and jumped up from his chair. Only then did he see Sepkin. His disreputable appearance did not seem to inspire much confidence, for Luka Antipovich started shouting, 'Help! Thieves! Robbers! Help!'

'No, no, Father dear,' said Yelena soothingly. She ran to the kitchen doorway. Her father had forgotten the pirozhki, which were burning on the stove. The kitchen was full of smoke.

Pushkin turned round, stared at his daughter and took a deep breath. 'It's well after midnight,' he shouted.

'Yes, I know, Papushka.' She snatched the pirozhki off the stove, tipped the charred pancakes into a bucket by the sink, and opened the window. 'I'll explain.'

'And who's that?' Luka Antipovich pointed at Sepkin. 'Is *he* your reason?'

'His name's Pyotr Mironovich.'

'Oh, and couldn't you find anything better in the whole of Moscow? He doesn't even have a jacket!' Then, at last, he took in the fact that Yelena was wearing a man's jacket, and her dress was dirty and torn. He snorted, glared at Sepkin, weighed him up, realized that the young man was infinitely stronger than himself, and confined himself to words. 'Did *you* do that to Yelena? And you dare come back here with her?' He made for the door, past the surprised Sepkin, and flung it open. 'Well, we have plenty of good neighbours here who'll be happy to deal with you.'

'Oh, come in and close the door, Father,' said Yelena calmly. 'You've got it all the wrong way round. Pyotr Mironovich saved my life.'

'Saved your life?' Pushkin was at a loss. The strange young man, who had not said a word yet, took his daughter's jacket off, and Pushkin saw the extent of the damage to her dress for the first time. 'Who did that?' he asked in hollow tones.

'Two soldiers; they were drunk,' said Sepkin. 'I turned up in time.'

'Pyotr killed them, Father, with his bare hands.'

'Is that true?' asked Pushkin, respect in his voice. 'You killed two soldiers to save my Yelena?'

'I don't know if I killed them or not; I didn't wait to find out. I thought it was more important to get Yelena safely home.'

'Thank you,' cried Pushkin, embracing Sepkin. 'Whoever you are, you saved my child, and I won't ask any more questions.'

Later, however, he did, and heard Sepkin's supposed life-story as they sat eating bread and cheese, and drinking red wine obtained by Pushkin from a cousin in the Crimea. He kept it for special occasions. Yelena made sweet blinis and spread them with carrot jam. When she brought the fragrant blinis in from the kitchen, her delicate face was flushed from the heat of the stove, and her eyes bright. She wore a simple dressing-gown belted round her waist. She looked beautiful, and Sepkin felt his heart lurch blissfully at the sound of her laughter.

'I tell you what,' said Pushkin, sliding a plump pancake on to his plate, 'I'll see if I can get you a job in my hospital. You'd be

207

surprised at all the important people I've got to know there. You saved my Yelena. You just rely on me, my boy. Have some more blinis. I'm not exaggerating when I tell you Yelena's blinis are the best in all Moscow.'

Luka Ivanovich Petrovsky spent the greater part of his first day in Moscow walking around the city like a tourist, deciding on his next course of action. He thought his supposed stomach ulcer might get him into a hospital, where perhaps he could find a niche as an orderly of some kind. That evening he sat on a bench in the sunlight outside Hospital Number 13 in the Petrovsky Boulevard; it appealed to him because of his own surname. He watched the comings and goings outside the building, counted the arrival of nine ambulances, enjoyed the sight of the pretty nurses passing by as they changed shifts, and at last, when the sun was sinking, rose, brushed himself down, and crossed the boulevard.

'Visiting-hours over,' snapped the porter at the big glass door, jerking his broad thumb at a notice. 'Come back tomorrow.'

'No, I have to come in. For examination,' Petrovsky insisted. 'I'm just back from the front.' He produced his medical certificate, with all its rubber stamps, and the porter reluctantly opened the door. 'Room 20,' he said. 'Straight ahead, then turn left and go along the corridor. It says *Reception* over the door. You knock, and if anyone calls "Come in" you go in.'

Petrovsky followed these directions, and found himself outside room 20, which contained a short-sighted old man in a white coat, playing chess against himself. His name was Dr Speshnikov, and he had been brought out of retirement because so many of the younger doctors were at the front. Petrovsky waited by the door, clearing his throat, but as nothing happened he came closer, looked over the doctor's shoulder at the board, and said, 'White knight to take the pawn.'

'I'm White myself, you fool. It's Black's move,' said Dr Speshnikov.

'Castle from E3 to—'

'That's it! Yes, that's it! The castle.' Dr Speshnikov's Black castle took a White bishop. Then he raised his head. His grey-blue eyes were sparkling eagerly behind thick, rimless glasses. 'Very well, you're Black now. You took my bishop. Sit down. My move. And don't count your chickens before they're hatched. I'll have you in four moves.'

Petrovsky sat down, pulled his chair up, and in six moves had checkmated Dr Speshnikov, who sighed, took off his glasses, cleaned them on his sleeve, and then looked at the man who had just beaten him at chess. 'Well, and who *are* you?' he asked.

'Case of *ulcus ventropoli*.'

'*Ulcus ventriculi*, you mean.'

'I expect you know best, comrade doctor. That's what I thought they said.'

'Who?'

'The comrade army doctor himself. "Luka Ivanovich Petrovsky," he said, "sorry, but you can't march to Berlin with the others and smash the Germans, not with that *ulcus ventro*—"'

'*Ventri*.'

'Well, whichever it is, it hurts like hell, comrade, so here are my papers, and I'm reporting for examination.'

'Rather late in the day for that.' Dr Speshnikov cast an eye over the much stamped paper, impressed by the number of official bodies apparently concerned with a simple stomach ulcer. 'The doctor you want to see closed up the X-ray department and went home hours ago.'

'I can't help it if the trains run late, can I?' Petrovsky folded his hands and looked guilelessly at Dr Speshnikov. 'I seem to remember someone telling me, some time or other: "Luka Ivanovich, did you know there's a war on?"'

Dr Speshnikov smiled wryly, shifted in his chair, and played with his defeated White king. 'Well, what do we do with you now?' he asked. 'Yes, what indeed? I'm Dr Speshnikov, and I'm only holding the fort. Night duty—they reckon that's all I can cope with. Ah, well, I suppose I'd better examine you. Get undressed.'

Petrovsky obeyed. Still playing with his chessman, Dr Speshnikov looked his patient over. 'Extremely long,' he murmured.

'Can I have that in writing?' inquired Petrovsky.

'What?'

'Anfissa—that's my fiancée back home—she says it's nothing out of the ordinary.'

'Your legs, man, your legs. You are an extremely long-legged type. Good sportsman, are you? Long jump, high jump, sprinter or what? Well, never mind. How about this stomach ulcer?' Dr Speshnikov rose, went over to Petrovsky, pinched his abdominal wall, tapped his stomach, and asked whether it hurt. Luka Ivanovich let out dutiful cries of 'Ouch!' The doctor listened to his chest and back, pushed up his eyelids to examine the pupils, and went back to his desk. 'Right, you can get dressed again.'

'Is that all?' asked Petrovsky, disappointed.

'All we can do at present.' Dr Speshnikov was setting out the chessmen again.

'Will I get a bed here?'

'Not a chance.' The doctor looked at Petrovsky over the top of his glasses. 'I can suggest something, though. Suppose I stamp your papers, to the effect that you're admitted to this hospital as an ambulant patient, and you can stay here and play chess with me? You're an excellent opponent. Obviously a fool in most ways, of course, but with a natural talent for chess. You can share night duty with me, and no one will ask any questions. Once your name's gone into the records, everything just follows on. Oh, we'll deal with your ulcer for you, too. How about that?'

'I need a bed, comrade.' But Petrovsky thought this sounded promising; under the protection of Dr Speshnikov he would have considerable freedom of movement. 'And food.'

'No problem about that,' said Dr Speshnikov cheerfully. He glanced at the chessmen and rubbed his hands with glee at the prospect of the coming game. 'There's a camp-bed in the corner, and I'll see about food.' He readjusted his glasses and made the first move. 'Surprised you, eh?' he said happily. 'An opening of my own. Now, see if you can get out of that one, Luka Ivanovich.'

At eight in the morning Dr Speshnikov went home, a baffled man. As soon as the laboratory and X-ray departments were open, he had taken Petrovsky round for examination, but all the tests were negative. No trace of any stomach ulcer. Much as Petrovsky complained of pain, he was the healthiest patient Dr Speshnikov had ever encountered. 'Well, there's only one explanation,' said the doctor, looking at the X-ray plates. 'It's psychosomatic, Luka Ivanovich. Your stomach ulcer is a hysterical syndrome.'

'Is it incurable?' inquired Petrovsky. 'How long do I have to live?'

'You idiot, you're perfectly healthy.'

'But the army doctor. . . .'

'That's a mystery. What on earth did he think he saw? Well, never mind; you're registered as an ambulant patient, even if you don't need a bed – and if anyone asks awkward questions just say you're from the research department, and they'll back off in case you're carrying germs about.'

Petrovsky thanked Dr Speshnikov, enjoyed a hospital breakfast of bread, marmalade substitute and slimy porridge, slept for three hours, and then went to wash in the outpatients' department.

The huge hospital building was full of people now. Petrovsky explored the place, wandering along corridors and past wards and winking at the nurses, most of whom looked haughtily past him. Back at the outpatients' department, he suddenly stopped by one of the benches. A girl with blonde hair, a pert little snub nose and a face sprinkled with freckles was sitting there on her own. She looked worried, and was shuffling her feet nervously, as if waiting for news from the examination-room. Petrovsky felt a quickening of the blood at the sight of her. Physically, she was exactly the type he liked.

'An accident?' he said. The girl looked up, her face quivering with emotion.

'Oh, are you a doctor, comrade?' she asked in a pleasantly soft voice.

'Do I look like it?'

'Well, it's hard to tell without a white coat on. . . .'

'I'm the *ulcus ventriculi*,' said Petrovsky impressively.

The girl nodded, awed. 'Goodness me. Er – is that a very high-up sort of doctor? I mean, someone important?'

'So to speak,' said Petrovsky gravely. 'Can I help you?'

'I brought my girlfriend in. She's being examined now. She suddenly fainted and fell off her tractor.' Petrovsky sat down beside the girl, who smiled shyly at him. 'I'm a tractor driver, too,' she said hesitantly, rather in awe of this distinguished Ulcus Whatever-it-was, whose manners were so much better than those of the men at the tractor-plant. They were well aware of their

211

rarity value, with almost everyone at the front, and it was a nice change to be sitting beside a man who did not open the conversation by asking when she'd last had it off with anyone. 'I test the new vehicles out before they're delivered.'

'That's a very responsible job.' Petrovsky looked at the door into the outpatients' department. Two ambulance men had just brought in an old man, leaving the door open, so that one could get a glimpse of the room beyond. Two doctors were talking, and a nurse came out with a basket of bloodstained linen. 'How long have you been waiting?' he asked.

'Half an hour.'

'I'll find out what's up,' Petrovsky promised grandly. 'What's your friend's name?'

'Viera Petrovna Orkol.'

'And yours, comrade?'

'Larissa Alexandrovna Khrulankova.'

'Well, don't worry.' He smiled encouragingly at her. 'You'll soon have some news.'

She nodded, looking admiringly at him as he rose. 'I don't know how to thank you, Comrade Ulcus—sorry, I forget the rest.'

Petrovsky waved a hand. 'Never mind that; it's only a kind of title. My name is Luka Ivanovich Petrovsky.'

'Oh, just like the Boulevard here!'

'Yes, it's a distant relation of mine.' Petrovsky shook hands with Larissa, smiled at her in a way that made her blush to the roots of her fair hair, and disappeared into the duty-room.

By a fortunate coincidence, a nurse did come out five minutes later, and told Larissa Alexandrovna, 'She went into premature labour. Much too early. The baby's dead. It was a girl. You can go now, comrade; we'll see that the father is informed.'

'Viera isn't married,' confessed Larissa.

'Oh.' The nurse looked at Larissa in what she thought a very snooty way. 'Well, I don't suppose she found the baby under a gooseberry-bush.'

'It was the foreman of the axle-fitting department. . . .'

'Very well, we'll inform *him*.'

'He's married, nurse. . . .'

'Well, really, I don't know.' The nurse scratched between her

212

breasts. 'You factory girls – running about like bitches on heat, all of you.'

'How would you know what it's like in the factories?' Larissa was suddenly furious. '*We* don't have ways of taking precautions, like you when you're having it off with the doctors. You needn't make out you're so much better than us.'

The nurse flushed, and Larissa swung round and ran out of the hospital. Outside, she changed her mind, and decided to complain of the nurse to that friendly and undoubtedly influential Ulcus, Luka Ivanovich. Turning to go back, she bumped straight into Petrovsky, who had seen her leave from the duty-room window and was about to go in pursuit.

'All right?' he asked, taking her hand.

'I want to complain,' she said firmly.

'Then you've found the right man, Larissa. Tell me about it. I'm ready to hear anything you want to say.'

No one had ever spoken to Larissa quite like that before. 'It was the nurse,' she said more mildly. 'She thinks we're all just tarts.'

'Never!' Petrovsky frowned dramatically. 'Tell me all about it, Larissa Alexandrovna. Let's go and have a lemonade, shall we?'

'Well, my tractor's waiting. I have to take it back.'

'Then I'll come with you.'

And so Petrovsky rode through Moscow on a brand-new tractor, driven with great skill by Larissa.

Later she showed him round the tractor plant, almost bursting with pride. 'He's an Ulcus,' she whispered to her friends, whenever she got a chance. 'Very important. He's nice, too.'

Petrovsky was introduced to the supervisor of the assembly-plant, a dried-up man with yellow whites to his eyes, who suffered from a metabolic disorder, and listened to a description of his symptoms with gratifying sympathy. He also learned that the men in the place were all after Larissa Alexandrovna, who was constantly having to fend them off. Further, she was twenty-two, lived alone in a little room; her parents were dead, and she was alone in the world.

'Well, so what about it, friend?' asked the supervisor, offering Petrovsky a mixture of machorka and home-dried tobacco to roll himself a cigarette. They were sitting in his office, which had glass walls from which they could see the assembly-hall. Larissa had a crowd of girls around her, and seemed to be telling them about Petrovsky. 'Does it make any difference?'

'What do you mean, comrade?'

'I mean, are you going to jump into bed with Larissa?' The supervisor laughed. 'A high-up comrade like you would stand a very good chance — no wonder, when you're an Ulcus.'

'*Ulcus* only means stomach ulcer,' said Petrovsky gently.

'What?' The supervisor chewed his cigarette. 'Oh. I thought—'

'A mistake, comrade. I was just giving my imagination free rein. I haven't had a chance to set Larissa right about it yet.'

'You're not an important doctor at all?' The thin, yellow-eyed man began to laugh, coughing on his cigarette-smoke. 'Of all the things to happen to our Larissa,' he crowed. 'Oh, that's a good one. But how d'you think she'll take it, Luka Ivanovich? I wish I could be there to see.' He drew a deep breath, calmed down slightly, and asked again, 'Well, *are* you going to sleep with her?'

'Maybe.'

'Of course you are. Good thing for all of us. We'll have more peace around here if everyone knows Larissa has a man she likes. What do you really do, Luka Ivanovich?'

'I was at the front till two weeks ago. Then they found this ulcer.'

'And now what?'

'I'm looking for a job — any sort of job.'

'If you ask me, we blokes with stomach trouble ought to stick together. How'd you like a job here, Luka Ivanovich? If I have a word with the personnel manager — *he* has a very sensitive stomach, too, and once he knows about your ulcer he'll sign you on. We're important to the war effort here, you know — and you can provide Larissa with all the babies she wants.'

It was a useful offer, and Petrovsky decided to accept it. Where would he be safer than in a tractor-plant, important to the war effort, and on good terms with a personnel manager suffering from a stomach ailment?

That evening, Luka Ivanovich and Larissa lay on the bed in her little room, naked and content after their lovemaking.

'I don't mind at all about an *ulcus* just being a stomach ulcer,' said Larissa. 'I never loved anyone the way I love you, Luka. Let's just pray we beat the Germans and the war is over soon.'

You can go from one end of a tramline to the other. That is what it's there for; that is what you're paying for. The tram is to transport anyone and everyone. None the less, Lyra Pavlovna, driving her tram along, gradually lost patience with her recalcitrant passenger, who sat behind the partition between her cab and the rest of the tram, staring as if there was something wrong with her and not getting out at any of the stops. He gave her a cheerful nod when she glared at him. Just before they reached the terminus, she put her head round the partition and almost hissed at him, 'Are you glued to that seat, or what?'

'Not that I know of.' Boranov rose and passed his hand over the seat of his trousers. 'No, nothing like that, little sister.'

'I am not your little sister. Then why don't you get out?'

'Why? Do I have to? I like trams, always did, even as a child.'

Lyra decided her passenger was slightly touched. She rang the bell and went on again. They reached the terminus where two other tramlines ended in a large, round paved area, with a shelter for the drivers, who took a ten-minute break before setting off again in the opposite direction. The last few passengers got out here, except for Boranov, who stayed put even when Lyra came round and stood in the doorway.

'This is the end of the line,' she said. 'Everyone out, please.'

'I'll be going back again.' Boranov jiggled some coins about in the palm of his hand. 'Fifteen kopecks, right?'

'You have to get out.'

'But I told you, I'm riding back again.'

'Passengers are not allowed to stay in the tram while it waits,' said Lyra Pavlovna. She climbed the two steps up into the vehicle and faced Boranov, her large eyes blazing. 'And for a very good reason; it needs airing after certain people have been sitting in it.'

'You have a point there.' Boranov rose, sniffing in the general direction of Lyra's pretty brown hair with its red lights. He shook his head. 'I know. It's the soap you wash it in. Rancid.'

Lyra Pavlovna opened her mouth, left it open, and stared at Boranov in horror. 'My *hair?*' she said at last. 'Now, you just listen

215

to me. I'm going to call Comrade Pavlov over from the number 3 line.'

'He provides the soap, does he? Poor Comrade Pavlov — doesn't he have any sense of smell?'

'You're an imbecile. Are you getting out, or do you want to be thrown out?'

'Oh, I'm a peaceful character; I'll get out,' said Boranov, leaving the tram and stretching his arms and legs out in the sun. Lyra Pavlovna locked the vehicle, hurried into the drivers' shelter and shut herself in the ladies', where she looked at herself in the cracked little mirror, moistened her fingertips, ran them through her hair and then sniffed them. Nothing at all. She tried the experiment again, then combed her hair, and left the shelter, her lips compressed. Boranov was talking to the number 3 driver, learning that Lyra Pavlovna Sharenkova was a remarkable young woman, only twenty years old, from a very educated family — father an architect, mother a teacher — and had got this good job with the tramlines through an uncle who was a senior clerk in the Civil Service. No, the driver did not know about her private life. She wasn't engaged — he was sure of that — but he didn't know about boyfriends. 'Never talks about herself much,' he added.

Ten minutes passed, and Boranov presented himself at the tram door again. Lyra was already in position, keeping the passengers out, and the game was repeated all over again, although there were only seven passengers at this end of the line waiting to storm the vehicle.

Finally Lyra Pavlovna rang the bell, shouting, 'Leaving now! Time to get in. Right, where to?' she hissed at Boranov, the last to board the tram this time.

'Fifteen kopecks, my dear.'

'Where *to*?'

'As far as I can go. The terminus — or the end of the world, with you. I like friendly people such as yourself, Lyra Pavlovna.'

'How do you know my name?'

'Your colleague on the number 3 tram told me.'

'The stupid old chatterbox! All right, give me your fare.' She counted it, and looked up warily. 'There's thirty here.'

'The rest is for the way back, Lyrashka.'

'I shall throw you out.'

'No, no, that would be against the rules. Anyone who can pay has a right to public transport unless he misbehaves. And it isn't misbehaving to think the driver's so pretty you can't bear to part from her. I've worked it all out, Lyra Pavlovna: I can spend four roubles riding in your tram until you go off duty. I can look at you for hours, for just four roubles. It's a gift.'

Lyra did not answer. She took fifteen kopecks, dropped the other fifteen on the floor in front of him, and started the tram. Boranov got to know her route through the city very well indeed. At each terminus, he paid another fifteen kopecks for the ride back, and there was nothing Lyra Pavlovna could do about it. She was seething with rage, but her self-control finally broke only when Boranov suddenly disappeared at the original terminus after riding back and forth four times. She waited there in the tram, staring first impatiently and then with lips quivering at the clock, clutching the tram's electric handle, and feeling her heart thump wildly. She ventured to delay her departure by a whole six minutes. Quite inexplicably, she was near tears by the time Boranov finally reappeared and got into the tram, whistling, to offer her his fifteen kopecks.

'For goodness' sake, where were you?' she said huskily.

'Only having a lemonade. Yours is thirsty work, Lyrashka. I don't know how you stand it.'

'We're nine minutes late.'

Boranov sat in his usual seat and crossed his legs. 'Right, off you go, then,' he said, with an affectionate smile which made her heart lurch. She hastily turned her back. 'We can make up the lost time between stops 7 and 10 and then stops 14 and 18,' he told her.

On this fifth journey, Lyra felt as though she were riding on air instead of on her hard driver's seat.

One might have expected that when Lyra Pavlovna came off duty she would walk straight away from Boranov, but no. She got through the formalities of handing over to her colleague driving the next shift as fast as she could, keeping an eye on the street all the time to see if Boranov was still around. Yes, there he was, stretching his legs and rolling a cigarette. He smiled at Lyra as she came towards him, leather bag slung over her shoulder.

'I've been warning my friend there,' she said frostily. 'If you insist on riding back and forth in that tram any more, she's going to call the police.'

'Well, I wouldn't like that, comrade,' said Boranov helpfully. 'I'll deny myself the pleasure of riding in trams, just to please you. Though how I'm to live without the sound of your bell I don't know.'

'Look here, who are you?'

'My name's Kyrill Semyonovich Boranov.'

'I'm not interested in that.'

'Well, you did ask.'

'I only wanted to know what kind of institution you've escaped from.' She took a comb from her bag, passed it quickly through her hair, and looked at her tram setting off with its new driver. 'You seem to have plenty of time on your hands. Well, I'm riding home now, and I hope I never see you again.'

'Riding home? In another tram?'

'No, on my bicycle.'

'Good,' said Boranov. 'I'm an excellent cyclist. I'll pedal you home.'

She got a man's bicycle out of the stands, and slung her big bag over the handlebars. It was an old machine, painted red, and looked very solid. 'Right, where will you sit?' Boranov asked. 'On the crossbar or on the carrier?'

'Oh, I wouldn't dream of sitting on the crossbar. My hair would get in your face, and it smells of rancid soap.'

'Let's forget all that nonsense, shall we, Lyrashka?' said Boranov affectionately. 'Believe me, at this moment I am a truly happy man. You give me that bicycle.'

He took it from her and mounted it, and Lyra sat behind him, her arms round his waist — a necessary precaution if she were not to fall off, and one which gave him great pleasure.

'Right, where to?' he asked, his voice husky. 'Georgia? The Amur? The Arctic? Across the taiga? Just say the word and we'll go anywhere, Lyra Pavlovna.'

'Home to Poltekava Street. Our building's painted yellow, and you have just about nineteen minutes left.'

'Before what?'

'Before my father gives you a black eye. I'm really going to enjoy that.'

Naturally, Lyra's father did not give Kyrill Semyonovich a black eye, although he was fairly cool in his manner at first; the Sharenkovs had never known Lyra to bring a man home before. Her mother, Marya Ivanovna, steered her into the kitchen for a private word with her, while her father, Pavlov Ignatovich, regretted that all he could offer his guest was cold tea flavoured with synthetic lemon extract. He warmed to Boranov, however, on learning that he was just out of the Army.

'How are things up at the front?' he asked. 'We hear so few details here. Can it be much longer before the Germans give up? Tell us, Kyrill Semyonovich, what does the situation look like from the point of view of the men at the front?'

Boranov told his host what he wanted to hear. The march to Berlin had begun, though half of European Russia, Poland and Prussia still lay in between the men and their goal. 'But nothing can hold us back now,' he said. 'Yes, we shall crush the Germans. I just wish I was still with my friends.'

'You'll recover from your wound all right here, Kyrill Semyonovich.'

'Yes, but the bullet lodged in my shoulder won't go away. Apparently they can't operate; I'm told I just have to live with the wretched thing.'

Boranov looked up as Marya and Lyra came out of the kitchen, with a tall tin of round biscuits which were evidently kept as emergency provisions, just in time to hear this. Lyra Pavlovna's cheeks were rather red, and she seemed to have been having a heated discussion with her mother in the kitchen.

'Oh, goodness,' she exclaimed softly, concern in her eyes. 'A bullet? You didn't tell me about that.'

'I didn't get a chance, did I?' Boranov grinned broadly. 'I was having to fight for my seat in the tram the whole time.'

'Was it as crowded as all that?' asked Sharenkov unsuspectingly. 'You should have told them you were a war veteran, invalided out, and they'd have made way for you.'

Boranov caught a pleading glance from Lyra, and nodded almost imperceptibly. Don't worry, my little pigeon, I won't give you away; my ride with you was the best tram ride of my life.

'And why have they sent you to Moscow?' asked Marya.

'To find work here.' Boranov took one of the biscuits, which were rather hard. 'They need everyone for the war effort.'

'What's your job in peacetime?' Sharenkov placed his fingertips together. He was an elegant, slim, grey-haired man of aristocratic appearance. Several of his architectural plans were tacked to the walls – plans for superb edifices which he would never build; they were especially dear to him. Beside them, in a simple wooden frame, hung Marya's teaching diploma, and there was also a commendation of Sharenkov from the Architectural Academy, praising his work on the design of a new Institute of Technology.

'I'm a biologist,' said Boranov.

He was not entirely happy about this, and had said so to Colonel von Renneberg. But Canaris's experts had found out that Kuehenberg's best subject at school had been biology, and only his responsibility to the family estates, and then the war, had kept him from studying the subject at university. 'They respect biologists in Russia,' Renneberg had said. 'You may find a job where you have plenty of freedom of movement, and what more could you ask for?'

However, Sharenkov said thoughtfully, 'A biologist. H'm. I don't know just what use they could make of you at the moment. What exactly is your line?'

'Breeding.' Lyra Pavlovna blushed, compressing her lips, her eyes begging him not to say anything outrageous, but her parents merely nodded. 'Plant breeding, that is,' said Boranov, avoiding Lyra's eyes. 'We bred nineteen new sub-species of orchids in Kazan.'

'Well, one doesn't win a war that way,' remarked Sharenkov. 'The things people do in peacetime – as if Russia didn't have enough roses and carnations and sunflowers of her own, without new orchids. My dear Kyrill Semyonovich, I'm afraid your biological qualifications may not get you very far just now. What do you expect?'

'I'm prepared for disappointments.'

'I think you'd better be.' Sharenkov rose, went into the bedroom, and soon came back with a little silver box. When he opened it, it proved to be half full of golden yellow tobacco with long fibres. 'Oriental,' said Pavlov Ignatovich. 'I was given two packets of it by a Turk with some unpronounceable name who visited the Academy in 1939. This is the last of it. So let's roll ourselves a good thick cigarette each, and get down to thinking about a job for you, Kyrill Semyonovich.'

And Boranov realized, to his great delight, that he had been accepted as a member of the family.

Little Nikolai Antonovich Pleyin, formerly Alexander Dallburg, flew from Stettin military airfield and had no trouble, until his plane approached its target-area. Then the pilot pointed down through the pitch dark. He flew lower, down through a blanket of cloud, and glided silently through the night. Below them lay a shimmering band of light going west: a chain of tiny, winking stars. It was the Yaroslavl-to-Moscow highway, carrying convoy after convoy of vehicles. Vast quantities of supplies were passing through the country, and men were surging westward with the sole aim of crushing Germany.

'Well, that's our target-area: Pyereslavl-Salyeressky,' said the pilot drily. 'Where d'you fancy landing? On the barrel of a gun or the radiator of a truck?'

'How about the region round Lake Pleyeshchyeyeva, to the north?' asked Pleyin.

'Probably swarming with infantry.'

'Farther on, then. The Nyerl marshes?'

'We can take a look.' The plane climbed again, described a wide arc over the lake and the little River Nyerl, then lost height. Beyond them, they saw the floodlights stabbing the sky at last, groping for the source of the engine noise. It was a pure formality: no one would suspect the presence of a German plane here.

'We're near Mikhailovskoye,' said the pilot. 'Looks all right. I'll go down to the right height for you to jump, OK?'

'OK,' said Pleyin, clutching his parachute harness. Suddenly he thought of Grandchamps-les-Bains on the shores of the North Sea, and the little apartment where he had felt Gabrielle's kisses and heard her voice whispering sweet nothings in his ear. She had been his first real sexual experience: she had taught him that the human body was capable of all kinds of amazing variations in its expression of love.

'Ready?' asked the pilot.

Pleyin nodded. 'Ready.' He went back to the hatch, where an NCO was sitting on a canvas stool. 'Right,' said Pleyin.

The hatch opened. The wind almost tore Pleyin out of the aircraft of its own accord, and he fell out with his arms spread wide, enjoying the sensation of free flight. He could not feel the speed at which he was falling, and was almost sorry to pull the cord. The crack of the opening parachute struck at his eardrums. Then came the jerk as the parachute unfolded, and his body felt its own weight again, dangling in the harness. Well, I've done it, he thought. Nikolai Antonovich, you're on your way down, so now you must forget everything that went before. Don't think of anything but Moscow and Stalin. Think Russian. You're Pleyin, a music student who was going to be a singer, who doesn't like the war and never wanted to be a hero.

An area of woodland, then a wide meadow with long grass. . . . Pleyin kicked out, drew up his legs, and landed on the ground in a crouching position. It felt remarkably soft. He rolled over, the way he had learned, and lay there listening intently. The night around him was silent, but for the silk of his parachute rustling faintly in the tall, coarse grasses.

Pleyin hauled the parachute in, crumpled it into a thick bundle, and put it under his head like a pillow. He looked up at the starry sky with its drifting cloud-bands and drew a map of his surroundings in his mind.

Mikhailovskoye to the west, where he could reach the road from Uglich on the Volga to Moscow. At Zagorsk the road would join the Yaroslavl highway. Yes, Pleyin decided he had landed in an ideal spot. Finding that huge column of supplies on the road had really been a stroke of luck. He could join it on its way to Moscow. One man, among so many, would not be noticed, whereas a solitary traveller walking across country might well be stopped and questioned.

After resting for a while, Pleyin carried his parachute into the wood, hid it among the bushes, and brushed down his clothes. Then he set off. He found a farm path, rutted by tractor wheels, leading west, and he went along it. No houses here, he thought. No, there won't be any till I get near the road, assuming this is a huge State farm administered by a sovkhoz.

It took him three hours to reach houses: he saw them ahead,

in the twilight, and sat down behind a bush to wait. When the first few vehicles came down the road — two flat farm-carts drawn by thin old horses stumbling over their own feet — he rose, checked his appearance again, to make sure there was nothing unusual about it, and then walked confidently towards the village. It was a small one, the houses built of stone, and not the traditional wooden huts with their carved gables and window-frames. A functional, modern place, obviously part of a big sovkhoz. Milda Ivanovna had not mentioned it, and he did not think he had seen it on the maps.

He said a polite 'Good morning' to a peasant passing by in a cart drawn by a tired old horse. The man looked at the stranger, and stopped his cart.

'Where are you going?' he asked. 'And where d'you come from?'

'I'm going to Moscow.'

'On foot?' The old peasant blew his nose vigorously into the air, and cackled with ancient laughter. 'On foot! Well, they say there's one born every minute. Why do you want to go to Moscow?'

'I've just come from the front.'

'On foot, too? Went the wrong way, didn't you, if you've come from the front? Should've been marching to Berlin, and here you are in Dushansk instead.'

'So this is Dushansk?' said Pleyin. 'I've seen prettier places.'

'Yes, some clever Party member designed it, ten years back. Supposed to be going to be a real town, till they discovered there wasn't enough of something or other — we never did find out what. Still, there were the houses, so we took 'em over from the sovkhoz.' The peasant looked at Pleyin suspiciously. 'How come you're here in Dushansk?'

'It's quite a story, comrade. I dare say you'd hardly believe it.'

'Well, jump up, then.' The man slapped the wooden seat. 'I'm making for Mikhailovskoye, though whether I'll ever get there with this old nag I don't know.'

Pleyin quickly climbed up beside the old man. The horse ambled on. The peasant assured him that, in Mikhailovskoye, he would be likely to find a car to give him a lift to Moscow. 'But what brought you back from the front?'

223

'It's my eyes. Trouble with my vision. A very rare ocular disorder,' said Pleyin.

'A what? Very rare?' The peasant peered at him.

'That's right, little father.'

'The name's Avraam Porfirivich.'

'Well, it started like this, Avraam Porfirivich. There was I behind my gun in a crater, when I suddenly saw triplets coming. Three officers, all of them second lieutenants, all with the same face, the same uniform, the same decorations, not to mention the same voice and the same movements. And I went on seeing triplets everywhere. Would you believe a whole battalion made up of no one but triplets?' Pleyin sighed. 'So I ended up being examined by army doctors—and they were triplets, too. They gave me injections, they shone lights into my eyes. And there were three professors who were triplets, showing me off to a whole lot of students, telling them I was an unusual variant of monocular diplopy, in fact I was the first case ever known of triplopy.'

'Er?' said the peasant, staring at Pleyin, baffled.

'And that's not all.' Pleyin raised a forefinger dramatically. 'They called it a hysterical accommodation reaction—you see, there weren't really any triplets at all.'

'There weren't? But I thought you said. . . . ?'

'Amazing, isn't it, little father? I don't blame you if you're surprised. Took me weeks to get used to the idea myself. But then the doctors decided I was too dangerous to be in the Red Army, seeing three people where there was only one, so they said I must go off to Moscow and see a specialist.'

'I get it. I get the idea,' cried Avraam Porfirivich, light dawning. 'And it's on account of seeing everything three times over you ended up in Dushansk. Well, fancy that.'

Pleyin was not called upon for further explanation. Avraam Porfirivich was so fascinated by his story that he stopped and offered Pleyin a share of his breakfast—bread, goat's milk cheese, and kvass from a battered tin flask.

Then, after another three versts of slow progress, they suddenly found the narrow road barred by an open, brown-painted motor vehicle of curious construction. Four uniformed figures were standing around it, arguing. They seemed to be very angry, and one of them, a slim young man, kicked one of its back tyres as if it were a stubborn ox.

'Oh, God help us,' said Avraam quietly, crossing himself. 'Police. Son, I think we're in for trouble. They won't believe all that about you and the triplets.'

'Oh, I have a medical certificate here with me,' said Pleyin. 'Covered with rubber stamps. I'm a special case.'

They approached, got down from the cart, and stood there looking at an American jeep, far superior to the German variety. The policemen looked at the old horse and grinned.

'Where are you going?' asked one of the men.

'To Mikhailovskoye,' said the old man.

'Unharness that horse.'

'Why, comrades?'

'It can take this thing to the garage.'

'But I'm on the sovkhoz's business,' protested Avraam.

'We'll give you a receipt.'

'It's urgent,' cried Avraam.

'Well, our business is more urgent,' bellowed the policeman. 'Come on, get that horse out of the shafts.'

'What's the matter with your car, then?' asked Pleyin amiably.

The leader of the police patrol, a lieutenant, the one who had kicked the back wheel, turned round. Pleyin caught his breath and felt the palms of his hands go damp. The lieutenant was a woman. He saw a face which must have Tartar blood in it: she had high cheek-bones and a passionate mouth. Black hair flowed out from under her cap, lying against the olive skin of her temples. Her eyes were a dark, flickering amber colour, the pupils stamped into them like great dark holes.

'It's not going,' she said in an extraordinarily musical voice.

'Why don't we look at the engine?' he suggested.

'Comrades, we appear to have come across a genius.' Her sarcasm hurt, and he felt himself begin to go red. She kicked the tyre again, and put her hands on her hips. 'Well, go on, then, comrade. It's an American vehicle, damn the thing.'

'I can see that.'

'A "jeep" they call it.' The lieutenant waited until one of the policemen with her had opened the bonnet. 'Right, so you're a Lenin Prizewinner in technology, I'm sure; you can tell us what's

225

wrong. Just looking at it gives one the horrors. The Americans make everything differently.'

Pleyin went up to the jeep, bent over the engine, and investigated the cables and connectors inside. Then he straightened up, and asked mildly, 'How did it stop?'

'Is there more than one way to stop?' The alarming lieutenant laughed. 'All of a sudden it wasn't going any more.'

'Who was driving?'

'I was.' The lieutenant's delicate chin jutted, and her Asiatic eyes narrowed even further; she obviously resented any implied criticism of women drivers. 'And I have been driving for six years,' she added.

'Did it smell?' asked Pleyin.

'Oh, for heaven's sake! As if a bad smell was enough to stop a car.'

'Did it dance about the road?'

'This is a motor vehicle, comrade, not a ballerina.'

'There's an ignition cable burned out,' said Pleyin, closing the bonnet. 'But, if there wasn't any smell, maybe that wasn't the trouble.'

'Are you a motor mechanic?'

'Not exactly, but I know a bit about electrics.' He produced his toolkit from Eberswalde.

'It did smell bad for a moment. Kind of a smell of hot rubber,' said one of the policemen, avoiding the lieutenant's eyes. 'That could have been it.'

'That *was* it.' He bent over the engine again. 'By the way, my name's Nikolai Antonovich Pleyin.'

'So who's interested?' The lieutenant drummed her fingers on the jeep. They were long, beautifully shaped fingers, and their pink nails had big half-moons. Her amber eyes sparkled dangerously. 'Can you actually do anything helpful, instead of talking nonsense?'

'I can try. Got any spare cables?'

'How should I know?'

'Comrade,' said Pleyin boldly, but careful to avoid her glance, 'you may have spent six years behind the wheel, but you should have spent at least a year under the bonnet, getting to know the insides of an engine.'

226

Avraam Porfirivich chuckled, but instantly fell silent when the lieutenant snapped, 'Nikolai Antonovich, you are under arrest. From now on you do what I say. Right—in a word, can you repair this jeep?'

'In a word, Comrade Lieutenant, yes.' Pleyin did look at her now. He felt his heart thud violently. Surely there never could have been, never could be again, such a beautiful woman.

'Then get on with it,' she said coldly. 'If all mechanics talked so much—'

'I'm not a mechanic, comrade. I told you.'

'What are you, then?'

'I was training to be an opera singer.'

'A singer?' The lieutenant looked at Pleyin again, unsure whether or not to believe him. 'Then what were you doing riding in this cart?'

'It's a long story. I'll tell you when I've got this thing going again.'

Here Avraam Porfirivich started to insist that, if he did not go on his way to Mikhailovskoye, he would be in trouble with the sovkhoz.

'Oh, let the old fool go,' said the lieutenant impatiently. Pleyin was hanging over the engine, cutting a piece of lighting cable to graft on and use as an ignition cable; naturally there had not been any spare cables when he found and investigated the car's toolkit.

'Not without my friend here,' said the old man bravely. But Pleyin called out, still head downwards, 'I'll follow you, little father. You go on ahead.'

Avraam had long since disappeared along the road, leaving only a pile of horse droppings as if by way of protest, when Pleyin finished repairing the engine. He leaned against the radiator, rubbing his oily hands, and said, beaming happily, 'There we are.'

'At last.' The lieutenant got into the driver's seat. Pleyin rubbed his hands on the grass by the roadside, but the oil would not come off. The engine roared, and the jeep shuddered violently.

'Don't give it too much gas,' yelled Pleyin. 'And remember, that repair's only a temporary job.'

'Get in,' she ordered, looking straight ahead. The policemen got into the jeep, grinning gratefully at Pleyin. 'You, too,' she added.

'Am I still under arrest?'

'Did you hear me say anything to the contrary?' She gestured to the policeman beside her, who changed over to the back seat, and then she looked at Pleyin. 'Come on, get in. You *do* want to go to Mikhailovskoye, right? Or are you keen on hiking?'

'Well, this is a new experience for me.' He sat down beside her, holding his oily hands well away from him. 'I never rode in a jeep before. By the way, you'll remember there's only one head-light working now, won't you? I used the other one's cable.'

'I'm dumping this damn jeep in Mikhailovskoye anyway. I'm not taking the wretched thing on to Moscow.'

Pleyin looked at his hands, feeling his stomach turn over. Moscow! She was going to Moscow. Now, how could he persuade her to take him all the way? He could hardly arrive in the city more safely than along with a police patrol.

'I have to go to Moscow myself,' he said.

'I don't believe you.' She looked sideways at him. 'You're a liar.'

'Why, comrade?'

'I don't even believe you can sing!'

'Want to hear me? What would you like me to sing?'

'I wouldn't.'

'I could give you Tamino's first aria from *The Magic Flute* — "O loveliness beyond compare". Or how about *Manon* — "Ah! Begone, vision fair!" Take your pick, comrade.'

'My name's Lyudmila Dragonovna Tcherskassya,' she said suddenly, out of the blue. Pleyin nodded. But of course, he thought. Lyudmila Dragonovna Tcherskassya — what a marvellous sound!

'What are you going to Moscow for?' she asked.

'The army doctors sent me off to see a specialist in Moscow, about my eyesight. I'll admit I did go the long way round, to visit my uncle — he's my only living relative, and I don't suppose I'll see him alive again. Actually, you took me by surprise as I was setting off for Moscow again, Lyudmila Dragonovna, and it's just my bad luck if you report me.'

Lieutenant Tcherskassya looked at him with interest, her amber eyes like liquid honey in the sun falling full on her face. 'Are you sick, then, Nikolai Antonovich?'

'I see three of everything. At least, I did. That was what they diagnosed, Lyudmila Dragonovna, and until four days ago it was right. But since then I've been seeing normally again. I guess it was the knock on the head I got from one of the low beams at my uncle's place. I practically stunned myself on it, but when I came round I was fine.'

'I don't believe a word of it,' said Lyudmila Dragonovna curtly.

'Well, I have all the medical reports here. They said I was a phenomenon. The point is, what do I do in Moscow now I don't suffer from triplopy any more?'

'Suffer from what?'

'It's a new word. They had to invent it. I've been privileged to enrich the vocabulary of medical science.'

'If you're not careful, I personally shall knock you over the head and start you seeing triple all over again,' said Lyudmila Dragonovna, in her strange, musical voice. 'Oh, do shut up, Nikolai Antonovich. I mean, it's not as if you had an unprepossessing exterior — it's a shame to hear such nonsense coming out of it.'

Shortly afterwards, a curious sight might have been seen on the way to Mikhailovskoye: a jeep bouncing crazily along the road, containing four police officers and one civilian — a young man singing operatic arias, and singing them so well that, after the first two, Lieutenant Tcherskassya took her foot off the accelerator and drove more gently, so as not to miss a note. Arias from *Tosca*, *Il Trovatore*, *Madame Butterfly*, *La Bohème*, *Carmen* — and after each one the policemen applauded loudly and asked for more. So Pleyin sang his way on through the lyric tenor repertoire until they reached Mikhailovskoye.

Here they had to be dignified and official again, so they drove to the local police station in silence. Just before they got there, Lieutenant Tcherskassya asked Pleyin, 'How are you off for money?'

'I have enough to see me to Moscow. And once I get there I'm supposed to go to a hospital, and no doubt they'll shut me up.'

'Why should they shut you up, Nikolai Antonovich?'

'For not seeing triple any more. The doctors will think I'm off my head.'

229

'And not just the doctors.' She braked, resting her elbows on the wheel. 'D'you want to find somewhere to stay the night yourself, or would you rather spend it at the station here?'

'I'm under arrest, aren't I? Do I have any choice?'

Lieutenant Tcherskassya thrust out her pretty lower lip. 'Oh, get out of this jeep,' she snapped. 'I really don't know why I'm bothering with you. Let's see your papers.'

Pleyin produced them, bedecked with all their rubber stamps, and handed them to Lyudmila Dragonovna, who glanced cursorily through them and gave them back. It seemed he had been telling the truth about his triple vision, which only went to prove that fact is stranger than fiction. Mollified, Lyudmila Dragonovna smiled at him. 'Well, where do you want to stay?'

'Where are you spending the night yourself, Lyudmila Dragonovna?'

'At the station here.'

'Then I will, too.'

For a moment she hesitated, her eyes darker, and slanting more than usual. But all she said was, 'Well, we shan't be seeing much of each other.'

The officer in charge of Mikhailovskoye police station was a portly old retired lieutenant, recalled to service because of the absence of so many young men at the front. He welcomed his guests with open arms; there was very little of interest going on in this town, though convoys had been passing through almost uninterruptedly for the last three weeks. The three male policemen carried straight on to Moscow with one of the convoys, but as she had to dispose of the jeep she was staying the night, and Pleyin himself was given an empty cell to sleep in. An attempt had been made to make it look like an ordinary bedroom, with a couple of white blankets, an enamel bowl, and a wardrobe that seemed to have been left over from the time of the Tsars, but the place still looked like a police cell, with whitewashed walls and a barred window near the ceiling.

It was not true, as it turned out, that he and Lieutenant Tcherskassya would not be seeing much of each other. Once she had taken the jeep to a garage and got hold of a new vehicle, an open green Ford, she walked around the little town with Pleyin, arousing great alarm in the breasts of the local people, who took her

230

for a newly appointed police commandant accompanied by a member of the Secret Police. And in the evening Lieutenant Dychkin produced roast chicken, and cauliflower garnished with chopped hard-boiled egg, and introduced them to his wife, a homely soul as stout as her husband, with her hair in a bun. She was very timid, and disappeared as soon as she had served the meal.

Dychkin quite soon got drunk on his home-brewed blackberry wine. He cursed the war, drank Stalin's health, and then tottered off to bed. Pleyin, too, rose to go back to his cell, but Lyudmila Dragonovna remained seated, her long legs in their tight boots stretched out. She was almost lying in an old armchair, turning her glass of blackberry wine in her hands. She had opened the collar of her uniform jacket, and her black hair tumbled down over her neck, brushing her cheeks. Her amber eyes were dark and shining. Pleyin felt the blood throb in his temples. Her unbuttoned jacket showed firm, mature and very feminine breasts under her blouse.

'Sleep well, then, Lyudmila Dragonovna,' he said huskily.

She nodded, looking at the wine in her glass, and asked as if casually, 'How old are you, Kolka?'

Much to his embarrassment, he felt himself blush; it was not something he could help.

'Twenty,' he said.

'Nine years younger than me.'

'I'd never have thought so. I was wondering how anyone so young could possibly be a lieutenant in the police force.'

'Oh, don't talk like that, Kolka. I don't care for that sort of compliment.' She sipped the light-red wine, holding it up to the light. 'You're twenty. I was twenty in 1935. How long ago that seems now. I was studying archaeology at Alma Ata.' She laughed briefly. 'I wanted to dig up the past of Kazakhstan. Ah, it's wonderful to be so young.'

'Why didn't you go on digging?' asked Pleyin. He sat down opposite her in an old basket-chair, a table between them like a barrier.

Lyudmila Dragonovna tossed back her black hair, and it swirled around her fine-boned face. 'I met Georgi.'

'I see.'

'No, you don't. Georgi Ivanovich Amelyev. Haven't you heard of him? Doesn't the name mean anything to you? No, why should it? You were only twelve at the time. He was the best runner in all Russia. The 800 metres, the 1500 metres, the 3000 metres. Unbeatable. He had such curly fair hair. Every day I saw him I almost died of love for him. Every kiss was like lightning striking, every embrace consumed me.' She sipped her wine again. 'That was 1936. Hitler was holding the Olympic Games in Berlin, to demonstrate his power. Georgi was one of the athletes going to represent the Soviet Union. He trained every day in the stadium at Alma Ata, and I sat there beside the track timing him. Four days before he was to leave for Berlin, on his last training run, he fell and broke his ankle. A day later, the doctors told him he'd never run again; his ankle would be stiff for life. When they broadcast the opening of the Games on the radio, and the fanfares sounded, and an athlete ran into the stadium with the Olympic torch, Georgi stabbed himself to death in his hospital bed.' She drank the wine left in her glass and handed it to Pleyin. 'Pour us some more, will you, Kolka?'

Pleyin poured the wine, and sat perched on the edge of the table. The barrier between them seemed lower. 'That must have been a dreadful shock for you, Lyudmila Dragonovna.'

'I was numb at first. I couldn't bear to stay on in Alma Ata. I went to Moscow. My uncle, my mother's brother, was a major in the police force there. I stayed with him, and wept till I had no tears left. Then he introduced me to his command headquarters, and I joined the police.'

'And you never married?' said Pleyin.

'Who would I have married?' She laughed, with that haunting musical tone. 'Whenever I look into a man's eyes, all I see there is greed. Lust. I've never met another man who asked who *I* was, what I thought. They were only interested in my body.'

Pleyin decided to have another glass of wine himself, less because he wanted it than because he could turn away from Lyudmila to pour it, and prevent her seeing a similar look in his own eyes. As he poured the wine, he asked, 'If you're stationed in Moscow, what were you doing when I met you?'

'Oh, I had to escort a convoy of prisoners of war to Ivanovo.

232

German officers. They'd been questioned in Moscow and were being sent on.'

Pleyin felt a chill around his heart.

'Can I ask you something?' he said.

'Go on, Kolka.' The room was hot; she took off her uniform jacket and tossed it on to the table. Her breasts were taut against her green blouse. She thrust back her black hair with both hands, and her dark amber eyes gleamed in the light from the electric bulb overhead. 'What do you want to know? Another glass of wine, and I dare say I shall be telling you about all the men who've tried to get into my bed — or did get into it. Oh, why am I going on like this, Kolka? You're so young, it's just like some kind of fairy-tale to you, isn't it?'

Pleyin breathed deeply, wounded by the realization that she did not regard him as a proper man.

'I'm not interested in the men you've had,' he said brusquely. 'I only wanted to know if you'll take me to Moscow with you, or whether I should try my luck getting a lift on a truck tomorrow, or go by rail.'

'Oh, I'll take you, Kolka.' Lyudmila hauled herself out of the armchair, and Pleyin hurried to support her, because she was swaying on her feet. She laid her head on his shoulder. He was not much taller than she was, and he could feel her lips on his throat. 'That wine of Dychkin's is strong stuff,' she said, her words slurred. 'D'you know where my room is?'

'No.'

'But you know where you're sleeping?'

'In a cell.'

She clung to him; her legs were giving way beneath her, her arms wound round his neck, her lips wandered over his throat and cheek. 'Take me away Kolka,' she said, her mouth quivering. 'Oh, my dear, young little Kolka. . . .'

Clasping her hips and lifting her slightly, he helped her away. She clung close to him. Somehow he got her to his cell, laid her on the wooden bedstead, and closed the door. It was hot here, too, and Lyudmila Dragonovna stretched out on the bed, unbuttoning her green blouse and raising one leg in the air. 'Will you take my boots off, Kolka?'

Pleyin did, freeing her lovely legs from the soft leather. Then he sat down on a stool, once again with a table between himself and Lieutenant Tcherskassya. She put her hands behind her head, laughing now and then for no obvious reason. Her green blouse was wide open. She wore a plain white bra, and her skin shone like dull gold.

'Sing me something,' she said suddenly.

'Here? Now?'

'Yes. I want you to sing.' She looked at him with wide eyes that no longer seemed so Asiatic. 'Please sing to me, Kolka.'

Pleyin went over to the bed, sat down by Lyudmila's outstretched legs, and saw that she was wriggling her toes; she did not stop till he took them in his hands. 'Oh, that's good,' she said softly. 'Now, sing.'

His eyes travelled over her breasts, her throat, her chin, her half-open mouth. 'If you make love to me,' she said, her voice tender, 'I'll have you shot at dawn!'

'Well, I think I might like to survive. What shall I sing, Lyudmila Dragonovna?'

'Anything. Just *sing*, damn it!'

He nodded, took a deep breath, massaged her restless toes, and sang, *sotto voce,* Nemorino's aria from *L'Elisir d'amore.* He did not look at her until he began on the second stanza, and then saw that she was fast asleep, a smile on her delicately shaped mouth, her fingers buried in her tangled hair.

Pleyin stopped singing, slowly let go of Lyudmila's toes, tiptoed back to his stool and sat down. Weary beyond belief, he looked at her. No, said Pleyin to himself, closing his eyes. No, Lyudmila. I'm here to kill Stalin. To change the course of world history. That's what they expect of me. I'm here to save Germany. Oh, Christ, I'm scared. . . .

And he fell asleep.

They reached Moscow next afternoon. Lieutenant Tcherskassya had become very official again. Pleyin had made sure she had the chance of creeping quietly out of his cell at daybreak when he went to wash and, sure enough, on his return the bed was empty. Later, at breakfast, they hardly looked at each other. They made desultory conversation, and remained silent for long periods on the way to Moscow. Much of the time they were caught up in slow-moving convoys of trucks carrying military supplies. But, as they were driving down the broad Yaroslavskoye Prospect, Lyudmila braked by the roadside, stopped, and turned to Pleyin.

'What are you proposing to do now?' she asked briskly.

He shrugged his shoulders. 'We're in Moscow. Thank you very much. Just drop me off, and I'll manage for myself.'

'Where are you going to stay?'

'In a psychiatric clinic, I imagine. Now I don't see things triple any more, the doctors won't be very keen on me.'

'No, they'll send you straight back to the front.'

'Very likely. A healthy young man certainly should be fighting for victory.'

'You wait here in the car,' said Lieutenant Tcherskassya brusquely, 'and we'll see how things turn out.'

They drove the brief way to Lyudmila's own police station, and Pleyin waited in the car while she disappeared into the building. Twenty minutes later she came out again.

'I got two days' leave,' she said. 'Bonus for getting the job done to everyone's satisfaction. So let's leave the car here for them, and we'll take the Metro.'

'Where to?'

'Turgenevskaya Station. We get out there and go to Markhlevskogo Street.'

'Sure, but why?'

'There's an apartment building opposite the Polish Church. My place is on the second floor. I have three small rooms.'

'Three rooms. That's luxury.'

She laughed a little. 'I told you, my uncle's a major in the police force.'

'Lyudmila Dragonovna, are you inviting me back to your apartment?'

'I think we should discuss this eye trouble of yours, Kolka. There's plenty of time for you to report to the doctors tomorrow.'

He nodded silently.

A little later he was in her small living-room. The only ornament was a huge picture of Stalin in a massive wooden frame. The furniture was light beechwood, upholstered in green with a yellow pattern: the place was bright but impersonal, a machine for living in rather than a home.

235

'Don't you like it?' asked Lyudmila, changing out of her uniform jacket. She put on a full Bukhara jacket gleaming with silk embroidery; she had left her boots and breeches on.

Pleyin stood looking at the picture of Stalin in silence. He looked like a benevolent uncle.

'You respect Stalin?' he asked.

'Of course. I'm devoted to him. Where would Russia be today without Stalin and Lenin?'

'Where, indeed?'

Pleyin turned away from the picture, but Lyudmila had already gone into the kitchen, and was taking a dish and several paper bags out of a cupboard.

'What are you doing?' he asked.

'Aren't you hungry? I'm ravenous,' she said. She lit the gas-stove, and looked for an egg-whisk. 'There's no meat in the shops today, but I do have milk and flour and sugar and eggs, so I could make a yeast cake. Would you like that?'

'I'd love it,' he said. They ate the yeast cake steaming hot when it was done, and since Lyudmila had no tea in the house they drank lemonade sweetened with saccharine. Then they sat side by side on a wooden window-seat, looking out at the Polish Church. The street below them was empty, with long evening shadows falling over it.

'We could play some music,' she said.

'We could?'

'I have a gramophone — and thirty-two records. One of them's tango music. Can you dance the tango, Kolka?'

A tricky question. Pleyin thought fast. A loophole in their training here. How widely known was the tango in Russia?

'Can *you*, Lyudmila Dragonovna?' he asked cautiously.

'Well, yes, but most men just look blank when I ask them.'

'I'm afraid I'm looking pretty blank, too.' Pleyin inwardly heaved a sigh of relief. 'We were going to learn dancing at the Opera School — you need to, for the stage — but they got me into uniform before the course began.'

'Then I'll teach you, Kolka.' She jumped up and hauled the gramophone — a large, square wooden box — out of the next room. She wound it up and put on a black shellac disc. And then they danced. Pleyin acted clumsily on purpose, frequently treading on

236

Lyudmila's toes, and asking her to explain the steps repeatedly. They danced three times to each side of the record. It was getting dark, and they did not put on the light; they were surrounded by the twilight of a warm summer night. As if on impulse, they danced into the next room, where a bed stood against the wall. There was a large wardrobe, a round table, two old chairs, and a brass hook from which hung a Chinese dressing-gown, black, with a pattern of huge red flowers and golden tendrils on it. And then they were not dancing to the music any more; their bodies merged together, and found melodies of their own. They fell on the bed. She had already shed her Bukhara jacket, and was pressing Pleyin's hands to her breasts, kissing him and nibbling the base of his throat with her teeth at the same time.

Confused and breathless, he felt her hands and lips everywhere. He lost all sense of reality, and plunged into mists where he heard her voice, close to his ear – 'Darling, I'm burning ... burning! Help me, Kolka, please help me. Don't leave me burning like this.'

His own breath was coming fast now. She collapsed on top of him, burying his face between her breasts, and then rolled over on her back, lying there with arms and legs spread wide, while Pleyin knelt above her.

Afterwards Pleyin fetched more of the over-sweetened lemonade from the next room, and they drank as if parched. Then they caressed each other again, exploring each other's body. Their happiness was idyllic.

'You've been reported missing,' said Lyudmila later, when they were lying side by side. 'You left the front, but you never got to Moscow. You went missing on the way.'

'That could be very dangerous for me, Lyudmilashka.'

'Only if people find out. But no one *will* find out if you're here.'

'No, it's too dangerous, to my mind.' I'd be delivering myself up to her, he thought. She could decide whether I live or die.

'But it's so simple, Kolka,' she said, stroking his genitals skilfully with her fingertips, and he felt himself begin to stir again. He gritted his teeth, and shook his head silently.

'No, it's terribly simple, I promise you,' she said. 'I can bring you a police uniform back from the station.'

The idea struck Pleyin so forcibly that all the unearthly magic around them was dispelled: even Lyudmila's clever fingers could not bring it back. His thoughts were cold and clear.

'That's impossible,' he said.

'No, it isn't. I can easily get hold of an NCO's uniform. You don't think anyone stops a police officer asking to see his papers, do you? They'd be as likely to stop Stalin and ask if he was really Stalin.'

'You'd really do that?' Pleyin leaned over her, kissing her nipples. That could be one way in, he thought. In fact, what could be better? If she brings me a police uniform, she's making herself my accomplice. That will keep the balance between us.

'It's not for long, Kolka.' She wound one leg around his hips, drew him towards her, and sighed deeply. 'Once the war's over, no one will ask where you came from. And it can't go on much longer now. The Germans are already beaten, though they may not know it.'

They stayed there together all night, their bodies merging, falling apart again, melting into passion once more. When the sun shone into the bedroom, Pleyin was lying on his back, exhausted. Lyudmila was sitting cross-legged beside him, watching him, caressing his chest very gently with her forefinger. 'My little Kolka,' she said, like a mother soothing a convalescent child. 'So young – far too young to be shot by the Germans.'

The Haller family was used to its new lodger by now. Wanda had made it plain that Ivanov was not in the same category as the lost dogs she used to bring home.

'Good-looking young fellow,' said the neighbour who had lent the Hallers the mattress for Ivanov to sleep on, when Wanda and Fyodor Panteleyevich had gone off to the Metro station hand in hand, like happy children. 'All that fair hair. Comes from the north, does he?'

'Haven't asked him yet,' said Semyon Tikhinovich, who was on late shift today, but had got up for breakfast, to see his daughter fluttering attentively round Ivanov, even spreading his bread and pouring his tea for him. 'Very polite comrade, anyway; good chess player, too.'

And now, the building job obtained, Fyodor Panteleyevich was on his way to the Kremlin with two trucks of builders' materials and other members of the construction brigade, though he had had to part temporarily from Wanda. However, a foreman, Lumyanov, introduced him to the rest of the party, who were mainly old men or very young boys. Ivanov had only to show off his scar to be accepted.

The moment he had feared, when he had to pass the Kremlin guards, turned out to be sheer farce. Everyone knew the construction workers' trucks, and the drivers only stopped at all as a formality, or for a swift bartering of papyrossi for sausage. There were differences in the rations for the military and the civilian population: manual workers on heavy duties got extra coupons for meat and fats, while the soldiers got more cigarettes. The builders did a good trade in sandwiches, jam, and a spread made of semolina, onions, salt and herbs, poured into small round stoneware pots to set. The soldiers prized this spread, and would give more cigarettes for a pot of it than for a piece of smoked sausage.

Slowly, the trucks drove down the broad road the other side of that high wall, past the Council of Ministers building with its huge cupola, turned to drive past the Church of the Twelve Apostles and the Patriarch's Palace, the astonishing façades of the Cathedrals of the Assumption and the Annunciation, and stopped beside the Great Kremlin Palace, by one of its side-walls. There was scaffolding almost up to the roof here, with poles, ladders, planks and beams stacked in the square beside the Palace of Facets.

Ivanov was the last to get out of the truck. He looked around. It was a clear, warm day; the golden cupolas of the Kremlin churches were dazzlingly bright, and the many hundreds of windows in the palace shone like mirrors. Isolated military patrols stood around. Limousines carrying high-ranking officers drove into the Kremlin through the gate of the Borovitzky Tower and up to the door of the great administrative building, where they discharged their cargo of men wearing broad epaulettes and the ribbons of their orders, and went off to their parking-places.

So this is where the fate of the world is decided, thought Ivanov. Behind that magnificent façade lie the controls of a power that calls itself invincible. In fact, he was less impressed by what he saw than he had expected. His training in Eberswalde had been so intensive that, standing here inside the Kremlin for the first time, Ivanov almost felt at home. Why, I could find my way around the place with my eyes shut, he thought. I know every corner, every angle, every path, every little tower and niche in the walls. We even learned the position of the groups of trees and bushes off by heart from the hundreds of detailed photographs of the Kremlin we had to put together like a jigsaw puzzle. The place isn't strange to me at all. I know my way around the tangle of little courtyards, the stairways and corridors, the side-entrances, the underground labyrinths. No one had asked just where Milda Ivanovna got her detailed knowledge of the Kremlin, and Canaris had instructed Renneberg to ask no more questions than was necessary. 'She knows the place all right,' the Intelligence people had said. 'In fact, her knowledge is phenomenal. There's a good deal we can't even verify ourselves, not having the information. For instance, a secret way out of Stalin's own quarters, supposed to be known only to a handful of trusted men. However, it's known to us, too, now. But Fräulein Kabakova doesn't answer questions on the subject of where she gets her information, so all we can do is trust her when she offers it.'

Ivanov jumped. The sturdy foreman, Lumyanov, had come up beside him and was chuckling.

'Quite a sight, eh?' he said. 'You wouldn't see things like this anywhere else. They can't keep their secrets from us. Up there, on the fifth platform of the scaffolding, nineteenth window from the left, you can see the officers having a pee. And farther down, twenty-third window from the right, are the secretaries' offices. Two weeks ago, we were all clustering on that bit of scaffolding like a swarm of bees, comrade. It was nearly dark, but we could still see a major with his trousers down, bending a little piece with dark curly hair over a chair. It's a good job, this, comrade. People trust us. We're picked men; we have to be — we can see into every room in the place from our scaffolding.'

'Yes, that's quite something, Comrade Lumyanov,' said Ivanov, as if much impressed. 'You mean we can see all the top brass?'

'Marshal Budienny was here yesterday. And Zhukov three days ago. We see Beria every day. And Molotov — he's practically an old friend. The other day he'd put his pince-nez down somewhere and couldn't find it, so Comrade Femyav, up on the scaffolding there, tapped on the pane and called out, "On the bookcase to your left, comrade!" And Molotov put the pince-nez on and called back, "Thank you, comrade!" Yes, we really get to know them in this job.'

'What about Stalin?' asked Ivanov, keeping his voice casual. 'Do you see Stalin, too?'

'Not very often. He's been seen three times lately, though not by me. Comrade Vishnovsky found himself looking Stalin straight in the eyes. He was so surprised he couldn't move. They were right opposite each other, face to face, only the window between them. Stalin waved his hand for Comrade Vishnovsky to go away, so Comrade Vishnovsky saluted, up there on the scaffolding, and went off. Couldn't eat a thing all day, he was so excited, and he's been a nervous wreck ever since. We had to take him off the pointing up here and give him a job mixing concrete.' Lumyanov patted Ivanov's shoulder. 'You see, you'll be needing good strong nerves here.'

'Don't worry. If I ever see Stalin, I shan't fall off the scaffolding in alarm. I'll get on with my job all right,' said Ivanov.

That day they were putting up scaffolding outside the windows of some more secretaries' offices, the men indulging in antics which had the girls at their desks inside squealing and giggling. Ivanov worked hard, hauling up planks and nailing boards together for the platforms. In so doing, he glanced into several rooms, and found himself coming to offices where army personnel or civil servants sat looking very busy, phoning, writing, reading letters, receiving visitors. There was a conference going on in one big room with three windows. A large map hung on the wall, and a general was explaining something in considerable detail to the officers present.

The map aroused Ivanov's curiosity. It showed the area between Polozk and Gomel, and extended all the way to Warsaw and Königsberg. There were red circles on it, and lines and arrows, all pointing west, and then bending aside in two different directions, only to curve back round and meet again.

Our central sector, Ivanov realized. With the Army Group Centre under Field-Marshal von Busch. The very heart of our front line—and what that map shows is the planned annihilation of our armies. According to the red marks on that map, there could, he realized, be no escape for the German forces now. The Russians would be driving huge wedges between their already thin lines. The first aim of the offensive was already determined; past Minsk, the circle closed, while the thrust went on northwards towards Lithuania and south through the Pripet marshes to Brest. A battle of encirclement, and one of vast extent.

Ivanov clung to his scaffolding, staring at the map and the general standing there calmly explaining it. He felt the blood beat fast in his throat. When is it going to start? he wondered. Or has it already begun? Right at the front of the map, encircled by two fat red arrows, he saw the town of Mogilev. And three numbers: 33A, 49A and 50A. Good God—three Soviet armies against Mogilev alone. How well he knew the German positions there: the bunkers and advanced posts connected by narrow communication-trenches and, behind the front line, the bases, the staff head-quarters, a few artillery divisions, some anti-aircraft guns, a company of tanks with very little petrol—the exhausted German 4th Army, half of it made up of sketchily trained boys brought in from the Reich, crouching there in holes in the ground, home-sickness in their eyes, wincing at every shot.

Ivanov thought of the Mogilev field-hospital from which he had been summoned to Eberswalde. And Elfriede, the lovely Germanic blonde who thought he was the author of one of Hölderlin's poems and who wore one of his fair curls between her warm breasts. Better get out fast, Elfriede. And all of the rest of you, friends—run for it. Elfriede, soft, warm Elfriede, no doubt you'll be serving lunch in your ward about now, with no idea of what's brewing a few kilometres to the east. Run, Elfriede, run....

The foreman Lumyanov swung himself up beside Ivanov and looked over his shoulder.

'Briefing session,' he said knowledgeably. 'I wonder why here. Never seen one held there before. The rooms were used for a museum. The secretaries are new, too.'

'How long have you been working in the Kremlin?'

'Over ten years. There's always pointing and repairs to be done.' Lumyanov was proud of it. Workmen came and went, but he had been on duty as a foreman in the Kremlin all this time. 'It's like home to me.'

'Does Stalin ever come to briefing sessions like that?'

242

'Stalin? No, and he wouldn't come here. He has his offices in the Praesidium of the Supreme Soviet building. We drove past it this morning.'

Ivanov nodded. He had the plans of the administrative and governmental buildings in his head just as clearly as the ground-plan of the Great Kremlin Palace, and he knew exactly where Stalin's offices lay, but on seeing that even the historic rooms of the Palace had been brought into use for military purposes he had wondered whether Stalin, too, might be working elsewhere.

'He never leaves the building, I suppose?'

'Hardly ever.' Lumyanov laughed. 'Really keen to get a sight of him, aren't you? Maybe you will in two weeks' time.'

'What happens in two weeks' time?' asked Ivanov, tightening a connection.

'There's seven chimneys to be repaired there. We'll be putting up the scaffolding. And a cornice, fourteen metres long, got to be restored. Could be we'll see Stalin then. The place is quite near his quarters.' Lumyanov helped Ivanov haul another plank up on the pulley. 'Listen, are you planning to marry Wanda Semyon-ovna?' he asked directly.

'We haven't discussed it.'

'But you're staying with her folks, I hear?' Lumyanov nailed the board in place. He had a powerful arm. 'I was thinking of marrying her myself.'

'You?'

'I'm a widower. No children, and only forty-nine — that's not too old to make a girl happy, is it? I'm strong and healthy!'

'What does Wanda Semyonovna say?'

'She doesn't know. Haven't got around to asking her.' Lum-yanov scratched his head. 'Hard to start on that sort of thing, in among the sacks of cement and concrete-mixers. I was thinking of taking her for a walk, and now you turn up.'

'I'm sorry, comrade. I was hoping we might be friends.'

'We shall, Fedya, we shall.' Lumyanov gave him a fraternal hug. 'Just one thing: if you don't make Wandushka happy, I'll chase you all the way to Siberia if necessary to wring your neck, understand?'

'You won't have to,' said Ivanov, laughing. 'I promise you that.'

He watched Lumyanov climb down the scaffolding again. Two

weeks' time, he thought. Friends, I think we may have to change our plans. I can't wait the four weeks we'd intended to bide our time before meeting at Milda Ivanovna's to decide on the next step. I must be able to act sooner than that. In two weeks' time I must have a hand grenade or a bomb. He leaned on the scaffolding and looked into the big room, where the general was still briefing his officers. To make quite sure, I must get really close to Stalin. A shot is not certain enough, and whether I use a bomb or a hand grenade it will blow both of us up.

He turned and looked at the big cupola of the Council of Ministers building. The sun shone on its windows, and the golden onion domes of the churches seemed to hover in the air. It was hot. A flock of pigeons was circling around the Bell Tower of Ivan the Great. He saw a small van driving along from the direction of the Tsar Bell itself and stopping by the scaffolding. Wanda Semyonovna got out in her working-clothes, spattered with plaster. Lumyanov spoke to her, pointing up. She raised her head and waved both arms.

'Come on down, Fedya,' she called. 'I've got something for you — a jar of pickled mushrooms. Come down.'

I love that girl, thought Ivanov, climbing down the scaffolding. I've fallen in love with her. This isn't just an adventure, like Elfriede or any of the other girls I've had. It suddenly means so much to me that I'm afraid of dying. Dear, sweet Wandushka, we must steal every moment together we can.

Down on the ground he took Wanda in his arms and kissed her, mentally cursing Stalin, the war and his mission.

On 22 June 1944, the Red Army attacked. Shells bombarded the enemy along a front of five hundred and sixty kilometres. Thousands of tanks rolled out of their positions and over the German bunkers and trenches. The sky was swarming with Soviet fighters, bombers and reconnaissance-planes, for the main part of the German Luftwaffe was concentrated in the west, where the Americans and English had a firm foothold now, with Rommel in a hopeless position.

The 3rd Belorussian Front, under General Cherniakhovsky, made for Vitebsk, with five armies. There was only one army to face them: the small German 3rd Army. Zakharov's 2nd Belorussian Front, with three armies of picked troops, attacked the German 4th Army, which had been continuously in action. The 1st Belorussian Front, under Rokossovsky, marched towards Minsk and right through the Pripet marshes to Brest-Litovsk, tearing open the whole German flank with tremendous force.

All at once eighteen Russian armies began to move against four exhausted German ones. Their superiority was something that even Hitler, in the Wolf's Lair, could not fail to understand. He had nothing with which to counter it but his saying that one German soldier was worth ten Russians. And the offensive rolled on. All Belorussia was on fire.

The daily news bulletin from High Command of the German Armed Forces, as broadcast over German radio and printed in the newspapers, said merely that, south of the Eastern Front, local attacks by the Russians had been repelled on the Strypa, to the north-west of Tarnopol and south of the Pripet marshes, while the Bolshevists had begun their expected offensive in the central sector of the front. Their onslaughts had been repelled in fierce fighting. Breaches of the front had been immediately made good.

While the German reports glossed over the desperate situation, the Soviet divisions streamed on, and the Soviet radio broadcast frequent news bulletins, interspersed with military marches and folk songs.

They all sat by their radio sets listening: Larissa Alexandrovna and Petrovsky; Lyra Pavlovna and Boranov with Pavlov Sharenkov and Marya Ivanovna, who burst into tears of joy at the news of the victories, while Boranov felt a tug at his heart. The doctor, Anya Ivanovna, sat by her radio with Duskov, listening to the news; he had come back to her apartment after their train journey from Zagorsk. They were eating biscuits she had brought home from the hospital. Sepkin folded his hands tightly as he heard the names of the places overrun that day. Yelena sat beside him, her head on his shoulder, while Luka Antipovich made sandwiches. Pleyin was naked in bed when the first news of the victories came through. Lyudmila Dragonovna, who was roasting a piece of pork bought on the black market, looked round the corner of the kitchen door.

'The time has come,' she said, in her wonderful, ringing voice. 'The Germans are done for. And they'll run faster yet.'

Ivanov and the Haller family sat at the kitchen table eating jacket potatoes with curds and chives, listening intently to the radio reports. Semyon Tikhinovich had torn a map out of an old school textbook, and kept indicating the places mentioned with his spoon. 'They're on the run,' he said. 'Yes, the Germans are on the run. It'll be a great victory. Look, Fedya, once they retreat past Minsk no one can stop us. And where will the Germans get more soldiers now? No, they're finished.'

They all listened until the end of the news programme. Then Pleyin and Lyudmila made love again, to the sound of martial music. The Sharenkov family discussed Pavlov Ignatovich's pet plan for a triumphal arch in the neo-classical style, to commemorate the names of all the fallen Russian soldiers, built to last for all eternity. The merriest party was at the Pushkins', where Luka Antipovich produced some vodka saved for special occasions to mark the day. It was so strong that he himself was almost overcome by it at the end of the radio programme, and lay back in his chair singing army songs before lapsing into unconsciousness. That was the night when Yelena Lukanovna first slipped into bed with Sepkin. She was still a virgin, and as he initiated her into a whole new world of feeling he thought that by tomorrow the Russians would have taken Vitebsk.

The sun shone more brightly over Moscow now. Of course, there were food shortages, but everyone understood that provisions must be sent to the front, where the gallant soldiers needed butter more than the civilian population, who could make their own contribution to the war effort by eating less.

Time was running out for the six Wild Geese who had infiltrated Moscow. Ivanov went on building scaffolding, waiting for a sight of Stalin. Pleyin caught up with his sleep while Lyudmila was on duty, then rose to cook a meal and prepare for his day's work: making love to her until she herself admitted to exhaustion.

Petrovsky had gone along to see the personnel manager of the tractor assembly-plant, and been taken on as a tractor testing driver, which meant he was on the same job as Larissa Alexandrovna and could see her during working-hours as well as at night. On the evening of his third day's work, they visited Larissa's friend Viera, who had had the premature baby, and Petrovsky looked in to see Dr Speshnikov, who was sitting over his chess-board in the duty-room again, evidently half-drunk. He gazed at Petrovsky with sad, watery eyes.

'Dogs are more trustworthy than humans,' he said, slurring his words. 'Can't expect a human being to stick to his friends, can you? Even a nice fellow like you. Well, what is it?'

'I thought you might like to know I'm in love, Dr Speshnikov. Her name's Larissa Alexandrovna, she tests tractors at an assembly-plant, and I've got a job there, too.'

'Well, congratulations,' said Dr Speshnikov drily. 'And on those X-ray pictures of yours, too. I've been thinking about them. Not a trace of an ulcer on them. And I know an ulcer when I see one, Luka Ivanovich.'

Petrovsky sat down, looked at the chessboard, moved one of the pieces, and nodded. 'Check. It was going to happen one way or another, in any case.'

'Damn you. You're right. Check it is.' Dr Speshnikov swept the chessmen off the board, and offered Petrovsky a bottle. 'Potato spirit.'

Petrovsky looked at it warily. 'That stuff's enough to castrate a man.'

'Better than nothing. The idea is to drink it, not pour it over your balls.'

Petrovsky took a cautious sip, held his breath, swallowed, and sat there open-mouthed. 'Am I breathing fire?' he inquired.

'Well, if you'd really had an ulcer, I dare say that would have burned it out.' Dr Speshnikov took his bottle back, drank, his eyes closed, and put it down by the chessboard. 'Well, now, what shall we do?'

'Larissa will be waiting for me. . . .'

'I mean, what shall we do about you and your ulcer, damn you. Don't forget you're in our files now. What do I write in my report? "Result of tests: negative"? They'll send you straight back to the front. Do you want that?'

'I'm a good Russian, Dr Speshnikov.'

'Oh, God knows why I bother with you. You're a born survivor, Luka Ivanovich, that's what you are.'

'I hope so. I have this good job now, testing tractors.'

Dr Speshnikov sighed, and slouched forward in his chair.

Petrovsky caught him and held him upright. 'Tell you what I'll put: "We have nothing to add to the findings of the army doctors."'

'That's a brilliant idea, Dr Speshnikov. I only hope I get a chance to thank you properly some time.'

'Shall I see you again, I wonder?' Dr Speshnikov clutched the arms of his chair to keep himself steady. 'I'm interested in you, Luka Ivanovich. What a nerve you have! I don't think you ever had a day's illness in your life. But somehow you managed to get discharged from the front.' He shook his head. 'Now, I don't know what it's all about, but it so happens that I like you, Luka. Well, you go back to your Larissa, my friend. Come and see me now and then; let me know how you are. And if Larissa has a baby, and I'm still alive, I'll deliver it for you. More potato spirit?'

'Doctor, why are you drinking so heavily?'

'Because we're winning the war, and I don't think the world knows what it's let itself in for. But I shan't see it. I'll have drunk myself to death first, praise be!'

With Luka Antipovich Pushkin's help, Sepkin obtained a job in the Sklifossovsky Accident Hospital. It was not a job to everyone's taste: they needed a man to tend the incinerator burning debris and rubbish from the operating-theatres. The incinerator was connected to the operating-area by a long corridor. Outside the furnace itself was a white-tiled room, full of buckets both large and small, made of enamel or zinc. Everything was spotlessly clean, and you might have thought you were in a well-run butcher's shop, but for the fact that the buckets contained amputated limbs, human intestines and muscle tissue. Still, work was work, and Sepkin was glad to have found friends, and an inconspicuous niche in Moscow.

Boranov found work, too. After that family conference in the Sharenkovs' apartment, it was decided that Lyra should introduce him to the manager of Moscow Tramways.

It should be mentioned that the people of Moscow are extremely proud of their tram services, and the tramway employees feel honoured to wear their uniform. Comrade Afonasev, a white-haired, distinguished-looking man, with the fine features of a

Georgian and the manners of an aristocrat, received Lyra Pavlovna as an old friend, and shook Boranov's hand. 'What a shame, getting a bullet in you just when we're marching on Berlin,' he said sympathetically. The upshot was a job for Boranov as Inspector of Readiness for Service. This sounded most impressive, but was something of a sinecure. Boranov had nothing much to do but go from depot to depot, making sure all the trams were roadworthy and reasonably clean. The great advantage was that he was free to come and go as he pleased. It would be easy enough for him to get to Milda Ivanovna's, or anywhere else, when the time came.

'I really never thought I'd have so much luck,' said Boranov at the end of his first day's work. The family were sitting by the radio set again, eating turnip soup with a little bacon in it.

'Well, we're all due for good luck now and then,' said Marya Ivanovna. 'Have another piece of bacon, Kyrill Semyonovich.'

It was really quite hard to say whether mother or daughter had fallen more heavily for Kyrill Semyonovich Boranov.

The Botkin Hospital is like a small, self-contained town, swarming with thousands of people from its basements to its upper floors. You could easily get hopelessly lost in its corridors and complexes of buildings. One needed to know the vast extent of the place to appreciate the significance of the fact that everyone in it knew Dr Anya Ivanovna Pleskina. And not just on account of her beauty; she was a famous surgeon. Women physicians were common in Russia, but it was less usual to see a woman, let alone one of Anya's extraordinary beauty, standing at the operating-table in a bloodstained apron, often for hours without a break. Her skill was a legend in the Botkin Hospital; she had been known to take responsibility for operations which the senior consultant declined to perform.

So it was hardly surprising that Leonid Germanovich Duskov instantly got a job as an auxiliary in the Botkin Hospital through her good offices. An excellent job, too, not a menial one in the wards. He had claimed experience as an undertaker's assistant, and he got the newly created job of welfare worker in charge of corpses, dealing with the bereaved relatives. He was given a room with box-trees in big tubs, two branched silver candlesticks borrowed from the church in the Vagankovsky Cemetery, dark curtains at the windows, and a piano. When a comrade died, and the grieving family came to the hospital, the corpse was not, as previously, shown to them in the bleak atmosphere of the mortuary: a handsome bier stood between the candlesticks, the corpse lay there as if he were only asleep, and Duskov sat at the piano in the background, playing soothing and melancholy music, usually Chopin nocturnes. Then he would mingle with the mourners, talking tactfully about the dead man as if he were an old friend, praising his good qualities, and comforting the relatives. The hospital professors, watching Duskov at work, were rather impressed. Not that his job was strictly necessary, but the famous Pleskina claimed that medicine ought to be given a more human and approachable face, and they saw her point.

Very soon Duskov was a firmly entrenched institution. Seeing weeping mourners enter the hospital, the porter would say, without even being asked, 'Block 2, corridor 17, go straight ahead and it's the last door, and may the comrade rest in peace.'

On the evening of 24 June, Duskov reached Anya Ivanovna's apartment first. While she made her last rounds of the day, visiting patients on whom she had recently operated, he made curd pancakes, stuffed them with minced meat eked out with breadcrumbs, and got the old samovar bubbling. When Anya Ivanovna came home, the table was laid, there was a candle alight on it, surrounded by six roses which Duskov had picked in the hospital garden, and a delicious smell of pancakes in the place.

'Is there no end to your talents, Leonid Germanovich?' said Anya Ivanovna, laughing. 'Oh, that does look good! So you can cook, too. Cobbler, undertaker, pianist, self-taught medical expert, car mechanic, thief and notorious liar. What tall tale will you tell me to explain how you learned to cook?'

'I dare say you won't believe this one, Anya Ivanovna,' said Duskov solemnly, 'but the undertaker ran a café, too, next to the funeral parlour. They were side by side. So when the relatives had chosen a coffin he'd show them the way to the café and suggest a drink to the memory of the dear departed, and then—'

'No, really, Leonid Germanovich,' said Pleskina, 'you can't expect me to swallow that.' She had a gleam in her eyes; she tossed back her hair and tied it with a red ribbon. She looked

250

lovelier and more challenging than ever. 'Can't you ever be sensible?'

'I don't feel in the least like being sensible,' said Duskov, looking at the flickering candle.

She stared at him, the candlelight throwing her face into strange and breathtaking relief. 'What do you mean?'

'Anya Ivanovna, I want to thank you for all your help.' Duskov rose and came round the table. 'But I must look for somewhere else tomorrow. I can't stay here.'

'Why not?' Her eyes were wide with alarm. 'What's wrong with it here?'

'I love you. That's what's wrong.' Duskov pulled her up from her chair, held her close, and was agreeably surprised to find that she did not resist. 'Can't you understand?' he cried roughly. 'I love you! I'm crazy about you! Me—discharged from the Army, notorious liar and so on—in love with the great surgeon Pleskina! I know it's madness, so let me go, Anya Ivanovna, let me go now, or God knows what I may do. . . .'

'Oh, Leonid Germanovich, how lovely to be nothing but pure feeling,' she said in her low, velvety voice, her arms going round his neck. 'My notorious liar. . . .'

'Don't say I didn't warn you.' Duskov's throat was constricted, and his heart thudding.

'I don't want warnings. I see death every day; I long for life so much.'

He picked Anya Ivanovna up—either she was lighter than he had expected, or he was stronger than he thought—and carried her to the bedroom. As they reached the doorway, she was biting his shoulder, digging her fingernails into the back of his neck, and moaning softly with pleasure. . . . And afterwards, when they had eaten the cold pancakes, and drunk tea with a few drops of vodka in it, they sat side by side listening to the news on the radio. 'What luxury,' she said, gently caressing him. 'To sit here naked and listen to the news bulletins.' She laid her head on his shoulder, spreading her long black hair over his chest. 'Do you understand German?' she asked abruptly.

Duskov felt a stab of alarm. 'What?' He tried to go on breathing normally. A cheerful marching tune came over the radio; the last news bulletin was over. 'No, they never taught us German. Do you know it?'

'Not much, but we did do some at school. Sometimes I listen to other radio stations, and it's quite hard to know who's telling the truth.'

'German stations, you mean? You can get them on your radio?' Duskov made his voice sound indifferent.

'Shall I try now?'

'If you like. I told you I don't understand the language.'

'Oh, but it's interesting. I'll translate for you.' She rose and walked over to the radio, naked, to retune it. When she turned to smile at Duskov the light of the candle flickered over her body. He thought: Let's use the short time remaining to us; let's drink it all down like intoxicating poison. Anyushka, you don't know that you have been making love to a dead man. Dear God, don't let her ever find out who I am. . . .

'It'll be on in a minute,' she said, raising a finger. 'There.' Dance music: foxtrots and American jazz. 'Wait a minute,' she said. 'Here we are.'

The music broke off. A calm, pleasant man's voice spoke, in German. 'This is the Western Military Radio. Friends on all the fronts you are now hearing the true facts. Here is the news. . . .'

'It's from an Allied transmitter,' put in Anya Ivanovna quickly.

Duskov leaned his head back and stared at the ceiling. The news was almost identical with that broadcast on Soviet radio. Penetration of the front in the Vitebsk sector, tank spearheads making for Orsha, men marching on Mogilev, the taking of German positions in the Pripet marshes. 'And now a comrade of yours will describe the situation,' said the voice.

Anya Ivanovna twiddled the knobs of the radio. 'They all say the Germans are retreating. We're winning, darling! Aren't you glad?'

'It's a real triumph,' said Duskov dully. 'How about some music, Anyushka?'

She looked at the clock. 'It's nearly time for the German news — do you want to hear it?'

'No.' Duskov closed his eyes. We must hurry things along, he thought. We can't wait any longer. There'll be no point in killing

Stalin if the Red Army is already marching up to Berlin. I hope to God the others are listening in and thinking the same.

The others. . . . Duskov took a deep breath. How many of them, and which of them, would he meet again at Milda Ivanovna's?

Anya found the German station, pleased to be able to demonstrate it. 'Listen to this. . . .'

'But I don't know German,' said Duskov hoarsely.

'High Command of the Armed Forces has issued the following bulletin: "Bolshevist thrusts all along the southern part of the Eastern Front have been repelled. In the central sector of the Front, the main Soviet offensive has increased in force, extending to other sectors. While enemy attacks between the Pripet marshes and Chaussy were unsuccessful, our advanced positions have been attacked by strong Soviet infantry and tank divisions east of Mogilev, on either side of the Smolensk highway, and either side of Vitebsk. The defending forces are fighting with increasing vigour in these areas. Yesterday the Bolshevist losses in the central sector were seventy-three tanks and fifty-three aircraft." '

'Lies!' cried Pleskina, clenching her fists. 'Sorry — you didn't understand it. But the Germans are the biggest liars in the world.'

'Turn it off,' said Duskov. 'Anya, turn it off.'

He spoke with such intensity that she turned the volume right down in alarm.

Was there still any point at all in Operation Wild Geese? Duskov wondered whether the German front would have disintegrated before they could get close enough to Stalin to carry out their mission.

'Come here, Anyushka,' he said, watching her body move in the candlelight. 'Come here to me. Let's forget what times we live in, at least for a while. . . .'

The German news bulletins did their best to keep the truth from the German people. On 28 June, Pyotr Mironovich Sepkin was sitting with Radolov, the operating-theatre assistant. They had made friends in the course of their distasteful but necessary work. Radolov had a radio set in his room in the operating-area, and as Sepkin happened to have nothing to do at the moment he had come up to see his new friend and hear the news from the front.

'We've taken Vitebsk and Orsha,' Radolov exulted, clapping his hands. 'And all in four days. The Germans are truly on the run. Pyotr Mironovich, I know you won't tell tales—I put something aside for when there was an occasion to celebrate.'

He searched in a cupboard of cleaning materials and produced a bottle of mauve liquid. Marching music was playing on the radio again.

'Good stuff, this,' said Radolov. He uncorked the bottle and held it under Sepkin's nose. 'Pure medicinal alcohol, diluted a bit and flavoured with juniper berries. Try it, comrade. In four days, our brave men will have reached the Beresina.'

That evening Sepkin decided to get in touch with Milda Ivanovna. He would go to her place next day.

Five

COLONEL IGOR VLADIMIROVICH SMOLKA, head of Internal Intelligence of the NKVD, had been feeling ill at ease since the unmasking of Major von Labitz. He read the evidence of all the witnesses over and over again, he listened to the tape which had been running during his conversation with Sassonov, and stared suspiciously, as if it were a live bomb, at the tiny but powerful transmitter Sassonov had carried with him. He could not shake off the suspicion that this German officer was not the only one to have been sent into Russia. Why would a solitary man be trying to get at the Perovo steelworks, carrying impeccable papers proving his Russian past? It didn't make sense.

Colonel Smolka had kept the file on his own desk. Every employee at the Perovo works was being examined and briefly interrogated, but Smolka felt sure nothing else would turn up there.

It was like a bolt from the blue when a report arrived in Moscow from the NKVD offices in Kalinin. So did two corpses, in lead-lined coffins, with four policemen guarding them. In addition, a police report from Moscow goods-station had just landed on his desk. After it had gone the rounds of seven offices who decided it was none of their business, a civil servant had had the bright idea of unloading it on the NKVD.

One of the corpses from Kalinin was that of a man who had stated while alive that his name was Ivan Petrovich Bunurian, which would make him either Armenian or Georgian, and who had been clubbed to death by a party of woodcutters in the forest near Maximovo. They had found a parachute – a Soviet parachute – and then discovered this man Bunurian with a broken ankle. When the woodcutters searched him, they found a tobacco-tin which turned out to contain a miniaturized radio transmitter.

They had then fallen on Bunurian in a fit of patriotic fervour and killed him. The report said they later regretted it.

The corpse had been collected by the Kalinin NKVD men after two witnesses, Oleg Viktorovich and Pal Tikhonovich by name, rang them from Maximovo. They would probably have dealt with the case locally instead of troubling Moscow with it, but for the fact that a second corpse had turned up in Volokolamsk and been brought to them. A tiny place like Volokolamsk — it was odd. A patrol of three police officers had arrested a man bathing in the River Lama. He claimed to be going to visit his uncle in Volokolamsk, one Dementi Russlanovich Kozeboshkin. There was no such person as Comrade Kozeboshkin, but the man, who called himself Sergei Andreyevich Tarski, had bitten a capsule of potassium cyanide and died directly, on the post office floor. His papers were all in order, but a tiny radio transmitter of unknown origin was found in the hollow heel of his left shoe.

The report stated soberly that the corpses were being sent separately. There they were now, down in the NKVD cellars, awaiting Smolka's reaction.

'Extraordinary,' said Colonel Smolka, after reading the report. The evidence lay on a table: the dead men's identity cards, certificates of discharge from the Red Army, medical certificates, transfer slips for the Central Labour Office in Moscow, all quite correct, quite convincing — and all obviously brilliant forgeries. The two radio transmitters were there, too: a tobacco-tin, with the battered remains of the device built into its false bottom, and a tiny lidded box which could rapidly become a radio, small enough to fit into the hollow heel of a shoe. The latter was the twin of the transmitter found on Sassonov — a device of such precision as Smolka had never seen before. Plainly a great advance in the field of radio electronics.

The dead men's clothes had been sent along as well, in two bags. Smolka did not open them, taking the Kalinin report's word for it that they contained ordinary Soviet clothing of poor quality.

And then along came the police report from the goods-station, with a small package containing a bloodstained identity card and other papers, and a collection of wires, contacts and smashed metal along with the remains of a shoe heel.

The connection between these and the objects found on the two

Kalinin corpses was unmistakable. Smolka lit one of the sweetly perfumed Turkish cigarettes and read the report.

While hosing down a cattle-truck, a cleaning brigade had found the remains of a human being in it. 'Remains' was the only word to describe it; the cows in the truck had trampled the man until he was unrecognizable. Since the animals had last been fed and watered at Stupino, a bright police lieutenant had worked out, the man must have boarded the cattle-truck there, hoping to steal a ride to Moscow. His death would have looked like an ordinary accident but for the curious wires sticking out of the heel of one of his shoes. According to his papers, the man's name was Alexander Nikolayevich Kraskin. Kraskin's remains were in cold storage at the Second Institute of Forensic Medicine.

Smolka sent for a big map of Moscow and its surroundings, hung it on his wall, and drew large red circles round the places where these four men seemed to have been found: Stupino, Volokolamsk, Perovo, Maximovo. They formed an arc, a neat semicircle around Moscow, each at a distance of some fifty to eighty versts from the capital. Smolka, smoking his second cigarette, said out loud to himself, 'Prussian perfectionism if ever I saw it.'

He summoned his staff, and sat staring at the four red circles while a major read out the two reports to them. He pointed to the map.

'What does that tell you?' he asked. 'I know what it says to me: a commando unit of German officers dropped into the neighbourhood of Moscow by parachute under cover of darkness. Here we have a semi-circle. But why shouldn't the circle be complete? Why shouldn't other Germans have dropped in, to the east and north of Moscow? I can't believe our enemies would have used only half the space available. There's no doubt that they *were* Germans, like the man Sassonov. They had the same forged papers, the same radio transmitters, and, as the papers show, they were all making for Moscow. Now, assuming that the four men discovered were only *part* of this group, the other members of it will have managed to reach the city. Comrades, we have among us an unknown number of saboteurs prepared, judging by the man we interrogated here, to take desperate measures.'

Colonel Smolka rose, went to the window, and looked out at the wide, busy street. The great offensive was under way, the

German front had been broken, life in Moscow was returning to normal—but danger, of a magnitude as yet unknown, had silently penetrated the heart of Russia.

'I shall inform Generalissimo Stalin,' said Colonel Smolka heavily. He turned and looked keenly at his men. 'Where do we start looking? Whom are we to protect? Who or what is in danger? You don't know, comrades, and neither do I. We're groping in the dark. All we *do* know is that there are German agents in Moscow prepared to carry out some very unusual mission.'

Before Colonel Smolka drove to the Kremlin, after making a long telephone call to Stalin's staff there, he went down to the cellars and looked at the two coffins from Kalinin. The four policemen were still on guard, shivering in the cold vaults in their summer uniforms.

'Shall we open them up?' asked the sergeant.

Colonel Smolka hesitated. The sight of the corpses would not tell him anything more. 'It's not a pretty sight, comrade,' added the sergeant drily.

Smolka nodded, turned away, and left the place. He gave orders for the coffins to be taken to the Forensic Institute, got into a big black car and drove to the Kremlin.

And on that short car-journey a thought began to form in his mind—so audacious an idea that Smolka told himself: I can't say it out loud, not now, not yet. They'd think I was crazy and shut me up. . . .

Smolka was not admitted to the presence of Stalin himself, but he was received by General Yefim Grigoryevich Radovsky. Colonel Smolka was conscious of the honour; it was rumoured that Radovsky was one of the very few people to enjoy Stalin's confidence. The Generalissimo's suspicion of people was notorious; his fear of treachery kept him living in seclusion within the Kremlin, seldom seeing even his sons or his daughter Svetlana except during the brief periods he spent at his dacha. But General Radovsky was said to have access to him at any time.

The General was in a good mood. The offensive was going even better than Operations Staff had hoped. The weakness of the Germans was apparent everywhere. 'Well, what's all this, Igor

Vladimirovich?' asked Radovsky, shaking hands. They knew each other only slightly, but Radovsky, a sturdy man of medium height, with short grey hair and a taste for sartorial elegance, liked to adopt a genial manner. 'Something about a German commando unit on its way to Moscow? With a white flag, no doubt. And about time, too. Have you heard the latest from the front?'

Smolka wondered if the General would be so cheerful in a moment. 'May I make my report?' he asked formally.

Radovsky nodded, sat down, crossed his legs and looked at the Colonel. 'I'm listening.'

Smolka told his story. Then he unfolded the map he had brought with him and handed it to Radovsky, who immediately noticed the red circles.

'This is where they were found, or traced to?' he asked.

'In a semi-circle around Moscow. Now, why a semi-circle? Put yourself in the Germans' position — or, better still, think what *we* would do if we wanted to infiltrate Berlin with a commando unit on a special mission. We'd drop them into Germany in a circle around the city. Well, it might not be feasible there, where the country is so crowded, but at a distance of some eighty versts from Moscow there are plenty of isolated places where — to name a purely imaginary figure — thirty or so men could jump into Russia unnoticed. With the kind of papers we found, they'd reach Moscow without difficulty, they'd even get employment as men discharged from the Red Army. Who would suspect those documents?'

Radovsky nodded. He put down the map and looked very thoughtful. 'Supposing you are right, Igor Vladimirovich: a group of German officers has reached Moscow and is hiding out here, having suffered the loss of these four men. But what can we do? Nothing. Are you going to question every man who applied for employment at the labour offices over a period of several days? Are you going to check up on every sick or wounded soldier in the Moscow hospitals? However, we must somehow discover the purpose of their mission. This operation seems too well planned to be anything but important.' Colonel Smolka nodded; Radovsky was approaching the unthinkable idea of his own accord. 'But what *can* they do to harm us in Moscow at the moment, now our offensive is going so well? Blow up power stations? Sewage works?

Radio stations? No point in any of that; it wouldn't affect the men at the front. So what would they be aiming to do, Smolka?'

Smolka took a deep breath. 'Assassinate Stalin,' he said boldly. Well, it was out now.

'Igor Vladimirovich, you're mad!' said General Radovsky.

'I'm inclined to think so myself, Comrade General.' Smolka tugged nervously at his uniform. 'But it's the one thing the Germans could do that might influence the course of the war.'

'If you should be right, we must do something at once,' said Radovsky gravely, but calmly. 'We must make him invulnerable.'

'Can it be done?'

'I would rather he didn't know about this himself. We're all aware how deeply suspicious he is. If he thought there was a unit of assassins in Moscow, he wouldn't take a step out of the Kremlin or see anyone at all. And we can't have that; it would have a very bad effect on public morale, now that reports of new victories are coming in hourly. Stalin belongs to the people now; he should be showing himself to them in triumph.'

'But that's out of the question.' Smolka passed trembling hands over his eyes. 'It's what his unknown assassins are waiting for.'

'We shall find some way to protect Stalin,' said General Radovsky. He rose. 'Well, my dear Igor Vladimirovich, we are much indebted to you.'

'Only doing my duty, Comrade General.'

'No need to be so modest about it. It's over and above the call of duty to think as clearly and logically as you have done.' Radovsky shook hands with Smolka, and actually accompanied him to the stairs.

Back in his office, Smolka sat lost in thought. An old plan reawoke in his mind — something he had thought of at the very beginning of the war, and then suppressed. At the time, he had seen it as a way of shoring up Stalin's security; now it could be an almost certain guarantee of his survival. Smolka had never lost sight of the men who were to be instrumental in this plan; they were, so to speak, always on call, and had been ever since he had carried out certain tests on them, performed with uncanny precision, in a dacha outside Moscow which belonged to his brother-in-law, an eminent chemist. It was at his brother-in-law's insistence that he had abandoned the idea. 'Igor Vladimirovich, this thing could rebound on yourself,' his brother-in-law had said. 'Stalin will see it as a threat, not a means of protection — proof that he could be quietly removed from the scene without anyone's noticing. I suggest you don't put this to any higher authority — just burn any records you have. In Beria's hands, they could well be fatal to you.'

Smolka had not burned his records, but he hid them well, and now and then he got in touch with his 'colleagues', as he called them. Radovsky had seemed well disposed to him. Why not try it out on Radovsky?

The lovely Milda Ivanovna Kabakova remained a mystery to her friends. She had been chaste as a nun in Eberswalde, her artistic and literary acquaintances had never got anywhere with her — and now she was having this tremendous affair. Her friends were surprised and envious. But Major Volonov was now like putty in her hands. He was obsessed by her.

He brought her everything he could in the way of special rations and, since the Kremlin staff officers got privileged allocations, Milda no longer had to stand in line outside the butcher's or baker's shop at five in the morning. Her artist friends, who profited from his generosity, thought it could not just be the uniform. After all, Yanis Mikhailovich did not go to bed with his decorations on his chest. He must have something special about him. . . .

Anything useful Milda learned from Volonov she passed on by radio, very early in the morning, to her contact. She did not know his name or where he lived, only a wavelength and a codeword. He must, she thought, be a cold-blooded character, for when she suggested that the present offensive meant changes should be made to Operation Wild Geese he only said, 'Wait and see. No further instructions.'

And no further instructions came.

At OKW and Canaris's Abwehr headquarters the operation was now officially regarded as written off. On hearing this from Keitel, Colonel von Renneberg protested. 'But the men have been dropped into Russia, sir.'

'Well, then, the war's already over for them, isn't it?' said

Keitel sarcastically. 'Weren't they reported missing, presumed dead?'

'Officially, yes. The relatives have been informed. Sir, may I ask you a question quite off the record?'

Keitel looked at Renneberg in surprise. 'Go ahead.'

'*Can* we halt the Russian offensive?'

'The Führer can do anything.'

'Because, sir, there won't be much point in killing Stalin once the Red Flag is flying over the Chancellery.'

'We shall halt the Russians at the Weichsel, if not before,' said Keitel. 'As for your Wild Geese, though I don't see them carrying out their mission, any time would be the right time to kill Stalin — now, or in four weeks' time.'

Renneberg drove back to Berlin, where Canaris saw him at once.

'Well? Your Wild Geese?' he asked briefly.

'Keitel says the Führer can do anything.'

'About a hundred and forty thousand of our men have died; the number of German prisoners of war is estimated at forty-six thousand — and that's all in the last few days.' Canaris rose and came round his large desk. 'Mistake after mistake is being made, Renneberg — but of course the Führer can do anything. How can we communicate with your men?'

'We can't.'

'You can't reach them at all?'

'No, sir.'

'But they do have a contact in Moscow, that girl — what's her name?'

'Milda Ivanovna, sir.'

'Does this Milda have precise instructions?'

Renneberg shrugged his shoulders. 'The men's own instructions were not to contact her until four weeks after landing, to give them time to get well established in Moscow.'

'That would make it the middle of July.'

'At the earliest.'

'Renneberg, have you any idea where the Russians may be by the middle of July?'

'We didn't reckon on quite such rapid developments on the Eastern Front, did we, sir?'

Renneberg drove home to his little apartment and drank two glasses of French cognac. No help from Canaris, either, he thought. The men are written off, and we shall never see them again. Our only hope is that they will assess the present situation correctly and turn up at Milda's sooner than instructed.

This was just what was about to happen.

On the evening of 30 June 1944, Major Volonov sat down to eat a good supper of minced meatballs and fresh cabbage with Milda Ivanovna. He was enjoying his meal, drinking kvass, and looking forward to bed afterwards. The radio was turned low, playing Borodin. Milda wore a Japanese kimono with bright silk flowers on it, and Volonov knew she was naked underneath. The knowledge excited him, and he was looking at Milda with gleaming eyes when there was a knock on the door. Milda Ivanovna looked up, perplexed. All her friends were aware that she was not to be disturbed in the evenings.

'Who's that, I wonder?' said Volonov, glad he was still wearing his uniform.

'I'll go and see. Maybe someone's got the wrong number.'

As she went to the door, she noticed a distinct rhythm to the continued hammering. Volonov, no fool, noticed it, too. He put down his fork, pushed back his chair and rose, buttoning up his uniform tunic.

Milda opened the door just a crack and looked out. Her heart missed a beat, but then she recovered herself with aplomb, and was about to shut the door again. However, she was prevented by Volonov, who suddenly found himself in the grip of violent and uncontrollable jealousy.

'Come in,' he snapped in military tones. 'Wrong door or not, come in.'

Milda's face froze. She stepped back from the doorway. Yes, as Volonov had feared, it *was* another man. A tall, strong, athletic man, too, though in civilian clothes of poor quality and a shabby cap. He was carrying a bunch of flowers, which he gave to Milda. She hesitated, and then took them. Volonov felt this was going too far. 'Who are you?' he barked.

The visitor looked silently from Milda to Volonov, and then said, in what appeared to Volonov a positively provocative tone,

263

'Pyotr Mironovich Sepkin.' He avoided Milda's eyes. *The alternatives are that either this man and I become bosom friends within the hour, or else one of us is carried out feet first.*

'Yes? What do you want?' asked Volonov condescendingly.

'Oh, Pyotr Mironovich is an old friend,' said Milda quickly. 'We've known each other since we were children.' She laughed, quite spontaneously. 'Goodness, how you surprised me,' she said. 'Turning up so suddenly without a word of warning – and with an armful of flowers, too.'

'Why aren't you in the Army, comrade?' snapped Volonov.

Sepkin took his cap off. 'Er – sorry, I didn't catch your name, comrade, though I can see you're a major, of course.'

'Isn't that enough for you, Pyotr Mironovich?'

'Could be.' Sepkin gestured in a casual way which seemed to Volonov to indicate lack of respect. 'What's in a name, comrade? However, as I said, mine's Sepkin, and I *have* been in the Army. I'm just back from the front.'

'Wounded?'

'Afraid not, Comrade Major. Trouble with my lungs. Supposed to be a danger to the company. . . .'

Volonov wrinkled up his nose, as if at an unpleasant smell. He stepped back. 'Then please leave this apartment, Pyotr Mironovich,' he said sternly, 'and don't come anywhere near Milda again. They shouldn't let you walk around infecting people; you ought to be in hospital. Get out.'

But Sepkin stayed put. He looked at Milda, who was trying to tell him, with her eyes, to do as Volonov said. However, Sepkin felt that, even if he did go, this major could represent a danger. Sepkin walked on into the room.

'Oh, good,' said Sepkin gleefully. 'Do I see cabbage and meatballs? You always were a good cook, Milda Ivanovna, as I'm sure you've found out, Major. My mouth's already watering.'

'I think you'd better go, Pyotr Mironovich,' said Milda, her voice rather hoarse. 'Don't you remember what Mamushka told you?'

Mamushka. Sepkin smiled wryly. *Mamushka, of course, was Colonel von Renneberg. But, my dear Milda, he thought, Orsha has fallen, Borissov has fallen, and we must move our plans forward. Never mind Mamushka.*

Sepkin summoned up a cough which sounded genuine enough to cause Volonov to retreat to the wall. Like so many Russians, he had a horror of infectious disease. Unwisely, he reached behind him and took his pistol out of its holster. It was a 9 mm Makarov, a smaller weapon than the standard Tokarev pistol. Sepkin nodded, braced his legs wide apart, picked up the serving-dish of meatballs and looked at Volonov.

'There are some people who just never feel fear,' he said in friendly tones, 'and I happen to be one of them, comrade.'

'We'll see about that.' Volonov's voice was cold and unyielding.

'Yanis Mikhailovich, he's here now,' said Milda Ivanovna hoarsely. 'And he's hungry. He'll be off again when he's had something to eat. Why make so much fuss?'

'He'll be off at once, to wherever he came from. Going around with rotten lungs, infecting people. Mildushka, you keep out of this — I'll see to him.'

Sepkin sighed deeply. 'And those meatballs looked so good,' he said sadly. 'I could smell them outside the door. Milda, little pigeon, life is hard.'

Raising the big earthenware dish with its pattern of poppies as if at least to sip the liquid in it, he suddenly flung it through the air. Before Volonov knew what was happening, it had struck him full in the face. Supple as a big cat, Sepkin leaped on him. Milda Ivanovna turned away. She did not hear the crack as the edge of Sepkin's hand struck first Volonov's throat and then his neck. As Volonov fell, Sepkin struck a third blow at his throat, but he did not feel it. His neck was broken. He fell to the ground with a crash, striking the earthenware dish with his shoulder. It shattered with a louder sound than that of Sepkin's blows. Volonov lay there with his face in a pool of cabbage and meatballs.

'Have you finished?' asked Milda expressionlessly.

'Yes,' Sepkin said. He looked at his hands; they were reddened and beginning to swell.

Milda slowly turned. The sight of Volonov made her feel sick. She looked at Sepkin, a silent question in her eyes. He nodded.

'Yes, he's dead.' He looked around for the kitchen, went into it and put his hands under the tap. The cold water felt good. Milda followed him.

'Was that man your lover?' he asked.

'Yes,' she said calmly. 'His name was Yanis Mikhailovich Volonov.'

'Evidently your hatred of Bolshevists only starts above the waist.'

'There was no call for you to say that, Pyotr Mironovich. Volonov was a Kremlin staff officer.'

'Oh, I see,' said Sepkin, turning off the tap.

'He was close to Stalin.'

'Well done, Mildushka.'

'Oh, for God's sake, never mind pet names now, Sepkin. What are you doing here? Your instructions were—'

'Don't you listen to the news, Milda Ivanovna? The Soviet armies have already taken Borissov; they're advancing on both sides of the highway. It makes a difference to our whole plan. We must get at Stalin sooner than we thought.'

'And just how do you think you'll do that, my clever and murderous friend?'

'I wish you could think of something nice to call me, Milda.'

'Did you murder Volonov, or did you not? Pyotr Mironovich, I had hold of a superb source of information from right beside Stalin. I could have had advance knowledge of every step Stalin took outside the Kremlin—and you've killed off my source of information.'

'You expected me to let him march me off with a pistol to my head?'

'I could have calmed him down. He was deeply in love with me.'

'Well, not surprising, either.' Sepkin went back into the living-room, his hands still smarting. 'Has anyone else reported here yet?'

'No, you're the first, Pyotr Mironovich. And you're too soon.'

'Look, I'm sorry about that, Milda. By the way, you don't think jealousy influenced me, I hope.'

Milda didn't reply.

'Well, don't. I'm in love with the most delightful girl in the world. Her name's Yelena Lukanovna.'

'Well, congratulations,' said Milda coldly. 'That's your own business.'

'No, that's just where you're wrong, Milda Ivanovna. I'm lodging with her and her father, a nice old boy called Pushkin;

266

he's a nurse, and he got me a job in the same hospital. But Yelena herself works in the Kremlin. You had your Major there – I have my secretary. Admittedly, it was pure chance I got to know her, and I may have killed a couple of men on that occasion, too—'

'Your speciality, Pyotr Mironovich?' inquired Milda ironically. She sat down, making sure her back was to Volonov's body. 'Can this Yelena help you?'

'It's possible, though she isn't actually breathing down Stalin's neck like your Major. Come to think of it, we'll have to get him out of here.'

'A brilliant idea, comrade,' said Milda. 'I suppose you take his arms and I take his legs, and we carry him across Moscow to the Kremlin Wall to join the illustrious dead there?'

'Something like that.' Sepkin knelt down beside Volonov, searched his pockets, and then replaced their contents. He even put the uniform belt back on the corpse, returned the pistol to its holster, found a cloth in the kitchen and wiped the dead man's face with it. There was an expression of surprise in Volonov's eyes, even in death. Sepkin closed them, and rose to his feet.

'I expect you'll want a blanket,' said Milda.

'You're very well trained, Milda Ivanovna.'

'This is going to be very dangerous.'

'It'll be more dangerous if he stays here.'

During the night, Sepkin and Milda Ivanovna made their way down Grusinskaya Street with a small handcart belonging to one of the other tenants of number 19, Lesnaya Street, who kept it in the basement. They took it to the Zoo, tipped Volonov out among some bushes and arranged the branches around him. The corpse was not immediately visible, but it would be found; people walked along a nearby path in the daytime, and children played games there.

They took a different and longer route back to Milda's apartment. It was three hours before they were home again. They were in luck: no one had noticed them. One police patrol drove past without a second glance: two comrades with a handcart was a familiar sight these days.

'We must get the others here, too, Milda,' said Sepkin, after they had both washed thoroughly, repeatedly scrubbing the tiled floor to remove any traces of the contents of the serving-dish, even using a knife to clean out the cracks between the tiles. 'But now I need vodka. I must be well and truly drunk; it's the only explanation Yelena will accept. Do you have enough for the purpose?'

'I'll see.'

Sepkin stayed in number 19, Lesnaya Street, until nearly dawn, discussing the next steps to be taken with Milda. Then he drank two glasses of her small supply of vodka, and poured another over his head to intensify the smell of it.

Sure enough, Yelena Lukanovna had been sitting up all night on the sofa, and her eyes were red with weeping when Sepkin stumbled into the apartment babbling, 'Where are you, my little pigeon? Let me smooth down your ruffled feathers.' The smell of spirits preceding him stopped Yelena asking the questions she had ready. She rose and glared at him — furiously angry precisely because her worst fears were set at rest — left him there, went into her father's room and shook him till he woke.

'He's back,' she said, sitting on the side of the bed.

'Good,' mumbled Pushkin. 'There, what did I tell you? I said he'd be back.'

'He's drunk, Father. Dead drunk,' said Yelena. 'It's disgusting.'

'Ah. Well, let's have a look.' Pushkin got out of bed and looked at Sepkin enviously. He made a mental note to ask about the secret source of all that liquor next day. 'Must have fallen into a vat of vodka, stinking of it like that,' said Luka Antipovich, with some awe. 'Here, what are you crying for, Yelena?'

'How *could* he get drunk like that?'

'Ah, he's a good lad, he's all right, my dear,' Pushkin assured her. 'All he wants now is a kind word from you. You know what? I really feel he's one of the family. . . .'

Next day, a small personal announcement was inserted in both *Pravda* and *Izvestia*. It ran: 'Mamushka is dead. Come round and mourn her with me.'

Duskov read the announcement sitting at his piano, in between dealing with two funeral parties. Petrovsky had bought a copy of *Pravda* in a Moscow suburb where he was testing a new tractor.

Pleyin read *Izvestia* sitting at the table, dressed in a silk Tartar dressing-gown Lyudmila had found for him. Ivanov had stopped for a break on his building site in the Kremlin when the friendly foreman, Lumyanov, lent him *Pravda*. Boranov was sitting in one of his beautifully clean trams, being driven to terminus 6, when his eye fell on the small advertisement in the paper. Sepkin, who had of course been looking out for it, was pleased, and handed his paper over to his new friend Radolov. Once again they toasted the latest Red Army victories in diluted medicinal alcohol.

That evening Milda Ivanovna sat in her apartment, receiving reports, at brief intervals, from those men present in Moscow. The only signal that came over the radio was the chirping of a number, followed by silence. And each time, Milda replied with the number eleven.

Then she waited on, until late into the night, but no one else reported. Thoughtfully, she sat reading over the numbers she had scribbled on a piece of paper by the light of a flickering candle. What had happened to the other four?

She burned the slip of paper with the numbers on it, crumbled up the grey ash, and scattered it over a pot of geraniums. Then she turned up her radio to take refuge in the music flooding from it.

After his visit to General Radovsky, Colonel Smolka had moved fast. He summoned his colleagues to Moscow. They arrived at the big NKVD building in Dchershinsky Street under cover of night. Smolka sent the nightwatchman away and met them at the entrance himself. Without encountering anyone else, the men were taken up to the fourth floor. Three rooms had been set aside for them just beyond Smolka's own office, at the end of the corridor, and these four rooms had been shut off from all the others by a special door in the corridor itself. Colonel Smolka had the only key to this door.

His colleagues did not think very much of their rooms, but they were in good humour and laughed a great deal, mainly at each other. They kept examining one another curiously. Colonel Smolka had provided several bottles of vodka, paid for out of the Special Purposes Fund, and a meal of cold roast pork and pickled cucumbers.

His colleagues were enjoying their first evening in Moscow. They had not met until now, at NKVD headquarters, but they immediately felt as if they were all part of the same family. Smolka was not so happy; he had a nasty feeling that if and when he put his plan to Stalin it could be the last official duty he ever performed.

'There was one old lady fell down in a faint when she set eyes on me, on the way,' one of his colleagues remarked.

'You let yourself be seen?' cried Smolka, alarmed. 'But you had the strictest orders—'

'Couldn't be helped, Comrade Colonel. That long journey – my bladder was full to bursting. So I got them to stop in a wood, very lonely sort of place, and I was out there with my flies open when this old woman came round the bushes collecting firewood, and fainted clean away, bless her heart.'

'I hope no one else saw you, Nikolai Ilyich?' asked Smolka gravely.

'Not a soul. We spent the night in the car, according to instructions.'

Smolka looked at his two other colleagues, sitting with their glasses of vodka, smiling at him.

'What about you two, comrades?' he asked.

'I didn't meet anyone,' said one of them.

'No, nor did I.' The third man waved his hand in what was obviously a habitual gesture. It set Smolka's blood pulsing to his temples. Perfect, he thought, both satisfied and alarmed. Absolutely perfect.

Next morning, Smolka rang General Radovsky, who sounded tired. Smolka guessed at one of the long drinking sessions which were compulsory for Stalin's intimates when he wanted drinking companions.

'Have you spoken to Comrade Stalin, I wonder, Comrade General?'

'I've been speaking to him all night, till I could hardly stay on my feet.'

'You didn't mention our suspicions to him?'

'No, he was doing the talking. Got very merry, even danced, and then complained he was surrounded by a pack of traitors.

270

But I've informed his staff of what we suspect. We shall look after Stalin, Smolka.'

'Comrade General, do you have time to call and see me after lunch today?'

'So long as you don't offer me anything to drink – I never want to touch a drop again.'

'No, I have something rather different to offer you.'

'What time?'

'Three o'clock, Comrade General?'

'I'll try to make it.'

Radovsky's car drove up to the NKVD building at three precisely. A major came forward, saluted, and escorted him to the lift. Smolka was waiting for the General on the fourth floor. They shook hands.

'Have you ever been to a performance of *Faust?*' inquired Radovsky curiously.

Smolka nodded. 'Yes, I've seen it several times, Comrade General.'

'You know, when Faust signs his pact with the devil, Mephistopheles usually smiles in just the way you are smiling now.'

Smolka said nothing, but went ahead, opened the new door, let Radovsky through it, and locked it again after him.

'What's the idea of that?' asked Radovsky warily.

'Safety precautions,' said Smolka, opening his office door. There was a smell of cigarettes and aromatic tea. Smolka invited his guest to sit down in a chair opposite the door into the next room. He waited for the General to light a cigarette, then went to the window, closed it, and drew the curtain. Radovsky pursed his lips.

'You obviously have a taste for drama, Igor Vladimirovich.'

'Perhaps I should explain first, Comrade General.'

Radovsky dismissed this. 'No, no, if a play requires explanation beforehand it's a bad one. The audience should be enthralled as soon as the curtain goes up.'

'As you please.' Colonel Smolka went slowly to the door. 'But don't blame me if you get a shock.'

'Stage monsters in the wings?' laughed Radovsky.

Smolka remained grave. 'That depends on how you look at it.' He opened the door to the next room, nodded, and then stepped aside, arms folded, leaving the doorway clear.

A man came in.

Radovsky stared, utterly taken aback, but only for a second. Then, in obvious confusion, he jumped up from his chair, stood to attention, and remained perfectly still. The newcomer said nothing. Finally, Radovsky said, 'Well, Comrade Generalissimo, Colonel Smolka promised me a surprise, and this certainly is one!'

Then Radovsky stopped short and went quite pale. He began to sweat. A second man had come in, stationing himself beside the first, in silence. He smiled at Radovsky, and waved a hand in that characteristic, inimitable gesture.

Smolka nodded again.

A third man entered the room, stood beside the other two, and smiled pleasantly as he, too, raised a hand to greet the General.

Radovsky stared at the three men, breathing heavily, and then dropped into his armchair and reached for a cigarette.

'But this is monstrous,' he said. 'Igor Vladimirovich, you could have killed a man with weaker nerves than myself. You're crazy.'

'I did offer to explain, Comrade General.'

'But who could ever have guessed at something like this?' Radovsky closed his eyes, then opened them again. Yes, the incredible sight was still there.

Before him, that familiar smile on their faces under three familiar bushy moustaches, stood three Stalins.

The same bulky, stalwart figures. The same lead-coloured complexion, with the beginnings of a double chin. The same grey hair cut *en brosse*. The same bushy eyebrows, strong nose, broad chin. The same plain uniform with broad epaulettes and only one order on it: the Order of Lenin. Three copies of the same man. Radovsky swallowed. 'Mephistopheles, indeed!' he said hoarsely. 'This is amazing.'

'It's not done with make-up or wigs. The whole thing is genuine.'

'I just can't grasp it.' Radovsky rose heavily, and went from one Stalin to another, looking them up and down, staring into their faces. Shaking his head, he returned to his chair. 'Igor Vladimirovich I see Stalin every day of my life. . . .'

Smolka filled five cups with aromatic, greenish tea from a samovar. As he handed them round, he introduced the three men.

'This is Vladimir Leontinovich Plesikovsky. A joiner, from

Temir-Tau in Kazakhstan. He's sat as a model for all the monuments to Stalin in the villages and towns along the Nura.'

Radovsky nodded. Plesikovsky smiled amiably, and hooked his right thumb through his buttonhole. That, too, is a characteristic gesture, thought Radovsky.

'Here's Nikolai Ilyich Tabun.' Smolka was introducing the next man. 'A carter. He lives in Oza on the Kama, south of Perm, where they used a photograph of him for the Party poster at the October Revolution celebrations of 1943. They wanted a picture of Stalin waving to the people with both hands, but in fact he never raises his right hand above his forehead.'

'Correct.' Radovsky sounded quite exhausted.

'And our third comrade is Anton Vassilyevich Nurashvili.'

'Aha!' Radovsky slapped his thigh. 'A distant relation?'

'Nurashvili comes from Akhalkansi, south of Tbilisi; he's a doctor, and modestly attributes much of his medical success to the fact that, though they know it's only an illusion, his patients feel Stalin himself has been treating them.'

Radovsky sipped his tea. At a gesture from Smolka, the three Stalins went out, taking their own teacups with them. As the door closed behind them, Radovsky loosened the collar of his uniform tunic.

'Do you realize, Igor Vladimirovich,' he said, 'just what you have there? Look on the dark side first. In theory, you could replace Stalin himself by one of these doubles. It's an idea that will certainly occur to Stalin. It would be enough to get them liquidated, and you along with them. You do realize that? I imagine you have your men there very well trained.'

'They walk and talk like Stalin, drink, shout, sleep, smoke and make love like Stalin – all to excess. They're perfect copies.'

'That, Igor Vadimirovich, adds up to four sentences of death.'

'We're in private here, I hope, Comrade General.'

Radovsky sipped his tea again, and lit another cigarette. 'I have to admire your courage.'

'I want Stalin to meet them.'

'Aren't there easier ways of committing suicide?'

'Comrade General, I want you to get me an opportunity of introducing Stalin to his three doubles.'

Radovsky stared at Smolka. 'Listen, the man is obsessed by

pathological suspicion of everyone, and you mean to present him with proof positive that he could be removed from the scene and no one would notice?'

'Look at it on the bright side, Comrade General. These doubles are Stalin's best possible protection against an attempt on his life.' Smolka sat down facing Radovsky. 'Whenever Stalin appears in public, over the next few weeks or even months, it would really be a double of him. It's the *only* way of protecting him against these Germans. Just let me explain that to him. And we could also put it to him that, supposing there really are any conspirators in the Kremlin, they themselves wouldn't know which Stalin they were seeing.'

'Igor Vladimirovich, you leave Mephistopheles standing,' Radovsky rose. So did Smolka. 'What do you suggest I say to prepare Stalin for this encounter? Any ideas?'

'Just tell him the facts.'

'An idea so brilliantly unusual, it could stem only from the NKVD,' said Radovsky ironically.

Smolka escorted the General to the lift, and then returned to his office and the adjoining rooms. The three 'Stalins' were sitting in Nikolai Ilyich Tabun's room, which was darkened, waiting in front of a screen with a 16 mm film projector in place.

'End of the first Act, and a very good performance,' Smolka told them.'General Radovsky is close to Comrade Stalin, and I think we've convinced him.' He went over to the projector and pressed a button. The first pictures came up on the screen: jubilant soldiers. 'Stalin visiting victorious troops. One of the few occasions when he's moved around freely among the people. Watch his movements: watch the expression on his face, and in particular the way he carries himself. Then we'll go right through it again in slow motion. Every detail matters.'

Smolka glanced at his three copies of Stalin as the film ran. Radovsky is right, he thought, pleased with himself. They're so like the real thing it's positively uncanny.

It turned out to have been a good idea for Milda Ivanovna to take this particular apartment at number 19, Lesnaya Street. The road was such a busy one that no one would notice several men strolling past a building, looking at it with interest, turning to

274

glance inside, and then going in. An old woman was sweeping the pavement with a birch broom, gathering the rubbish into heaps. Ivanov, always a friendly character, gave her a cheerful 'Good morning!' as he went into number 19. Then he stopped on the stairs, listening warily. The sound of music, faint but clear, came from above. A Tchaikovsky piano concerto.

The door of the building opened again. Ivanov bent, pretending to tie a shoelace, and waited. He looked up as the new arrival came level with him. It was Sepkin.

Ivanov hugged his friend. 'Peter!' he cried.

Sepkin clapped a hand over his mouth. 'Ssh!'

'Sorry — Pyotr Mironovich,' stammered Ivanov. 'You made it. My God, I'm so glad to see you.'

'Come on, let's go up to Milda's,' said Sepkin. 'We're ten minutes early, but that won't hurt.' He glanced at Ivanov. 'You're looking well. Very brown.'

'I got an open-air job — putting up scaffolding with a construction brigade. We're actually at work on part of the Kremlin Palace walls.'

'Congratulations, Fyodor Panteleyevich.'

They climbed the steps towards the strains of Tchaikovsky.

Milda opened the door at once, smiling radiantly at Ivanov. 'It's good to see you,' she said, letting them in. 'You two are the first. There'll be four more coming.'

'Four?' Sepkin looked inquiringly at Milda. She only shrugged her shoulders and shook her head. 'What about the others, Mildusha?'

'No sign of life from them.'

'Which ones?' asked Sepkin, his voice husky.

'Later — wait till the others are here. . . .'

They had all arrived by eleven o'clock, embraced, slapped each other on the back. The tension that had been weighing on them all relaxed.

Petrovsky was the last to burst into the apartment, letting out a yell of joy, and brandishing two dark-brown paper bags. 'Comrades, it's great to see you again,' he cried. 'Look what I've got here. Sausage, bread, butter, cheese, cucumbers and chicken breast. And a bottle of potato spirit. . . .'

'We're all here now, then,' said Duskov gravely.

275

Petrovsky looked around, and understood. His happy mood burst like a bubble. He bowed his head, saying quietly, 'I'm sorry. I didn't know.'

He broke off, biting his lip, and stood there in silence beside Boranov. Little Pleyin, looking rather paler and thinner than before, was fiddling with a horseshoe charm on a small gold chain which Lyudmila Dragonovna had given him.

Duskov, as the man appointed by Colonel von Renneberg to take over command if anything happened to Sassonov, raised his head, and spoke just loud enough to be heard above the sound of the music.

'We must assume', he said in German, 'that we shall never see our four friends again. Let us honour them with a brief tribute.'

Milda Ivanovna started, as a sudden sharp sound rang through the room: the six men had clicked their heels and were standing stiffly to attention. She stared incredulously at her friends. It was an odd sight: six shabbily dressed Soviet workmen in the middle of Moscow, standing to attention like German officers at the funeral of a companion being buried with full military honours.

'We mourn for our friends,' said Duskov, his voice husky.

'For Major Bodo von Labitz

'For Lieutenant Berno von Ranovski

'For Lieutenant Detlev Adler

'For Second Lieutenant Dietrich Semper

'Who fell in action at the front, true to their oath of allegiance.'

'Have you finished?' asked Milda Ivanovna.

Duskov turned, as if waking from a dream. 'Yes.'

'Good.' Her voice was harsh. 'You're here to kill Stalin, not play soldiers.'

Boranov relaxed, and sat down on a chair behind him. Pleyin swallowed, and cleared his throat. Ivanov sat on the sofa where Volonov and Milda used to lie, listening to music and making love.

'We can recount our experiences later,' said Duskov. 'For reasons you'll all appreciate, Sepkin was quite right to move the date of our meeting forward.'

'I was coming here very soon myself, in any case,' said Ivanov. 'I need some hand grenades. I could well meet Stalin somewhere in the Kremlin.'

'Events on the Eastern Front are moving at alarming speed.' Duskov looked at his hands. 'And things are no better in the west. Rommel can't stop the extension of the Allied bridgehead. We're short of men and supplies everywhere.'

'But of course the Führer will bring us through,' said Petrovsky sarcastically. 'What are such minor inconveniences to a man of his genius?' Milda was pouring wine for them. 'So now what? Do we have to wait for a military parade, or for him to go to his dacha or open some establishment or make a public speech? No, we must go to him. But how?'

'I can have a good try.' Ivanov sniffed the wine in his glass; it smelled sour. 'Over the next week or so, I should surely find a way to get close enough to Stalin to carry out our mission.'

He spoke quite casually. Simultaneously, however, Duskov and Boranov shook their heads.

'Well, why not?' said Sepkin. 'Ivanov really does have the best chance.'

'Not alone.' Boranov put his glass down without drinking. 'The uncertainty factor is too great. If Fyodor Panteleyevich should try and fail, we won't get another chance.'

'Lyudmila says he drives around in an armoured car,' said Pleyin. 'But that's not often, because he suffers from claustrophobia.'

'Who's Lyudmila?' Sepkin asked.

'A lieutenant in the police. We're lovers.'

'Well done you,' cried the irrepressible Petrovsky.

'Kyrill Semyonovich has a good point,' said Duskov. 'Now, if a couple more of us could infiltrate the Kremlin.... Fyodor Panteleyevich, could you get your construction brigade to take on a couple of your friends?'

Ivanov shrugged his shoulders. He was not friendly enough with the supervisor, Comrade Skameykin, to feel sure of it. He'd be more likely to listen to Wanda, but Ivanov's instincts told him it would be better for him not to introduce his friends to her yet. The Hallers, particularly Wanda's father, would surely see something suspicious in such a coincidence: one discharged soldier meeting two friends discharged for similar reasons.

'I think it's too soon for that,' said Ivanov. 'I'm lucky to be in the brigade myself; I have my girlfriend Wanda Semyonovna to thank for that.'

'You, too?' said Petrovsky. 'Hands up anyone who hasn't found a warm bed in Moscow yet. What, none of us? Brothers, I'm beginning to feel we've done pretty well for ourselves.' Suddenly he was more serious. 'I have a girl, too. Larissa Alexandrovna is her name. And I'm in love with her.' He looked round. 'Can any of us honestly say we're making love to these girls only to make use of them?'

'Let's not discuss that,' said Duskov. 'We have our mission to complete; nothing else matters.'

He thought of Anya Ivanovna and knew it wasn't true.

'I want a gun and hand grenades,' Ivanov was saying. 'I can't bear to think I might come face to face with Stalin tomorrow, with no weapon but my bare hands!'

Milda Ivanovna, who had taken no part in the conversation so far, went to a wardrobe and opened it. Some dresses hung inside, two coats, a fur, a quilted jacket—and when she pushed the clothes aside they could see the back wall of the wardrobe. Three Soviet submachine-guns stood against it, two automatic rifles, and two rifles with telescopic sights. And there were pistols, hand grenades and explosives lying there in ordinary paper bags. 'Milda Ivanovna, are you crazy?' Sepkin asked hoarsely. 'Just keeping them there, at the back of an ordinary wardrobe?'

'Tell me a better place to hide them.'

'Suppose someone had opened it?'

'Who?'

'Yanis Mikhailovich.'

'He was more interested in me without my clothes.'

'And who, for heaven's sake, is Yanis Mikhailovich?' asked Petrovsky.

'A Russian major,' said Sepkin calmly. 'One of Stalin's staff officers. I killed him the day before yesterday, here in this room.'

They all stared at him.

A couple of children playing ball found Volonov's corpse. The police acted fast. Once photographs had been taken, Volonov's body was taken to the NKVD building. Clearly a case of murder.

The man's neck was broken and his carotid artery ruptured. The first injury would have killed him instantly.

Smolka went down to the cellars at once. The dead man looked as if he were asleep; the one jarring note was traces of vegetable broth in his hair and on his uniform.

'Major Yanis Mikhailovich Volonov,' said the police lieutenant who had brought the body in. He handed Smolka the police report. The Colonel put it in his pocket, walked slowly round the corpse, then nodded and turned to go out.

'Keep him here,' he said.

Back in his office, he rang General Radovsky, who sighed on hearing his voice. 'No, Igor Vladimirovich, I have not had access to Stalin today.'

'Comrade General, the Germans have struck.'

'Where? I can assure you Stalin is alive and well.'

'It's one of his staff officers, according to the papers on him. Major Volonov was murdered by a karate chop.'

'Smolka, this is atrocious.' Radovsky's voice shook. 'Who knows?'

'Not many people.'

'Where was he killed?'

'He was actually found by some children at the Zoo, but that's not where the murder was committed. There are traces of food on his clothes and hair. He must have died in a room where a meal was in progress. The corpse was removed and hidden in the bushes where it was found.'

'What do you know about this Major Volonov, Smolka?'

'Not much yet. We're busy investigating his private life, of course. He lived on his own, a quiet sort of character. Very fond of the theatre. No one knows for certain if he had a mistress, though he hadn't been spending the night at his own place recently.'

'Ah, a quiet sort of character,' Radovsky laughed. 'Come on, Smolka, your obsession with these Germans is affecting your judgement. This sounds like some ordinary *crime passionnel*. First she throws a plate at him, then she strikes an unfortunately fatal blow—'

'Which broke his neck?' asked Smolka. 'A woman's hand?'

'I've known some women with very hard hands, Igor Vladimirovich. Well, what are you going to do? Publish Volonov's picture in the papers?'

'No, hush it up, I think,' said Smolka. 'Publicity might make the murderers lie low.'

'Why do you think it was your German officers who killed Major Volonov?'

'I have a theory, Comrade General, that he could have chanced upon some clue that alerted him. Then, following it up, he entered their hideout, and found himself facing them, probably while they were eating. They murdered him and disposed of the body.'

'You're making life complicated for yourself, Smolka,' said Radovsky. 'Not every crime committed in Moscow has your Germans behind it, you know. Well, don't panic—and I'll see what I can do with Stalin for you.'

Colonel Smolka thanked Radovsky politely and hung up.

After the six Wild Geese had said good-bye, they left the building separately, at intervals of a few minutes. Milda Ivanovna went out shopping, taking her basket to stand in line outside a fishmonger's where a consignment of dried cod had just arrived. Sepkin went for a walk in the sun, sat on the bench in the Zoo where the children's grandmothers had been sitting earlier, glanced casually around, and guessed that the man leaning against the nearby fence, reading a copy of *Pravda*, was a secret policeman. Volonov's body had been found. He rose, strolled on, stopped at the Zoo gates for a view of a magnificent peacock spreading his tail, and then went down to the Metro station and back to the accident hospital and his incinerator.

Ivanov was the only man to leave armed, with a pistol and three hand grenades. The others inspected the weapons available, and agreed to keep in constant touch from now on through Milda Ivanovna. They would transmit a signal to her every evening, merely to report their presence. Only if Milda sent back a certain signal—the same number three times running—would they know that it was a summons to come at once.

That evening they were all back with their girlfriends, listening to the radio news describing their brave brothers' victories at the front.

Semyon Tikhinovich Haller had brought off a splendid piece of bartering at work that day, and came home with a good joint of beef, to the delight of his wife Antonia Nikitayevna. She served it with a piquant sauce and dried, soaked and cooked potato slices. After the meal, Wanda and Ivanov sat on the sofa hand in hand. At first, Semyon Tikhinovich had looked askance when he saw his daughter sitting so close to Fyodor Panteleyevich, devouring him with her eyes. But they were gradually becoming used to the idea that Wanda had brought them home a son-in-law. Now she would even kiss Fedya in front of her parents.

'But I'm not having them hopping into bed together, not before they're married,' Semyon told Antonia. 'There are limits!'

These things were not discussed so openly in the Sharenkov household: Pavlov Ignatovich, the architect, was a tactful and educated man. Lyra Pavlovna was plainly in love with Kyrill Semyonovich Boranov; her parents did broach the subject with her one day when Boranov was working late.

'Lyra, are you two planning to get married?' asked Sharenkov.

'Yes,' said Lyra Pavlovna.

'Why?'

'Because I can't imagine life without Kyrill Semyonovich any more.'

'A very good answer, too,' said her mother, Marya Ivanovna. 'I said the same to my own father twenty-two years ago, as you may remember.'

'Ah, the times were different then,' said Sharenkov.

'But love was the same.'

'Well,' said Sharenkov thoughtfully, rolling himself a cigarette, 'I must admit Boranov is a decent fellow, and what more can one ask, in these days?'

When news of the Russian victories began coming over the radio, Sharenkov had tacked a large map of Russia to the wall, and brought home little flags from the office to stick on it—red flags for the Red Army, yellow flags for the Germans. Every evening they sat in front of this map, marking the areas the Russians had taken as the news bulletins came through. Later, they would have a cup of tea, and after that Boranov and Lyra would usually go for a walk in the mild summer evening. They could kiss, standing in dark doorways, or out in the Botanical

Garden, whose benches were full of pairs of lovers, all needing some quiet, private place to be. Lyra Pavlovna said, 'Who'd have thought it possible for me to love you so much?' Her tone was teasing and affectionate. 'A man like you.'

'I know, it's incredible.' They kissed, and when Boranov put his hand on Lyra's breast she began to tremble, her fingers digging into the back of his neck. She was twenty, and no man had ever touched her like that before. 'Oh, I do love you,' she repeated, her eyes wide with mingled fear and longing. 'Kyrill, people can see us here. . . .'

'We can lie on the grass. We have so little time, Lyranya.'

She nodded, nestling close and putting her arms round him as his hand slipped inside her blouse, caressing her. She felt sensations like little electric shocks running right through her body. 'Oh, can't you find a room somewhere?' she whispered breathlessly. She felt hot between the thighs, a sort of arousal she had never guessed at. 'Kyrill, we need a room so much. What shall we do — oh, my darling, what shall we do?'

She was trembling. She took Boranov's hand from under her skirt, and covered his face with rapid little kisses, as if in apology.

'We'd get a room to ourselves once we were married,' she said. 'I know Father could see to that, at the office. We are going to get married, aren't we?'

'Yes,' said Boranov, holding Lyra's face against him and staring over her head at the quiet park, its benches so full of closely entwined couples. 'Yes, we'll get married, if luck's on our side.'

Lyudmila Dragonovna Tcherskassya had kept her word and brought Pleyin a police uniform. She laid her spoils on the bed, hugged Pleyin, calling him 'her little eagle', almost tore her own clothes off, and made love to him there beside the uniform.

Pleyin was overwhelmed by so much pleasure. Surely there could be no one like her in the world! He never tired of looking at her smooth-skinned body, her slanted, glowing eyes, her full lips which opened to show two rows of small white teeth. She was like a lovely beast of prey.

It was a very curious feeling for Pleyin when he first tried on the uniform. It had a sergeant's stripes on it, and was a little too big, but a tuck or so could soon put that right, and it changed

Pleyin's appearance completely. He looked in the mirror, and could not help smiling wryly when Lyudmila, stark naked, appeared behind him and put her arms round him. What the glass showed him was a beautiful woman, vibrant with life, embracing the living dead.

'No one will dare to ask you any questions now,' she said in her low, thrilling voice. 'You can go anywhere you like in that uniform. Are you pleased, my little eagle?'

Pleyin nodded. What a chance it could give me, he thought.

Petrovsky, so resilient, ready to make light of anything and never at a loss for words, was suffering from a sense of depression which he could not explain to Larissa Alexandrovna on the day the Wild Geese met.

As usual, they went home together from the tractor-plant. Petrovsky had been driving tractors around all afternoon, knowing that four of his companions had apparently never reached Moscow. No one would have expected it of him, but he was mourning; thinking of those days in Eberswalde, the cheerful evenings he and the others had spent with Kraskin, Sassonov, Bunurian and Tarski, of their farewells before they were driven off to the various airfields and their waiting parachutes. Of course, they had known very well at the time that there was almost no chance of coming home alive, but it was hard, at first, to accept it when you knew for certain that a particular man, a friend of yours, had died.

'Let's go and see Dr Speshnikov, Larissa,' said Petrovsky, as they waited at the Metro station to change trains.

'Are you sick?' she asked, eyes wide with alarm. 'Luka — oh, darling, is it that ulcer again?'

He shook his head. 'I just feel like seeing him, love. I'm quite all right now, really.'

'But what about the ulcer? Does it hurt?'

'It's cured now; the doctor said so.' Petrovsky put his arm round Larissa's shoulders. She's trembling, he thought, comforted by her affection. She's afraid for me. My dear little girl. She's already making plans for after the war — a little wooden house with a tiny garden, so our children will have somewhere pleasant to play, and she can grow vegetables and sunflowers, and have cherry-trees and currant-bushes. Oh, Larissa, if only there were no Stalin. . . .

'Dr Speshnikov was a good friend to me, and he's a lonely old man. We ought to visit him now and then to cheer him up, so why not today?' he said.

So they did visit Dr Speshnikov, which cheered him considerably and even, to some extent, consoled Petrovsky himself.

Duskov sat in an armchair, leaning forward, listening to the German news. He could hear Anya Ivanovna clattering plates in the kitchen, and smell braised cucumbers, one of her specialities: there is an art in cooking braised cucumbers so that they are tender but not mushy, and the stuffing is important. Anya made a delicious minced-meat stuffing.

'What are they saying?' she called from the kitchen.

Duskov raised his head. 'No idea,' he called back. 'It's in German; you had it tuned to that damn Nazi transmitter again.'

She came out of the kitchen, tossing back her black hair, and licking the wooden spoon she had used to stir the cucumbers. A pleasant voice, well calculated to get the listener's attention, was being broadcast from Berlin, reading a piece outlining the general situation and the necessity for reducing the fronts, and going on to praise the Führer's irresistible will and his intention of turning these severe trials into a glorious victory any time now. 'Never has the iron will of our people been stronger than now, never has our faith in our Führer been greater.'

I believe that's Hans Fritzsche, thought Duskov. We used to hear him every Saturday, broadcasting Goebbels's leading articles from the *Reich* to the nation. And the nation felt it was a privilege to live in such stirring times.

Duskov presented a picture of boredom as he leafed through a newspaper, but all the time he was listening intently to the radio. 'No, really, German is a barbarous language,' he told Anya Ivanovna.

'If you could only understand it. . . .' Anya sat down on the arm of Duskov's chair and pointed her wooden spoon at the radio. 'Now he's saying Germany will soon have beaten Russia. Really, you should hear him. I almost feel sorry for the Germans.'

'Why?' Duskov bent his head. The broadcast had ended; another announcer was saying, 'That was Hans Fritzsche speaking.' Yes, I was right, Duskov thought.

284

'Because they believe all they're told,' she said. 'They even believe it when they hear they're going to crush Russia.'

Duskov leaned over to retune the radio to the Moscow station, and turned down the volume. There were military marches on again.

'They'll be sorry,' she added.

Duskov took a deep breath, looked up, and tapped Anya's wooden spoon. 'Why should that bother us?' he asked. 'Is it even worth thinking about the Germans? How about those cucumbers – they're not burning, are they?'

After supper they listened to extracts from *Lohengrin, Tannhäuser, Die Meistersinger*. Duskov had clasped his hands and was resting his chin on them, sitting well forward in his chair, his eyes closed. There were deep lines at the corners of his mouth, carved into a face almost too good-looking for a man's.

Inwardly, he was bleeding for his country. What will become of Germany? he thought. Dear God, what will happen?

Anya Ivanovna sat on the floor at his feet, her head against his thighs. She looked forward, all day, to this brief evening hour, when the room was lit by a single candle and filled with music, and she was alone with Leonid Germanovich, feeling him near her, until the night brought tenderness and fulfilment.

'Why Wagner?' asked Duskov. She looked up at him; his voice was odd, almost as if he were having difficulty in suppressing tears.

'I just love his music,' she said.

'He was German.'

'So were Bach and Beethoven.'

There was a record of Franz Volker on the gramophone, singing the part of Lohengrin, and he remembered vividly the Baldenov family's visits to Berlin. As befitted their rank, they had always stayed at the Adlon hotel. And they always visited the Berlin State Opera, his mother in a long silk dress, his father with the ribbon of his order in his buttonhole.

'Turn it off,' he said hoarsely. 'Please turn it off, Anyushka. Put on a waltz, something from an operetta, anything – but not this music today.'

She rose at once, turned off the gramophone, went back to Duskov and bent over him. 'You're tired,' she said solicitously, stroking his face. 'Let's go to bed.' She passed her fingertips over the deep lines at the corner of his mouth. 'What are you doing with those? Let me smooth them out for you.' Her lips fluttered over his eyes and mouth. 'I love you so much,' she said. 'I don't know how to put it into words.'

'Oh, Anyushka, I wish I need never hear about the war or think of it any more.' He held her head close to his shoulder. 'How wonderful that would be, Anyushka.'

Every night, radio signals came through to Milda Ivanovna. No words or letters, just the identifying number announcing that they were in touch.

Duskov, Pleyin and Sepkin usually transmitted their signals from the lavatory, where they could unscrew the heels of their shoes in private. Boranov could wait for the last tram to arrive at a depot, sit in it and transmit his number from there. Petrovsky and Ivanov transmitted their signals earlier than the rest, when they came off work. Ivanov hid behind a pile of planks, amazed at his own audacity in sending his radio signal from the Kremlin itself, and Petrovsky found places to hide, unseen, among the shelves full of engine parts in the spares store of the tractor-plant.

Every night, each time, Milda Ivanovna radioed back a brief 'Zero'.

Not many people were privileged to speak to Stalin in private. But General Radovsky had given Colonel Smolka the opportunity he wanted. Smolka felt the palms of his hands begin to sweat when Radovsky rang him at the NKVD building and said, almost casually, 'Tomorrow. Eleven at night. I'll be waiting outside to take you in through the side-entrance.'

'Eleven at night?' Smolka inquired.

'Stalin needs only two or three hours' sleep.'

'I'll be there at eleven,' said Smolka. 'What about the guards on the gate?'

'They have orders to let through two NKVD cars without checking them; if you show your own pass, that will do. Captain Soliakov is the name of the duty officer.'

'Suppose he sees our three men?'

'Captain Soliakov is being transferred to a special unit at the front, the day after tomorrow.'

Colonel Smolka hung up. He did not know Soliakov, but he felt a certain sympathy for him.

That evening, he rang Radovsky back. 'What will Stalin be wearing?' he asked. 'It could be important to know.'

'His usual style of uniform.'

'And he's prepared for anything?'

'I propose to spend my retirement peacefully, in the country,' said Radovsky drily. 'And by "the country" I do not mean Siberia.'

Everything went smoothly when Smolka stopped at the gate of the Spassky Tower, a quarter of an hour before his appointment, and Captain Soliakov came up to the first of the black cars. Its driver was a young NKVD lieutenant. Smolka showed his special pass at the window. The Kremlin guard, usually fairly numerous at this point, had been sent off, and Captain Soliakov bore sole responsibility. He gave Smolka's identification only a cursory glance, as he had been told to do, and waved both cars on.

The windows of the second car were covered with blackout material. Three stocky men sat in the back of it, wearing a simplified version of a field-marshal's uniform. A partition had been erected between them and the front of the car, so that no light could fall on them, and their driver, who had not been allowed to get behind the wheel until they were safely inside, did not know who his passengers were. His instructions, and those of the driver of Smolka's car, were to leave the cars and go away as soon as their occupants were out.

The cars drove slowly in, and stopped at the entrance to the Council of Ministers building. General Radovsky stood there, alone. He got into the leading car beside Smolka. 'Drive on to the Nikolski Tower,' he said, 'round the building and along the inside of the Kremlin Wall. I'll tell you when to stop.'

Smolka nodded. He had thought his nerves were pretty strong, but as they drove around the building, and stopped at a small door opposite the Kremlin Wall, where the illustrious dead were entombed, he felt his pulse beat harder.

'Here we are,' said Radovsky. Smolka gestured, and the two drivers marched off into the darkness.

Radovsky had the key to this small door. He opened it, and nodded to Smolka. Smolka opened the door of the second NKVD car, and said, into the darkened interior. 'You can get out now, Comrade Generalissimo.'

The door on the other side of the car was opened, too. Three Stalins got out. They looked around them, eyes narrowed, straightened their coats, cursorily smoothed down their bushy moustaches with their forefingers, and then went towards Radovsky with that familiar firm tread.

'This would really be too much for most men's nerves,' murmured Radovsky. 'How the hell do you stand it, Igor Vladimirovich?'

'I've got used to it, Comrade General.'

'I suppose it's all right for you; you're only dealing with the outer man. If you saw him every day. . . .' Radovsky did not finish his sentence. 'You're in luck, Smolka.'

'I hope so.'

'Stalin's had a couple of drinks, maybe more. He's in a good mood. He's even told a couple of jokes.'

'Programme 4,' Smolka told his companions. They were just mounting a rather steep and narrow staircase.

Radovsky stopped. 'What does that mean?'

'During our rehearsals, we've analysed the behaviour of Stalin in various situations. Stalin as field-marshal, Stalin at a parade, Stalin viewing exhibitions, Stalin supposedly in private but still on view to the public, Stalin at lectures, Stalin at receptions. . . . Well, Programme 4 is Stalin in a small circle of intimates, after a moderate intake of alcohol.'

'Igor Vladimirovich,' said Radovsky, his voice hoarse, 'you could be a dangerous man.'

They entered a large hall, went down a long corridor, and found themselves in a room of medium size, with remarkably bourgeois furnishings. Its standard- and table-lamps had pleated silk shades, and the windows were thickly curtained. What struck Smolka the moment he came in was the smell of acrid tobacco hanging around the room.

The three doubles showed not the slightest concern. Smolka chewed his lower lip as Radovsky went to a telephone and raised the receiver. He dialled a single digit. It was ringing somewhere: the signal Stalin was expecting.

The three doubles took off their caps. Their heavy iron-grey

288

skulls dominated the dimly lit room. Frowning, they watched the door. It *is* uncanny, thought Radovsky. That is precisely the way he looks at someone when he is displeased. Sometimes he can be expansive, jovial, relaxed, but generally his glance is hard and hypnotic.

At last the door at the far end of the room was flung open. Stalin stood in the doorway himself. He was wearing the uniform Radovsky had described. His hands were behind his back, his pipe, with its curved stem, in the corner of his mouth. His eyes were a little larger than Smolka had expected. His face, with its leaden complexion and broad planes, might have been modelled out of clay. He tucked in his chin, looking at Colonel Smolka, and did not move a muscle when Smolka, feeling that the frantic beating of his heart must be clearly audible, stood to attention.

The three doubles reacted rapidly, as they had been taught to do. They produced pipes from their own pockets and put them in the corners of their own mouths. Stalin came a couple of steps on into the room and, without a word, looked around him.

One Stalin stood by the window to Stalin's own left, pipe in mouth, glaring at him in a chilly manner.

Another Stalin stood in the middle of the room, beside a round coffee-table, pipe in mouth, a look in his eyes that boded no good.

Another Stalin stood to Stalin's own right, beside the Colonel, pipe in mouth, looking as if he disliked the world in general.

'That one in the middle is too fat,' said Stalin, pointing at Plesikovsky with his pipe. 'Should be ten pounds lighter.'

Plesikovsky removed his pipe from his own mouth and pointed it at Stalin. 'The measurements are quite correct,' he said, in precisely the same voice and with precisely the same tone.

'Ten pounds too heavy, and I should know,' barked Stalin. He turned away, went up to the Stalin on the left, and looked at him as if he were a piece of sculpture on exhibition. As he did so, he tamped down the tobacco in his pipe with his thumb. The other Stalin copied the movement exactly with his pipe. 'Cow's eyes!' said Stalin. 'Cow's eyes!'

Smolka felt his alarm increasing. He remained motionless, standing to attention. Radovsky was standing inconspicuously behind a standard-lamp.

Treading heavily, Stalin passed on, taking no notice whatever of Smolka, who might as well have been part of the furniture, and stopped in front of the third Stalin. Yet again he tamped down the tobacco in his pipe; yet again his double performed the identical movement. Stalin raised his bushy brows. So, simultaneously, did the man opposite him.

'As for this one, his nose is no good at all,' said Stalin. 'Hairs growing out of it. Do *I* have a hairy nose?'

'Yes,' said his counterpart. 'There was a drip hanging from the hairs, too, at the last October Parade.'

Radovsky, stationed behind his lamp, was on the point of collapse. Smolka, still standing to attention, closed his eyes. The man is quite right, he thought. You could see that drip clearly on the photographs I gave them to study, but did he have to say so to Stalin's face?

'It was cold,' said Stalin, after a moment's surprised silence. 'Very cold. *Your* nose would have been running the whole damn time. Mine only had a drip on it.' He put his left hand to his nostrils, felt the small hairs in them, and returned his pipe to his mouth. The three doubles did so, too.

Radovsky emerged from behind his lamp.

'Comrade Generalissimo,' he said, carefully casual, 'may I introduce Colonel Igor Vladimirovich Smolka of the NKVD?'

'Ah.' Stalin looked at Smolka, frowning. 'This was your idea?'

'Yes,' said Smolka hoarsely.

'Why didn't Beria mention it to me?'

'Er—Comrade Beria doesn't know yet. . . .'

For a moment, Smolka felt that he had said the disastrously wrong thing. Then Stalin's face relaxed, split into a smile, and he laughed—laughed uproariously, brandishing his pipe in the air and poking Smolka in the chest with it.

'Beria doesn't know,' crowed Stalin, delighted. 'Beria doesn't know, the little rat-face. There are three more of me about the place, and Beria has no idea!' He punched Smolka playfully in the chest, laughing again. 'Igor—what was your name?'

'Vladimirovich.'

'Igor Vladimirovich, I like you. Men with original ideas are few and far between. You might not know it, but I have to do everything myself—everything, all by myself. I'm the only one who can think in this place. The rest of them are solid bone between the ears.'

Radovsky cast Smolka a quick glance, behind Stalin's back. It said: Don't answer back, just keep smiling and listen. I told you he'd had a few. At this point he likes to deliver a monologue. The great dictators all act the same.

Suddenly, Stalin stopped short. He was breathing heavily, with a hollow snorting sound. Then he poked Smolka in the chest with his pipe again, and said, in a milder tone, 'Well, we'll see, Igor Vladimirovich, we'll see. An idea is a good idea only if it works. We'll see.'

He went to the door, indicating to the three other Stalins that they were to follow him. They left the room. Smolka relaxed. Radovsky blew his nose hard.

'It should be all right,' he said, putting his handkerchief away.

'Where's he taken them?' asked Smolka. 'What do you think, Comrade General?'

'Better not to think, Smolka. Not here. Just wait.'

At last, the door opened again, and the Stalins came back. Four of them stood there in the room side by side, a broad smile on their faces, the smile that beamed down genially from Stalin's picture on the hoardings. Radovsky had never had a moment's trouble with his eyesight in his life, but even he began to doubt if his optical nerves were really working properly.

Colonel Smolka looked keenly at the four, and then he understood.

'Well, which is the real Stalin?' asked one of them. 'Come along, Yefim Grigoryevich, it shouldn't be hard for you to tell,' he added.

There's no mistaking that voice, thought Radovsky, relieved. He can't take me in. That particular undertone, that accent — they're unmistakable. It's the details that give you away, Comrade Chairman. You should have got one of the others to do the talking.

He stepped forward, looked at the speaker, and said, 'You are, Comrade Generalissimo.'

'Igor Vladimirovich?' Stalin looked at Smolka. 'What's your opinion?'

Smolka was not so sure as Radovsky. He looked hard at the four men, in search of differences, and he found them, but he still could not say for certain which was the man himself. He decided on the Stalin standing on the extreme left. The faint trace of a mocking smile at the corners of his mouth seemed a good enough clue.

Radovsky's choice of Stalin put his hands in his jacket pockets, as if his uniform were a dressing-gown: another favourite mannerism of Stalin's. Yes, that's him, thought Radovsky, with satisfaction. And I should know, after so many drinking sessions with him.

'I am Nikolai Ilyich Tabun,' said Radovsky's Stalin.

Radovsky gestured helplessly. 'I give up,' he said.

Smolka looked at his own choice. 'And I'm Anton Vassilyevich Nurashvili,' said Smolka's Stalin. Smolka took a step backwards. The perfection of his own creation left him speechless.

With that familiar wave of the hand, the Stalin on the extreme right came forward, walked to an armchair with his characteristically firm tread, and sat down. 'Well,' said Stalin. 'If even you two don't know me – and you in particular, Yefim Grigoryevich – how could anyone else expect to do so? Colonel Smolka, your plan is excellent.'

'Thank you very much.' Smolka was annoyed to find himself sounding like a schoolboy getting praised for something, but Stalin's goodwill was to be received in a spirit of simple thanksgiving. 'This should disarm any potential enemies. . . .'

The second Stalin from the right suddenly roared with laughter, laughing so much that he bent double. 'They fell for it again. That was a double bluff. I'm the real Stalin, comrades.'

He took the pipe from his pocket, lit it, and waved his hand around the room. 'Well, let's all sit down. What's the matter, Radovsky?'

'How do we know that you *are* the real Stalin?' asked Radovsky.

'Well, I am. Ask the others.'

'They'll nod – and, if the real Stalin is among them, so will he. It – it's a dangerous game, if no one can tell you apart.'

'I was coming to that,' said Stalin. 'We'll discuss it. Smolka, you have successfully proved that I could disappear, and a substitute could take my place. Do you really think I'm going to stand for that?'

And then Radovsky knew, not just that they had proved their

case, but that this speaker was the true Stalin: the man who went in fear of treachery all his days, insecure even behind the high walls of the Kremlin.

Sharenkov had learned the news three days in advance, before there were any notices in the papers, or Stalin's inspiring speech was read out over the radio, against a background of military music. They heard of such things early on in the Reconstruction Planning Office. He was so late home that Marya Ivanovna said, 'I suppose he's working away on that triumphal arch of his.' She began to worry. Boranov and Lyra Pavlovna did their best to calm her; Boranov even went out to a public phone and rang the Planning Office, where they assured him that Comrade Pavlov Ignatovich was perfectly all right. However, his late return home was puzzling.

At last, Sharenkov did come through the door, swinging his briefcase happily, kissed his wife with great fervour, and even hugged Boranov, though he did not usually approve of such demonstrations of affection between men.

'Wonderful news,' cried Sharenkov. 'If it's true, 17 July will be a day to remember for ever.'

Marya Ivanovna, dishing up a delicious onion-and-cabbage soup, was baffled. Pavlov did not actually smell of vodka, but he sounded distinctly intoxicated. She sat down, asking in her quiet way, 'They're not really going to build your triumphal arch after all, are they?'

'Better than that,' cried Sharenkov. He looked at Boranov, who was dividing a piece of bread into four equal portions on a wooden board. 'Kyrill Semyonovich, you're a war hero, this will mean a lot to you. On 17 July thousands of German prisoners will march through Moscow. It will take all day. They're being brought to the city from all over the place, to big camps in the woods outside. On the night of the sixteenth they will be brought right into Moscow, and on the seventeenth – ah, on the seventeenth they'll be marched through the streets!' Sharenkov was quite carried away by his patriotic enthusiasm. 'A great day for all of us. Forty thousand German prisoners, they say.'

He ate his soup, drank some kvass, and rubbed his hands with delight.

'Oh, Papushka, we must go and see it,' said Lyra Pavlovna.

'Indeed we shall. Every Soviet citizen should see it. The shops are going to be closed, everyone will have the day off work, all the children will be out to watch. Of course we'll be there, too.'

Sharenkov's information turned out to be correct. The news-papers urged everyone to turn out and watch, the radio kept broadcasting Stalin's speech, in which he proclaimed that he was going to disprove the lies of the Germans, who claimed that they had broken the force of the Soviet offensive.

It was said that fifty-seven thousand captured Germans would be on show.

Sepkin borrowed a newspaper from the supervisor of the hospital crematorium and read the article about the march with growing indignation. When he was alone, he unscrewed the heel of his shoe, assembled the transmitter and tried, four times, to contact Milda Ivanovna, but she did not answer. Nor could he reach her in the evening, when she acknowledged his call, but merely answered, 'Zero,' as usual.

'Stupid woman,' said Sepkin, blind with rage. His future father-in-law, Pushkin, met him when they both came off shift. Pushkin was in a state of great excitement. As soon as he saw Sepkin coming he ran towards him, crying, 'Did you read it? Did you hear about it? They're going to parade a whole German army through Moscow. And we shall stand in the very front row and spit in their faces, that's what we'll do.'

When they got home, Yelena Lukanovna's reactions were much the same. She was sitting by the radio set, drinking in the patriotic speeches.

'Oh, Pyotr!' she cried flinging her arms round Sepkin's neck. 'Darling, darling Petya, do you think they'll shoot those German monsters afterwards?'

Sepkin bowed his head, kissed the girl he loved more than anything else in the world on the forehead, and locked himself in the bathroom, where he ran cold water into the basin and immersed his head in it. It was the only way he could think of to shake off the feeling that his skull was about to explode at any minute.

On 17 July, Moscow was quiet, waiting. Most of the shops were closed, a skeleton staff kept the industrial plants going, three regiments of Red Guards had cordoned off the streets through which the procession of German prisoners would march. There was no motor traffic at all, except for a great many trucks converted for use by the film-camera units. The police had diverted all other vehicles out to suburban areas. Lyudmila Dragonovna was commanding a platoon of police cordoning off the forecourt of Kursk Station. Pleyin, safe enough in his sergeant's uniform, took the Metro to Lesnaya Street and went to number 19.

He found Milda Ivanovna's apartment occupied by three tubercular poets and a composer with only one eye. They looked warily at him. Milda pretended that there was some mistake, and accompanied Pleyin out to the stairs. 'Are you crazy?' she hissed at him. 'What on earth are you doing going around in that uniform? I suppose it's the one your Lyudmila got you. Well, if anyone stops you to question you, you'll have to use your cyanide capsule at once.'

'No one'll stop me, not in a police uniform,' said Pleyin, very confident. 'Where are the others?'

'Not here, and why should they be?' Milda was steering him towards the top of the stairs. 'My friends and I will be out in the streets in a minute, too.'

'But it's horrible, Milda Ivanovna.' Pleyin's face was pale, and he looked much older than usual, alarmingly so. 'Fifty-seven thousand of our comrades, led about like a great herd of cows.'

'Why should you care, Kolka?' Milda Ivanovna gave him a little push to start him on his way. 'Surely you're Nikolai Antonovich Pleyin, a good Soviet citizen, aren't you?'

Pleyin heaved a deep sigh and left. The spectators were already gathering in crowds, very thick around the Belorussian Station. Cossacks on their fast ponies came trotting down the road, shouting to the crowds, 'They're on their way! They'll soon be here! Be patient, you'll soon see them, and what a sight!'

Military music was relayed from a truck equipped with big loudspeakers. Another truck, carrying a platform with two cinecameras mounted on it, drove slowly past the waiting crowd, filming them. Pleyin himself came into the picture for a moment as the camera passed him.

And then the procession arrived – down Rusakovskaya Street

from the Solniki Park. A broad, grey and apparently endless river of heads, bodies and feet making their way down the road. A column of vehicles preceded them, and they were followed by a detachment of cavalry: proud, bright-eyed Cossacks on prancing horses, laughing as they passed the crowds.

The Sharenkovs and Boranov, who had his arm round Lyra Pavlovna's waist, craned their necks to watch the procession as if it were a circus show. They were in the square outside Yaroslavl Station: since two trucks with cameras on them had been positioned at this spot, the Germans would be coming very close here. Guards formed a chain, arms linked, to keep back the crowd, which surged forward as the German prisoners came in sight. Sharenkov, usually a quiet and courteous man, was in a perfect frenzy of patriotism. The endless, marching procession came closer and passed them by. The men marched in ranks thirty abreast, either bareheaded or wearing peaked caps or field-caps, shirts open at the neck, their uniforms dirty and dusty, their faces haggard and unshaven. The defeat of Germany was made plain.

But many of the prisoners put a brave face on it, passing through Moscow with heads held high, treading as firmly as weariness, hunger and hopelessness would allow. Red Guards armed with automatic rifles and submachine-guns accompanied the column, but it was the Cossacks, riding up and down on their fiery horses, who stole the show.

On and on the prisoners went, dusty, sweating. The sound of their marching feet echoed back from the walls of the buildings. Some of the men looked straight ahead, some looked around them. Many of the onlookers fell silent as they passed, while others shouted threats. The Germans saw faces that marvelled at them, were curious, scornful, hostile or sometimes sympathetic, but never indifferent. Some of the Germans showed relief at having survived the war, though what lay ahead was unimaginable.

Sepkin, Petrovsky, Duskov and Ivanov, with their girlfriends, were in the crowd watching the great grey procession go by. Pleyin had joined the policemen cordoning off the Belorussian Station. When about half the prisoners had been paraded past, he slipped quietly away, worked his way through the crowd, and disappeared inside the station. He ran to the empty lavatories, shut himself into one of the cubicles, sat down and wept like a wretched child, his face and the palms of his hands against the wall, weeping out all his pain, weeping for the tragedy of his twenty years of life, and the pointlessness of the present.

Then he collapsed on the floor, putting both hands to his ears. The sound of the fifty-seven thousand marching men could be heard even inside the Belorussian Station.

On 18 July, Ivanov saw Stalin in the Kremlin for the first time.

Fyodor Panteleyevich was pushing a barrow full of wooden wedges over the Trinity Bridge to the Trinity Tower, when he saw Stalin walking in a private part of the Alexandrovsky Garden. It was a very hot day, and Stalin had taken off his jacket and was walking in the shade of the trees, talking to a general. Ivanov stopped on the bridge, looking down. No doubt about it, that was Stalin: he was an unmistakable figure.

But too far off, thought Ivanov. Much too far off. I need a rifle with telescopic sights now. I wouldn't get him with a pistol or a hand grenade from here. Pulses hammering, he observed his surroundings. No, there was no chance of getting down from that bridge to the garden. Given two or even three of them in the place, it would have been different, but Skameykin, damn the man, had refused to sign on any more discharged Red Army soldiers, complaining that he was not running a convalescent home.

Stalin stopped once or twice and even looked up at the bridge, but naturally he took no notice of Ivanov with his barrow, looking down at his intended victim.

Then, that same day, Ivanov saw Stalin for the second time.

He was closer on this occasion. Stalin was driving from the Council of Ministers building to the Praesidium of the Supreme Soviet. He had wound down the window on his side of the car, and he glanced at Ivanov for a second without interest. Ivanov, though he had his pistol in the pocket of his boiler-suit, was taken utterly by surprise and did not even react until the car had passed. He leaned on the plank he had been carrying and decided not to mention this second encounter to the others.

Ivanov worked poorly for the rest of that day. In the evening he, Wanda Semyonovna and her parents went to the cinema. Semyon Tikhinovich had heard that the film being shown was about a steelworker who had risen to become District Commissar at the time of the Revolution and had twenty Tsarist officers hanged. 'Should be worth seeing,' he said. 'You find good men in the steel industry, that's what I always say.' Antonia Nikitayevna was willing enough to see the film: she liked the film star Ivan Petrovich Yedemsky, a strong, handsome man, who was playing the leading part.

'You're so quiet,' whispered Wanda when the lights went out, reaching for Ivanov's hand. 'What's the matter? You look so angry, too. Have I annoyed you or something?'

'It's nothing, Wandushka,' said Ivanov, sitting farther back in his seat. He laid his hand on Wanda's knee and stroked it. Semyon Tikhinovich happened to glance at them just then, and grunted, 'Keep your hands to yourself, will you?'

While the handsome star Yedemsky made a fiery speech on the screen, and Wanda held hands with him tightly, Ivanov decided that he must have a hand grenade in his pocket every time he went to the Kremlin, and be ready to use it at any moment.

That evening, Colonel Smolka rang General Radovsky, as usual, to ask how his three Stalins were. They had been accommodated in a separate part of Stalin's private suite of rooms, and had been introduced to his closest intimates, who, much to Stalin's delight, were in a state of complete confusion. Neither Khrushchev nor Malenkov, neither Bulganin nor Kosygin, neither Kaganovich nor Mikoyan knew for certain whether the Stalin to whom they were talking was the genuine article.

Beria had rung Colonel Smolka at once to express his disapproval, but in cautious terms, since by now Smolka seemed so high in Stalin's favour that it would be unwise to complain too bitterly. Smolka had justified his actions, but Beria remained quietly seething: he and only he was responsible for Stalin's protection. Why had he not been informed?

'I have an idea,' said Smolka, when he rang Radovsky on this particular evening.

'For God's sake, not another of your ideas, Igor Vladimirovich.'

'The German officers will be all the more anxious to carry out their mission now that our armies are winning the war.'

'But, thanks to you, we have four Stalins. As long as Mother Russia is so fertile, she will be invincible.'

'However, our Germans don't know that.'

'Igor Vladimirovich, are you planning actually to introduce our false Stalins to these Germans?'

'Well, yes. It is the only way we can get them to see how hopeless their plan is. And we'll never have a better opportunity. Fifty-seven thousand German prisoners of war have just marched through Moscow. What a slap in the face for the Germans. They hoped to take Moscow and march past the Kremlin, parading on the boulevards themselves—and so they did, but with an army of wretched, starving prisoners of war, betrayed by their Führer, their illusions shattered. At this moment, Comrade General, the people of Russia would be ready to go down on their knees to Stalin if he'd go out and show himself to them on the Kremlin Wall.'

'That's out of the question. Better go and put your head under the cold tap, Smolka. You can abandon that idea at once.'

'Look, Comrade General, we have four Stalins. Can you imagine an assassin who wouldn't throw down his weapons and withdraw in despair at the sight of them? It would be another triumph for Stalin: a quiet one, a secret one but, all the same, one which could have a tremendous effect on history. How can I convince you?'

'Smolka, are you genuinely afraid of these German officers of yours?'

'Yes, on Stalin's behalf. An assassination attempt does have a chance of getting the right man still.'

Radovsky seemed to be thinking hard. He himself could not imagine how any such attempt could be made, with so tight a ring of security around Stalin. However, Smolka was the Intelligence expert, and he seemed to think it possible.

'Well, I'll speak to Zhukov about it,' said Radovsky at last. 'And Khrushchev. But don't be too hopeful, Igor Vladimirovich.'

Smolka hung up, sat back in his armchair and turned on the radio.

The main theme was still the parade of the German prisoners of war. Captured German generals were interviewed. Private

299

soldiers haltingly expressed their grief. One officer, a captain, said, 'This is one hell of a war. Yes, we had to come to Moscow before we knew how they had lied to us. I didn't want to believe that could be true. Like millions of us, I trusted the Führer. You ask what I wish for now? I pray to see my wife and parents again. They live in Wuppertal.' And then, very quietly, almost in tears: 'I only hope Wuppertal is standing when I get home.'

Colonel Smolka leaned back, watching the smoke rise from his Oriental cigarette. Yes, a great day. A day on which to allow oneself a glass of red Crimean wine, as he did now.

Of forty German divisions in the central sector of the Eastern Front, twenty-eight had been encircled.

Duskov, too, was listening to the radio. Anya Ivanovna had fetched her special rations from the Botkin Hospital canteen, and had come home with two pounds of flour, three eggs, some butter eked out with margarine, and a can of goulash. Now she was cooking them a feast: pancakes stuffed with goulash and baked in the oven.

'When I get home ...,' the German captain said. Duskov rose, went into the kitchen, and put his arms round Anya Ivanovna.

'What is it?' she cried in alarm. 'Leonid, you're squashing me!' She dropped the saucepan lid and knife she was holding, and turned into his arms. 'What is it, my darling? Oh, my dear heart, what is it? My love. ...'

Duskov breathed out all the air in his lungs in a heavy sigh, and buried his face in Anya's hair. He was glad she could not see the distortion of his mouth in soundless weeping.

Wuppertal will still be standing, friend, he thought. But he knew, to his bitter grief, that there would be no Neu-Nomme any more.

'The pancakes will burn,' said Anya Ivanovna.

He nodded silently, let go of her, went into the bedroom, threw himself on the bed and covered his face with both hands.

Six

ON THE EVENING of 26 July 1944, Yelena Lukanovna came home radiant and rosy-cheeked. Pushkin and Sepkin were sitting over the chessboard, as grimly intent upon their game as if they were controlling the movements of real armies. They merely grunted when Yelena cried, 'Listen to what I've heard in the Kremlin.'

'There's going to be less bread about, I dare say,' growled Pushkin. 'Now, don't disturb Pyotr. I'm about to checkmate him in two moves.'

'Stalin's going to come out of the Kremlin and see the people of Moscow.'

Yelena jumped in alarm as Sepkin knocked over the chessmen lying closest to him.

'Oho!' said Luka Antipovich triumphantly. 'That's one way of getting out of it — pretending to be clumsy. Go on, admit it — you were beaten!'

'Who says so?' Sepkin managed to say.

'I do,' exulted Pushkin. 'I won that game.'

'Yelena, what was that about Stalin?'

'He's going to drive to the Stadium to address the Guards regiments going to the front next week.' Yelena Lukanovna was fluttering around like a little bird, her large eyes shining.

'When?' Sepkin leaned back. After the first shock of surprise, he was furious with himself for having lost control. It was, he thought, a warning sign; it showed how his life had imperceptibly changed. This was his home now. After that parade of the prisoners of war, a dangerous thought had come into his mind; a hope that time might run out, that the war would be over before they could kill Stalin. He was horrified to find himself thinking along these lines, but he could not help it, and the thought stayed with him.

Sepkin reached for Yelena's hand, kissed it, and pulled her on to his lap. She put her arms round his neck, laughing at him and smiling radiantly.

'When? The day after tomorrow – 28 July,' said Yelena.

The twenty-eighth. So that was to be the day for Operation Wild Geese.

Yelenushka, my dearest love, it's *our* time which has run out. Forgive me if you can. All the things I haven't told you – they're far outweighed by our brief happiness. Oh, God, how banal that sounds.

He kissed her shining eyes, and tried to suppress his feelings. They had just one thing to live for, Renneberg had told them. They were to change the course of history.

Three days after the parade of prisoners through Moscow, another event, whose significance could not be assessed at once, had shaken the six Wild Geese. It was reported that Hitler had been blown up at his headquarters, the Wolf's Lair.

They all met at Milda Ivanovna's again. They might have been expected to display horror and indignation at such an act of treachery, but their reactions were quite different.

'If the Führer is dead,' said Duskov, 'then our mission is over. Well, the next day or so will tell.'

But they knew within hours. That same evening, Moscow broadcast the news that Stauffenberg's plot against Hitler had failed. The Führer was still alive. The would-be assassins and their closest associates had already been shot out of hand, and a wave of arrests was being made, purging the German officer corps and the ranks of the old aristocracy.

'Shit,' said Petrovsky. 'Oh, bloody hell. For four whole hours I was hoping I could marry Larissa. Is – is he really alive?'

Hitler was indeed alive. Milda had heard the news from a German radio station, which broadcast reports, news bulletins, and an interview with Major Remer, commander of the battalion on guard, who, having made inquiries at the Führer's headquarters, had spoken to Hitler himself. Goebbels made a short speech, thanking Almighty God for saving the Führer's life. Himmler was appointed head of internal German security. The spectre that had threatened the country for years became flesh: the SS was taking over.

'So nothing's changed, as far as we're concerned,' said Duskov, when they parted again later. 'Our mission goes ahead. Well, the main thing now is to think of good reasons to explain why we're home so late tonight.'

For three days, Milda Ivanovna had been trying to get in touch with her unknown contact in Moscow. She sent out a signal once an hour. But her brief call went unanswered. They had no radio contact at all with Berlin now; the umbilical cord was cut. Milda told Sepkin, the only one who could easily receive a radio message in daytime, working alone at his incinerator.

'You've been left entirely to yourselves,' she said. 'It's up to you to make all decisions. From now on, we're on our own.'

They still had to carry out their mission, now scheduled for 28 July.

Having heard Yelena's news, Sepkin went into the lavatory, unscrewed the heel of his shoe, and got through to Milda Ivanovna.

Milda Ivanovna answered briefly, just with her code number. Sepkin radioed back '28.7,' and the answer came at once: '12.X.'

From that moment the operation was set in motion. Sepkin returned to the living-room, sat down with Pushkin, and replaced the chessmen as Yelena served up steaming kasha. Luka Antipovich, drinking kvass from a patterned mug, gave Sepkin a broad grin.

'Look at that, my little pigeon,' he told Yelena. 'See how sour our strong man looks—limp as a rag, just because he lost a game.'

Sepkin smiled wryly, and made the first move of a new game. It was so bad that it aroused Pushkin's suspicions. He was thinking: At least three of us should have him in our sights, and we must not shoot or use explosives until we are absolutely sure.

They arrived at Milda Ivanovna's apartment at noon next day, at intervals of ten minutes. The last to appear was little Pleyin in his police sergeant's uniform, looking unusually pale, with dark circles round his eyes. Duskov's glance rested thoughtfully on him.

'I couldn't sleep,' said Pleyin. 'No, no, it wasn't Lyudmila—

don't grin like that. I — I've been thinking what a short time we have to live.'

'We agreed never to talk about that,' said Duskov roughly.

Ivanov grunted. He was seated on a chair in his working-clothes, hands still covered with cement dust, just as he had left the building site during the midday break. 'I couldn't sleep, either. In the end I crept in to look at Wanda. She sleeps in the same room as her parents, you know. I stayed looking at her for what must have been an hour. It was a clear night, and I could see her hair lying on her shoulders. . . .' Ivanov swallowed. 'I was saying good-bye,' he said, his voice harsh. 'Damn it, why shouldn't we talk about such things?' He looked at the others, who were all staring at the tiled floor. 'Well, did *you* dance for joy?'

'We'd better practise with the weapons again,' said Boranov tonelessly. He, too, had said his good-byes to Lyra Pavlovna. They had gone to the cinema, one of the few places where they could be alone together, and watched a stupid propaganda film about a villainous boyar living a life of luxury and eventually being stabbed at a banquet by the servant whose daughter he had got pregnant. They sat in the back row, where no one could see them, and then they hurried to the tram depot, for which Boranov had a key, threw themselves on the wooden seat of one of the vehicles and made love as a matter of urgency.

Tonight they all knew that their lives did not belong to them any more. They must turn themselves into automatons to accomplish Stalin's death.

Milda Ivanovna fetched the weapons from her wardrobe: automatic weapons with telescopic sights, capable of being folded up but easy to assemble within seconds; hand grenades with such a fast action that there would be no chance for anyone to pick one up and toss it back. Six pistols with elongated magazines. Three small submachine-guns. Forty special cartridges for each man. Petrovsky played the part of Stalin, coming unexpectedly out of the next room. The weapons were raised to fire at once. Pleyin and Ivanov practised pulling the pins from hand grenades to throw them, using tennis balls.

'Two seconds' delay,' said Milda, pressing a stopwatch. 'That's too long. It shouldn't be more than one second.'

They practised until it was nearly two o'clock. They could not get the manoeuvres down to a single second; the best time was 1.42.

'That may be good enough,' said Milda Ivanovna coolly. Sepkin still admired her; he loved Yelena, but Milda, he thought, was like a lovely, dangerous, incalculable animal. 'The parade's to be at eleven,' she said. 'They've already announced it.'

'Half of Red Square will be cordoned off while Stalin leaves, Lyudmila told me,' said Pleyin. 'He's to come out of the Spassky Gate, turn right towards the Moskva, drive past St Basil's Cathedral, and then along the river-bank towards Gorky Park.'

'Well done, Kolka.' Duskov leaned over a map of Moscow spread out on the table. The others surrounded him, while Milda Ivanovna handed out glasses of mineral water flavoured with fruit vinegar. It was a hot, oppressive day; they were sweating from every pore.

'Pleyin, you're to be in full view of the Spassky Tower, stationing yourself either near the Lenin Mausoleum or the GUM department store. You will radio the information on to us when Stalin leaves.'

'Yes,' said Pleyin, 'and then what?'

'That's all.' Duskov did not raise his head; he did not wish to look at the young man. Yes, he thought, I know what you want to say: that means you will survive. And quite right, too. You are the youngest. Keep your life and your lovely Lyudmila — but don't let's talk about it now.

'Unless,' Duskov added tactfully, 'you find yourself close enough to Stalin to be able to throw a grenade or you can be perfectly sure — and I mean *perfectly* sure — of getting him with a sub-machine-gun.' He tapped the map. 'Right, Ivanov, you station yourself by St Basil's Cathedral, opposite the Nabatnaya Tower. Stalin will have to go that way to reach the Moskva. If he is being driven too fast, or if he is not close enough for *you* to be sure, let him through, Fedya, just let him through. We don't want to leave anything to chance. Report to us by radio if Stalin passes you.'

Duskov looked at Petrovsky. That saved Ivanov, too, the second youngest of the party. When peace comes, you can let your curls grow as long as you like again, thought Duskov, and how happy Wanda Semyonovna will be, burying her hands in them.

'Petrovsky,' Duskov asked. 'What about that motorbike you were going to borrow?'

'Yes, I can get it all right. Comrade Kurkurin in the spares depot promised to lend it. Believe it or not, it's a German Zündapp machine.'

'Then you follow Stalin's procession on the bike and keep in constant radio contact with us,' Duskov went on. 'When Stalin comes round the Beklemsky Tower and down to the road by the river, the street is broad enough for you to be able to overtake him on the bike. But you'll have to assess the situation for yourself. You'd need to be quite sure you can race in among his escort and make use of the momentary confusion to throw a grenade accurately. If that's not possible, if you're not entirely sure it will come off, let him drive on and let us know.'

Petrovsky nodded. He was thinking: My darling Larissa, my little blonde with your snub nose and pretty freckles, I hope to throw that grenade, but don't be too bitter.

'Sepkin, Boranov and I form the main strike-force,' said Duskov. 'We shall direct concentrated fire at Stalin from three sides as he drives over the Crimea Bridge, on his way from the Kropotkin Embankment. At the corner here, where the car will have to slow down to turn, would be the best place for us to get at him.' Duskov looked up. 'Any questions, comrades?'

'No,' said Sepkin grimly.

'We take up our positions at ten.' Duskov smiled, a rather forced smile. 'Good luck, everyone. Well, perhaps we'll meet here at Milda Ivanovna's later.'

It was a dry joke which they would hardly have expected of Duskov. They smiled wryly, raised their glasses of mineral water to each other, and then embraced. At the door, Milda gave each of them a kiss. Not a sisterly kiss; if nothing else told them that they would not return, that kiss did so.

At two minutes past ten on the morning of 28 July 1944, a sunny day, so hot that the asphalt already seemed to be steaming, Pleyin, Ivanov and Petrovsky got in touch by radio from their respective positions. Duskov, Boranov and Sepkin had fetched their weapons from their overnight hiding-place in the cold furnace of Sepkin's incinerator, where they were sure to be left undisturbed.

Petrovsky saw that Pleyin and Ivanov had their own weapons; he had been able to hide hand grenades, pistols and small sub-machine-guns in odd corners at the tractor-plant. He thundered across Moscow on his borrowed motorbike, met Pleyin and Ivanov by the annexe to the Historical Museum, and gave them what they would need.

At twenty minutes past ten, Colonel Smolka was facing General Radovsky, palms sweating, feeling very nervous.

They could hear Stalin on the phone in the next room. His deep voice came through the door. He was speaking to Marshal Konev of the 1st Ukrainian Front, who had been carrying out a vast pincer movement with his 13th and 16th Armies, and had encircled several German divisions east of Lemberg. He was so sure of himself that he even proposed leaving two armies in reserve well to the east, behind Tarnopol.

Stalin was obviously delighted. He was full of praise for Konev.

'We're in luck,' said Radovsky. 'Igor Vladimirovich, we really are in luck. Stalin will drive through Moscow in an excellent mood. Do you keep a diary? If so, you should enter the fact that, on 28 July 1944, you became the only man in the world ever to induce Stalin to appear as a play-actor. Though I hate to think what might happen if your crazy plan goes wrong. . . .'

At ten-thirty, the guard came out of the Spassky Tower. A chain of police and soldiers keeping back the crowd stood to attention. Behind the iron barriers, people craned forward. There were not, in fact, very many present here; most had gone to Gorky Park to see the parade. But several officers appeared in the entrance, themselves forming a barrier.

Pleyin put his transmitter to his lips. They had adjusted their sets so that they could all communicate freely with each other. He was stationed by the Lenin Mausoleum, with a good view of the gate. If Stalin came out in his car now, Pleyin would get a good view of him, too, but he would be too far off to be sure of picking him off with his submachine-gun, or throwing a hand grenade accurately.

'The guards are out,' said Pleyin quietly. He was, of course, in his police uniform, and anyone watching him speak into a small

transmitter would suppose he was in touch with policemen elsewhere along the route.

'Ivanov?' asked Duskov.

'In position.'

'Petrovsky?'

'Ready to start the bike any time.'

'Don't do anything silly, Luka.'

'What d'you think I am?' asked Petrovsky, hurt.

Pleyin came in again. 'Three cars just driving out. Open cars
with armed soldiers in them. And six motorcyclists.'

'Good,' said Petrovsky. 'I should be able to buzz in among
them. . . .'

'Wait and see what the situation looks like first,' Duskov told
him.

He, Boranov and Sepkin were stationed on the Crimean Bridge,
hidden behind a wooden hoarding used for propaganda, with a
huge photograph of Stalin on it. A perfect place: as Stalin drove
slowly past his own picture, he would be in the sights of their
three rifles.

'He's coming out himself now.' Pleyin spoke so soberly that
Duskov looked at Boranov with a nod of slight surprise. Sepkin,
perfectly calm, concentrating hard, checked the lock of his gun
yet again.

'He's in a car with its window open,' said Pleyin. 'I can see
him quite clearly. He's smiling – and the window's open. Damn.
And I *am* too far off.'

'Splendid.' Duskov shook his head. 'Making himself the perfect
target.'

Ivanov came in. 'I can see him coming, with the escorting cars
in front.'

'Just starting my engine now,' said Petrovsky.

Then they heard a quiet and quite unexpected little cry of
surprise. Pleyin's voice – trembling, incredulous, rising to a
childish note.

'It's not possible – it just isn't possible – good God in
Heaven. . . .'

'What's the matter, Pleyin?' called Duskov urgently. 'Pleyin –
Kolka – what's up?'

Out through the Spassky Gate drove the twin of the car in which Stalin had just turned off to the right. A sleek black limousine, its window wound down. And there in the passenger-seat, looking out cheerfully and nodding to the people behind the barriers, sat another Stalin.

'It's—it's a second Stalin. There are two of him,' faltered Pleyin.

'Kolka, pull yourself together,' Duskov replied angrily.

A third came out. The same model. The officers saluted. At the open window, Stalin smiled broadly, raising his hand to the level of his forehead in his characteristic gesture. The sunlight lay full on his iron-grey hair as he leaned slightly forward.

'A third Stalin,' cried Pleyin desperately. 'Don't shoot—for God's sake, hold your fire. There are three of them coming.'

'Damn it all, boy, you must be drunk,' snapped Petrovsky, ready on his motorbike. 'Duskov, he's gone off his head with fright.'

'And the third Stalin is turning left.' Pleyin's voice was shaking pitifully now. 'He's coming my way, passing me now—*waving* to me. . . .'

'Fire, Kolka!' shouted Petrovsky.

'That—that was the third one. And there's a fourth Stalin coming out of the gate! Another one! Leaning out of the window —I can see him. We—we have *four* Stalins!'

'Crazy,' said Petrovsky. 'He's gone quite crazy.'

But before Duskov could react Ivanov's voice cut in.

'I'm here at the Cathedral. Here comes the escort—and now the car with Stalin in it—no, two cars, quite close together—coming up level with me. Not close enough for me to attack. Oh, my God. Kolka's right: there *are* two Stalins driving past me. Duskov, there really are two of them coming.'

Pleyin's piteous voice came in again from Red Square.

'The second two Stalins are turning into Gorky Street. Don't shoot! Don't! How can we know which is the real one?'

Duskov stared at Sepkin and Boranov. His eyes were red-rimmed. Sepkin was crouched behind the hoarding, sweating. Boranov had put his head back and was gazing at the cloudless, hot, pale-blue sky.

Now it was Petrovsky, calling them from the Belemsky Tower. 'Oh, shit!' They could hear the roar of his motorcycle engine over their radios. 'They're coming, and there really are two of them Duskov, there are *two* Stalins coming towards you. . . . Oh, Christ!'

'The second two Stalins have parted company now. One's going right, around the Museum, the other's turning off to the Arsenal Tower.' Pleyin's voice was as thin as a child's. 'I—I'm signing off now. Nothing more to report.'

Duskov bowed his head. What was supposed to have been one of the great moments of history had turned to pure farce. The Wild Geese had become common sparrows.

'Well, that's the end,' said Duskov dully. 'And God protect our country. We can't do any more.'

As the column passed Duskov, Sepkin and Boranov—the escort vehicles, the motorcyclists, the two black limousines, all reducing speed to turn on to the Crimea Bridge—the three men stood by the roadside, saluting. And from the two cars, sitting by the open windows, Stalin waved to them, in unusually jovial mood.

The three of them watched the cars drive over the bridge, then picked up the bags they had hidden behind the hoarding, and walked slowly away, like passers-by enjoying the summer sunshine, along the Kropotkin Embankment, towards the Kremlin.

Petrovsky rode to meet them, braked, and got off the motorbike. 'Now what?' he said. His face was so distorted it might have been that of a stranger. 'Duskov, for God's sake, say something.'

'When we go home this evening,' said Duskov slowly, 'I think we should take flowers to our girls. After all, they are the winners. . . .'

On 2 October 1944, Ivanov suddenly found himself facing Stalin.

Again, it was in the Alexandrovsky Garden, and near the Arsenal Tower. But this time Ivanov was not wheeling a barrow across the Trinity Bridge; he was putting up scaffolding for the pointing of part of the wall of the Arsenal building. It was midday, and Ivanov was alone, with one other workman, whose name was Belyayev. Belyayev was sitting in the shade of the wall, eating a pickled cucumber and telling Ivanov a story about a girl he knew with a big mole just above her mons veneris. Ivanov was so well educated: did he know if a mole like that could be removed successfully?

And then Stalin was suddenly there in front of them. Casual, smoking a pipe, wearing a loose, light-coloured summer jacket, showing none of the cares of state. Russia's little father, just as he appeared on the big pictures on the hoardings.

Belyayev, not the brightest of souls at any time, gaped, then sprang to his feet and stood to attention by the wall, feeling his heart thudding so loud that he thought he might die of shock at any moment.

Ivanov ran forward. He was not even thinking; it was pure reflex action of the kind he had practised so many times in training.

Stalin stared at him, surprised, but he could not avoid him. As Ivanov and Stalin collided, Fyodor Panteleyevich was pulling the pin from the grenade in his pocket: the hand grenade which would go off instantly.

For a brief fraction of a second, while they were so close as to be merging together, Stalin's suddenly horrified glance registered in Ivanov's expressionless eyes. Ivanov was already a dead man, and knew it. And then the explosion shattered the sun-drenched peace of the midday break. Belyayev fell to the ground winded, but still able to see the two bodies before him splinter like red glass and mingle with each other.

'We have clamped right down on all information,' said Colonel Smolka, half an hour later. He was watching the remains of Stalin and Ivanov being carried away in two zinc coffins. Radovsky, elegant as usual, stood aside, a handkerchief to his mouth, suffering from nausea. Two utterly wrecked bodies, though the heads were unharmed. One was that of a young man with curly fair hair; the other had Stalin's angular face and iron-grey skull.

'Well, do you believe in my German officers now, Comrade General?' asked Smolka.

'Am I expected to strike up a hymn of joy?' Radovsky asked sharply. 'Who was it?'

'Nikolai Ilyich Tabun.'

'Stalin is likely to withdraw entirely from public view now,' said Radovsky gloomily. 'You know what that means, Igor Vladimirovich? More suspicion all round, more intrigues. Well, it's all right for you; you're not close to him the whole time. Those of us who are will just have to endure.' Radovsky gestured apologetically. 'Be a good fellow, Smolka; forget what I just said, will you? Not a word about this incident, then?'

'Certainly not, Comrade General.'

'What about the eyewitness — that carpenter? He only sustained slight injuries.'

'He will be sent to a very good special clinic for them,' said Smolka casually. 'In Omsk.' Omsk lies on the far side of the Urals, in Siberia.

Radovsky looked at Smolka, saw his eyes smiling slightly, thrust out his lower lip, and turned to go.

Over the next four weeks, Wanda Semyonovna went everywhere she could think of to make inquiries — hospitals, police stations, anywhere that might have information. She was desperate. No one could help. Her mother, disregarding her husband's disapproval, arranged a corner of the room for prayer. She put up an icon, arranged flowers round it, lit a candle and knelt down.

When Wanda came home she fell on her own knees beside her mother, raised her clasped hands and cried out, 'Dear Lord, give him back to me! Help me, Jesus! Where is he? What's happened to him? How can someone simply disappear? Christ have mercy upon us. . . .'

Semyon Tikhinovich could stand it no longer. He left the apartment and got very drunk. When he came home he staggered around calling his womenfolk and Ivanov names. But when he was alone at work he stood beside the rolling mill, staring at the red-hot metal, unable to make it out, and shaking his head helplessly.

He had loved Ivanov like a son, though he had never said as much, Semyon was not a man to wear his heart on his sleeve.

The war was over. The victory celebrations in Moscow lasted a week, and a magnificent firework display lit up the sky above the city with shimmering cascades of light. A vast parade marched across Red Square. Stalin stood on the Kremlin Wall, surrounded by his most intimate associates, and by generals sparkling with decorations. He waved and smiled and shook his field-marshals' hands, and the tens of thousands watching were moved to tears.

That day, Boranov and Lyra Pavlovna were on their own. Pavlov Ignatovich Sharenkov and his wife had been invited out to a victory party.

'Lyra, there's something I have to tell you,' said Boranov. He and Lyra were sitting on the sofa; they had been kissing, and Lyra had taken off her blouse and was stretched full length, her body quivering as Boranov caressed it.

'Oh, why talk now?' she asked faintly. 'They say women talk too much – but, if you ask me, men never stop talking. . . .'

'This is something I have to say.' Boranov took off his left shoe, twisted the heel off, and showed its contents to Lyra. 'That', he said, 'is a miniaturized radio transmitter. An American invention. I don't need it any more now. The war is over. But I am a German, Lyrashka. A German officer. My real name is Asgard Kuehenberg.'

She looked at him, her eyes wide and shining, stretched her half-naked body, nestled close and put both arms round him. 'What nonsense are you talking, Kyrill Semyonovich?' she asked, in a very small voice.

'Lyra, I'm a German.'

'No, your name is Boranov. Kyrill Semyonovich Boranov. You've never been anyone else. And you're going to be my dear husband Kyrill. You have a wife called Lyra Pavlovna, don't you? Or, at least, you soon will. And aren't you going to have children whose name will be Boranov? Who wants to alter that?' She smiled at him, took his hand and laid it over her breasts. 'Your life is here,' she said. 'Don't talk, my darling, don't talk it away. Don't give it any other name – bury everything else deep inside you, for good. . . . Oh, Kyrill look at the clock! Time goes so fast – and we're wasting time talking!'

When Sharenkov came in, well after midnight, he was taken aback to see his daughter Lyra lying in bed with Kyrill Semyonovich, asleep, covered by a blanket. He could tell from the sight of their shoulders that they were naked under it.

'Dear me,' he muttered, as Marya Ivanovna drew him out of the room. 'And under my own roof, too. What do you think I ought to do?'

'Let them get married as soon as they can,' said Marya Ivanovna. 'We'll go and put their names down at the Palace of Marriage tomorrow.'

Milda Ivanovna still lived at number 19, Lesnaya Street. She had a secretarial job in the Central Textile Controls Office and was able to get hold of all sorts of material, and even made-up clothes. She was living with a man who was the precise opposite of Volonov. Comrade Ivan Yanovich Volodin spoke five languages, among them German, and taught the History of European Art at Moscow University. He loved Milda to distraction, bore with her many friends, and enjoyed discussing all kinds of subjects with Sepkin, Duskov, Pleyin and Boranov and their wives. He admired the animal beauty of Lyudmila Dragonovna Pleyina, the sheer loveliness of Anya Ivanovna Duskova, the radiant youth of Yelena Lukanovna Sepkina, the cheerful nature of snub-nosed Larissa Alexandrovna Petrovskaya, and the infectious gaiety of Lyra Pavlovna Boranova. And he never stopped wondering why, when Milda Ivanovna shone even in such a circle as this, she should have chosen to marry him of all people.

In that year after the end of the war, Milda's job was extraordinarily valuable. She got dresses and materials for her friends' wives, permits for new shoes, and even brought home three of the shopping permits which allowed the holders into the special shops reserved for important Party functionaries. Life was back to normal, more or less. There was little news from Germany, but it was said the people there were cold and hungry, resorted to the black market, and would walk miles trying to barter a few grammes of cooking-fat. When Milda turned her radio to Berlin, they got American jazz, and voices which Lyudmila Dragonovna said sounded like wolves howling.

One September day in 1946, Milda Ivanovna rang her friends and asked them all to come round to her apartment. Her voice was choked with tears. When Duskov, Boranov and Petrovsky arrived, she was sitting on the sofa weeping. Ivan Yanovich Volodin was trying to comfort her, attempting to ply her first with wine and then Georgian brandy, but she would only shake her head. She sat there like a broken doll, and kept saying, 'It's dreadful. Dreadful. Sepkin rang from the hospital to tell me, an hour ago. They were brought in bundled in three sacks, because the people who found them didn't want any fuss. . . . It seems she was still alive when they took her out of the sack. He says she took just one more very deep breath, with her eyes open, and then she died, too. Sepkin thinks she recognized him.'

'Who? Who, for God's sake?' asked Duskov.

'Lyudmila Dragonovna.'

They were stunned for a moment, unable to take it in.

'It—it can't be true,' said Boranov in hollow tones. 'What happened? Who were the other two?'

'Kolka. . . .'

'Our little Kolka?' stammered Petrovsky. He slumped into a chair. 'An accident. . . . What sort of accident?'

Milda Ivanovna sobbed convulsively, and Volodin got her to drink some cognac after all. She sipped it and wiped the tears from her face with both hands.

'She shot him. Four times. And then the other woman, twice. And then she had one shot left. She shot herself.'

'The—the other woman?' asked Boranov tonelessly. 'What other woman?'

'A waitress. Lyudmila Dragonovna found them in a wooden hut by the Moskva. I suppose she'd been watching him for some time, and she followed him there. She shot them at once.'

'My God, it's incredible.' Duskov reached for the wine-bottle and put it straight to his mouth, swallowing the wine convulsively. 'He must have been crazy,' he said, putting it down. 'Deceiving a woman like Lyudmila Dragonovna.'

'She was nine years older than Kolka,' said Milda quietly. 'And the waitress was a year younger than he was. It's dreadful, yes—but I do understand Lyudmila.'

It was a quiet funeral, with only a few of Lyudmila Dragonovna's friends from the police standing by the two coffins. The family of the other girl had taken her corpse for burial in a different cemetery. Slowly, Duskov, Petrovsky, Sepkin, Boranov and their wives filed past the open coffins. Pleyin lay on the pillows like a sleeping boy, his mouth twisted into a slightly defiant smile. There was no crucifix between his fingers, only a single red rose, the kind of rose Lyudmila had always loved.

Lyudmila Dragonovna, in her own coffin, was a picture that burned itself into their minds. If she had been beautiful in life,

315

death seemed to enhance that beauty. The high cheek-bones stood out under the smooth, luminous olive of her skin. Even in death, her curved lips summoned up thoughts of sensuality and passion. And around her face lay the black, silken cloud of her hair, stirring slightly in the breeze blowing over the cemetery.

They filed past Pleyin and Lyudmila, laid flowers on their bodies, and stood with folded hands, looking at them. They found themselves at the limits of their own understanding. When the coffins were closed and lowered into the double grave, and the earth thudded down on their lids, Duskov said, 'He always dreamed of going back to Germany some day, poor boy. He often told me so.'

They stood in the shade of a group of chestnut-trees, and looked back at the new grave from time to time. The grave-diggers had taken off their jackets, and were shovelling the earth in. It was a fine autumn day, the trees and bushes lovely in their autumn colouring, Nature generous with her hues before the cold came down.

'What was that you said then, Leonid Germanovich?' asked Boranov. 'The boy was homesick? He wanted to go back to Germany ...?' He put his arm round Lyra Pavlovna; he did not want her to be alarmed by what he was about to say. 'It's not too late to think about it,' he said. 'Surely the question must sometimes occur to us all: do we want to go back to Germany?'

'I was afraid someone might ask that,' said Sepkin.

'We are Germans, after all.'

'We *were* Germans. Now we're Russian citizens.' Duskov offered everyone cigarettes. Even Anya Ivanovna smoked one, quickly and nervously. 'Anya has put in an application for me to become a Party member. It's an honour, you know.'

'And I have a better job in the hospital now,' said Sepkin. 'Assisting in the operating-theatres, instead of tending the incinerator. It's better paid. Yelenushka wants to buy a fur coat, and I've had a good offer on the black market.'

'As for me, my name's down to take the examination to become departmental head of the testing department in a tractor-plant.' Petrovsky stroked Larissa Alexandrovna's fair hair. Her cheerful face was still freckled, in autumn and winter as well as in summer. 'I'm spending all my evenings studying. ...' He shrugged

316

his shoulders in a silent plea for understanding. 'How about you, Kyrill Semyonovich?'

'I'm driving a number 3 line tram now.' Boranov watched the smoke of his cigarette. 'And I've been guaranteed promotion to inspector in six months' time. As you can see, Lyra's baby is due in three months.'

Boranov regarded his friends. 'In a few years' time, maybe, comrades?' He trod out his cigarette. 'The world's always changing ... and so are we. Couldn't it happen that, some day, we may say to ourselves it would be good to see Germany again?'

There were ten of them, and one came back to tell the tale. The other three are still alive somewhere in Moscow, with their wives, their children, their grandchildren:

Leonid Germanovich Duskov

Pyotr Mironovich Sepkin

Luka Ivanovich Petrovsky.

One should not try to find them now.